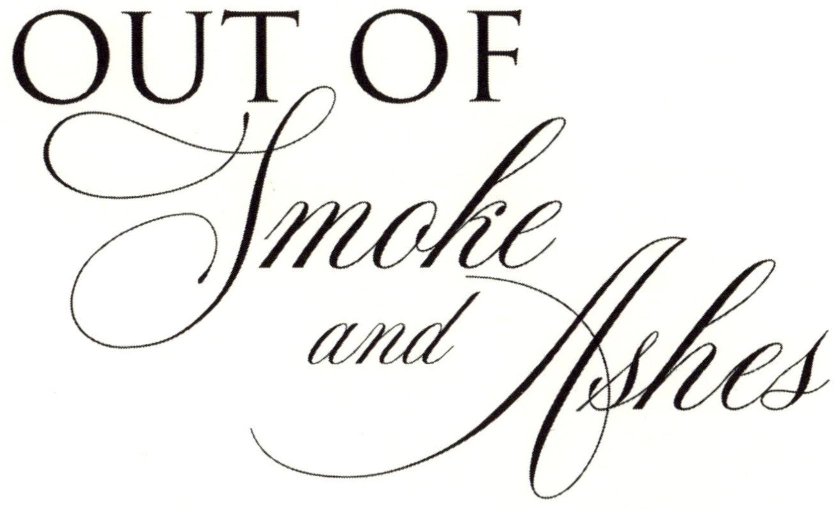

#3 FLAMES OF WINTER SERIES

BY BREE WOLF

Out of Smoke and Ashes by Bree Wolf

Published by WOLF Publishing UG

Text by Bree Wolf
Cover Art by Victoria Cooper
Paperback ISBN: 978-3-98536-160-1
Hard Cover ISBN: 978-3-98536-161-8
Ebook ISBN: 978-3-98536-159-5

This is a work of fiction. Names, characters, businesses, places, brands, media, events and incidents are either the products of the author's imagination or used in a fictitious manner.

Any resemblance to actual persons, living or dead, or actual events is purely coincidental.

WOLF Publishing - This is us:

Two sisters, two personalities.. But only one big love!

Diving into a world of dreams..

...Romance, heartfelt emotions, lovable and witty characters, some humor, and some mystery! Because we want it all! Historical Romance at its best!

Visit our website to learn all about us, our authors and books!

Sign up to our mailing list to receive first hand information on new releases, freebies and promotions as well as exclusive giveaways and sneak-peeks!

WWW.WOLF-PUBLISHING.COM

Also by Bree Wolf

Flames of Winter Series

Some stories can be told in one book. Others cannot. This is one of those stories.

In the Flames of Winter series by USA Today bestselling and award-winning author BREE WOLF, a young English miss dares to break society's strict rules as she flees from her parents' house the night before her wedding. This one decision ends up leading her from one adventure into the next...and, of course, into the arms of a fiercely protective highlander. He may not be a peer, but he is the one man she never knew she always wanted.

#1 Flames of Winter

#2 Shield of Fire

#3 Out of Smoke and Ashes

#4 On the Wings of Cinders

OUT OF *Smoke and Ashes*

Chapter One
ON THE RUN

England, Early March 1804 (or a variation thereof)

As the carriage rattled over the frozen ground, Sarah Mortensen, youngest daughter to Baron Hartmore, gazed out the window at the sky streaked with shades of orange and violet. Each branch of every tree had been coated in ice and was glittering in the fading light. The frigid air of winter chilled Sarah to the bone, and she knew that once the sun disappeared for good, it would cool even further. Thankfully, Sarah was tucked away in the carriage, sheltered under a pile of heavy blankets and with a hot brick at her feet. Next to her, her sister Kate was equally bundled up, her arms cradling her newborn daughter Frederica. Frederica's older sisters, Augusta and Dorothea, sat opposite them, only their little faces and the tips of their fingers peeking out of the cozy nest the Whickertons had made for them before their departure from Whickerton Grove. Only Loki, Sarah's recently adopted cat, appeared unaffected by the cold weather. He stretched and yawned lazily next to the basket of provisions the Whickertons had provided for their journey, then hopped onto Sarah's lap. He kneaded her blanket with his little paws and then circled a few times before finally snuggling down and closing his eyes.

"How long?" six-year-old Augusta asked into the stillness of the carriage, her wide blue eyes sparkling with adventure.

Sarah frowned, running a hand over Loki's fur. "How long? What do you mean?"

"Until we reach the island, of course." A chiding look came to Augusta's young face. "*He* said we're going to an island." She jabbed a finger out the window at the shadowed rider. "Is that true?"

Sarah turned her head, her eyes settling upon the tall, broad-shouldered man accompanying the carriage. He and his steed almost seemed to blend into the approaching dark, only their silhouette visible. His dark hair was hidden under a wide-brimmed hat, and his face lay in shadow. Upon occasion he would ride ahead, scouting the road, before returning to the carriage, keeping careful watch. His movements were unhastened by unease or concern, and his calm demeanor soothed Sarah's tense nerves.

"Yes, it's true!" Dorothea exclaimed the moment her elder sister ceased speaking. The four-year-old wrinkled her little nose, her bright green eyes shifting from her mother to her aunt as though daring them both to contradict her. "I heard him say it! Honest! It's true!"

Sarah chuckled and looked at her sister, seeing a warm, almost enchanted smile upon Kate's face as she gazed at her beloved daughters. "*He* told me so as well," Sarah assured her two nieces, delighted finally to have the chance to get to know them. "And his name is Keir, Keir MacKinnear. It is his home we're going to."

The girls' eyes widened in awe. Indeed, the island in the far north Keir called home had to seem like a fairytale land to them. Sarah could not say she disagreed. Kate, however, looked far from enchanted by the prospect of their long journey, a shiver shaking her delicate frame and gritting her teeth. *Of course, this is difficult for her. If only we could be certain not to be found out!*

Sarah briefly closed her eyes, praying that they would reach their destination without delay, without being overtaken on the road by Kate's enraged husband.

"Then it is true?" Augusta insisted for clarity's sake. "We're going to an island?"

Sarah nodded. "We are."

Little Dorothea frowned. "How will we get there? The carriage has wheels. It can't swim."

"With a boat, silly!" Augusta rolled her eyes at her younger sister in a rather overbearing gesture that almost made Sarah laugh out loud. "How else can you get across the water?"

Dorothea continued to frown. "But we don't *have* a boat," she pointed out matter-of-factly.

Two sets of expectant eyes turned to Sarah. "Oh, well... I don't quite know. However, I'm certain Keir will know what to do when the time comes."

"He speaks funny," Dorothea remarked with all the directness of a four-year-old.

Even Kate had to chuckle. "He is not English, dearest," she told her daughter. "He's a Scot."

Again, that scrunched-up expression came to Dorothea's face. "Then what is he doing in England?"

Kate's mouth opened... and closed before she looked at Sarah, an almost pleading look in her eyes.

Caught off guard, Sarah stammered a few rather unintelligible words before reminding herself to be simply honest with her nieces and use words that held meaning for them. "Well, he is a friend of the Whickertons, and—"

The girls' faces lit up. "The fairy!" Dorothea exclaimed, and Augusta nodded vigorously.

"Yes," Sarah agreed, "the fairy."

As far as Sarah knew, Harriet—youngest daughter to the Earl of Whickerton—had posed as a fairy as she had sneaked onto the estate where Kate's husband had hidden away their daughters. She had found the girls and gained their trust by promising to make their most-desired wish come true.

Of course, their most-desired wish had been to be reunited with their mother after months of separation.

"Well," Sarah continued, choosing her next words most carefully, afraid to frighten her nieces, "while Harriet—the fairy!—went to fetch you, Keir came to fetch your mother."

"Oh." The sound left Augusta's lips in a puff of cold air, the look in her young eyes suddenly far too mature. She looked at her mother and then held out her hand to her. Kate took it, tears brimming in her eyes as she gazed longingly at her child, undoubtedly filled with thankfulness to have Augusta by her side.

"I didn't thank him," Dorothea remarked in a somber tone, her wide green eyes staring out the window at the shadowed rider. "I must thank him for bringing Mummy back to us."

A muffled sob escaped Kate's lips before she pressed them shut, her hand tightening upon Augusta's.

Sarah offered her sister a tentative smile, then she gently placed her hand upon Dorothea's. "Thea?" she whispered, waiting until the girl looked at her. "Keir knows you're grateful. He often helps people because... it's simply who he is."

"He's a hero," Dorothea whispered, and her gaze once more strayed to the window and the rider beyond.

"Yes, he is." Sarah knew it was true. After all, Keir had initially come to England to save *her*. The Dowager Countess of Whickerton had called upon him, asking him to aid her in freeing Sarah from a forced match. That was how they had met almost two months ago. He had come to London and *kidnapped* her from her parents' home the night before her wedding.

Involuntarily, Sarah smiled when she thought of the night he had stolen her away. He had been a stranger, and she had been utterly terrified of him. So much so that she had fainted, waking later to find herself on top a horse and in her *kidnapper*'s arms.

Thus, their story had begun.

Blinking his eyes open, Loki lifted his head to look at Dorothea. Her little face still held something deeply melancholic. As though, the often-times haughty feline understood the girl's need for distraction, he rose, stretched and then jumped across onto her lap.

Dorothea's eyes went wide, and she stared at Loki, her hands in midair as though she were uncertain what to do with them.

"He is very friendly," Sarah tried to reassure her. "There is no need to worry. You can pet him." Sarah refrained from mentioning how ferocious Loki had proved when he had thought one of his clan threatened, namely her. Indeed, he was almost as fiercely protective of her as Keir. *Perhaps he might extend his protectiveness to the girls,* Sarah thought. *Indeed, they could do with a loyal companion!*

Dorothea petted Loki while Augusta watched her little sister with envious eyes. "His eyes glow in the dark," Augusta remarked in awe. Then she reached out a tentative hand to let him sniff it. When Loki licked it affectionately, the girls burst out into giggles.

Soon, all gloomy thoughts had vanished, and the girls laughed and chatted happily. "Thank you," Kate whispered, leaning her shoulder against Sarah's. "A part of me still cannot believe," her voice choked with tears, "that you came for us." Her gaze fell from Sarah's eyes and drifted to the bruise forming upon her left cheek. Kate's husband had struck Sarah there the night before when she and Keir had helped Kate and her daughters escape their gilded cage.

Sarah grasped her sister's hand. "Of course, I did." She smiled at Kate, ignoring the apologetic expression upon her sister's face. After all, Kate was not responsible for what her husband had done. "I could not have done it alone, though."

Kate's gaze strayed past her to the window. "Thea is right," she murmured, her eyes fixed upon the shadowy figure outside. "I need to thank him. If he had not come..." Her voice trailed off, and her arms tightened around the sleeping child she held cradled against her chest. "I would have lost you as well," she murmured to the babe, and a lone tear fell from her eyelashes and down onto Frederica's cheek.

The little girl stirred for a moment but then continued to slumber peacefully. Augusta and Dorothea had settled down as well, Loki curled up in their arms, their eyes closing as exhaustion overtook them.

"That will never happen," Sarah said firmly, needing her sister to know that she was no longer alone... and never would be again. "I won't allow it." Kate looked up and met her gaze. "*He* won't allow it."

A tentative smile came to Kate's face. "I did not know you would accompany us to Scotland."

Sarah exhaled a sudden breath, realizing how trying the past few hours had been for her heart. "I didn't think I would. I thought I would have to bid you farewell."

Kate swallowed, and again, her gaze traveled out the window. "You thought you'd have to bid *him* farewell."

Forcing back the tears that threatened, Sarah nodded. "I... I knew he cared for me, but... but he never spoke of... He never said he..." She closed her eyes and inhaled a deep breath. "Of course, neither did I."

"He asked you to come?"

Sighing deeply, Sarah nodded. "He did. He said he did not want to say goodbye just yet, perhaps not ever."

Kate smiled at her. "It is obvious that he cares for you, Sarah, and deeply. I saw it that first day when you came to Birchwell. It's in the way he looks at you, speaks *of* you and *to* you. He respects you, admires you." Her lips twitched into a tearful smile. "Loves you." She wiped a tear from the corner of her eye, regret upon her face. "My husband never did."

Sarah grasped her sister's hand. "Today is a new beginning. Today you're leaving behind all the heartbreak and regret, all the pain and suffering of the past. Today, you're taking your first step into your new life." She nodded at Kate encouragingly.

"You're right," her sister murmured, a brave smile coming to her face. "I have my daughters with me again, and soon, they'll be safe. We'll all be."

"Yes." Sarah wrapped an arm around her sister's shoulders, her eyes drifting to the smile that briefly danced across Frederica's face as she slept. "We'll all start over in Scotland."

"He's a good man," Kate murmured, a touch of disbelief in her tone as she looked out the window at their protector. "I... I'd forgotten that men like him existed."

Sighing deeply, Sarah nodded. "I'd forgotten it, too." But then Keir had come, reminding her what it meant to have someone to lean on, someone who made you feel safe and protected, someone who... cared for you. Though he had frightened her in the beginning, it had been Sarah's experiences that had put her on her guard, not Keir himself.

The forlorn expression upon Kate's face pained Sarah. No doubt her mind was consumed by thoughts of her husband and what he would do now that she had so openly disobeyed him. Sarah, too, struggled to put that thought from her mind. Would he come after them? How could he not? After all, everything Lord Birchwell had ever wanted was an heir, and thus far he only had three daughters.

And with his wife gone, that would never change.

"He hates me," Kate suddenly murmured into the stillness, her voice hard with anger. "He never cared for me, not truly. He never looked at me the way Keir looks at you. Not for a single moment." A heavy sigh left her lips, and yet Sarah could sense that there was more than regret in her sister's heart. "I deserved more."

"Of course, you did!" Sarah scooted back and looked at her sister. "You're wonderful, Kate. You've always been wonderful, and he is a fool for not having seen that."

Kate smiled at her. "I'm sorry that you had to work so hard to convince me, and I'm grateful that you didn't give up when I all but threw you out of my house." Tears glistened in her eyes. "You're right. This is a new beginning, and I will do what I can to see my daughters happy." She looked down at Frederica before shifting her gaze to Augusta and Dorothea. "To make them feel safe."

Sarah hugged her sister, praying that Kate, too, would find happiness again. Yet from personal experience, Sarah knew it to be far from easy to leave behind the confinements of a life drilled into one since infancy.

Perhaps, now, at least, her young nieces would never know what that meant.

Chapter Two
OLD HABITS

As the first rays of light streaked across the dawn sky, Keir gestured toward a small clearing to the east with a stream running through it. Mr. Garner, seated atop the box of the carriage, nodded and then directed the horses off the frozen road. The clearing glistened in the morning light, ice crystals clinging to every branch and blade of grass. Mist hung in the air, giving the world an almost magical touch, making it seem like a place from one of the old legends.

Patting Scout's neck, Keir murmured words of comfort to the gelding, sensing the animal's fatigue beginning to set in. Keir, too, could feel weariness upon his bones, something heavy that weighed them down and urged him to close his eyes. The time for rest, though, had not yet come.

Keir lifted his head and looked towards Mr. Garner, who just now pulled the carriage to a stop. The hunter then jumped off the box, alert as always; yet Keir saw signs of exhaustion upon his face as well. Of course, that was to be expected. After all, they had not slept in almost two days.

"I'll see to the horses," Mr. Gardner remarked as Keir swung himself out of the saddle. He glanced back at the carriage. "You see to the ladies." A good-natured grin came to the man's face before he took Scout's reins and led the gelding away.

The frosted grass crunched beneath Keir's boots as he approached the carriage. Everything seemed still inside, and so he quietly opened the door. His eyes blinked into the dark interior until they settled upon Sarah's face, her eyes closed in slumber.

For a moment, Keir was reluctant to wake her, knowing that she, too, had been through a lot these past two days. Still, he did not wish to rob her of the chance to move her limbs and breathe in fresh air. He gently placed a hand upon her shoulder, giving her a soft shake. "Sarah! Wake up, lass."

To Keir's surprise, the one responding to him was not Sarah but Augusta instead. The girl rubbed her eyes and yawned widely. "Are we there yet?"

Keir smiled at her. "Not quite, lassie. But we stopped for a bit, and I thought ye'd like to step outside."

Sarah stirred as Augusta shook her little sister awake without another thought. "Thea, wake up! Wake up!" Only moments later, the two girls bounded out of the carriage with such eagerness that Keir had to jump aside to avoid being overrun.

He laughed, relieved to see their joy.

"Is it morning yet?" came Sarah's voice, and Keir turned back to look at her.

Although she had slept at least a little, dark circles still rested beneath her eyes, and her skin seemed pale. Yet the touch of red that came to her cheeks as their eyes met warmed Keir's heart. Aye, he had always managed to make her blush. Sometimes it was only a faint hint of crimson, while at other times her cheeks shone like a beacon in the night sky.

Only now, her left cheek also sported other colors, and Keir gritted his teeth at the memory of Birchwell's attack on her. He did not even want to contemplate what could have happened if he, Keir, had not returned the moment he had.

Determinedly, Keir pushed those thoughts aside as he took Sarah's hand and assisted her out of the carriage and down the two steps to the frozen ground. Her blue eyes were wide as she looked around, and she ran a tentative hand through her hair, brushing unruly wisps behind her ears. "Where are we?" She turned around to meet his eyes.

"Still a good bit away." Out of the corner of his eye, Keir noticed Sarah's sister awaken. For a moment, Lady Birchwell seemed disoriented, fear widening her eyes as she searched her surroundings. Then, Keir saw recognition flare up before she exhaled a deep breath.

"Are you all right?" Sarah inquired, stepping back toward the carriage. She held out her hand to her sister, and Lady Birchwell grasped it, her other arm wrapped tightly around her infant daughter.

"I'm well. Thank you." Her gaze moved from Sarah to him, something knowing coming to her eyes before she nodded to them and then stepped away. At first, Lady Birchwell seemed unsteady upon her feet, but then as she stretched her limbs and breathed in the fresh morning air, Keir saw her truly awaken. Her demeanor changed, and something tentatively hopeful appeared upon her face. She gently rocked Frederica in her arms, her eyes moving to her other two daughters as they chased one another around the clearing, laughing as Loki followed them, shaking his little paws against the wetness upon the ground.

"How is she?" Keir asked Sarah when she came to stand beside him.

Sarah shrugged. "I don't quite know. She's grateful to have escaped him, and yet I think at the same time there's still a part of her that doubts the wisdom of that decision." She raised her eyes to him. "It is not easy to leave behind the only life ever meant for one."

Unable not to, Keir reached out to take Sarah's hands within his own. "And how are ye?" He loved the feel of her tender skin against his own, but not nearly as much as the blossoming blush upon her cheeks.

On impulse, Keir pulled her gently into his arms, unable to suppress the sudden urge to embrace her. Swiftly, he pulled her aside, around the carriage and away from view. His arms came around her, gathered her close as he gazed into her blue eyes. "I missed ye," he murmured, torn between gazing down at her upturned face a moment longer and dipping his head to steal a kiss.

The smile that graced Sarah's face was reply enough, and without another thought, Keir inclined his head and brushed a loving kiss onto her lips. Then he exhaled softly and pressed his forehead tenderly against hers, relishing the moment of holding her close. "Is there anything ye need?"

Sarah's eyes met his, and her dainty hands came to rest upon his chest. "How long shall we be on the road?"

Keir noticed her gaze stray sideways and guessed that her thoughts were lingering upon her sister. And rightly so. After all, Lady Birchwell had only just given birth, not even a month ago. "I'm afraid 'tis a long journey. Perhaps a sennight if I were traveling alone. Now, considering weather and road conditions and stops for the night, I suppose 'twill take twice as long."

Although clearly discouraged by his answer, Sarah merely nodded. "How many stops? Shall we sleep outside?"

Keir chuckled, remembering the last time he had taken Sarah across country. Then, they had spent a few nights in a tent outside. "No, not this time, lass. But we need a head start and shall push on until nightfall. However, starting tonight, we shall spend the night at inns along the road. Warm beds and warm food."

Relief came to Sarah's face, and Keir knew it was not for her but for her sister and her young nieces. "So, we'll ride on until nightfall?"

Keir nodded. "Do ye wish to ride Autumn, little wisp?"

Sarah shifted upon her feet to peer around the corner of the carriage to where Mr. Gardner was watering the horses. Her mare, Autumn, stood beside Scout. Thus far, she had trotted after the carriage. Like Loki, the two horses had become trusted companions.

"I'd like to," Sarah admitted with a longing look at Autumn. "But I think Kate needs me. She cannot hold Frederica all day as much as she would like to."

Keir nodded. He had seen the fearful look in Lady Birchwell's eyes, overshadowed by past pain. *What sort of man would separate a mother from her children?* Keir pondered. *'Tis unthinkable!*

Shaking off that thought, Keir tugged Sarah closer, smiling at her as she turned wide eyes to him. "And ye? How are ye, little wisp? Regretful? Or—?"

"No, no regrets!" Sarah exclaimed, shaking her head vehemently. "No, I want to be here." She bit her lip, and her eyes closed as though she could not believe what she had just blurted out. "My mother would be scandalized, of course."

Keir chuckled, purposefully tightening his hold on her. "And ye?" He arched his brows meaningfully. "Does it bother ye to know that yer mother would disapprove?"

Sarah's lips thinned, and for a moment, she seemed thoughtful, undecided. Then her eyes focused, and she smiled up at him. "I cannot deny that it does. At least, a little." She shrugged. "I was raised to care more for the opinion of others than my own. It is like an instinct, nothing I can simply shake off."

"Aye, 'tis not easy to abandon old habits."

"But I'm trying," Sarah replied insistently. "I'm doing my best to ignore her voice in my ear and to make up my own mind."

"And what does yer mind say?"

A luminous smile lit up her face. "My mind is still confused," she admitted a little sheepishly, which made her look utterly adorable, "but my heart just sighed with contentment." Then, bold as she could be at times, Sarah pushed herself up onto her toes and kissed him.

Chapter Three

FOR FAMILY

Sarah's head snapped up as the carriage pulled to a sudden halt. Her eyes blinked against the darkness, then focused as they detected faint light from outside the carriage. Leaning forward, Sarah peered out the window and instantly heaved a sigh of relief as she spotted the simple, two-story inn half-hidden in the dark.

Across from her, the girls were asleep, Loki once more curled upon their laps. Kate, too, was lost in slumber while Frederica was lashed to her chest as before. As much as Sarah had tried to persuade her sister, Kate could not seem to part with her infant daughter for longer than a few moments. Consequently, exhaustion lingered upon her every feature, her arms now hanging limply at her sides.

The sound of footsteps drew Sarah's attention, and as she turned her head, the door was opened, and Keir appeared in the dim light from the inn. "Are ye well?" His gaze moved from her to her sister, and she could see his brows draw down in concern. "She needs rest," he murmured, a touch of anger in his voice—no doubt directed at Kate's husband. "Mr. Garner is procuring rooms. Come! Can ye walk, lass?" He held out his hand to her, his own features marked by fatigue.

Sarah nodded, accepting his hand. "And you?" she asked, climbing out of the carriage. At first, her limbs protested, a slow ache burning through them. Then, however, the movement relieved the tension that had been lingering these past hours. "You look exhausted as well."

Keir offered her one of his teasing grins. "Aye, lass. Truth be told, I feel as though I could easily sleep standing up." He pulled her to his side for a quick moment, his arm wrapping around her shoulders. "We'll have to carry the girls," he murmured then. "Perhaps they'll not wake. 'Twould be best for them." Then his gaze moved to Kate before he looked down at her. "Ye should wake her. I reckon she'll be frightened if I pick her up and she wakes without knowing where she is."

Sarah nodded. As much as she hated robbing her sister of the sleep she so clearly needed, waking to find oneself in the arms of a stranger was deeply unsettling. Sarah knew so from experience, her thoughts instantly drawn back to her first day with Keir.

"What?" he asked with a sudden chuckle, his dark eyes lingering upon her face. "Are ye thinking of me, lass? Of the first time I carried ye in my arms?"

'I still cannot believe you allowed him such liberties!' her mother's disapproving voice chided in her ear. 'I raised you better than that!'

Sarah felt heat rise to her face, averting her head to hide the traitorous blush. Keir would not allow her, though. His hand gently grasped her chin, urging her to meet his gaze. "Why would ye hide that?" Keir asked, tightening his hold on her. "Are ye afraid to admit that ye care for me? Did ye not already do so only the day before?"

A part of Sarah wanted to sink into a hole in the ground—as she always did when embarrassment heated her cheeks. Still, the look in Keir's eyes was mesmerizing. She felt warm and tingly, her skin humming with something unexpected and unfamiliar. "It's my mother's voice," she whispered, closing her eyes and willing it away. "I feel as though she is standing right beside me." She sighed, then met his gaze again. "For a time, I thought I'd banished her for good, but now, I hear her again. I don't know why."

A challenging gleam lit up Keir's gaze. "When do ye hear her, lass? When I hold ye?" His hands settled more firmly on her back. "When I kiss ye?" Sarah felt her heart almost beat out of her chest as Keir lowered his head purposefully, then paused a hair's breadth from her lips. "Can ye hear her now?"

"No," Sarah gasped breathlessly.

Keir brushed his lips against hers. "Now?" A teasing note lingered in his voice.

Sarah smiled against his lips. "No."

"Good," was all he said before his mouth claimed hers in a kiss that would have given her mother a heart attack had she been here to witness it. For many reasons, Sarah was quite glad that she was not.

"I was able to secure two rooms."

At the sound of Mr. Garner's voice, Sarah flinched, almost jumping out of Keir's arms. He, in turn, merely chuckled, giving her one of those looks that never failed to make her toes curl.

Turning toward Mr. Garner, Keir nodded toward the girls. "We'll have to carry them inside." The other man nodded, and Keir looked down at Sarah. "Ye ought to wake yer sister now."

Sarah nodded and stepped up into the carriage again. Gently, she shook her sister's arm, careful not to wake the sleeping baby. "Kate, wake up! We're at the inn."

Only with continued persistence was Sarah able to pry her sister from the claws slumber had dug into her. Eventually, though, Kate was sitting upright, her arms once more wrapped around her youngest daughter. "I'm all right," she murmured, her eyes blinking rapidly as though her vision had not yet cleared.

Sarah frowned, worried for her sister. In fact, she looked far from all right. "Keir and Mr. Garner will carry the girls inside. Can you walk?"

Kate nodded, and Sarah helped her out of the carriage, Loki upon her heels. He looked suddenly alert, his amber eyes aglow in the dark as he looked up at Kate, a soft meow drifting from his mouth.

In the next instant, Kate swayed, her eyes blinking rapidly. "Keir, help!" Sarah called, wrapping her arms around her sister to keep her from plummeting to the ground and crushing her daughter.

Within a heartbeat, Keir was there. He gently pulled Kate out of Sarah's claw-like embrace and then swept her and Frederica into his arms as though they weighed nothing. "Dunna worry, my lady," he murmured in that calming tone Sarah had grown so fond of. "We shall see ye and yer daughters settled."

Kate mumbled something unintelligible, her eyes still closed, and her head resting against Keir's shoulder.

"Go ahead." Sarah nodded to Keir. "I'll take Thea," she added when she saw Mr. Garner emerge from the carriage with Augusta in his arms.

Keir held her gaze. "Are ye certain? I'll be back out in a moment, and then I can take the wee lassie."

Sarah squared her shoulders. "She's only four. I can carry her." Almost desperately, Sarah wanted to be helpful. She wanted others to depend upon her. After all, this was her sister.

Her nieces.

Her family.

Keir nodded. "Go ahead, lass."

As Sarah gently gathered Thea into her arms, she heard Keir say, "Mr. Garner lead the way." The girl's head ended up upon her shoulder, her limp arms slung around her neck. For a moment, Sarah feared the girl would wake, but she merely mumbled something under her breath and then went on sleeping, oblivious to everything around her.

Following Keir into the inn, Sarah could not deny that she felt Dorothea's soft weight in every fiber of her being. Her arms and legs were exhausted, and her four-year-old niece seemed to grow heavier with every step she took. Still, Sarah gritted her teeth and continued on. They moved past the innkeeper's desk, who gave them a friendly nod, and then toward the stairs leading to the upper floor.

Sarah suppressed a groan at the sight of it.

"Wait here," Keir remarked over his shoulder as though he had once again read her thoughts.

At his words, Sarah paused. However, some part deep inside instantly urged her onward, urged her not to hand over this responsibility to another. Was that not what Kate was doing? Was that not what it meant to be a mother? To continue on for one's children no matter the hardship?

'You'll never be a mother!' came her mother's hateful snarl, echoing through her head again and again. 'You could have been, but now you're ruined, and no decent man will want you.'

Tears gathered in Sarah's eyes as she took the first step up the steep staircase. *Yes, I'll never be a mother, but I'm an aunt and I can do this.*

Halfway up the stairs, a familiar *meow* echoed to Sarah's ears, and she looked up to see Loki seated on the landing, his amber eyes holding hers. Again, he mewed, giving Sarah heart.

Gathering every last bit of strength, Sarah climbed the last few steps to the top, her arms and legs aching beyond compare. Her heart, though, soared, tears of accomplishment running down her cheeks.

Quick strides sent Keir out of the chamber at the end of the corridor and propelled him back toward the stairs. The moment he saw her, though, he slowed, and Sarah could feel his gaze sweep over her. She wondered if he would chide her, ask why she had not waited. Yet Keir understood; she could see it in his eyes, in the soft twitch at the right corner of his mouth. "This way," he beckoned and stood aside, allowing Sarah to carry Dorothea the last few steps into the chamber.

Mr. Garner tipped his hat and vanished before Sarah even had a chance to settle Dorothea onto the bed next to her sister. Kate lay in the other one, a relieved smile stealing onto her face the moment she saw her middle child laid down gently. Her eyes closed, then opened once more, exhaustion plain as before upon her face.

Now free of Dorothea's weight, Sarah's arms ached as she turned back to Keir. He stood upon the threshold, that concerned frown back upon his face. "Ye look pale, lass," he remarked in a whisper, raising a brow at her. "Ye need sleep."

Sarah chuckled, allowing him to pull her closer, savoring his warmth as much as the steady arms that held her. "And you do not?" she challenged, suddenly loathe to be considered less. "After all, you've been up as long as I have."

Keir chuckled. "Aye, in fact, I'm asleep on my feet." He grinned down at her. "Can ye not tell I'm sleepwalking?"

Sarah shook her head at him, wishing she could remain in his embrace all night.

"Lock the door," Keir urged suddenly, his gaze insistent as Sarah stood back and raised her eyes to his.

"Do you think we were followed?" She swallowed hard, hoping her sister could not hear their whispered words.

"If I did," Keir murmured, leaning in until she could feel his breath upon her lips, "I wouldna be sleeping in another room."

Sarah's blush was instantaneous, and the wide grin that came to Keir's face told her he had said those words so on purpose. Indeed, he loved teasing her, loved making her blush. He always had, and deep down, Sarah could not rightly say that she minded.

Still...

"You're impossible!" she chided him with a laugh, giving him a shove while Keir allowed himself to be pushed out into the corridor. "Good night."

His gaze held hers a moment longer. Then he nodded his head. "Good night, little wisp."

As Sarah locked the door behind him, she wished that Keir could have stayed. Indeed, the room next door was too far away, and for a split second, Sarah considered slipping back out into the corridor and going after him.

"I'm glad," came Kate's strained voice from the bed behind her, "that he is out there." Sarah turned to meet her sister's eyes as she settled herself comfortably to nurse Frederica. "I feel... safer knowing he is watching over us."

Seating herself beside her sister, Sarah nodded. "I do as well." She sighed. "I can no longer imagine a life without him."

It was a shocking truth, one that held great sway over her life. Sarah knew it, and a part of her feared it.

She could not help that.

Chapter Four

ROOTS & WINGS

Moments before dawn, Keir knocked on Sarah's door. He had already been outside, seeing to the horses and the carriage with Mr. Garner before asking the innkeeper to have a large breakfast readied and packed up for the journey ahead.

Fortunately, the taproom was empty, and he could not detect any signs that someone had followed them here the night before. Still, Keir felt a nagging sense of unease settle in the back of his head. After all, he had overlooked signs of danger once before when Sarah's former fiancé had sent men to find them in the woods. That night had almost ended badly, for Sarah had become too much of a distraction for him.

Whenever she was near, Keir struggled to remain focused. His thoughts strayed to her, and her alone. Keir chuckled as he climbed the stairs to the upper floor. What could he do? He was long past the point where he could have given her up.

As though on cue, Keir could all but hear his father's voice. 'Why are ye bringing her home, lad? There's only one reason, is there not?'

Aye, there was only one reason. Keir had always known so. Yet now was not the time to dwell on such matters.

"Who is it?" came Sarah's voice in answer to his knock upon her door.

"'Tis me, lass."

The door opened, and Sarah's face appeared in the gap. Her blond hair was disheveled, wild wisps billowing around her head. The blue of her eyes shone in a darker shade this morning, and her cheeks glowed in rosy red. She looked utterly fetching, and for a moment, words failed Keir.

"Is something wrong?" Sarah asked, a look of concern coming to her lovely face as she squeezed through the gap in the door, no doubt concerned her sister would overhear. "Keir!"

A part of Keir was utterly disappointed that Sarah had already changed out of her nightgown and into a thick woolen dress. As his gaze traced her yet untamed curls, he wondered if she always looked like this in the mornings.

"Keir!"

Keir started chiding himself for his inattention. *Aye, the lass is a most awful distraction!* "We need to be off, lass. Can ye rouse yer sister and yer nieces?"

Sarah frowned. "That is all? Nothing is wrong?" She exhaled deeply when Keir shrugged. "Then why would you frighten me so? You looked at me as though... as though..." Her voice broke off, and slowly her eyes grew larger as understanding dawned.

Keir chuckled, then leaned in, whispering, "Ye look utterly fetching this morning, little wisp."

Sarah blinked before her gaze rose, and she lifted a hand to finger her wayward curls. "Oh, you're awful!" she chided, slapping his shoulder. "I rather detest how annoyingly cheerful you're this morning." Then she spun on her heel... and almost closed the door upon Loki's tail.

The feline growled in protest, and a moment later, Sarah vanished inside.

Feeling the smile upon his face stretch from ear to ear, Keir shook his head at himself. "She's one of a kind, is she not?" he asked the feline as they headed back down the stairs. "Have ye ever met another like her?" He sighed. "Neither have I."

Aye, Keir loved that bold side of Sarah. He loved seeing it break through a little more each day after being suppressed for far too long.

He was certain that when she came fully into her own, she would take the world by storm.

The air outside was still cold, but the sun peeked over the horizon, casting a warm glow upon the world. Ice crystals glistened wherever he looked, and the roads were slightly frosted. Keir breathed in deeply, taking in the crisp scent of morning. He loved how the cold air filled his lungs, invigorating him. *Hopefully, we'll make good time!*

Keir could not help but picture their arrival in Scotland. He wondered what his family would say about him returning with Sarah and her family. He knew that they would be welcoming; still, he wondered what conclusions they would draw. Keir could all but imagine his grandmother's shrewd look—not unlike Grandma Edie's. She would know even without any sort of explanation that he cared for Sarah.

She knew him too well!

Of course, she did. They were family!

When the sisters and the girls stepped outside a little while later, Keir saw with one glance that Lady Birchwell was still struggling with what little strength she had left. Her limbs seemed to tremble, and he guessed she kept herself upright by sheer will alone. Augusta and Dorothea, however, were eager and cheerful, their little legs carrying them around with ease, their faces aglow with thoughts of adventure.

"My lady." Keir held out his arm to Sarah's sister. "May I escort ye?"

Lady Birchwell tensed briefly, then relaxed, her breath a bit labored as she nodded. "Thank you, Mr. MacKinnear, and... please, call me... Katherine." A touch of reluctance clung to her voice, and Keir wondered why she was offering the use of her first name. After all, it was far from common in her circles. Still, his family was a rather informal bunch, and he supposed it would be better for her to get used to it.

"May I escort ye, Katherine?" Keir asked, waiting until she took his arm, her other held protectively over Frederica. "Call me Keir."

Kate gave him a tentative smile and then allowed him to help her into the carriage.

"Thank you," came Sarah's voice as he stepped back. Her blue eyes shone with gratitude, and yet he detected a hint of unease in them.

"What is it, lass?" Keir asked, pulling her aside.

Sarah glanced at her sister, then looked back at him. "She needs to rest, but she will not allow me to take Frederica. Not for long, at least." She swallowed hard, something dark overshadowing her face. "She's still terrified of losing them."

Keir nodded, unable to imagine what a forced separation from her children did to a young mother. He was certain if Katherine could, she would cling to all her children as she did to Frederica.

Sighing, Sarah called to her nieces, then helped them bundle up in the carriage. All the while, Keir saw Katherine's watchful eyes linger. Aye, it was not distrust he saw, but fear.

"Listen," Keir spoke up cheerfully, his gaze directed at Augusta and Dorothea, "we'll be on the road for a few more days, and I was wondering if ye'd like to ride with me sometime."

While Augusta all but squealed with delight, Dorothea looked at him with that skeptical expression upon her face. *Aye, the wee lassie is a cautious one!*

"Yes!" Augusta answered without hesitation, unabashed delight upon her face. Then her eyes snapped to her mother. "Mother, can I? Please?"

Unmoving like a stone column, Katherine stared at her daughter. Keir could see that she wanted to refuse; still, the yearning expression on Augusta's face would not allow her. "O-Of course, my darling." She swallowed hard before her eyes met his.

Keir nodded to her. "I promise I shall take the utmost care of her and return her to ye without delay. Ye have my word, my lady." Keir added a formal bow, hoping Katherine would see the sincerity of his words.

A faint smile flitted across her face, and her shoulders fell on a deep exhale.

"When?" Augusta demanded the moment her mother relaxed.

"Soon," Keir replied, deciding to give Katherine a little more time to settle in before spiriting her daughter away. Although Augusta looked a bit disappointed, she said nothing, no word of complaint leaving her lips. Sarah smiled at him as she moved past him, seating herself in the carriage beside her sister.

And then, they were off, back on the road north. The sun shone brightly, offsetting the fierce wind that tugged on Keir's hat and coat. Mr. Garner kept his head low to shield his face, and even the horses seemed displeased by the harsh tug upon their coats.

Fortunately, no one came upon them on the road. There were no thundering hoof beats catching up to them. No shouts of pursuers giving chase. Only the occasional traveler who would tip his hat in greeting and then continue on his way.

After pausing for a quick bite to eat and to allow the horses a moment of rest, Keir approached Augusta, determinedly keeping his gaze fixed on the girl, not allowing it to stray to her mother. "Are ye ready?"

Augusta clapped her hands with joy, then paused, her eyes wandering upward, beginning at Scout's hooves and stopping when they reached his saddle. "I'll never get up there."

Keir chuckled, then swept Augusta up and settled her on Scout. The girl squealed in delight, and yet Keir could all but sense her mother tense. Still, he did not look. Instead, he swung himself into the saddle behind the girl, careful not to upend her balance. "Gather the reins," he instructed as the carriage pulled out onto the road ahead of them. "Aye, then give them a little tug, gently, so Scout knows where ye want him to go."

Augusta held her breath, and Keir could all but sense her little body quivering with delight as Scout moved. "I love this!"

"Do ye never ride?"

Augusta shook her head. "I always wanted to, but... but there were no horses. I mean, there were, but they were too tall, like... like Scout. Only there was no one to ride with me." She craned her neck and looked up at him. "Do you think I'll ever be able to ride by myself?"

Keir smiled at her. "Aye, certainly. All ye need is a little practice."

A sigh of longing left Augusta's lips, and Keir knew that the best he could do for Katherine in the coming days was to keep her daughters engaged and happy. Perhaps then she would see that loosening her grip on them would not tear them from her side.

Chapter Five

A FAERIE TALE?

Over the next few days, as they continued to travel north, Kate noticed her gaze move toward what lay ahead. Thus far, all her thoughts had been focused upon the past, upon how it would affect her present and future. Every day had felt paralyzing, her mind and heart terrified of what was to come, unable to notice what was around her, right in front of her eyes.

Now, though, Kate felt herself beginning to blink, to clear her eyes, her gaze focusing on her children, not with fear but with hope.

For days now, Augusta had seized each and every opportunity to ride with Mr. MacKinnear—Keir. At first, of course, Kate had felt every inch of her body tense at the thought of her precious daughter leaving her side. It was irrational; of course, she knew it to be. Unfortunately, that knowledge did nothing to dissuade that tense, terrifying, utterly paralyzing emotion that seized her chest the moment Augusta moved a step too far away.

Yet with repetition, Kate's body finally eased into a more relaxed state. Her gaze lingered upon Augusta with curiosity, seeing her eldest daughter laugh and smile, her blue eyes sparkling with joy and adventure. Kate could not remember the last time she had seen Augusta like this, and the thought broke her heart. Children should know joy, and yet her daughters' lives had been shaped by emotions far darker.

Kate closed her eyes and heaved a deep, sorrowful sigh. *I allowed it to happen. I failed them.*

"Mother! Look how I'm doing this!" Augusta called, her voice echoing through the window of the carriage.

Instantly, Kate's eyes flew open. She watched her child fly by, the reins tightly in her hands. For a split second, Kate felt a memory tug upon her mind, a memory of her seated upon her own pony chasing the wind across an endless meadow. It was a memory accompanied by joy and a sense of utter freedom, of a tomorrow full of promises and dreams that had not yet abandoned her.

And Kate smiled.

She felt an honest smile claim her face, and her heart remembered that this was what life was supposed to be.

"Our governess said that ladies are not to ride like that," Dorothea remarked with a pout as she glanced out the window at her sister. Her right hand continued to stroke Loki's fur as he lay curled up on her lap, purring softly. "She said it is not ladylike."

Kate tensed, uncertain how to respond, how to—

"Things are right when they feel right," Sarah answered Dorothea's unspoken question, her voice steady and ringing with conviction. "Augusta is enjoying herself, and there's nothing wrong with that." She gently took one of Dorothea's little hands into her own. "Never believe another over yourself, Thea."

A tentative smile came to Dorothea's face, and she gave an almost imperceptible nod. "Do you think... I could try it, too? Sometime?" With her teeth set into her lower lip, she glanced up at Sarah, hope shining in her green eyes.

"Of course, you can." Sarah squeezed her hand in encouragement. "Life is full of possibilities, but we need to be brave enough to seize them."

Thunderstruck, Kate stared at her sister. Never had she known Sarah to be so confident and daring. Indeed, when they had been children, Kate herself had been the one to test the limits set for their lives while Sarah had simply tagged along. Now, it seemed their roles had been reversed. How had this happened? How had Sarah found such strength?

Kate's gaze moved toward the window where Augusta was still riding in front of Keir. Only now, her eyes did not linger upon her precious child but upon the man who had brought them here. Without a doubt, Kate knew him to be the reason for the change she saw in her sister. She had suspected so for a while now. He was a man unlike any she had ever met, urging Sarah to hold her head high, to brave whatever was coming at her, to make her own way. In Kate's experience, men did not do that. Men liked being in control, having power over others. Her father was like that as was her husband and countless others she had encountered over the years.

But this was a new beginning, was it not? And the world at large was not like the small part she had lived in, was it? Indeed, Kate refused to believe that it was. After all, the Whickertons were different as well. That she had always known. Only for a time, it had slipped her mind. And now, there was Mr. MacKinnear.

Keir.

Kate smiled, another one of those smiles that felt honest. *Yes, I do feel safer with him around!*

While Mr. Garner kept to the background, driving the carriage and seeing to the horses, Keir spent his days trying his utmost to make her daughters laugh. Kate could see that he had already conquered Augusta's heart, her love for horses paving that path. Dorothea, however, still looked a bit skeptical. Kate could not quite say what made Thea eye Keir with a hint of apprehension. Was it a natural sort of distrust? Or was it learned? Had life taught little Thea not to place her trust easily?

Kate hated that thought, and so, when she came upon Keir and Dorothea one afternoon as they took a break in a small grove near a stream, she could not bring herself to leave, to venture over to Mr. Garner who was seeing to the horses or to Sarah and Augusta who were gathering firewood.

Instead, Kate remained half-hidden behind a tree, Frederica sleeping in her arms, and listened.

"I hear that ye like fairies," Keir remarked as he set to work on making a fire.

Seated upon a small rock, Dorothea nodded, her right hand curled into Loki's fur. As most days, the feline lay sleeping in her lap. "A fairy brought us back to Mother."

"So, I hear." Keir smiled at her, carefully feeding the orange flames as they grew, licking at the dry wood. "Would ye care to hear a story about a faerie dog?"

Even from a distance, Kate could see the slight widening of Dorothea's eyes, the way her slender shoulders tensed in anticipation. Her teeth once more sank into her lower lip before she nodded her head up and down.

"But I warn ye," Keir remarked with a serious expression upon his face. "'Tis not a story for the faint of heart." As the fire crackled softly, he sat back, his blue eyes fixed upon Dorothea in a contemplative way. "But yer heart knows how to be brave, does it not? Ye have the look of it."

Kate held her breath as Dorothea seemed to straighten, her shoulders pulling back. Again, she gave a quick nod. "I *am* brave," came her tiny voice, and to Kate's ears, it seemed to echo across the small grove. "You cannot frighten me with a story."

Keir settled himself across from her. "I didna think I could," he assured her with an acknowledging nod.

For a moment, he remained still, his gaze distant as though moving to a faraway place. Then, his eyes moved back to look into Dorothea's. "The faerie dog is a bad omen," he began softly, a slight cock to his head as though meant as a last warning. "'Tis massive, the size of a young bull, and wolf-like in appearance. Have ye ever seen a wolf, Thea?"

Dorothea shook her head, her arms now curled around Loki, her eyes wide.

"They have sharp fangs, and this particular one has paws the size of a grown man's hand." He held up one of his hands in front of Dorothea's face, and her eyes grew even rounder. "Faerie dogs are said to roam the Highlands, and people whisper that sighting such a beast would see ye stripped of yer soul, for the faerie dog carries it away to the afterlife."

Kate felt a shiver run down her back, and her arms tensed upon

Frederica. For a moment, she felt compelled to interfere, to cut the story short and assure Dorothea that there were no such creatures as faerie dogs.

"Where do the faerie dogs come from?" Dorothea asked, to Kate's surprise, her voice full of intrigue.

Keir shrugged. "No one can tell. They appear as though out of nowhere."

"Perhaps they have a secret place somewhere."

"Perhaps." Keir paused, not another word leaving his lips as he watched Dorothea.

"What is the afterlife?" Dorothea asked, and Kate tensed. *Oh, this is not good! Why didn't I stop this?* "Does it mean you're dead?"

Keir nodded.

A sigh left Dorothea's lips, and yet Kate saw nothing dark in her daughter's eyes. "And the faerie dogs can go there and come back?" she asked, her voice still ringing with fascination. "Are there other places people cannot go? Places only faeries know about?"

Keir grinned at her. "'Tis a good question, but since I'm not a faerie, I wouldna know."

Dorothea chuckled. "Have you ever seen a faerie dog?"

Keir shook his head.

"Are you afraid you might?"

For a moment, Keir held her gaze. Then he leaned closer in shared confidence. "Are ye afraid ye might fall off a tree?" He nodded to a tall oak nearby.

Dorothea frowned. "No, I never climb trees."

"But ye could, couldn't ye?"

She nodded, a calculating gleam coming to her face that Kate did not quite care for.

"Well," Keir said, tossing another log onto the fire, "I think 'tis good to be afraid when there's something to fear."

Dorothea eyed him curiously. "And there's no faerie dog around, is there?" She grinned at him and then resumed stroking Loki's fur.

"Not that I can see," Keir answered with a matching grin.

Kate exhaled a sigh of relief, amazed by Keir's subtle way of addressing Dorothea's fears. Indeed, her daughter had been fearful, had she not? Kate had not even been aware of it. Now, though, she saw a new lightness in the way Dorothea smiled and laughed, as though a heavy weight had been lifted off her young shoulders.

With the flames dancing nimbly, everyone gathered around the fire. They spent an hour in the small grove, eating together and listening to another one of Keir's stories. It seemed he possessed an endless memory, countless legends to share at a moment like this one. Kate watched the entranced expression upon her children's faces as he spoke, and in that moment, she truly believed that all would be well.

Listening to the soft rhythm of Keir's voice, Kate saw the way his gaze moved to linger upon Sarah every so often. Her sister, in turn, would smile at him, a shared look between them that held secrets and confidences.

Kate burned to know what passed between them.

And so, as Augusta and Dorothea jumped up to help Mr. Garner ready the horses, Kate remained behind, her gaze following Sarah and Keir as they slipped away through the trees. She knew she ought to remain where she was or perhaps already seat herself in the carriage.

Yet she could not.

A deep need to understand, to look deeper and see what connected Sarah and Keir made her walk after them. Quiet steps carried her onward, her arms softly rocking her sleeping baby daughter. More than ever, Kate was grateful that Frederica was such a good sleeper!

Glimpsing Sarah's blond curls, Kate pulled to a halt behind a tree, and then she carefully peeked around to look at them.

Suddenly, Kate felt reminded of when she had first observed Sarah and Keir from her bedchamber's window as they had walked the garden. Then, too, they had stood close, their hands linked and their bodies almost leaning into one another. Kate could not explain it any better. Words seemed to elude her, and those that did come to mind did not do justice to what she saw.

There seemed to be a bond between them, unseen, that linked them, urged them closer, as though... they had once existed as one and longed to return to that state.

The thought brought tears to Kate's eyes, and that longing Kate had felt awakening within her heart, when she had first seen them together that day, once more made its presence known. *If only!*

Whispered words passed between Sarah and Keir before Keir reached out and touched the tips of his fingers to Sarah's temple. Sarah's eyes closed as his fingers trailed down to the curve of her ear. Keir leaned closer and whispered something that had Sarah open her eyes and look up at him.

Kate held her breath...

... and then Sarah nodded.

Chapter Six

BONDS & ALLIES

Utter giddiness surged through Sarah's body as she met Keir's eyes, their blue deep and compelling. "Yes," she breathed, nodding her head for emphasis, lest the wind carry away her feeble answer.

Keir's smile made her knees go weak, fueling that heady feeling that had swept her away the moment his fingertips had touched her skin. She could still feel their soft caress, light and almost fleeting, but overwhelmingly real. "Ye truly wouldna mind, lass?" He dipped his head slightly, his gaze settling more firmly upon hers. "If ye dunna—"

Sarah stepped forward, her right hand moving to touch the small braids upon Keir's temple. For a moment, her gaze lingered upon them before her eyes flickered sideways to meet his. "Truly, yes."

Honest joy, no longer hampered by caution, now rested in Keir's eyes, and he moved to stand to her side. Then he gently gathered a few strands of her blond curls together and began braiding them backward, away from her face.

Sarah loved the feel of his touch, wished she could sink into his arms, regretted the physical distance that seemed to keep them apart these days. For a moment, she allowed her mind to wander back to their days in the woods, hidden away in that lone cabin, all but cut off from the rest of the world. No one had been there but them. No one to take affront at the closeness between them. How often had Keir reached out to touch her cheek, to take her hand, to pull her close? Sarah could not even begin to count all those precious moments, longing for that natural ease between them to return. Only now, there were always people around, and Sarah knew that at the very least she would face a myriad of questions if she were found in too intimate an embrace with Keir. Of course, Kate knew—or at least suspected—that Sarah cared for Keir, that there was something between them. Still, if she were to come upon them in each other's arms, what would she think?

'She would be appalled!' her mother's voice offered rather unhelpfully at that moment. 'Like me, she would be utterly disappointed.' Sarah could not deny that her mother might be correct. As compassionate a woman as Kate was, Sarah knew she was herself shocked by her own behavior and still struggled with the fact that she had disobeyed her husband, that she had robbed him of his children and of every chance for an heir. Sarah understood her well; after all, they had both been ingrained with values they had now tossed to the side of the road, choosing a path that led them far away from the one they had been meant to travel.

Sarah knew that there was no going back. And she, at least, did not even want to. No, she wanted to move forward.

With Keir.

If... at all possible.

"What are ye thinking, lass?" That teasing chuckle rumbled in Keir's voice. "I can see the cogs turning in yer head again."

Sarah smiled as he stepped around her and then began braiding the hair upon her left temple. "I... I was just thinking that I... miss our cabin." She sighed deeply, unable to help herself.

Keir grinned. "Our cabin?"

Heat once more surged into Sarah's cheeks, and she kept her gaze fixed upon the trees ahead of her. Still, she would not hide. "Yes, I miss... when it was only the two of us." She chanced a glance at him, feeling emboldened by the soft touch of longing that lingered upon his face. "I wish I never had to stop wearing my hair like this." She reached up to touch the finished braid on her right temple.

Keir nodded, then moved behind her, combining the two braids in the back of her head. "No one forced ye to stop." A hint of regret lingered in his voice.

Sarah sighed. "I know, but... people would have... wondered."

"I suppose they would have," Keir agreed, yet the tone in his voice suggested that he did not deem that reason enough to alter one's behavior.

"Your life was never like mine," Sarah replied, suddenly feeling the need to defend herself. "Nothing I did was ever quite right, quite good enough, and to betray everything I was raised to be so openly..." The air rushed from her lungs when a sudden wave of finality washed over her. Indeed, no matter what she did now, her old life was gone. There was no going back, and although Sarah had no desire to do so, the thought still sent a chill through her body.

Keir's hands settled upon her shoulders and then turned her to face him. "'Tis yer life, Sarah, yer choice. It always should have been." He paused, his gaze daring her to contradict him. "All I'm saying is that... I missed yer braids." A soft smile came to his lips as his gaze darted to her right temple.

"Why?" Sarah dared him, suddenly feeling bold.

"Because they remind me of *our* cabin as well," Keir replied with a grin. Then his expression suddenly sobered, and he reached for her, gathering her close. "They remind me of ye, little wisp, of our time together."

"I know you wear the braids to remember your sister," Sarah heard herself say. "I always knew that. Still, a part of me wonders if—"

"Aye."

Sarah frowned. "Aye?"

Grinning, Keir dipped his head and gently leaned his forehead against hers. "Aye, they always reminded me of Yvaine, but now, they also make me think of ye, lass."

Sarah felt her heart skip a beat. "Truly?"

"Aye, truly."

About to sink into Keir's arms, Sarah stopped herself. "What if...?" She broke off, worrying her lower lip.

"Aye, lass?"

Sarah closed her eyes. "When we reach your home, will you want me to take them down?"

Keir lifted his head and looked down at her. "Why would ye think so?"

"Because... your family, they will think that... that we..." Unable to finish that sentence, Sarah bit her lower lip, doing her utmost to ignore that nervous tingling coursing through her veins.

"Aye, they will." Keir's hands upon the small of her back tightened, his gaze penetrating in a way that Sarah felt her head spin.

"And... And you don't... mind?"

Keir shook his head. "Why would I, lass? After all, they wouldna be wrong." His right brow quirked upward. "Would they?"

Sarah exhaled a shuddering breath as that earlier sense of exhilaration broke free, threatening to buckle her knees. "No," she breathed. "They would not."

"Good." Keir smiled, then dropped an achingly sweet kiss upon her lips. "Dunna worry, lass. Before ye know it, ye shall be one of us. Yer sister and her lassies as well." He chuckled. "Soon, ye won't even remember what it felt like being English."

Sarah laughed. "And what does it mean to be a Scot?"

A rather intense expression came to Keir's face. "Freedom." He all but exhaled the word as though it were deeply ingrained within his bones. "The freedom to choose yer own destiny, to be who ye are." He gently grasped her chin, and for a second, his gaze strayed to Sarah's lips. "I canna remember a time when 'twas different. I know from the legends that it was, that it was the old ways that gave rise to our new path. Still, my grandmother has always been devoted to that cause. She was granted freedom long ago, and she has never forgotten it. She's a Scot through and through."

Laughter bubbled up in Sarah's throat. "And yet she was born English."

"That doesna matter, lass. We choose who we want to be. 'Tis the only way to be at peace with yerself."

Sarah nodded, Keir's words reminding her of Grandma Edie. "I think I'll like your grandmother, and I have to admit, I'm curious to meet your family." *And also, a bit afraid!*

Keir chuckled. "Dunna worry; they willna bite, but I might as well warn ye, lass. My family is a nosy lot. Nothing is private, for they know no boundaries when it comes to sticking their noses into other people's affairs."

Sarah chuckled. "Something they have in common with the Whickertons."

"Aye, they certainly do." Smiling, he shook his head. "I suppose there had to be a reason why my grandmother and Grandma Edie remained friends all those years."

A warm glow rested in Keir's eyes that made Sarah wonder. "Do you have such a friend? Someone you've known all your life?" Sarah instantly thought of Christina, one of the Whickerton sisters.

Keir nodded, and that warm glow in his eyes deepened. "Aye, I do. His name's Eoghan. As lads, my brother Duncan, Eoghan and I were inseparable." He chuckled. "We got into a lot of trouble together, going off on adventures, but 'twas always worth it."

Sarah loved the joy in Keir's gaze as he spoke of his friend. "Why did he not accompany you to England, then? Or has he outgrown the need for adventure?"

Sighing, Keir shook his head, and the glow darkened. "Nah, I dunna believe so. Only Eoghan lost his wife a few years back, and she left him with a wee lassie, Augusta's age. Her name is Bonnie."

"Oh." Sarah swallowed hard, remembering the night Frederica had been born. There had been a moment or two when she had been uncertain if Kate would live. "I'm so sorry."

Keir nodded, the expression in his eyes one of deepest sorrow. "Aye, he loved her fiercely, and it broke his heart. But Bonnie needed him, and so he continued on."

Leaning closer, Sarah welcomed the way Keir's arms closed more tightly around her. "He misses her still?"

Keir nodded. "Aye. Most days, he seems fine, the way he was before he lost her." He exhaled slowly. "But then there are moments when I can see how deep the wound still is."

Sarah closed her eyes and rested her head against Keir's shoulder. "I cannot imagine his loss," she whispered, and her fingers dug into Keir's coat, holding on tightly. "I cannot imagine..."

More than once, Sarah had been on the brink of having to bid Keir farewell, and now, more than ever, she knew she could not bear a life without him. But could they have a future?

Of course, his family did not live by the standards and expectations of the English *ton*, but would they truly approve of her? And if they did not, would that mean the end to all Sarah's hopes? After all, Keir adored his family and to find himself faced with their disapproval would pain him. Certainly, he would not go against their wishes. How could he?

"What are ye thinking, lass?" Keir asked with frightening precision as he once more grasped her chin, urging her to look at him. "Ye have that look in yer eyes again."

Sarah swallowed, annoyed with herself for spoiling this moment. "Your grandmother is a duke's daughter, is she not?" Indeed, he had told her so once.

Keir nodded. "Aye, she is." The corners of his mouth teased upward ever so slowly. "But she forgot how to be English a long time ago." He leaned down and touched the tip of his nose to hers in a teasing way. "Dunna worry, lass. She willna judge ye. I can see that ye fear that. No, she will applaud ye for walking yer own path."

A shuddering breath left Sarah's lips, for her doubts would not be so easily silenced. "I could not have done so without you."

Keir nodded. "And she couldna have done so without Grandma Edie." He touched her cheek. "None of us can stand alone. 'Tis a universal truth and nothing to be ashamed of, ye hear me, lass?"

Sarah nodded as tears blurred her eyes, and a moment later, she found herself in an almost crushing embrace... and it felt wonderful!

Chapter Seven

AT AN INN IN GRETNA GREEN

The very moment they crossed the border into Scotland, Keir felt a hum in his bones. It was an odd sensation, and although he was still a good distance from the home he loved, he already felt its pull, tugging him onward, hastening his steps. *Aye, 'tis good to come home!*

The sun had already set, darkness falling over the world and the sleepy village of Gretna Green as they drew up to the inn. Its worn stone walls were light in color, set against a dark, but clear night sky, revealing a thousand stars. It was a moderate-sized, clean inn, and its windows glowed with candlelight, soft music and laughter spilling out into the night whenever the door opened.

Turning his head, Keir could all but see English soil; and yet it felt good to be on Scottish ground once more. On the morrow, they would continue their journey north, and Keir knew that feeling deep within him would only grow with each step he took. It had been too long, and a part of him could not wait to show Sarah his home, to have her meet his family. He could only hope that her heart would eventually feel at home in Scotland.

As Mr. Garner ensured that the horses were tended to, Keir assisted the ladies out of the carriage. The girls looked at this new place with wide eyes and curiosity, their sense of adventure not yet satisfied. Sarah, too, met his gaze with something akin to enjoyment and hopeful expectation. Certainly, there was a hint of nervousness about her, too. After all, everything these days was rather unknown to her, far away from what she had grown up with. Yet it was Katherine who looked deeply apprehensive. Although the last few nights sleeping in proper beds at various inns had restored some of her strength, the young woman still moved with great hesitancy, her gaze uncertain, as though she still doubted every step she took. Keir wondered how long it would take for her to truly feel at ease.

Together, they entered the inn and seated themselves in the taproom. Its wood beams were dark with age, the tables worn and the floor slightly uneven. Still, the light cast by the fire in the hearth illuminated the room with its flickering orange glow, warming not only their chilled fingers but their bodies, too. While Sarah saw to her sister and nieces, Keir ensured that they would be provided with a hearty stew, thick and meaty with carrots and potatoes, fresh bread on the side, toasted in the hearth and smothered with melted butter and honey. In Keir's experience, a full belly soothed many worries and allowed one to take in the world with fresh eyes.

Indeed, once their plates were empty, their bowls freed of all contents, everyone appeared more relaxed. Even Katherine had a small smile flicker across her face as she watched her two eldest daughters whisper to one another, their eyes aglow.

Keir smiled at Sarah, meeting her eyes, seeing how relieved she, too, felt. Indeed, the atmosphere was one of contentment. It had taken them a good bit of time and effort to get here, but slowly everyone was settling into this new routine.

Then Keir rose to his feet and stepped over to Sarah, gently placing a hand upon her shoulder as he leaned down and said, "I shall see to our rooms." He grinned at Augusta and Dorothea, both girls all but bouncing in their chairs. "And keep an eye on those little fleas. I have a feeling they might bounce away."

Sarah chuckled, then glanced at her nieces, well-aware that both girls were listening. "What fleas? I don't see any fleas." She spun abruptly toward the girls, and they squealed. "Do you see any fleas?"

The girls' giggles followed Keir as he crossed the taproom and approached the innkeeper's desk. The man's balding head shone in the firelight like a polished apple, and he wore a pair of round spectacles that made his eyes appear even smaller than they were. Again, Keir secured two chambers, one for the ladies and one for himself and Mr. Garner. As the innkeeper jotted down a few notes in a ledger and then rummaged through his desk for the keys to their rooms, Keir looked over his shoulder toward their table.

At Sarah.

By now, Keir knew every delicate freckle upon her nose, every shade of blue in her eyes, every minuscule wrinkle that showed in the corners of her mouth when she smiled and laughed. He knew how to read every expression, every sweep of her lashes, every tug upon her lips. He knew *her*.

And yet, Keir found he did not tire of looking at her. Every spark of joy upon her face echoed within his own heart, and every tear to escape her eyes weighed heavily upon his shoulders as well. He marveled at these sensations. Never had he been so attuned to another person before. As well as he knew Sarah, still every day he discovered a hundred new little things about her. Would this ever stop? He rather doubted it.

Aye, I could look at her forever!

In that moment, Sarah lifted her gaze and their eyes met, and Keir could feel the effects of that gentle smile that tugged upon her lips in every fiber of his being. It made him rock back on his heels. It stole the breath from his lungs. It made him want to rush across the room and pull her into his arms. It made him want to stand here and look at her forever.

"Will ye be needing an anvil priest, then?"

Keir stilled at the sound of the innkeeper's voice, turning to look at the man. Middle-aged with a balding head, the innkeeper still possessed a bit of an impish quality, his eyes glittering with amusement.

Caught off guard, Keir could not reply, his mind slow to catch up, to understand and find appropriate words. After all, he found himself across from a stranger who did not need to hear the story of his life.

Yet, Keir felt as though a simple *no* would not suffice. Would it not be a lie? Because deep down, Keir knew why he was bringing Sarah to Scotland.

Why he found himself unable to leave her side.

Why even a single look into her wide blue eyes changed everything for him.

He knew, and yet the time for open words had not yet come.

The innkeeper chuckled good-naturedly. "If ye require anything, please dunna hesitate to ask." He glanced past Keir's shoulder at Sarah. "I'm always more than happy to assist a young couple." And with that, he handed Keir the keys to their rooms.

Keir thanked the man and heard his father's voice echo through his head a moment later. 'There's no use running from the truth, lad. It'll catch up with ye, sure as daylight.'

Keir grinned. "I'm not running," he murmured quietly to himself. "I know what I want, and when the time is right..."

Aye, when the time is right!

Like a caress, Sarah could feel Keir's gaze upon her. It chased teasing shivers over her skin and made her catch her breath. Unable to deny herself, she lifted her gaze, and their eyes met.

The look in Keir's eyes chased an instant blush onto her cheeks, and Sarah quickly averted her gaze. Always had she marveled at the way she could feel him, sense him, even when he stood across the room. What did that mean?

Again, Sarah lifted her eyes, Keir's own gaze now directed at the innkeeper, his lips moving as he spoke. Sarah sighed, enjoying the chance to look at him, to watch without being watched. She loved the self-assured way he stood in this world, the way he addressed others with kindness and respect but also with determination. He would not cower, but neither would he bully. He was the kind of man Sarah had always imagined in her dreams, honorable in the truest meaning of the word. Not like the gentlemen of the *ton*, who had twisted the meaning of the word into something utterly grotesque.

"I never thought I'd ever find myself at an inn in Gretna Green," Kate remarked with a disbelieving chuckle.

Sarah resettled her gaze upon her sister, seeing her look around and take in their surroundings. "It does not feel quite real, does it?"

Kate nodded. "Sometimes I feel as though I strayed into a dream and that any moment now, I'll awaken. Only... I do not." She shrugged, looked down at Frederica as the girl began to stir and then back at Sarah. "Is this life? Is this real?" Again, she shrugged, then rocked Frederica gently as her daughter started to fuss. "There are moments when I cannot tell."

"I remember feeling like that when I left our parents' house that night," Sarah admitted in a whisper, quickly glancing at the girls to ensure that they were quite occupied seated in front of the large fireplace, Loki in their laps. "Perhaps it is something that simply happens when life takes an unexpected turn."

Kate chuckled, and Sarah savored the sound, happy to see that Frederica had calmed again. "There have been quite a few unexpected turns lately, have there not?" Again, she flicked her gaze around the taproom. "It does feel strange to be here." Then a sudden grin stole onto her face, and she met Sarah's eyes. "Do you remember how Mother warned us of gentlemen with dubious intentions, seeking to secure an heiress's fortune by luring her away to Gretna Green?" She chuckled, and the sound was even more powerful than before.

Sarah laughed, relieved to see that the Kate she had known all her life once again shone through, fighting her way back to the surface after years of cowering under her husband's rule. "Well, since we are not heiresses and have no fortunes to speak of, I suppose that means we are safe from such dubious gentlemen." Her gaze drifted across the taproom to where Keir still stood at the innkeeper's desk.

"Is this the place where Harriet was taken by her kidnapper?" Kate suddenly asked, her green eyes wide and curious. "Do you know?"

Sarah shrugged, looking around the taproom as though a clue might materialize out of thin air and answer that question for her. "I do not. Is this the only inn in Gretna Green?" She shrugged, then laughed. "Oh, I wish I could've seen Harriet challenge Lord Burnham to a duel!"

Kate nodded her head vigorously. "Yes, Harriet has always been one of a kind, and she has not changed a bit." A shadow suddenly crossed over Kate's face, and Sarah wondered what her sister could be thinking. Indeed, many of the young women she had known had been forced to grow up as time passed, forced to abandon childish fantasies and become the people society demanded. Yet somehow, Harriet had not. Did Kate perhaps regret *she* had bowed her head and not fought harder to remain who she was? Sarah knew that she herself did.

"If you wish, I could ask Keir if this was indeed the inn," Sarah suggested, hoping to draw Kate's thoughts away from the past and back to the present, to where hope still existed.

Kate blinked, and her chin rose, her eyes meeting Sarah's. "He was here when it happened?"

Sarah nodded. "He told me he stopped here on his way down from Scotland and ran into the Duke of Clements, who had followed Harriet's trail to an inn in Gretna Green, determined to save her from her vile kidnapper." Chuckling, Sarah shook her head. "Of course, Harriet was grateful for his help; however, she has always been the kind of girl who saves herself."

Kate grinned, clearly amused. "And so she challenged Lord Burnham to a duel?"

"She did, and I know she enjoyed every moment of it." Sarah exhaled a long breath, trying to picture Harriet standing out on some field at dawn, facing her opponent with a sword in her hand. "Oh, I so admire her! She's so brave and dauntless, never afraid to do what she deems right, to be who she is."

Kate, too, sighed, something wistful in her gaze. "Truthfully, I cannot imagine the life Harriet lives. I am not brave as she is." She met Sarah's eyes, the look in her own resigned. "Perhaps we are not all meant to be larger-than-life."

Feeling her sister's melancholy spread to her own heart, Sarah pulled back her shoulders and lifted her chin. "Kate, I admit that for the longest time I thought so, too. Now, though, I am no longer sure."

Kate frowned. "Sure of what?"

Sarah smiled. "That I'm not brave enough for this world." She looked back at Keir, and once again their eyes met, something new in his gaze that made Sarah wonder what thoughts went through his head in that moment. "I *am* brave," she whispered to herself as well as to her sister, her gaze lingering upon Keir. "More than I thought I ever could be. More than anyone ever expected from me." She met her sister's gaze, the smile upon her face giving her strength. "Who knows what the future will bring? All I know is that I am no longer afraid of it."

Chapter Eight

A TOUCH OF SALT

Keir could smell a faint trace of salt upon the air as they moved closer to the coast. The English border was now only a memory in the distance, and Keir found he was more than eager to return home.

Though the air remained cold this early in the year, the sun shone upon their journey, making traveling brighter and raising all their spirits.

More than ever before, Sarah seemed to glow with exuberance, new eagerness to experience the world, to see what it had to offer, taking one step after another, never afraid of where they might lead her. Keir loved that about her. Deep down, he knew that this was the Sarah she had always been meant to be, and every day he watched her come a little more out of her shell and rediscover her true self.

Fortunately, the same could be said for Katherine. Only she still stood at the beginning of her journey, her fears and uncertainties still there, seated upon her shoulders, weighing her down and making her suspicious and hesitant. Yet Keir could see that she was trying. She was doing her best to release her tight grip upon her daughters, to allow them to venture farther and farther away from her as she fought to step out of that shadow that still hung above her head.

Indeed, Augusta, in particular, now seemed like a child who had never known sorrow. Her smile and laughter were infectious, and she fluttered through each and every day with such lightness that it amazed even Keir. She utterly adored the horses, and after a few days, Keir agreed to allow her to ride Autumn by herself. Augusta was so excited that for a second Keir feared she might faint. Her breaths were coming so fast that she swayed upon her feet.

"Calm yerself, lassie," Keir murmured, placing a steadying hand upon her shoulder. "Ye'll spook Autumn. She can feel yer agitation, and I can tell ye she doesna care for it."

Holding his gaze, Augusta inhaled a deep breath, pushing it deeper and deeper into her body until she finally released it. "Better?" she asked, willing her breathing to calm.

Keir chuckled. "Aye, well done." Then he picked her up and sat her upon Autumn's back.

"When will I be old enough to get myself into the saddle?" Augusta asked as she gathered up the reins.

"'Tis not a matter of age but of height." Keir chuckled, reassuringly patting Autumn's neck, allowing the mare to familiarize herself with her new rider. "Give it some time, lassie. Not everything has to be done in a single day."

Before the day was done, though, Augusta felt completely at ease on Autumn's back. Every bit of doubt vanished from her eyes, and she laughed and chatted happily as they rode along. *Aye, 'tis what life is all about!*

With every step Augusta took out into the world, though, the frown upon Dorothea's face seemed to grow. Keir knew the lassie to be cautious, objections and concerns often falling from her lips. Still, every once in a while, her green eyes would light up with longing, with envy even.

"Will ye ride with me today, Thea?" Keir asked her one morning as they were preparing the carriage, getting ready to depart the latest inn.

The girl paused in her step and craned her neck, looking up at him. Doubt shone in her eyes, and for a moment, Keir thought she might refuse him outright. However, she did not.

"'Tis perfectly safe, I assure ye." He kneeled down in front of her. "Ye have my word."

Crossing her little arms over her chest, Dorothea regarded him quizzically, clearly trying to decide whether he was trustworthy. "You will not let me fall?"

Tempted to smile, Keir willed his face to remain serious. "I willna let ye fall."

"You will not go too fast?"

"I willna go too fast."

Pressing her lips together, Dorothea regarded him for a long moment, clearly torn. "You will not tease me about being a baby?"

Keir placed a hand above his heart. "I wouldna dream of it, my lady."

After another endless moment of consideration, Dorothea finally nodded her head. And so, Keir quickly whisked her away and placed her upon Scout's back.

For a moment, Dorothea's face paled, and her little hands clutched Scout's mane. Her body tensed as she clung to the horse's back. However, as Scout failed to move, to buck and kick, to try to throw her off, Dorothea slowly relaxed.

Keir looked towards Sarah and Katherine, the look upon their faces expectant. They seemed to be almost holding their breaths as they watched Dorothea cling to Scout's back.

"He's not moving," Dorothea observed with a sideways glance at Keir, apprehension marking her features.

Keir chuckled. "He can sense yer unease, Thea, and he doesna want ye to be afraid."

The expression in the girl's eyes changed, and her tight grip upon Scout's mane lessened. She inhaled a deep breath, then pushed herself into a more upright position.

"Come on, Thea! Let's go!" Augusta called as she urged Autumn out of the inn's yard. Sarah and Katherine were now seated in the carriage, and Mr. Garner clicked his tongue, urging the two mares onward.

"Not too fast, Gus!" Keir called after the young girl as he gathered Scout's reins and then swung himself into the saddle behind Dorothea. For a moment, the girl tensed, but then she exhaled deeply as his arms came around her, caging her in and keeping her from falling off.

And then they were off, continuing down the road and farther north. The sun shone overhead; the smiles Keir saw all around him made his heart feel lighter. He no longer looked over his shoulder as he had before, concerned that they might be followed. It seemed that the dowager's plan had succeeded in throwing Lord Birchwell off their tracks. Even if eventually, he were to find out which way they had traveled, he would be far behind, unable to catch up before they reached Keir's home and the safety of his clan.

"Men are not to wear their hair long," Dorothea suddenly remarked not long before midday. She had been rather quiet as they rode along, not a word falling from her lips.

Keir chuckled. "Says who?"

"My governess."

"Does she know everything?"

Dorothea paused for a moment, then said, "She says she does."

"And do ye believe her?"

Again, a pause followed before Dorothea's next reply came. "Well, she didn't know we were sneaking out to see Mama."

Keir grinned. "There ye have it."

Once again thoughtful, Dorothea leaned back in his arms, her little body more relaxed than he would have expected. Clearly, the girl had a lot on her mind, questions to sort out and opinions to weigh.

"Let us ride ahead and see if we can find a suitable spot to sit and eat, shall we?" He clicked his tongue and spurred Scout onward. "Gus, stay with the carriage!" he called over his shoulder, glimpsing a frown coming to the young girl's face. Still, she heeded his words and remained where she was.

Dorothea once again clung to Scout's mane as they galloped down a small slope, and so Keir wrapped his arm tightly around her middle, holding her against him, reassuring her she was safe with him. "That looks like a suitable spot over there, dunna ye think?" Keir pointed up ahead toward a small grove, a little ways off the road.

Dorothea nodded. "Why do you speak like that?"

"Like what?" Keir dared her, unable to prevent a grin. A sudden wail echoed to his ears from the carriage, and he wondered what had upset little Frederica.

As Scout slowed his steps, Dorothea twisted around to look up at Keir. "Like that," she said, her green eyes sparking with interest. "Why do you talk like that?"

"Because I'm a Scot," Keir replied by way of explanation. "In different parts of the world, people speak differently."

Dorothea frowned. "Miss Newton said we were to learn other languages." The frown deepened as she looked at him. "But I understand you. Only your words sound... strange." Before Keir could reply, her right forefinger came to rest against the corner of her mouth, a deeply thoughtful expression falling over her face. "Can I do it, too?"

"Speak like a Scot? Certainly. Give it a try." Amusement swelled in Keir's chest, and he struggled to keep it contained. *Aye, the lassie is adorable in her directness!*

"What shall I say?"

Keir drew Scout to a halt, then turned and waved toward Mr. Garner. A moment later, the carriage with Augusta alongside it moved toward them. Then Keir jumped to the ground and lifted Dorothea out of the saddle.

The second her little feet hit the ground, Dorothea looked up at him. "What shall I say?" she repeated, a bit of impatience in her tone now. "I don't know what to say."

Thinking, Keir kneeled down in front of her. "How about this," he suggested, "*I willna frown.*"

Dorothea nodded, then slowly parted her lips, deep concentration in her eyes. "I willna frown," she said slowly and with great emphasis on every word. "I willna frown."

Keir smiled at her. "Bravo!" He applauded, delighting in the joy lighting up her face. "Well done! If ye keep practicing, soon no one will be able to tell if ye're English or Scottish."

A look of accomplishment came to Dorothea's eyes, and as she continued to repeat the sentence he had suggested, that adorable frown vanished from her little face, replaced by a heartwarming smile. "I willna frown. I willna frown."

Keir chuckled, then turned to assist Sarah and Katherine out of the carriage while Mr. Garner once again saw to the horses. Augusta bounced around joyfully, the excitement of her ride still buzzing within her limbs. Only this time, Dorothea did not look at her sister with envious eyes. No, indeed, her mind was still focused on the words she kept repeating.

To Keir's surprise, Sarah managed to convince Katherine to hand her Frederica. The girl was wide awake for a change, her blue eyes open and looking out into the world with great interest.

After a moment of hesitation, Katherine stepped away from her youngest daughter and toward her eldest. "How was the ride, my dear?"

Augusta beamed up at her mother, her mouth not standing still. Katherine smiled, brushing a tender hand over her daughter's head, her expression growing more relaxed.

"I think she's feeling better," Sarah whispered beside him, hope ringing in her voice as she gently bounced little Frederica up and down. "As are you, isn't that right?" she cooed to her little niece. "Fed and changed and warm." She met Keir's eyes. "Did you hear her cry before?"

Grinning, Keir nodded. "The French probably heard her cry."

Sarah chuckled, and Keir smiled down at aunt and niece before his attention returned to Katherine. "Aye, she seems a bit more at ease." Again, his gaze strayed to the small braids upon Sarah's temples, and he reached out a hand to tug a small wisp of hair back behind her ear. "But 'twill take time, lass. Ye'll have to be patient."

Sarah nodded, and yet her blue eyes shone with exuberance. "I know. It's only that it's been so long since I've seen her like this. Part of me feared I never would again."

Keir nodded, watching Katherine as she ventured over to Dorothea, placing her hand upon the little girl's shoulder. "And how was your ride, my dear?"

For a moment, Dorothea did not seem to hear a word. Then, however, she looked up and met her mother's eyes. Instead of answering her question, though, she said, "I willna frown."

While Keir and Sarah burst out laughing, Katherine seemed taken aback. She clearly did not know what to make of her child's reply, and so Dorothea attempted to explain. "When I grow up, I'll be a Scot," she declared, the deepest conviction in her voice.

Glancing toward Sarah and Keir, Katherine's lips twitched. "Is that so?"

Dorothea nodded. "Keir said so."

Katherine chuckled. "Then, by all means, continue."

At her mother's words, Dorothea turned away, her little feet carrying her around the small grove, her lips whispering again and again, "I willna frown."

Even Augusta chuckled, and together, they prepared for the midday meal, stretching their legs and enjoying a moment of rest. Dorothea, though, seemed completely oblivious to the amusement her sudden obsession stirred within her family.

"Are there children where you live?" Augusta asked as they sat together, enjoying a bite to eat.

At her sister's question, Dorothea stopped muttering and looked up.

Keir squeezed Sarah's hand, sensing the amused tremble of suppressed laughter within her. He did not dare meet her eyes lest he lose his own struggle and offend the girl by laughing. *Aye, they're adorable!*

"Of course," Keir replied with as much earnestness as he could muster. "Ye long to make some friends?"

Augusta nodded eagerly. "I've never had a friend."

"Well," Keir elaborated, leaning forward as he spoke to the girls across from him, "my oldest friend Eoghan has a wee lassie right about your age." Indeed, the thought of the wee lassies robbed of all the delights of childhood angered Keir.

Augusta squealed with delight. "What's her name?"

"Bonnie. But I'm not sure ye'd like her," Keir added, glancing at them and drawing down his brows into a serious frown.

Augusta's eyes widened, fixed upon his face. "Why not?" Dorothea, too, looked at him with rapt attention.

Keir sighed, shaking his head a bit dramatically. "Well, she's not a well-behaved young lady like yerselves. She's got a bit of a mischievous side, always going off on some kind of adventure."

Again, an almost inaudible squeal emanated from Augusta. "She sounds marvelous! When can I meet her?"

Keir laughed. "I suppose as soon as we reach our destination."

Rising from her spot beside her sister, Dorothea walked around the fire Mr. Garner had lit and came to stand in front of Keir. "Do you know of a friend for me also?"

Keir grasped her little hand. "Dunna worry, lassie. We'll find ye a friend." He glanced at Sarah, seated beside him. "Ye know, I find the people ye end up caring about the most are the ones that find their way into yer life quite unexpectedly." He leaned closer and whispered confidentially, "Keep yer eyes open, will ye, Thea? One day, the one who's meant to be yer best friend will simply stand right in front of ye."

With shining eyes, Dorothea nodded. "I will," she promised breathlessly. "I promise."

Keir smiled, realizing in that moment that he would not mind having a little girl like Dorothea. Indeed, he would not mind at all...

... and his gaze strayed back to Sarah.

Chapter Nine
A CHILD'S HEART

Sarah looked up at the bright blue sky and thought that it had been a long time since she had last seen such a beautiful day. Not a gray cloud was in sight, and the sun shone brightly, warming her face despite the chill that still lingered in the air. She breathed in deeply, almost tasting a hint of salt upon her tongue as they ventured a little closer to the coast every day.

Seated once again upon Autumn's back, Sarah enjoyed the soft swaying of the horse's gait. It felt familiar and comfortable, and it made her heart feel lighter. Indeed, today was a beautiful day.

"Mother seems sad," Dorothea remarked in a heavy voice.

At her niece's words, Sarah felt her heart sink, her gaze lowering to the small child seated in front of her. She sighed, knowing that despite every little bit of joy they had found these past few days, a dark cloud remained. "She does, does she not?" Sarah murmured into Dorothea's ear; after all, there was no use in pretending.

Dorothea nodded, then craned her neck and looked up at Sarah. "Why is she so sad?"

Again, Sarah heaved a heavy sigh, her mind spinning with everything that had happened. How much of it ought she to share with a four-year-old? A four-year-old she had only met a fortnight ago?

Casting a glance over her shoulder, Sarah saw the carriage rumbling along behind them, Mr. Garner seated on top. Ahead, Keir rode with Augusta on Scout, one arm pointed toward the horizon as he spoke to the girl.

"Aunt Sarah?" Dorothea prompted, clearly demanding an answer. And, of course, she deserved one.

"Well," Sarah began tentatively, "why do you think she is sad?" Indeed, perhaps, it was wise first to ask the child's opinion. More than once on their journey had the girls surprised Sarah with something they had observed, with the way some things appeared to them she would never have seen.

Dorothea's little shoulders rose and fell with a deep breath. "I thought perhaps she does not like traveling," she murmured, then abruptly craned her neck to look at Sarah, as though a new thought had just occurred to her. "Will we ever go back home?"

Ice settled in Sarah's stomach. "Where is home for you, Thea?" she eventually asked, wondering why the girl was asking *her* and not her mother. However, perhaps Dorothea simply did not want to worry Kate. The little girl seemed to have a keen insight into another's feelings and needs.

Dorothea shrugged. "I remember the place we lived before... with Mother and Father." Again, she looked up at Sarah. "Where is Father? Will he come, too?"

At that, the lump in Sarah's stomach twisted and turned painfully. "Well... Thea,... No." She smiled at the little girl tentatively. "He is not coming."

"Why?"

Although Sarah had known that this question would come, she was not in the least prepared for it. Never had she had to search for words to explain the world at large to such a young soul. What if she said too much? What if she did not say enough? What if she simply chose the wrong words?

"Aunt Sarah?"

Closing her eyes, Sarah sighed for a moment, simply feeling the soft swaying of Autumn's gait. Then she looked down at Dorothea, meeting the girl's bright green eyes. "You see, sometimes life is very difficult, very complicated. There is not one right decision. There are simply many to choose from, each one bringing something good and also bringing something bad."

Dorothea nodded, her eyes becoming distant, as though she truly knew what Sarah tried to say. "Father didn't want us to see Mother, did he?"

Caught off guard, Sarah stared at her little niece.

Dorothea nibbled upon her lower lip, a contrived look upon her face. "I heard him say so," she whispered, as though afraid to betray a secret. "He didn't know I was there, but I heard him. He was angry, and Grandmother said mean things to him. Then he was sad."

Not knowing what to say, Sarah wrapped her arms around the little girl and held her tightly, savoring the feeling of Dorothea snuggling back into her. "If you could choose any place in this world where you would like to be more than anywhere else," Sarah whispered in Dorothea's ear, "where would you go?"

For a long moment, the girl remained quiet, and Sarah felt her body move with each breath she took. A slight tremble seemed to travel up and down her arms, and yet otherwise she remained perfectly still. "I want to be wherever Mummy and Augusta are," Dorothea finally said, moving to turn around and look at Sarah. "And I like being where you and Keir are." The ghost of a smile teased her lips. "And Loki. I truly like him."

Sarah smiled at her little niece. "He likes you, too, as do we all, and we are very happy to have you with us."

Dorothea's mouth twitched into a smile, and it was breathtaking and overwhelming and utterly mesmerizing. "Is this an adventure?"

"An adventure?" Sarah repeated, feeling puzzled.

Dorothea nodded. "I remember Mama reading stories about adventures, about people who go on quests and do heroic deeds."

Sarah chuckled. "Well, I don't know about heroic deeds, but if you ask me, this is definitely an adventure. We are going out into the world, to places we've never seen before, to meet new people and see new things. Yes, to me, that is an adventure."

"It is exciting," Dorothea remarked, then paused. "But it's also a little frightening." She met Sarah's eyes. "Will I like the place we're going to? What's it like there?"

Sarah shrugged. "Well, to tell you the truth, I've never even been there myself. It will be a new place for the both of us." She tugged an errant curl back behind Dorothea's ear. "Perhaps we can help one another fit in there and come to feel at home. What do you think?"

Dorothea nodded eagerly. "I'd like that, Auntie Sarah. I'd like that very much."

"Well, then it's agree—"

A sudden cry of joyous delight echoed to their ears from up ahead, and they both flinched. Sarah's arms instantly held Dorothea tighter as she lifted her gaze, trying to see what had happened.

A little ways down the road, where it sloped to a higher point, Keir had pulled Scout to a halt and he and Augusta were staring down at something Sarah could not see. Still, the look upon their faces held joy, and Augusta was looking back at them, waving her little arms, beckoning them forward.

"I suppose we better catch up," Sarah murmured, then spurred Autumn onward, and together, they galloped up the small rise. "What is it?" she called out to the other two as they neared. "What did you—?"

The words remained locked in Sarah's throat as her eyes found the far horizon and then the churning sea below. The sun glistened upon the waves, their sound now drifting to Sarah's ears, a soft, even gentle murmur, still a good distance away. And yet it was mesmerizing, whispering to her of something unknown but meant for her.

"The sea!" Dorothea exclaimed in awe, as though she had spotted a fairytale creature, her little hands clutching Autumn's mane as she stared ahead. "It's beautiful!"

Keir chuckled, looking from the girls to Sarah. "Ye've never seen it?"

"Not like this," Sarah murmured, torn between looking into Keir's eyes and watching the beautiful rhythm of the sea. "Not quite like this."

"What now?" Augusta demanded, craning her neck to look up at Keir. "Do we need a boat?"

Keir nodded. "Unless ye can walk on water, lassie, or perhaps sprout wings?" He looked questioningly from Augusta to Dorothea, brows raised.

With her eyes wide, Dorothea shook her head. "I wish I could," she whispered, still mesmerized. Then she blinked. Her eyes settled upon Keir. "Can we go down there?"

Keir nodded, and the joy that came to the girls' faces made Sarah's heart sing. As much sadness as these two had already known in their short lives, there was still happiness to be found, happiness to contradict everything that had gone wrong thus far.

While the two horses might have been able to pick their way down the steep slope to the beach, the carriage could not. Therefore, they were forced to take the longer way around, following the road that slowly narrowed and turned into little more than a trodden path. With each step they took closer, the sound of the waves grew louder until it became an almost deafening echo against their ears. Still, it was soothing somehow, and Sarah felt drawn toward it.

Nestled into a small cove, they found a cluster of houses, which could not rightly be called a village. Still, it looked utterly picturesque. An almost bewitching lightness filled the people Sarah saw going about their work, tending to boats and seeing to repairs.

Dismounting, they led the horses by the reins as they approached the house situated farther from the others near a dock. "Is this where the boat is?" Augusta asked, her feet unable to remain still. "Is this the right place?"

Keir laughed. "These people have small fishing boats they use; however, none are big enough to transport all of us and the two horses." He smiled at Sarah, and she was relieved to hear that, of course, Autumn and Scout would not be left behind.

"We need a bigger boat?" Augusta asked, her gaze narrowing as she swept it along the beach. "I don't see a bigger boat."

"Heavens!" A raspy old voice called from behind them. "If it isna Keir MacKinnear!"

Almost as one, they turned around and found themselves facing an old man with a thick bushy beard while his head sprouted not a single hair, his bald head glowing in the sunlight. He stood a bit hunched over, his thin body appearing rather fragile, his eyes the palest blue Sarah had ever seen.

"Angus!" Keir exclaimed and strode forward, then he embraced the man warmly, almost knocking him off his feet. "'Tis good to see ye!"

Angus looked up at him, a wide, rather toothless grin upon his weathered face. "Have ye finally found yer way home, lad? Took ye some time! We thought ye got lost down there!" Then his gaze shifted, and he looked past Keir at the rest of them. "Ye seem to have brought an entire household, dear lad." He slapped Keir's arm good-naturedly, a deep chuckle rumbling in his throat. "Dunna mind me saying so, but ye'll cause a bit of a stir!"

Keir nodded knowingly when they all turned at the sound of the carriage drawing to a halt nearby. Mr. Garner swept his gaze over the stretch of beach, the minuscule village as well as what he might suppose lay beyond. Then he jumped down and opened the door, offering Kate his arm to help her alight from the carriage.

Angus chuckled. "How many more are coming?" He grinned up at Keir. "I assume ye wish for me to send word to yer father. Looks as though ye be needing a boat."

"A big boat!" Dorothea stressed, stretching her arms as wide as they would reach as she looked up at Angus. "The horses are coming, too."

Angus grinned at her. "Well, of course, they are, lassie. We canna leave them behind, can we?"

Dorothea shook her head for emphasis. "No, we canna. Thank ye, Angus," she said, matching his accent.

Angus laughed a booming laugh, clearly delighted with Dorothea's imitation. "Ye sound wonderful, lassie. Truly wonderful! Clearly, ye belong here with us! There's no doubt about it!"

Sarah smiled at the joyous expression upon Dorothea's face. She knew that the girls, and Kate as well, were in dire need of a home, a true home. A place where they felt at ease, where they were welcome and wanted. And perhaps Keir's home would be that place.

Sarah chanced to look at him as he spoke to Angus, exchanging a few words and providing the old man with the details he needed to send in his message. Still, in that moment, all Sarah could think about were the words Keir had spoken to her the day they had left Whickerton Grove. Sarah had revealed her heart to him, and he had reciprocated, had he not? Of course, neither one of them had used the word *love*, and yet Sarah could not deny that it was something, at least, akin to love that was between them, was it not?

That question circled in Sarah's head, and she wanted to pull Keir aside and ask him. Yet this moment, like so many others before, was not their own. No doubt they would be interrupted. Indeed, first Kate and the children needed to be settled, and then, perhaps, Sarah might find the time and the nerve to speak to Keir.

"How will he send a message?" Augusta inquired, her gaze following Angus as he disappeared inside a small wooden shed. Then she looked up at Keir.

"We keep doves," he explained, gesturing from the small shed out across the sea. "They can quickly carry messages back and forth between the mainland and the islands. We always do it like this when a bigger boat is required." He looked at the girls, a deep smile upon his face. "Would ye like to play at the beach?"

Augusta squealed in delight, and Dorothea nodded her head vehemently. Both their eyes were wide and filled with temptation. "Can we?" Augusta inquired, dancing upon her feet. "Mother, can we?"

Kate smiled, then nodded. "Of course, you can." Her permission sent both girls racing off toward the water's edge, their arms stretched wide as the wind tugged upon their hair. "I've never seen them like this," Kate suddenly murmured, sorrow in her voice.

"That is the past," Keir remarked before Sarah could find any words in reply. His gentle blue eyes looked at Kate, waiting for her to raise her gaze to look at him. Then he smiled at her encouragingly. "Yer daughters are extraordinary, and they will find their place in this world. All they needed was a chance, and ye gave them that."

Kate was not the only one touched by Keir's words. Sarah had to blink away tears, grateful that he always seemed to know what to say.

"Yes, they are," Kate agreed, brushing away a tear. The look in her green eyes no longer overshadowed. Indeed, she stood taller, her shoulders back and her chin lifted as she watched her daughters chase one another along the beach. "They are extraordinary, and they deserve all this and more."

"Aye, they do," Keir agreed before his gaze settled on Sarah. "Go and enjoy yerself, lass," he whispered to her, reaching for her hand and giving it a gentle squeeze. "I shall see to everything. Before the day is out, we shall be home." Then he walked away, toward Mr. Garner and the carriage.

Sarah grasped her sister's hand, hugging her close, as Frederica began to stir. "It feels like an utterly new world, does it not?"

Kate nodded. "But a good one," she whispered to Sarah's surprise, brushing a gentle hand over Frederica's head. "You know," she murmured, then abruptly lifted her eyes to Sarah, "we never quite had a home, did we? I mean one that was truly ours and where we felt completely at ease."

Sarah sighed. "I suppose not."

"Do you think this could be it? Will we stay here for the rest of our lives? Will my daughters grow up here?" For a long moment, Kate looked out to sea. "I don't quite know what to expect of this new place, of its people," she whispered as she turned to smile at Sarah, "but I'm hopeful."

As the wind tugged upon their hair and skirts, the girls' laughter echoing to their ears, Sarah smiled at her sister, their eyes locked in a way that truly gave her hope. Thus far, Kate had seemed so subdued, full of doubt and regret and fear. Now, though, the look in her sister's eyes felt different. Something had changed, and Sarah knew that now there was a chance.

A chance for Kate to be happy again.

If she can be happy, Sarah thought to herself, *perhaps, I can be, too.*

Chapter Ten

A FORK IN THE ROAD

Gently swaying from side to side, rocking Frederica in her arms, Kate watched as her sister chased after her daughters along the beach. They had all removed their boots, their bare feet leaving prints in the wet sand as their laughter echoed closer, carried by the wind. Kate smiled, renewed hope in her heart.

Indeed, it had been absent for far too long. Still, now that it was back, Kate was almost terrified of losing it again. She willed herself to ignore that persistent voice that whispered words she did not want to hear. "This was not a mistake," Kate told herself, willing her voice to harden, to speak with conviction. "I did what I had to do to see my daughters like this again. Look at that joy! They are happy!" At her words, Kate felt her smile deepen and that doubting voice retreat.

Turning her head, Kate spotted Keir speaking to Mr. Garner. She had overheard their conversation before and knew that Mr. Garner was to take the carriage back to the Whickertons. He would not accompany them to the island, but do everything within his power to clear their tracks and keep them hidden for as long as possible. Indeed, he was the final tie that bound them to their life in England, and it would be cut soon.

Although Kate knew it to be a good thing, she could not help the moment of panic she felt at the thought. Perhaps it was simply the finality of everything, of her choices, everything they came down to.

Again, that persistent voice in her head gave voice to her doubts. In fact, it sounded a lot like her mother, chiding her as she had when Kate had been a child, telling her in no uncertain terms what she had done was wrong and what consequences she would have to suffer because of it.

Kate flinched when a shadow suddenly fell over her. Her arms tightened upon Frederica, and she spun sideways. Her heart beat fast in her chest, and yet it calmed instantly the second her eyes fell on Keir.

"I'm sorry for startling ye," Keir murmured softly, his gaze briefly dropping to Frederica.

Kate exhaled a deep breath, waving his concern away. "No, there's no need. I was simply... lost in thought."

His blue eyes held hers, and he nodded in understanding. "Aye, 'tis not easy to upend one's life."

Kate stilled at his words, wondering how he knew so precisely what she was thinking, what she was feeling. Indeed, even before today, there had been the odd moment when she had been all but convinced that he could read her thoughts.

Keir chuckled softly. "Dunna worry, lass. I dunna know yer thoughts, but I can see that ye are unsettled. The look in yer eyes tells me so." Something tender flickered across his face, and for a second, his gaze darted down to the beach to where Sarah was playing with Augusta and Dorothea. "Yer face is almost as expressive as yer sister's." He moved to stand beside her, shoulder to shoulder, his gaze directed outward to the sea. "What is it that worries ye? Of course, ye dunna have to tell me." He smiled at her. "Might ease yer mind, though."

Rather absentmindedly, Kate nodded, her attention drifting away from Keir to the far horizon, and her heart sighed as she looked into the distance and saw the world reaching far and wide around her. "I simply cannot help but wonder," Kate volunteered with a deep sigh, "if I did the right thing or... if this was an awful mistake." She gazed down at Frederica's sleeping face. "Did I have the right to tear my daughters away from their home? From the life they were supposed to have? A life of privilege and security?" Her eyes closed on a deep sigh, and she rested her chin gently upon the top of Frederica's head.

"Aye, I hear ye," Keir murmured gently, the tone in his voice thoughtful.

Kate opened her eyes, curious to see the expression upon Keir's face. Throughout their—granted! —short acquaintance, she had always seen him certain of his next steps, conviction in his eyes as he moved through life. How did he do it? How could he be so certain of the path he was to take?

Keir turned to her. "I suppose 'tis only normal to worry. We all do, from time to time." He glanced past her shoulder and then looked back into her eyes. "What do ye see when ye look at them?" He nodded down to the beach.

Kate turned and looked at her daughters and her sister. "They look happy," she whispered, feeling the wind tug upon her curls, as though urging her onward. "They do, don't they?" Her eyes returned to Keir.

"Aye, they do," he agreed with a smile. Then, however, the expression in his eyes changed, and Kate felt herself still, expectant of his next words. "Is that not the greatest privilege in life to find a reason to laugh every day? To wake in the morning and be around those ye love?" He remained silent for a long moment and simply looked at her. "I'd say ye only have to look at yer children to know whether ye made the right choice. Happiness and joy are not based on material goods, on one's station in life." Again, his gaze darted past her shoulder before it returned to her. "Ask yerself honestly, recently ye had all that, but did it make ye happy?"

Kate exhaled a deep breath, blinking her eyes as tears rushed forward. "No," she breathed, remembering the life she had led not too long ago. "No, I was not happy."

"And neither were they, were they?" Keir dared her.

A shuddering breath left Kate's lips. "No, they were not." She closed her eyes, all but pinching them shut. "Still, what if..." She struggled to sort through her thoughts. "But they will not remember, will they? These last few weeks, months, they will blur and fade. They are still so young. Eventually, they might not even remember these first few years of their lives. And what then? What if one day, all they know is that they ought to have had something that I took from them?"

Keir nodded thoughtfully. "We can never know what the future may hold. Still, are ye not worried what yer daughters might blame ye for if ye do nothing? Can ye not imagine one day preparing them for their own wedding day, seeing tears in their eyes because they were not free to choose? And if they knew in that moment that ye could have prevented it, what do ye think they would say?"

Kate felt tears run down her cheeks as she looked up into Keir's eyes, all but seeing the moment he spoke of before her eyes.

"Aye, with each choice, there's the possibility of regret. All we can ever do is follow our hearts, our conscience." He stepped toward her, his left hand coming to rest upon her shoulder as he urged her to turn and face down the beach. "More than our children can ever learn from us, we can learn from them. They teach us every day what it means to live, to enjoy life and make the most of it." He chuckled as Dorothea lost her footing and fell forward into the sand. Augusta laughed, then ran over and helped her little sister back onto her feet, both their faces aglow with excitement. "Dunna think too much of tomorrow. Instead, do yer best to enjoy the moment ye have. That is the secret to finding true happiness." He smiled down at her, then brushed a gentle hand over Frederica's head. "Sit down and rest for a bit. 'Tis a good place for it. I've always found the sounds of the tide deeply soothing." He winked at her and then walked away, down the beach and toward Sarah and the girls.

Kate watched him walk away and then settled herself onto the sand. She heaved a deep breath and directed her gaze back toward the far horizon. She watched the rolling waves and breathed in the salty scent of the air. Indeed, this was a deeply peaceful place, and she slowly felt all her worries slip away, even more so when the cheerful sound of her daughters' laughter echoed to her ears.

As Frederica opened her eyes, stretching her little arms, Kate smiled down at her. "Because of him," she whispered softly to her daughter, "you will never know what a gilded cage feels like. Instead, you will know freedom and the feel of the wind on your face." She snuggled her daughter in her arms, holding her close. "It truly is a priceless gift, is it not?"

Kate looked from Keir to Sarah and wondered what would become of them. Clearly, they cared deeply for one another. More than once, Kate had observed tender moments between them, each one stirring her heart and making her long for something she had never known herself. Yes, Keir was an unusual man, one of a kind, and she knew that more than anyone, Sarah deserved to claim him for herself.

Chapter Eleven

HOMEWARD

"There!" Keir gestured to the distant horizon as a faint speck slowly grew in size. It was heading in their direction, and eventually, its white sail became visible, taut in the strong wind that propelled the ship toward shore.

"Is that big enough for us all?" Dorothea wondered; one hand lifted to shield her eyes. "It looks so small."

"It looks so small because it is still far away," Augusta explained with all the bearing of an elder sister. "It is bigger than it seems, is that not right, Keir?"

Smiling at the girls, Keir nodded. "Aye, 'twill be big enough for all of us. Dunna ye worry." He tugged Sarah into his side, intertwining their fingers together. "How are ye?" he whispered down to her as the girls raced toward the water's edge, shouting to one another in excitement.

A slight tremble snaked down Sarah's arm, and the expression in her eyes betrayed her anxiousness. "I... I hope..." She lifted her chin and looked into his eyes.

Keir smiled. "Dunna worry, lass. My family will take one look at ye and never let ye go again." He chuckled, relieved to see her relax a little.

Sarah leaned into him. "That sounds wonderful."

Still, Keir could sense that she was not fully at ease. Of course, she worried. How could she not? After her own family had treated her so callously, she had now been forced to leave behind the only family that had ever cared for her well-being: the Whickertons. To venture out into the unknown was never easy, and Keir hoped that meeting his family would eventually restore Sarah's faith in people.

The sun was beginning its descent, and Keir was grateful that they would not have to spend the night in the village. Though the people were friendly and quite hospitable, he was eager to make his way back home. Squinting his eyes, Keir tried to make out the man standing on the ship's deck. From this distance, he could not quite make out his face; yet the man's burly physique made it obvious who it was.

His brother Duncan.

Moments earlier, they had bid Mr. Garner farewell. He would take the carriage back to the Whickertons and do his utmost to hide whatever tracks they might have left behind on their journey north. Katherine seemed particularly anxious about leaving her past life behind and moving forward into the unknown.

The quaint fishing village hardly held more than a few dozen people, but its dock extended far into the sea, so larger ships could make their way to shore. The ship currently approaching was of medium size, just large enough to transport the horses alongside of them. Again, Keir squinted his eyes and then laughed, finally able to make out his brother's face.

Even from a distance, Duncan looked like a bear of a man. The wind ensured that his wild hair stood on end, billowing around his head, giving him a bit of a savage expression. He was tall, taller than Keir even, with a booming voice that never failed to make people quake in their boots. Still, at heart, Duncan was the kindest man Keir had ever known.

"What is it?" Sarah asked, her hand tightening upon his arm. "What do you see?"

Keir gestured toward the vessel. "Do ye see that man? The one of hulking stature who looks like a bear?"

Sarah gave a slight nod, and Keir felt her tense up beside him. Her lips were slightly parted, and she stared at his brother with a stunned expression upon her face.

"Dunna worry, lass. My brother might look like a bear and growl like one, but he's truly a good man. I promise ye."

Sarah let out a heavy sigh and nodded her head, her gaze shifting from the vessel and Duncan back to Keir. Her eyes were a deep shade of blue, wide and almost unblinking, as she gnawed on her lower lip, anxiety reflected in her expression.

Keir grinned at her. "Ye're about to blush again, lass, are ye not?"

As though on cue, Sarah's cheeks glowed crimson. "You're truly impossible!" she chided him with an embarrassed chuckle. Then she elbowed him in the ribs, a playful scowl upon her face.

Keir smiled, watching her gradually become more and more daring, cautiously poking her head out of its shell to explore the world beyond it. Bit by bit, she ventured out into the unknown. *Oh, my little wisp is a brave one!*

On impulse, Keir tugged her closer, wrapping an arm around her shoulders. "I can see that ye're worried, and I know that this is not an easy step for ye. But I am at yer side, lass. Always." He placed a kiss upon her temple, relieved to do so again without worrying who might see. After all, before long, everyone would know.

And Keir did not mind.

He did not mind in the least.

Arm in arm, Keir and Sarah strolled down the pier, watching the ship arrive. Katherine and her daughters trailed behind them, the girls' chattering voices echoing through the air.

Two other men, both of whom Keir had known all his life, walked around on deck. He gave them a wave of acknowledgment before refocusing on his brother. He released Sarah's arm and then swiftly caught the line his brother tossed to him, securing it at the dock. The other two men lowered a gangplank, and yet as Keir knew he would, Duncan ignored it as he was wont to do.

Duncan swung himself over the railing of the ship, and the moment his enormous feet landed heavily upon the dock, Sarah's eyes widened and Keir heard Katherine draw in a shocked breath. While Keir had never thought of himself as short of stature, he did sometimes feel a bit dwarfed by his brother's size. More than once, he had seen Duncan inspire fear in those who did not know him—unjustified as it was.

After securing the ship with yet another rope, Duncan stood, and his blue eyes immediately found Keir. A broad smile spread across his bearded face. "Little Brother, I almost didna recognize ye! How long has it been? Five years? Ten?" With open arms, Duncan walked toward him.

Chuckling, Keir strode toward his brother. "It's not even been one, big Brother." They embraced one another, and for a brief second, Keir almost felt knocked off his feet. Then, they stood back, one hand upon the other's shoulder, and looked at one another. "Then again," Keir remarked with a chuckle, "ye've always been rather bad at maths."

Duncan laughed his usual booming laugh. "I canna fault that observation." He heaved a deep sigh, then looked Keir up and down from head to toe. "Do ye eat enough, Brother? Ye seem a bit weak upon yer feet."

Keir smiled warmly, realizing in that moment how deeply he had missed his family, to have people around who knew him, who knew everything there was to know about him, who had walked with him through life for as long as he could remember. "'Twas from yer embrace. It truly knocked the wind out of me."

Laughing, Duncan grasped Keir's shoulder. Then his gaze traveled past him. "I see ye've brought company, two beautiful lasses and two even more beautiful lassies." He paused, frowned for a second as his gaze swept over Katherine, noting the babe in her arms, and then added, "Make that three lassies." A question rested in his eyes as he looked back at Keir.

Keir waved the sisters and the girls forward, offering quick introductions. "This is my occasionally ill-mannered brother, Duncan MacKinnear." He grinned at Duncan, who regarded him with a scrunched-up expression. "Duncan, these are Miss Sarah Mortensen and her sister Katherine Dunley, Countess of Birchwell, as well as her three daughters, Augusta, Dorothea and wee Frederica."

A look of amazement flashed across Duncan's face as he gazed upon Katherine. "An English countess? I canna say we've ever had one of those here." He grinned at her, then offered what undoubtedly was supposed to have been a formal bow. “Welcome to Clan MacKinnear.” His gaze shifted back to Keir. “How do ye come to be here?”

“I shall explain everything later,” Keir told his brother. “We’ve had a long journey and wish to see it end.”

Nodding, Duncan turned to look out to sea. “Aye, the winds are favorable. We ought to head out right away.” He grinned at Keir, something wicked twinkling in his eyes. “Our parents are most eager to see ye, especially as ye were to return long before now.”

Keir smiled back at his brother’s good-natured teasing, then looked over his shoulder at Sarah, locking eyes with her. “Well, what can I say?” He turned back to his brother. “I was detained.”

A knowing twinkle came to Duncan’s eyes. “I know what ye mean,” he remarked, and Keir noticed the way his brother’s gaze seemed to remain fixed upon Sarah’s braids. Aye, everyone would see at first glance that she belonged with him!

Keir found himself curious about his brother’s words. After all, to his knowledge, Duncan had never been in love—or at least, not enough to tie the knot. Among their clan, whispers abounded about whether Duncan would ever seek a bride and settle down. At well past thirty, many considered it to be about time. Even Keir had felt the pressure to make the same decision; before meeting Sarah, he had never given marriage much thought. Now, though, the temptation of seeing her made his bride was growing more powerful with each day, and he knew that before long he would have to do something about it. Aye, he would wait until Sarah had a chance to settle in, and then he would ask for her hand.

Chapter Twelve

A GIANT OF A MAN

As Keir and his brother walked the horses down the dock and toward the vessel, Sarah stared at Duncan. Kate, it seemed, did the same. "The comparison to a bear seems quite accurate," her sister murmured, her arm linked with Sarah's. "I've never quite seen a man like him."

Sarah nodded. "Englishmen do not seem to come in that size." Indeed, Keir's brother was huge, terrifying in a way that Sarah had never experienced before. And then something happened that changed Sarah's perception of him in an instant.

While Scout followed Keir, unbothered, as they made their way to the ship, Autumn seemed reluctant. Her ears flickered back and forth, and Sarah could sense her unease. She was about to step forward and reassure the mare when Duncan pulled Autumn close, his voice soothing as he murmured to her. His paw-like hands stroked down her neck and back, and gradually the mare relaxed.

"He seems very kind, though," Kate remarked beside Sarah, her own voice no longer as tense as before. "I suppose first impressions can be misleading."

Sarah nodded, knowing it to be so. *After all, did I not fear Keir upon first seeing him?*

Watching with rapt attention, the girls whispered to one another. "I've never seen a man so huge," Augusta remarked as she stared at him open-mouthed. "Thea, do you think he's a giant?" She turned to her little sister. "After all, not too long ago, we met a fairy. I mean, she did not have wings, but she granted our wish. Do you think he could be a real giant?"

Dorothea was about to respond when Duncan stepped forward, obviously having overheard every word Augusta had uttered, a glimmer of amusement in his eyes as he gazed down at the girls. "Well, there's no use in denying it. Truth be told, I gobble up at least two or three children each morning for breakfast."

Augusta backed away from Duncan, her cheeks devoid of color. Dorothea, though, watched him with an inquisitive eye, not appearing frightened. "Do ye truly mean that?" she asked boldly, and Sarah and Kate exchanged a look of disbelief.

Duncan fixed his eyes upon the girl. "Do ye think it wise to question a giant, lassie?"

While Augusta took another step backward, Dorothea crossed her arms over her little chest. "Ye shouldna frown so much," she said in her best imitation of Keir's accent. Then she poked her forefinger at Duncan's furrowed brows before leaning in rather conspiratorially. "'Tis what makes people think ye're a giant."

A grin claimed Sarah's lips as she watched tiny Dorothea standing dauntless before Keir's giant of a brother. Then Duncan's laughter filled the air, and Sarah knew that this was a moment she would never forget.

"I like this lassie!" Duncan declared, winking at her. "Aye, she's a plucky one!"

"My name is Dorothea," the girl instructed him. "But ye may call me Thea if ye like."

Duncan smiled at her. "I'd be honored, Thea. Thank ye very much."

After Keir had taken the horses down to the hold of the ship, he returned to help the others on board. "Go ahead," Sarah told her sister, nodding to Keir. "I'll fetch the girls. Don't worry."

The expression upon Kate's face clearly stated that she did worry.

Her mouth opened as though to protest; however, she stopped herself, swallowed whatever she was about to say with great effort and then accepted Keir's arm. Still, her gaze drifted back to her daughters, her teeth worrying her lower lip.

Sarah waved over her little nieces, a smile coming to her face as she watched them almost trip over their feet in their eagerness to reach the boat. "Watch your step," Sarah warned with a chuckle then abruptly stopped and turned back toward the beach, her eyes searching. "Loki! Loki!"

Out of nowhere, a soft mew filled the air, and Sarah spun around to see the little feline sitting by her feet. "How long have you been there?" Sarah chuckled, then bent down and scooped him up into her arms. More than anything, she had feared he would be left behind. "Come, your highness, it is time to go aboard." She waved Augusta and Dorothea onward, and then they all followed Duncan up the gangplank. He offered each of them a hand as they clambered onto the vessel.

"I've never been on a ship," Augusta remarked, wide eyes sweeping over everything.

Dorothea nodded. "Neither have I."

"Do ye wish to go below deck?" Duncan asked, looking first at Sarah and then turning toward the girls. "There's a small cabin."

As one, the girls shook their heads. "We wish to stay here!" Each of them had one hand clamped upon the railing as if frightened that a gust of wind might blow them away. "We've never been on a ship! Never!"

With a grin, Duncan nodded. "Aye, as ye wish." He yelled out some commands in Gaelic to his two crewmates, and the three of them got to work preparing the ship.

"If you wish to stay above deck, we need to go and speak to your mother or she'll be worried," Sarah told the girls. Though clearly displeased to have to abandon their spot at the railing—even if only for a moment—the Augusta and Dorothea did not argue but rushed below deck in search of their mother. Half-way there, they ran into Keir, who was on his way to see to the horses once more. "Right over there," he said, pointing at a small door and the cabin beyond. "She seems rather pale," he whispered to Sarah as Augusta and Dorothea burst into the cabin like a horde of marauders.

Although reluctant, Kate gave her permission when Sarah promised not to let the girls out of her sight. "Rest," Sarah instructed her sister with an insistent look, Loki squirming in her arms. "You need it." Then she hurried after her nieces back up on deck.

Standing with the girls at the railing and looking out toward the sea, Sarah felt excitement well up inside her. Indeed, the past few months had led her to many unknown places, and yet she knew deep down that the greatest adventure was yet to come.

Holding Loki tightly in her arms, Sarah kept a watchful eye on her two nieces as they gazed with wonder down into the turbulent waters. All the while, she warned them not to lean too far over the railing. "Did you know that a sea serpent is rumored to live in these waters?" she whispered to them, remembering the story Keir had told her.

The girls' eyes instantly grew wide. "Is it friendly?" Dorothea asked, her eyes going back and forth between the waters below and Sarah.

Sarah nodded. "As far as I can tell, it is, and rather protective of the people who live on the islands."

Augusta exhaled a deep breath. "That is good because Keir and Duncan live on the islands, do they not? Does that mean the ship will be safe from the serpent?"

"Yes, if I did not believe it to be so, we would not be on it," Sarah assured the girls, suddenly fearful that she might have frightened them with her story.

"How do you know about the serpent?" Dorothea inquired, both hands now clammed upon the railing, her green eyes fixed upon the churning waters. "Have you ever seen it?"

Sarah shook her head. "No, I've never seen it. It was Keir who told me the story. It is one that has been handed down through generations of his clan. If you want to know more, you need to ask him."

"Aye, 'tis an old story," Duncan suddenly spoke out from behind her, and Sarah all but flinched.

Sarah raised her chin and looked up at Duncan, but when their eyes met, she quickly glanced away, her arms tightening around Loki. Despite Duncan's friendly nature, Sarah could not shake that last bit of unease she felt in his presence. Perhaps it was the way he looked at her, trying to get to the root of who she was; or, perhaps even, who she was to his brother.

Of course, it was only natural for Keir's family to wish to know her; yet Sarah could not shake the feeling that they would find her wanting. People always had. Why should this be any different?

"Did you ever see it?" Augusta inquired tentatively; her blue eyes wide as she peeked up at Keir's brother. "The sea serpent, have you ever seen it?"

Duncan grinned at her, then braced his large hands upon the railing, leaning forward to look down into the endless sea. "Well, of that I canna be certain." His gaze turned left and then right, moving from Augusta to Dorothea. Both girls were hanging on every word. "Yet I've seen the shimmer of scales in the water, green and blue like the waves themselves. I've seen enemy ships tipped over by massive waves and our own make it through terrible storms without a scratch." He lifted his gaze to the horizon, a contemplative expression upon his face. "Aye," he finally said, a deep breath rushing from his lungs, "I've seen it." He straightened, then looked at the girls, who were still staring up at him wide-eyed. "If ye watch the sea carefully, ye might as well."

Absolutely mesmerized, the girls stood motionless. Then, they abruptly spun around and darted away toward the front of the ship. Their little fingers curled around the railing, and they peered into the depths below, in search of glimmering scales.

Duncan laughed, something almost wistful upon his face. "Aye, there's nothing like the hearts of children." He sighed again; his gaze fixed upon Sarah.

For a moment, Sarah almost cringed, her arms tightening upon Loki.

Duncan studied her intently, and Sarah felt like he could read her thoughts in the way his eyes assessed her—it was something Keir always had the uncanny ability to do. "Ye needna fear me, lass," Duncan murmured gently. "I might look like a giant." The hint of a smile teased his lips. "But I promise ye I have never gobbled up a child for breakfast. Not one." He winked at her.

A deep breath rushed from Sarah's lungs, and she smiled. "That is good to know," she said around the lump still lodged in her throat. For a moment, she felt herself reminded of those first few days with Keir when she had barely spoken a word or two.

"How do ye come to know my brother?" Duncan asked with a directness that stole the air from Sarah's lungs. Again, his gaze touched upon the small braids upon her temple. Sarah had noticed it before, and she had wondered what conclusions he might draw. "Clearly, ye know him well."

Once again, Sarah's muscles tensed, and her arms wrapped around Loki a little tighter. The feline instantly shifted his gaze toward Duncan, his amber eyes studying the giant. He spat a warning hiss and growled menacingly.

Of course, far from intimidated by Loki's threat, Duncan grinned at him. "Oh, what an adorable wee kitty!" He reached out one of his large hands and patted Loki on the head.

Loki, in turn, clearly did not care for such treatment. His eyes narrowed further, and a low growl escaped from his throat as he lifted his paw and struck Duncan's hand.

Unimpressed, Duncan still grinned. "Aye, ye protect her." Then his gaze shifted to Sarah. "Ye're fortunate to have such a loyal friend."

Sarah nodded, well-aware of the expectant expression upon Duncan's face. He had asked a question, and he was still waiting for its answer. "Well, I... that is to say, Keir..." Every clear thought eluded Sarah as she worried how to put into words what had happened these past few months. Almost desperately, she longed to be accepted by Keir's family, and yet she was certain that they could not help but disapprove of her. After all, who was she? Sarah doubted that Keir's family cared in any way that she was the daughter of a baron. And even if they did, her father was a disgraced baron, after all; one who had gambled away his fortune and plunged his family into ruin. There was no honor there, nothing that would recommend her family. Indeed, they stood as paupers before Clan MacKinnear, begging them for help. Was that not precisely why they were here?

The sound of footsteps made Sarah and Duncan turn, and Sarah sighed in relief when she found Keir approaching. His watchful gaze moved back and forth between her and his brother, and she could tell that he understood what had happened here.

As always, as he had done countless times before, Keir did not hesitate to stand by her side, quite literally this time. He met his brother's gaze, then clasped a good-natured hand upon Duncan's shoulder. "I can see that ye have questions, Brother; however, I believe 'tis fair to say that everyone will ask the same questions, and I must admit I dunna relish the thought of repeating myself countless times." Duncan chuckled. "Therefore, I would like to postpone any questions ye might have until we're all gathered together. I promise ye that I shall explain everything. Agreed?"

Duncan nodded. "Agreed, Brother." He then mimicked Keir, reaching out his right hand and clasping his shoulder in a gesture of affection. "'Tis good to have ye back. 'Tis been a long time, and we missed ye." Sarah saw Duncan's hand momentarily tighten upon Keir's shoulder. "There must've been a truly persuasive reason for ye to stay away as long as ye have." He winked, then laughed his usual booming laugh and strode away, his attention shifting to the ship and the remaining journey ahead.

Seeing Keir smile as he looked at his brother made Sarah think of the very moment she had seen Kate again after years of distance. For Keir and Duncan, it had not been years; and yet they, too, had been apart for longer than ever before. "Only when we see them again," Sarah murmured, "do we realize how much we missed them."

Turning toward her, Keir sighed, then nodded. "Aye, ye might be right, lass." His eyes found hers, and he placed his hands upon her shoulders. "How are ye? Tell me honestly."

For a moment, Sarah closed her eyes. "I'm excited, but I'm also nervous."

Keir nodded knowingly.

"If you know," Sarah asked with a nervous chuckle, "then why do you ask?"

"Did ye not tell me that ye rather disliked it when I read the expression upon yer face?" His right eyebrow rose in challenge. "What are ye nervous about?"

In that moment, Loki finally had had enough. He squirmed, and

Sarah set him down upon the deck. "Will he be all right?" she murmured, then looked up at Keir. "You don't think he will jump overboard, do you?"

Keir laughed. "In my experience, cats rather dislike water. See, he's settling himself beside the girls." He turned back to look at her. "There's nothing to worry about."

Sarah nodded. "And Kate? How is she?"

Holding her gaze, Keir slowly shook his head, a knowing smile upon his lips. "Dunna try to distract me, little wisp. Ye know as well as I do that everyone is fine. What of ye, though?"

Sarah heaved a deep breath, lifting her shoulders and letting them fall. "I know it's foolish, but I... I cannot seem to shake the memory of the Whickertons' ball. It haunts me."

A frown slowly descended upon Keir's face, and he drew closer, his hands sliding up her arms and once again settling upon her shoulders. "It haunts ye? And here I thought ye had been pleased to see me again." He spoke lightly, and yet Sarah was surprised to see vulnerability in his eyes. *He does not truly doubt how I feel about him, does he?*

"No. I mean, yes, I was overjoyed to see you again," Sarah assured Keir, delighting in the way he looked at her, smiled at her. "What I did not care for, what I did not expect, foolish as I am, was the way... people looked at me. I knew I would be ruined after..." She grinned at him. "And yet I never quite imagined what it would feel like to walk among the *ton* and have them look at me and whisper behind my back." She scoffed. "Of course, I should have. Yet my focus was simply upon never again receiving an offer of marriage! I completely overlooked the inevitable disapproval, the censure that would be directed at me wherever I went." She shrugged, feeling helpless. "And then we arrived at Birchwell, and every word to fall from the dowager's lips was..." She pinched her eyes shut at the memory, that feeling of unworthiness that had somehow wormed its way into her heart. "I felt so small, so flawed. I..."

Keir simply wrapped his arms around her, and Sarah could feel some of that weight float off her shoulders as though carried away by the wind. "Words are odd sometimes," Keir murmured next to her ear. "They have the power to cut deep, wound us to the core of our being, and yet other times, it seems we are immune to them. No matter how often they are repeated, their meaning simply won't sink in." He kissed the top of her head. "I know I've said it before, and I shall say it again as often as ye need to hear it; no one will look at ye with disapproval. No one will blame ye for what ye did. On the contrary, I am absolutely certain that my family will be proud of yer courage, of yer daring spirit." Sarah chuckled as Keir continued, "and yer perseverance. Yer story is like the story of our clan. 'Tis not a simple story, one marked by many obstacles, yet eventually by going against convention, freedom and happiness are found."

Lifting her chin, Sarah looked up at Keir. "I love your stories," she murmured, savoring the way he held her close. "They are so beautiful, and the way you tell them always makes me feel..." She shrugged, unable to find words to do the feeling justice.

Trailing a finger down her chin, Keir smiled at her. "Once upon a time, these stories were nothing more than the simple retelling of a life. A life like mine... and yers. One day, perhaps centuries from today, people shall tell yer story." Keir dipped his head and touched the tip of his nose to Sarah's. "And feel inspired by yer strength and yer perseverance, wondering if ye ever had doubts walking the path ye knew to be yers."

As tears streamed down Sarah's face, she snuggled into Keir's embrace, grateful for every word of comfort and encouragement. Indeed, she loved his stories. She loved the way his voice rang with kindness and certainty alike, speaking of the past and the future as though they were forever connected. And perhaps they were. After all, people were people, each one with their own set of hopes and fears. In that moment, locked into Keir's embrace, Sarah's gaze drifted out across the waters toward the islands that slowly came into view. And she wondered if Yvaine—the young woman who centuries ago had gone against convention, brought her people to safety and become the origin of Clan MacKinnear—had ever felt uncertain.

Sarah knew she had to have. After all, she had been as human as Sarah herself, and the human heart worried and feared. It was a part of who they were, and no one was safe from that.

Not even those that lived in legends.

Chapter Thirteen

A FARAWAY LAND

To Kate, the ship felt like a teacup bouncing along upon the open waves. She had never been on a ship before, and she could rightly say she would not care to do so again. The idea of remaining on deck had frightened her from the beginning, and she had been grateful when Keir had led her below. Unfortunately, though, her own nervousness had stirred Frederica awake, and Kate had had a hard time calming her little daughter. By the time, a shout rang to her ears from above deck, Kate felt exhausted.

And slightly nauseated.

Stepping out of the small cabin, Kate looked up and found Keir climbing down the ladder. He turned toward her, a kind smile upon his face. "How are ye, Katherine? Ye look a bit green around the gills." He stepped forward and then held out his hand. "Here, let me take Frederica."

To Kate's surprise, her arms moved, handing over her child without another thought. *I trust him! I must or...*

"Go ahead," he urged her, nodding toward the ladder. "We'll follow." He looked down at Frederica. "Won't we, wee lassie?"

With a smile upon her face, Kate climbed the short ladder up onto the deck. The wind almost knocked her off her feet, and for a brief moment, she feared she would tumble back down the ladder. Then, however, she managed to right herself, and her eyes widened as they fell upon the island sticking out of the sea only a few ship-lengths ahead of them. It was lush in vegetation, and sharp rocks jutted upward, a natural fortification. Down by the water's edge, Kate spotted a small harbor town with people hurrying to and fro and a wide path leading upward toward a massive fortress seated upon a cliff overlooking the sea.

To Kate, it seemed like an entirely different world, one with its own set of rules and traditions, and she felt lost at the thought of entering it. *What will these people think of me?* After all, she had left her husband and stolen away his children. At the thought, another wave of doubt assailed her, its impact almost as strong as the wind that had threatened to knock her off her feet.

Then, however, her gaze fell upon her daughters, standing at the front of the ship, their little mouths hanging open as they stared in fascination at this new place. *Does it seem like a fairytale world to them?* Kate wondered, and once again she heard Keir's words echo in her head, reminding her that nothing was more important than her children's happiness. That was the measure of a life. *And they do seem happy, do they not?*

As the ship slowly glided towards the harbor, Kate realized Keir was still holding Frederica. Thus far, she had barely been able to part with her newest daughter for longer than a few moments, always afraid deep down—a notion that went against every rational thought—that if she were to release her for only a moment, something would snatch Frederica away for good. Still, now looking at Keir, seeing him coo under his breath to the child, making her smile, Kate realized Dorothea was right; he was a hero.

"Here," Keir murmured as he moved closer, "go back to Mama." He smiled at Kate and then handed her her daughter. "I shall help with securing the boat and then see ye all safely off board." He nodded to her, a deeply reassuring gesture, and then moved away to do as he had said.

As the ship docked, Kate felt every muscle in her body tense. A crowd of people gathered, staring not only at Keir but at all of them.

For a moment, Kate felt certain they were glaring at her, whispering behind her back about what she had done.

"That is nonsense!" she reminded herself in a quiet whisper. After all, no one knew! At least, not yet!

At a second glance, Kate saw that there was no hostility in anyone's eyes. What she saw instead was curiosity and joy also. Clearly, Keir's homecoming was a reason for celebration, and she saw many people call out to him, waving their hands, smiles upon their faces. He returned their greeting as best as he could as he assisted his brother in securing the ship.

Then he moved toward the gangplank, beckoning them forward. Within a second, Augusta and Dorothea were at his side, eager eyes sweeping past Keir and toward the gathered crowd. "There's a carriage waiting to take ye up to the fortress," Keir explained then held out his hand to Sarah. He escorted her off the boat before seeing Kate's daughters safely from board as well. Last, he returned for her, Kate, his presence reassuring as she put one foot in front of the other, joining Sarah and her daughters upon the dock. People crowded close, still calling out greetings, and for a moment, Kate closed her eyes, overwhelmed by this sudden racket. Then a sudden thought struck. *In such a crowd, my daughters could easily be lost!*

Instantly, Kate forced her eyes back open, only to see Sarah take Augusta and Dorothea by the hand, holding them by her side. "You go ahead," her sister said, nodding to Keir, her gaze meeting Kate's for a brief moment. "We'll follow. Won't we, girls?"

Augusta and Dorothea cheered.

Walking upon Keir's arm, Kate was grateful when they reached the carriage. She shifted Frederica from one arm to the other and then stepped inside, welcoming the thin barrier between herself and the rest of the world. Augusta and Dorothea quickly joined her, and then Sarah, too, seated herself in the carriage, Loki following on her heel. Keir stood in the open door, his hand still holding Sarah's, his gaze directed at her. "I shall follow with the horses," he told her reassuringly, then smiled at the girls. "I'll see ye soon." He squeezed Sarah's hand one more time and then left, closing the door.

As the carriage pulled away from the docks, rumbling along the cobblestone street, they all looked out the windows, taking in their new surroundings. Even with the harsh wind blowing in from the sea, everybody seemed to be outdoors, tending to some work or another. The girls stared wide-eyed, whispering to one another, completely lost in this fairytale come true.

"How do you feel?" Sarah asked, and she turned her head away from the window.

"I hardly know," Kate replied with a shrug. "All this is so overwhelming."

Sarah nodded, understanding clear in her eyes.

As the carriage moved up the small slope toward the cliff, they could see farther inland, their eyes drifting over endless meadows and thick woods growing in the far distance. "I've seen meadows and woods before," Kate remarked, "and yet this place feels so utterly foreign."

Again, Sarah nodded, and yet her gaze seemed distant. "It reminds me of the many stories Keir told me when we were alone in the woods. Somehow, I imagined his home just like this." A deep smile touched her face, and it took Kate a moment to realize what her sister had just said.

"Alone in the woods?"

At her question, Sarah suddenly became still. Then she lifted her gaze and met Kate's eyes. "I suppose I forgot you do not know." She shook her head, then glanced at Augusta and Dorothea, who were still whispering animatedly with one another. Scooting to the edge of her seat, Sarah leaned closer, her voice dropping to a mere whisper. "It was Keir who took me from our parents' house that night."

Kate tensed without quite knowing why. Of course, it made sense, perhaps on some level, she had already suspected it. Still...

"He brought me to a small cabin deep in the woods," Sarah continued in hushed tones, her blue eyes sparkling with something Kate could not help but envy. "We hid out there and waited for the ransom to be paid."

Even if Sarah had not yet revealed to Kate that her kidnapping had been far from an ordeal, any fool could see that... it was a cherished memory for her. "How long did you hide out? Only the two of you?"

Kate whispered, trying to imagine Sarah and Keir alone in a small cabin in the woods. What had they done all day? No doubt, Keir had told her countless stories, perhaps seated together by a roaring fire, a cup of hot tea in their hands.

Kate almost shook her head, trying to wipe away the image. Yet it remained, making her wish—

"About a fortnight," Sarah replied in that wistful voice again. "Oh, Kate, it was wonderful! I never expected it to be. Of course not! At first, I was terribly frightened of him. After all, he was a stranger. But then..." She shrugged, clearly helpless to explain how easily Keir had won her heart... because he had—Kate had known so for a while. She simply had not known how it had happened. "Within a matter of days, I knew that bidding him farewell would break my heart. We came to know each other so well, spoke of so many things. I spoke to him of you and your daughters, and he told me of his family, his home." Again, her gaze swept out the window, and Kate wondered what Keir had said to Sarah, how he had spoken of this place. No doubt he had painted a beautiful image, and Kate wished she could have been there to hear his words.

Uncertain why her chest suddenly felt so tight, Kate lifted her head, her eyes sweeping over the small houses lining the road until she caught sight of Keir. He sat upon Scout's back, leading Autumn behind him. He waved and exchanged words here and there. Then he suddenly drew to a halt, and Kate saw a red-haired man move toward him through the small crowd, a wide smile on his face.

Who is he? Kate asked herself, for it was a question much safer than the one she felt growing within her heart.

Chapter Fourteen
HOMECOMING

The moment Eoghan's voice echoed to Keir's ears, his head whipped around, and he felt utter joy seize his heart. "What kept ye away for so long?" Eoghan demanded as he strode toward him, his red hair aglow in the sunshine and a smile upon his face. "Do I dare guess that 'twas a lassie?" He glanced at the carriage, the smile upon his face turning into a wicked grin.

Keir pulled Scout to a halt and then leaned forward to clasp Eoghan's outstretched hand. "It has been too long, old friend."

Eoghan chuckled. "I canna fail to notice that ye have not answered my question." Then he nodded, dropping the subject. "'Tis good to see ye again. Verra good."

The carriage moved onward, and Keir cast his friend an apologetic look. "We shall talk later."

Eoghan nodded. "We shall. I will be up at the fortress when they call the gathering."

Keir frowned. "What gathering?"

Eoghan grinned at him. "Do ye not know yer own family?" he chuckled and then stepped away, waving to Keir, urging him to catch up to the carriage.

Eager to see his family, Keir spurred Scout onward, his gaze directed upward at the fortress that had been his home all his life. As he rode through the gates and into the courtyard, memories assailed him. Memories he would treasure forever. Memories that never failed to weigh heavily upon his heart, though.

Keir could not remember all the many times he had returned from a hunting trip or an exploration of one of the smaller islands nearby only to find Yvaine rushing down these very steps to greet him, her green eyes flashing with excitement and her unruly red curls dancing upon the breeze. Keir closed his eyes, and for a brief moment, a part of him felt utterly certain that he need only to open them again to see his sister. His mind argued against it, reminding him it could not be; yet his heart remained steadfast in its belief.

The moment Keir opened his eyes, his heart twisted painfully at the renewed sense of loss. For the thousandth time, he wondered if the day would ever come that he would finally find out what had happened to his sister. He doubted it, and yet his heart was not yet ready to abandon hope.

Focusing his gaze on what was right in front of him, Keir lifted his head and smiled as he saw his parents standing at the top of the stairs leading up to the front doors. Their faces showed their deepest joy at seeing him, and they looked at him in a way that made Keir push all other thoughts aside, jump out of the saddle and rush toward them. He took two steps at a time, meeting his parents halfway, and then embraced them just as much as they embraced him.

His father's hand clasped the back of Keir's neck as his mother's hands touched his cheeks. Both their eyes held a shimmer of tears, and the way they smiled at him reminded Keir of many wonderful moments throughout his life. Always had his parents been at his side, their words encouraging and their faith in him unshakable. "How dare ye stay away for so long?" his mother demanded, grasping his chin and meeting his eyes. "Ye made me worry I might never see ye again." She huffed out a deep breath, and Keir could see that she was trying her utmost to collect herself. Indeed, his mother rarely showed the world this vulnerable side of her, the woman he knew was strong and proud no matter the circumstances. Still, losing Yvaine had changed them all, and Keir knew it was hard for his parents to bear any sort of distance between them and their children. The world simply was no longer the same place.

Keir took her hand, holding it tightly. "I'm sorry, Mother. I didna mean to worry ye, and there's nothing in the world that could keep me away forever." He winked at her, and she smiled, rolling her eyes at him. "'Tis a rather long story, and I already told Duncan that I shall answer yer questions once we're all together."

Glancing past his shoulder at the carriage, his mother nodded, now a curious glimmer in her watchful eyes. "I see ye've brought visitors," she remarked, her voice rather innocent; however, the look in her eyes was not.

"It seems ye've had quite the adventure," Keir's father remarked with a wide grin as he stepped forward, one arm wrapping around his wife's middle and the other clasping his son's shoulder. "'Tis good to have ye back home, Son, and I canna wait to hear about yer journey." A chiding look came to his face. "Ye didna add many details to the note requesting the boat."

Keir grinned, far from unaware of how curious his parents were. "Indeed, there's much to tell." He looked from his father to his mother and back. "Where's Grandmother?" For a moment, his heart tensed—perhaps an echo of Yvaine's sudden loss—and he feared that he had stayed away for too long.

"She's waiting for ye in the great hall," his father said with a booming laugh that clearly proved his kinship to Duncan. "Be assured that she willna let ye slip away without providing answers."

Keir exhaled the breath he had been holding. "I never expected her to," he replied, then bid his parents to wait as he hastened back down the steps toward the carriage.

Duncan already stood there, the door open, and offering his arm to Sarah. With her face a scarlet red, she alighted, her fingers like claws upon Duncan's arm. "May I remind ye that this isna yer execution, lass," Duncan remarked with a chuckle. "Would ye be so kindly as to retract yer claws?" He winked at her, which made Sarah blush even worse, her other arm tensing upon Loki until he squirmed to get down.

In a flash, the feline bounded up the stairs, not bothering to extend any sort of greeting to their hosts and dashed past them into the great hall.

Keir laughed. "He already feels quite at home here, wouldna ye say?" He smiled at Sarah, relieved to see a smile tease her lips.

As much as Keir wanted to be the one to lead Sarah into the great hall, he stood back and allowed her to go with Duncan, knowing that Sarah always worried most for her sister. And so, he turned to Katherine, offering her his arm and assisting her out of the carriage. In contrast to Sarah, Katherine's face seemed rather pale, her green eyes wide as she looked around, seemingly trying not to meet anyone's gaze. "Dunna worry," Keir whispered as he waved Augusta and Dorothea forward. "Ye're most welcome here."

Katherine's eyes found his, and she smiled in gratitude.

Augusta and Dorothea poked their heads forward curiously as they stood half-hidden behind Keir and their mother. "Does a king live here?" Augusta inquired before craning her neck to look up at Keir. "Is your father a king?"

Keir chuckled. "My father is the chief of our clan," he explained, encouraging the girls to step forward and follow them up the stairs. "That means that 'tis his duty to see to the welfare of our people."

Dorothea's eyes grew wide. "There are a lot of people here!"

Augusta nodded. "I've never seen so many in one place." She looked at her mother. "Have you, Mother?"

With Frederica's head resting upon her shoulder, Katherine turned a bit awkwardly to look at Augusta. "Well, truthfully, London always struck me as a rather overcrowded city."

"More than here?"

Katherine nodded before she lifted her chin. They had reached the top of the stairs and now stood in front of Keir's parents.

Keir could see that his parents were deeply intrigued by the two young ladies he had brought back home. Meanwhile, Sarah and Katherine looked as uncomfortable as he had ever seen them. Only Augusta and Dorothea appeared rather unfazed by their hosts, their eyes round as they tried to peek past them into the interior of the fortress.

Keir offered a quick introduction, presenting his companions in the same manner as he had before. Indeed, not unlike his brother, his parents seemed to still briefly at the mention of Katherine's title. Yet they did not comment.

"Welcome," Keir's father greeted their guests, a warm smile upon his face. "We must admit we're quite surprised to find ye here but also most intrigued." He winked at his son.

Keir's mother laughed. "Ye must be famished from such a long journey. Please, come inside." Together, Keir's parents led the way through the two large wooden doors and into the great hall. Tapestries graced the walls, and large rugs covered the floors. Orange red flames danced in the massive fireplace, sending out their warmth into the far reaches of the large chamber. Long wooden tables were set up in rows, benches alongside them, offering enough seats for a large banquet. Near the fireplace, however, cushioned chairs had been placed, one of which was currently occupied by Keir's grandmother.

Keir smiled. Now that he had finally met the Dowager Countess of Whickerton, he saw something in his own grandmother's gaze that made him think of Grandma Edie. It was the same shrewd expression, the same sense of certainty with which both women tackled the world, determined to get their way, determined that they had every right to meddle as they saw fit.

While his grandmother's hair was still fairly dark, only a few gray streaks running through it, her brown eyes were as warm and welcoming as he remembered—as was the smile she bestowed upon him. "I knew the moment Edie's letter arrived that life would never be the same," she remarked with a chuckle before her gaze moved from Keir to the guests he had brought. "That you might not be coming home alone."

Keir felt Katherine's hand tense upon his arm, and he immediately looked past her at Sarah, eager to see her expression. Indeed, her gaze had dropped to the floor, her cheeks a flaming red.

"Who have you brought, dear boy?" his grandmother inquired, setting aside her blanket and pushing to her feet. Her brown eyes lingered upon Katherine for a moment before moving to Sarah. Although Katherine was the one upon Keir's arm, he could tell that his grandmother knew better than to assume she was the one who held his heart.

Once again introducing Sarah and Katherine and the girls, Keir stepped forward and embraced his grandmother. "'Tis good to have ye back, dear lady."

His grandmother chuckled, patting his cheek. "You were the one to leave. I've been here the whole time."

Keir smiled at her. "Ye have my deepest apologies," he replied with a teasing bow.

His grandmother slapped his shoulder. "If only you meant it."

Keir felt his heart sigh, reveling in that familiar sense of being home once more. "'Tis been a long journey, Grandmother. We've been traveling for a fortnight and are in dire need of rest." He looked at his parents. "Shall we speak on the morrow?"

His grandmother slipped her arm through his, her gaze directed at Sarah and Katherine. "Aye, you do look in need of rest, my dears." Then she chuckled. "Please, take no offense. You look quite fetching. I assure you." Her voice all but drifted away upon the last word, and as Keir looked down at her, he noticed his grandmother's gaze linger upon Sarah's braids. Then she looked up at him, and Keir knew she understood.

Clearing her throat, his grandmother stepped toward Sarah and Katherine, taking their hands. "Rooms have been prepared for you... and your little ones," she added with a wink at Augusta and Dorothea. "Go and rest. Mrs. Murray shall show you the way and provide you with something to eat." She smiled at them. "Welcome." She leaned forward, and her voice dropped to a whisper. Still, straining his ears, Keir heard her say, "Do not worry. You'll be safe here."

In the next moment, Mrs. Murray bustled over. She had been his family's housekeeper for as long as Keir could remember. While she was at least as old as his own grandmother, Mrs. Murray had never once thought of slowing down. Indeed, together, the two women ruled the fortress... and the clan, and no one in their right mind had ever minded.

"Welcome home, dear boy," Mrs. Murray exclaimed in her slightly gruff voice as she rushed past him, not bothering to stop and greet him properly, and pulled up next to his grandmother. Her eyes narrowed in a scrutinizing way as she regarded Sarah and Katherine.

Keir saw a frown come to Sarah's face, and her eyes found his a moment later, an almost pleading expression in them.

Instantly, Keir moved closer, coming to stand on Sarah's other side the moment Mrs. Murray opened her mouth to mumble, "Too thin," with a disapproving shake of her head.

Keir chuckled as dear moments of his childhood resurfaced, and so he leaned down to Augusta and Dorothea the moment Mrs. Murray stepped away to exchange a few quick words with his grandmother. "If ye ever want a treat," he told the girls, their eyes eager as they hung on every word, "that's the woman to get it from." He nodded toward Mrs. Murray.

"She seems a bit... fearsome," Sarah murmured quietly to him, her blue eyes wide and her teeth occasionally worrying her lower lip.

Keir grasped her hand. "She's like Duncan," he murmured. "She growls but she doesna bite."

Sarah's hand squeezed his as she leaned closer. Keir wanted to draw her into his arms, yet Sarah quickly retreated, well-aware of their company.

A heartbeat later, Keir's grandmother once more stepped toward them. "Go upstairs and rest, and I shall have supper brought up to you." She smiled at the girls. "And tomorrow night, we'll celebrate your arrival in the great hall." As Sarah's and Katherine's eyes widened with apprehension, his grandmother clasped her hands together, bid them a good night and then resettled herself by the fire, waving his parents and Duncan over.

"Follow me!" Mrs. Murray barked, the sound of her voice startling a frightened gasp from everyone's lips. "This way!"

Keir squeezed Sarah's hand, nodding at her to follow the housekeeper. "I'll find ye later," he whispered the moment his grandmother called him over, wanting a word with him.

From experience, Keir knew that *wanting a word* meant *wanting every little detail*. Indeed, it would be a long night after all! Still, it felt good to be home again.

Chapter Fifteen

MRS. MURRAY

Sarah felt dwarfed as she followed Mrs. Murray up the long staircase with Kate at her side and the girls trailing behind. A look over her shoulder told her that her nieces felt the same, their eyes wide, awestruck as they tried to take in everything at once.

The fortress was enormous, thick stone walls a testament to its original purpose. Yet colorful tapestries, curtains and rugs offset its harsh edges, giving it a gentler note.

As they walked, Mrs. Murray explained about every room they passed and every staircase that led elsewhere. Her gruff voice droned on, and despite her detailed explanations, Sarah knew she would be hopelessly lost if tasked to reach the great hall on her own. Augusta and Dorothea were clearly not burdened by such a notion, for their eyes glowed as though they had just stepped across a threshold into a fairytale world.

"Are there ghosts here?" Augusta asked, bored by Mrs. Murray's explanation about regular mealtimes and proper attire.

Sarah held her breath, exchanging a concerned look with her sister, as Mrs. Murray broke off midexplanation and turned to fix Augusta with a hard stare.

The girl swallowed hard, only now realizing what she had done.

"What sorta question is that?" Mrs. Murray demanded in a huff. "Of course, there are. What self-respecting fortress doesna have a ghost?"

Completely caught off guard, Sarah and Kate watched as the girls stepped forward, eager for more details. "Have ye ever seen one?" Dorothea inquired, once again slipping into her imitation of a Scottish accent.

Mrs. Murray eyed the girl curiously for a moment before nodding her head. "Aye, I've seen the occasional spook." Instantly, the girls looked about themselves. "Nah, they wouldna dare show themselves during the day and frighten my guests." She eyed the girls sternly, lifting her right forefinger. "One needa be firm if one is to be obeyed, ye understand?"

Both girls nodded, staring at the old housekeeper.

"If a spook dare frighten ye, come and tell me at once and I'll put an end to it," Mrs. Murray promised, her words like a vow written in stone. "Ye hear me? I willna allow ye to be frightened."

Again, the girls nodded, clearly awestruck at the thought that Mrs. Murray would dare chide a ghost.

Stunned speechless herself, Sarah saw tears brim in her sister's eyes as Kate turned to smile at her. "I love that woman," she murmured under her breath. "She's... She's like..."

"Grandma Edie," Sarah finished for her sister. "Not from this world."

Kate chuckled, then bounced a little on her feet to soothe little Frederica, who did not seem as entertained by Mrs. Murray's ghost stories as her sisters were.

For the first time since setting foot upon the island of the MacKinnears, Sarah felt her heart grow lighter. She was surprised that it happened in this moment, one that seemed rather insignificant. Yet Mrs. Murray's ways spoke to Sarah. While the woman had seemed cold and unfeeling before, with a few short words, she had now revealed herself to be a most caring person. She certainly had her ways, only revealing to those who knew her well what lived in her heart. It was a moment that once again proved to Sarah that first impressions could be terribly misleading.

Indeed, thus far, Keir's family had been incredibly welcoming and kind. They were rather direct, quite like him, but Sarah cherished Keir's honest way. Clearly, to him, it was a normal way of communicating, for he had learned it here in this place he called home.

Turning back down the corridor, Mrs. Murray gestured toward two doors on the right. "One is for ye," she explained to Sarah, not bothering to pause in her steps, "and the other is for yer sister and her wee ones." Outside Kate's door, Mrs. Murray suddenly did stop. She all but spun around and then fixed Kate with a rather stern expression. "Ye dunna mind sharing a chamber with yer wee ones, do ye?" Her brows drew together a bit more, almost connecting above the bridge of her nose. "I've heard it said that English ladies often have others care for their children."

Sarah could tell easily from the look upon Mrs. Murray's face that she disapproved of said English ladies and that there was clearly only one right answer to her question.

Kate beamed at Mrs. Murray. "I would never part with my children, not for all the gold in the world." Tears stood in her eyes as she hugged Frederica tighter against her chest, and Sarah understood how deeply the MacKinnears' sense of family and belonging touched Kate. Indeed, it stood in stark contrast to the way her husband's family, the Dunleys, approached life.

At Kate's emotional assurance, the ghost of a smile flickered across Mrs. Murray's face, and Sarah knew her sister had just won herself an ally. "Come on, then." Mrs. Murray waved them onward, unlocking the door to Kate's chamber and then handing her the key. "This is it. Come, have a look."

A large bed—larger than any Sarah had ever seen—stood at the back wall opposite the fireplace, its flames casting shadows across the chamber. Three windows faced the east, with a comfortable chaise beneath it. An old wooden chest stood in the corner, its lid not quite closed, revealing glimpses of wooden toy horses and straw dolls. "These used to belong to the lads and the Lady Yvaine," Mrs. Murray explained, nodding toward the chest, a touch of sadness in her eyes now. "I hope yer wee ones will enjoy them."

Clearly touched beyond words, Kate clasped Mrs. Murray's hand.

"Thank you, dear Mrs. Murray. You cannot know what this means to us."

Mrs. Murray gave a short nod, then quickly turned away, but not before Sarah saw her eyes soften. "I'll send a lass to help ye with the children and to bring ye some supper." She gestured for Sarah to follow her as Augusta and Dorothea settled upon the rug in front of the fireplace, eagerly digging into the toy chest. "Good night." Then she closed the door and headed a few more steps down the hall, Sarah following upon her heels.

"Yer chamber's right here." Mrs. Murray had just reached the next door when she suddenly paused. "Where did ye come from?"

Frowning, Sarah stepped sideways to look past Mrs. Murray and was surprised and overjoyed to see Loki sitting in the middle of the hallway. His amber eyes glowed brightly in the shine from Mrs. Murray's candle, and he angled his head as though he wished to offer a polite greeting. Sarah chuckled. "That is Loki," she explained as Mrs. Murray looked to her for an explanation. "He has a tendency to come and go as he pleases."

Mrs. Murray regarded Loki for another moment, then gave a quick nod. "He's got the look of a guard about him, doesna he?" She raised one eyebrow, clearly intrigued, then once more looked at Sarah. "Does he stay with ye?"

Sarah nodded. "If it's no trouble." She remembered only too well how Lord Birchwell, Kate's husband, as well as his staff, had reacted to Loki's presence.

Mrs. Murray looked almost aghast. "No, dear. Why would that be any trouble?" She turned and unlocked Sarah's door, handing her the key. Then she pushed it open and walked inside.

The moment Sarah stepped across the threshold, she was drawn to the beautiful bay windows, allowing a view of the sea to the east and a glimpse of the land farther south. Darkness was falling, and the moon's faint silhouette glittered upon the waves. "It's beautiful," Sarah whispered, completely entranced.

"Aye, it is," Mrs. Murray agreed, something wistful in her voice, and as Sarah turned, she saw a rather faraway expression in the old woman's eyes. "'Tis almost magical, is it not?" A deep sigh left her lips, then she blinked, and her gaze refocused upon Sarah.

Wondering if she might be overstepping, Sarah approached Mrs. Murray, meeting her eyes openly. "How long has Lady Yvaine been missing?"

A startled expression came to Mrs. Murray's face. "Oh, ye know what happened, then?" Sarah nodded, not bothering to offer more of an explanation. "Well, 'tis been three years." The old woman sighed again. "Three long years."

Sarah reached out and grasped her hand. "I'm so sorry. I cannot imagine losing a loved one like that."

Mrs. Murray nodded, making it clear that the old housekeeper mourned Yvaine's loss as much as her family did. Indeed, here, in this place, family had nothing to do with bloodlines and reputation. No, the meaning of family went far deeper to the core of human nature, to that place deep inside that made people who they were.

"And no clues were ever found about what might've happened to her?" Sarah inquired, unable not to. More than once she had been tempted to put these questions to Keir, and yet she dreaded seeing that look of sadness returned to his eyes.

Mrs. Murray shook her head. "Yet is that not a clue in itself?" She straightened, her brows rising meaningfully. "If ye ask me, lass, 'twas the fairies that took her back home. Aye, she was never quite of this world, was she? Ye could tell by looking into her eyes." Mrs. Murray smiled at her then, gently patting Sarah's hand. "Ye're a fine lass, and I'm glad the lad brought ye home. Sleep ye well then." And with that, Mrs. Murray turned and left.

For the longest time, Sarah simply stood in the middle of the chamber and breathed. Out of the corner of her eye, she saw Loki settle by the fireplace, stretching and yawning and finally closing his eyes. Sarah, though, did not feel tired. Not any longer. Somehow, every fiber of her being pulsed with energy, chasing away every bit of exhaustion she had felt before. Her feet moved across the chamber and toward the windows, her eyes seeking the land and sea below. Indeed, this was a magical place, made so by its people. Always had Keir spoken to her of his family's kindness, of their way of life, of their way of looking at life. Yet Sarah had never quite managed to believe him, not completely. Now, she stood here in his home, and Sarah finally realized what he had meant...

... and that people like his family truly existed.

Whatever questions they might be asking of Keir in this very moment, Sarah no longer feared Keir's honesty. The *ton* might have abandoned her but perhaps with a little bit of hope...

... and kindness...

... and love Sarah would find a new home.

Here.

Among the MacKinnears.

With Keir.

Chapter Sixteen
QUESTIONS & ANSWERS

Standing in his grandmother's salon, Keir inhaled deeply of the familiar scent: cedar and pine. This chamber had been his childhood sanctuary, a place to retreat to if he wished for solitude but not loneliness, needing counsel and a kind smile. Now, it brought with it images of warmth and companionship, hot tea and fresh pastries, stories told until dawn and stargazing until his eyes fell closed.

At the memory, a smile stole onto Keir's face before his family's chattering voices drew him back to the present. And he blinked, finding himself to be the center of everyone's attention. Not only his grandmother and his parents were present but also his brothers Duncan and Magnus as well as his aunt and uncle with their son, Hamish.

While Magnus also possessed the MacKinnear eyes—a deep blue like the sea surrounding the islands—and stood about as tall as Keir himself, Magnus was of a more slender build. Keir's younger brother had never fancied the outdoors. He had always preferred to experience his adventures through the pages of a book. Therefore, most often, Magnus could be found lost somewhere in the fortress's library or seated under a tree, his eyes glued to a page. Keir was often amazed at the knowledge his little brother had amassed, and he treasured

Magnus's gentle way of communicating what he knew without making another feel inferior.

"Welcome home, Brother," Magnus exclaimed as he strode into the salon, not bothering to pause or stop. Long strides carried him forward, a wide smile upon his young face, before he embraced Keir tightly. "I missed ye." He stepped back, grinning at Keir. "I heard a rumor that ye didna come home alone." His voice rose at the end of the sentence, giving it the touch of a question.

Amusement lingered in Magnus's gaze, and Keir chuckled. "Aye, ye and everyone else."

"So?"

"I promise I shall explain everything."

"We certainly hope so," his grandmother exclaimed from where she was seated near the fireplace. "After all, we're all bursting with curiosity, are we not?"

Everyone nodded their heads eagerly, and Keir turned to embrace his aunt Isobel and his uncle Conall as well as their son Hamish, his cousin, who was about Magnus's age.

Keir's grandparents had had three children: Keir's father, Aiden, as well as two daughters, Isobel and Catriona. While Catriona had found love outside of their clan, settling on the mainland, Isobel had married a MacKinnear man and remained upon their island all her life.

Once everyone was seated near the fire, all eyes turned to Keir, the expression on their faces one of checked curiosity. Keir laughed. "I feel honored to see ye all take such interest in my life," he remarked teasingly, then moved toward his grandmother. "Grandma Edie sends her love and asks ye to take care of her girls."

His grandmother chortled. "That's Edie! She never beat around the bush! Never worried for fancy words!" An almost wistful smile came to her face. "Grandma Edie," she murmured, then shook her head, chuckling. "It is odd to hear you call her that. As old as we've gotten, I always think of her as the young girl who told me not to worry and trust that everything would turn out all right." Something deeply enchanted rested in her eyes as her mind no doubt traveled back to the time she spoke of. Then, though, she blinked, and her gaze focused upon Keir, the touch of a frown creasing her forehead.

"Is her hair all gray?" Rather absentmindedly, her right hand rose and touched her own, the dark, almost-black strands streaked with silver.

Everyone chuckled good-naturedly.

"More or less." Despite his grandmother's teasing words, Keir could tell that she missed her old friend dearly but chose to remember the good things they had shared instead of dwell upon the many moments they had been apart.

"Now," Keir's father began, slapping a hand upon his knee, "are we ever to hear this story? Tell us, why did the famous Grandma Edie send for ye! I must say I dunna care for her secret keeping!" He grinned, then reached out and grasped his wife's hand, pulling her close as they all settled in to listen.

Keir could not say that he cared for Grandma Edie's secret keeping, either; yet that had never discouraged the woman. "Well, quite frankly, Grandma Edie wanted my help in breaking an engagement."

Rather stunned expressions met Keir. "An engagement?" his Aunt Isobel inquired, exchanging a frown with Keir's mother. "Grandma Edie was engaged?"

Keir laughed. "No, not her engagement. Sa-Miss Mortensen's."

At Keir's slip of the tongue, hushed silence fell over the room, and he could see that each and every member of his family knew or, at least, suspected the truth. "And why did Sa–Miss Mortensen," Magnus asked with a wink, "wish to end her engagement?" He paused, then continued a second before Keir could reply. "And why on earth did she need help to do so?" He looked at their grandmother as though asking for support. "Are engagements harder to break in England than they are here?"

Their grandmother chortled. "Among the *ton*? Most definitely! It is simply not done... except for, perhaps, in rather rare and unusual circumstances, and even then, it does leave a bitter aftertaste that might haunt those involved for the rest of their lives."

Keir nodded in agreement with his grandmother's words. "Sarah's parents were severely in debt," he explained, abandoning all attempts at concealing his close connection to her, "and so, *naturally*, they sought a beneficial match, seeing her betrothed to a... vile man." Try as he might, Keir knew he failed to conceal his contempt for Lord Blackmore.

"Without her consent?" his mother demanded, the outrage upon her face suggesting quite clearly that she would never have dreamed of forcing a match upon her own children.

Keir nodded. "From what Grandma Edie explained, this was not the first match they had planned for her. There had been others, all prevented because of the Whickertons' involvement. Yet they knew, at some point, they might not be able to interfere in time, and thus, Grandma Edie devised this plan in order to see Sarah permanently safe from her parents' matchmaking."

His family nodded in agreement; their eyes fixed upon him as they waited for Keir to continue. "So, what plan was this?" Magnus inquired, his blue eyes aglow with excitement, as if he were reading one of his favorite adventure stories. "And what was yer involvement?"

Without going into every detail, Keir explained how Grandma Edie had planned a feigned kidnapping the night before Sarah's wedding and how he, Keir, had been assigned the role of kidnapper.

Amused laughter echoed through his grandmother's salon, and Keir shook his head, remembering his own thoughts, his own disbelief at having agreed to such a ludicrous plan. Yet everything had worked out for the best, had it not?

"We remained hidden in the woods for about a fortnight, waiting for Lord Blackmore to pay the ransom, which, in turn, was then used to free Sarah's father of his gambling debts."

Keir's cousin Hamish frowned. "But how did that prevent her marriage? If, in fact, Lord Blackmore paid to have her returned to him?"

"She cried off afterward," Keir explained, remembering how Sarah had spoken to him of that moment. Lord Blackmore had been furious, and only because of Loki's as well as Grandma Edie's interference, had he been unable to unleash said fury upon Sarah.

Magnus's forehead remained furrowed. "But if she simply cried off, could she not have done so before? Why the kidnapping?"

Their grandmother chortled, a glimmer of anger coming to her eyes. "Because it would not have stopped her parents from seeing her betrothed again. After all, there are still those who seek a young bride of the peerage in order to elevate their own status." Her gaze looked around their small circle and then met Keir's. "The kidnapping was to ensure she would be utterly ruined, was it not? To prevent her parents from ever selling her off again?" Her brows rose questioningly.

Keir heaved a deep breath, then nodded. "Aye."

The right corner of his grandmother's mouth twitched in amusement. "So, you did not simply take on the role of kidnapper, but you were also the means of her ruination, were you not?"

Around Keir, jaws dropped and eyes widened as his family began to understand the implications of his grandmother's words. He remembered the day he, himself, had asked that very question of Sarah. He also remembered how deeply she had blushed struggling to explain why the kidnapping had been necessary.

Indeed, no reputation could survive such implications, and upon her return to society, Sarah had been deemed unmarriageable.

"Then why did she have to cry off?" Magnus inquired, that thoughtful expression upon his face once more, that desire to understand shining in his eyes. "If that kidnapping ruined her, why would her fiancé still wish to see her made his bride?"

Keir gritted his teeth, for a part of him wondered at Lord Blackmore's true motivation. "From what Grandma Edie said, it would have been impossible for him to cry off. A gentleman simply doesna do so. Just as he didna pay for Sarah's return out of the goodness of his heart or his concern for her well-being, he could not refuse because the *ton* would have crucified him for it. He did what he did to save his own reputation."

His mother frowned at him, softly shaking her head. "'Tis an odd world, one with very confusing rules and traditions." She looked up and met her husband's eyes. "I must say I consider myself fortunate not to have been born into that world, able to marry for love and love alone."

Keir's father wrapped an arm around his wife and pulled her close. Then he looked up at his son. "I am proud, my son, that ye stood by someone who needed yer help, and yet it saddens me that *Sarah* didna have a family to do that for her. After all, that is what family is for." He smiled, looking at them all, and Keir knew that his father, like his mother, understood how precious their deep familial connection was.

His mother nodded in agreement. "However," she continued, a chiding look in her eyes, "I would've liked for ye to inform us of yer decision in greater detail." Her eyebrows rose challengingly as her lips curled upward into a smile. "We couldna quite make sense of why ye'd stayed in England all this time. Next time—should there be a next time!—please write back with more details, agreed?"

Keir chuckled. "Agreed!"

"I have another question," Magnus remarked, lifting a hand to gain everyone's attention, before he looked at Keir. "Why ye?" he asked simply.

Keir frowned. "Why me what?"

"Why did Grandma Edie send for ye in the first place? Was there truly no other man in all of England who could have done what ye did?"

Oh, Keir had asked himself that very question before! And deep down, he knew the answer. He had known it for a while.

His grandmother chortled. "Edie being Edie, I know she had a good reason for choosing Keir." A wide grin came to her face as she regarded him curiously. "Would you not agree?"

Again, before Keir could think of any sort of reply, Magnus interrupted, his forehead still in a frown. "What do ye mean? What does she mean?"

Indeed, the only two who did not seem to understand were Magnus and Hamish. Everyone else nodded knowingly, amused expressions upon their faces as whispered words flew back and forth.

Duncan laughed a booming laugh. He sat a bit off to the side and had thus far remained quiet. Yet Keir knew his brother well and had often seen him stand back and observe before offering his opinion. "Are ye truly blind, little brother?" he demanded, slapping Magnus on the shoulder. "Can ye not see that Keir is quite taken with the lass?"

Keir felt an odd tingling as all eyes once more turn to him, regarding his face, his expression with such intensity, as though they wish to dig into his mind and heart.

Yet Magnus still frowned. "But how could Grandma Edie know he would... come to care for Sarah?" He looked from Duncan to his parents and then back to Keir. "She'd never even met ye? How would she know?"

A warm chuckle drifted from their grandmother's lips. "Oh, she knew! Edie's always been an excellent judge of character, and over the years, I've written to her of all of you." She nodded, meeting his eyes. "She had an inkling, and as always, she acted upon it."

For a moment, Keir felt utterly overwhelmed, thinking how close he had come to never even meeting Sarah. It was a dark thought that filled his heart with dread and sadness.

"And what of her sister?" Keir's uncle Conall asked, changing the topic with a meaningful look in Keir's direction. "The countess, how does she come to be here? What is her story?"

Grateful, Keir recounted how they had gone to visit Sarah's sister and discovered the truth about the seemingly perfect life she had led.

"He took away her children?" Keir's aunt Isobel exclaimed, clasping a shocked hand over her mouth. "What husband would do that? 'Tis unfathomable!"

Keir nodded, all amusement and laughter gone. "I promised the Whickertons," he looked from his parents to his grandmother, "that the sisters would be safe here."

For a moment, silence fell over the salon as his grandmother looked around their small circle, meeting everyone's eyes. Then she turned back to look at Keir. "They are welcome to stay here as long as they wish," she told him solemnly, "and for as long as they are here with the MacKinnears, they will be treated as such. I shall write to Edie and assure her that her girls will be quite safe here. After all," she continued as her gaze traveled around the room, "that is what the MacKinnears have always been about, new beginnings."

Everyone nodded in agreement. Indeed, like the Whickertons, the MacKinnears had always stood shoulder to shoulder, loyal and steadfast. It was precisely that which made them strong, that which had given their ancestors the courage to start over on these shores.

New beginnings, indeed!

Keir smiled at his grandmother. These days, she rarely got involved in the day-to-day of the clan as she preferred teaching the young all she had learned, ensuring that the children of Clan MacKinnear received a well-rounded education. Still, she was the heart and soul of their people, and Keir knew that she could not keep quiet where her old friend and those Edie cared for were involved.

Of course, her son, Keir's father and the current clan leader, understood so without words, stepping aside and granting her this moment.

As their small gathering broke off and everybody headed to their own chambers, Keir noticed his father staying behind, his gaze upon him. And so, Keir bid everyone a good night and waited until no one else remained but the two of them. Then he stepped toward his father. "Ye clearly have something on yer mind, Father," he remarked, eyeing him curiously. "What is it?"

His father rubbed his chin, the expression in his green eyes thoughtful. "A lot has happened lately," he began, clasping a hand upon his son's shoulder. "A lot has changed in yer life." He chuckled. "I admit I've only met the famous Grandma Edie once or twice in my younger years, and while I have no reason to doubt my mother's impression of her, I must urge ye to remain true to yerself no matter what others might plan for ye." His brows rose imploringly as he held Keir's gaze.

Keir understood his father's concern, and he wondered what to say to put it to rest. After all, as much as Grandma Edie enjoyed meddling and matchmaking, Keir knew how he felt. He did not feel directed by another, his path set before him against his own will. No, he had made his own choices along the way.

Indeed, it had been his choice to agree to the kidnapping.

His choice to stand by Sarah's side.

His choice to accompany her to her sister's estate.

His choice to...

"I'm in love with her," Keir said simply, shrugging his shoulders almost helplessly, unable to explain how it had happened or when. Yet he was certain of it, more certain than he had ever been of anything else. "She's the one."

For a moment, the expression upon his father's face stilled. Then, though, he nodded, eyes lit up in understanding. "Ye do have the look of a man in love," he remarked with a smile. "I simply wished to be certain."

Keir embraced his father, hugging him tightly. "I know, Father, and I'm grateful for it." He stood back and met his father's eyes. "It caught me by surprise as well, for it happened within a matter of days. At first, I suppose I was rather unwilling to accept that I had lost my heart to her." He shrugged. "Now, though, I no longer doubt the truth of my affections for her."

His father squeezed his shoulder, a smile coming to his face. "Then what do ye intend to do?"

Keir laughed. "I intend to marry her!" He paused, then sighed. "However, I wish for her to have some time to settle in first. I dunna think 'twould be right to force yet another decision upon her so soon after uprooting her life. I want her to... choose me out of her own free will and not because she's lacking a better option."

His father frowned. "Do ye think she would? Do ye doubt her affections for ye?"

Again, Keir laughed. "I dunna; however, I need her to be certain. I want her to know what it means to choose freely."

Pride rested in his father's eyes as he looked at him, and Keir felt warmed by it. "I'm glad ye finally returned, and I wish ye and Sarah all the happiness in the world." His father embraced him, and for a moment, Keir almost felt like the wee lad he had once been, wrapped in his father's enormous arms, safe from every harm that might ever befall him.

"Thank ye, Father. 'Tis truly good to be home."

Chapter Seventeen
A COWARDLY HEART

Although fatigue tugged upon her eyelids, Sarah simply could not bring herself to lie down, her feet carrying her across her chamber, away from the windows and then back toward them. Her eyes were drawn to the far horizon, the soft twinkling of the stars above, reflected gently in the waves of the sea. Indeed, magic seemed to live in this place, and Sarah wanted some of that magic—joy, happiness and love—for all of them.

For herself as well.

For Sarah, none of these things would ever exist without Keir.

As much as she had always prayed for a future safe from marriage, all Sarah suddenly wanted was the very thing she had struggled so hard to avoid.

Seating herself in the alcove, Sarah pulled up her legs, crossed her arms above her knees, and rested her head upon them. She heaved a deep sigh. "Sometimes life leads one down strange paths."

Indeed, here she was, among Keir's people, his family. And from the short moment she had spent in their presence, Sarah was certain that they were as good and kind as Keir had said, as Keir was himself. But would it be enough? Would they truly accept her? Even welcome her? Not only as a stranger in need of help, but...?

Again, Sarah buried her face in her hands. "I don't even know if he wishes for a future with me," Sarah whispered to Loki, still curled up by the fire. "He said he was not ready to bid me farewell, that he might never be, but does that mean he wishes..." Even finishing that thought was something Sarah shied away from.

Something she had learned in her life was that hope was a very dangerous thing. And yet, it came as it chose, did it not? Often unbidden, making her feel like a little girl standing before a fairy, revealing her heart's deepest wish.

Only there was no fairy, was there?

A soft knock sounded on her door, and Sarah flinched. For a moment, she stared at it, dumbfounded, before her feet moved, once more settling upon the floor and pushing her upright. "Who could it be this late?" she murmured to herself as she tiptoed across the rug in front of the hearth. "Perhaps Kate needs me!"

Swiftly, Sarah pulled open the door, concerned that something might be wrong with the children... only to find Keir standing there.

His face lay in shadow, his features barely illuminated by the soft glow from the fire in the hearth. His hair was tousled, windswept even, and his clothes looked rather disheveled. His coat and vest had disappeared, and he had rolled up the sleeves of his shirt, as though intent on tending to some sort of laborious task. Yet at the same time, fatigue clung to him like a heavy blanket, and Sarah realized how much Keir had done for her.

In the past few days alone.

"Are ye all right?" Keir inquired with a slight frown, his watchful gaze sweeping over her features, as though once more digging to unearth her secrets. "Ye seemed concerned just now. Has something upset ye, lass?"

Sarah shook her head and then beckoned him across the threshold. As he stepped into her chamber, she closed the door. "No, I'm perfectly fine. I simply thought that perhaps something was wrong with the children, that Kate..." She trailed off as she saw understanding come to his eyes.

"Have they settled in?" Keir asked with a look over his shoulder toward the door and the corridor beyond. "I know that this place—and its people—differs greatly from what ye were used to, but I hope that ye will feel at home here soon."

Keir's words made Sarah's heart sing... and hope once more. As much as she tried not to, she simply could not help it. "Your family seems very kind, and Mrs. Murray is a true treasure."

Keir chuckled, reaching for Sarah's hands and gently tugging her closer. "Aye, she is. She's a wonderful storyteller, too. Her ghost stories are legendary."

Sarah intertwined her fingers with Keir's, savoring this small touch, this closeness after a day filled with unknowns and new experiences. "Yes, she told the girls not to be afraid and to come speak to her should a spook dare frighten them." She smiled deeply, and an answering expression came to Keir's face. "The girls adore her, and so does Kate. She's one of those people who make you feel completely safe, is she not? At first, I thought her stern and cold." She shrugged, shaking her head. "But I was wrong. Indeed, first impressions are nothing more than a mere glimpse at a story."

Keir nodded. "Aye, I've always found that to be true." His eyes shone as they looked down into hers, and Sarah held her breath as Keir tucked a stray curl behind her ear. The tips of his fingers brushed against her temple and then traced along the curve of her ear. It was only a fleeting touch, and yet Sarah felt it in every fiber of her being. It made her want to sink into his arms and stay there forever.

Still, her mind would not allow her to give in to this longing just yet. "How did it go with your family?" Once the question was spoken, Sarah felt her insides tense. As much as she wanted to believe that Keir's family were the kind of people who easily opened their hearts to others, had they not just spoken about first impressions being misleading?

Keir grinned, and that teasing look upon his face eased some of Sarah's doubts. "Ye're doing it again, lass." There was a chiding tone in his voice. "Ye're overthinking everything. 'Twill only give ye a headache. Ye know that." He pinched her chin affectionately, his blue eyes looking deep into hers.

Sarah nodded. "I know," she whispered, leaning into his touch as he reached out to cup her cheek. "I haven't been able to sleep because of it. I keep thinking and thinking. The thoughts are going round and round in my head. No matter what I do, they simply won't stop." She shrugged, her hands reaching out to slink around his neck, pulling herself closer. "What am I to do? How can I make it stop?"

Something almost wicked flashed in Keir's eyes a second before his arms closed around her, all but lifting her off her feet. Then he inclined his head, capturing her mouth in a searing kiss that, at least for the moment, made the rest of the world disappear.

Sarah sighed against his lips, and before she knew it, her hands were in his hair, tugging him closer. Longing made her bold, and she returned his kiss with a fierceness that would have made her blush had her mind not been silenced.

Keir smiled against her lips, then deepened their kiss. Sarah could feel his longing for her grow in tandem with her own. They had kissed like this before, been in each other's arms before, and yet suddenly, it no longer seemed enough. *Is this love?* Sarah wondered. Or was she confusing this heady feeling with one that had nothing to do with the heart?

All Sarah knew for sure was that she had never felt like this before.

Breaking their kiss, Keir set her back down, her feet sinking into the lush rug in front of the fireplace. "Ye have a way of making me forget everything, little wisp," Keir whispered, then brushed his mouth against hers once more. He trailed the backs of his fingers down her chin, then gave it a teasing pinch. "I missed this. Only the two of us, with no one around." His gaze locked upon hers, and for a moment, he remained as still as a statue, as though debating something within. Then he suddenly dipped his head and kissed her once more.

Sarah's heart soared, and she felt almost weightless. Shivers teased her skin, and every touch—even a fleeting brush of Keir's fingertips against her skin—made her heart trip and stumble and rejoice. Never had Sarah felt like this.

Only ever with Keir.

"I... I..." Sarah bit her lip, willing the words to leave her tongue, to fly out into the world and make themselves heard. *I love you!* That thought rang loud and clear in her heart, and yet... she could not seem to speak those three little words.

Closing her eyes, Sarah heaved a deep sigh. "Have you already had a chance to speak to your family?" *Oh, I'm such a coward!*

"Aye." He smiled at her, still holding on tightly, not letting go, giving Sarah's heart yet another reason to trip, stumble, and rejoice. "Of course, they insisted upon knowing everything." He chuckled. "As I knew they would."

Sarah tensed. "And? How did they...?"

Again, Keir chuckled and yet did not comment on her fluttering nerves. "My mother chided me for staying away for so long while my father complained about Grandma Edie's secret keeping." The expression upon his face sobered, grew into something sweet and almost tender. "Yet they understood once they knew what had happened and why I had stayed."

A part of Sarah wished she could have been there to see their faces and hear their replies. Always had Keir done his utmost to ease her mind, and every once in a while, Sarah wondered how truthfully he recounted events and reactions. Had his concern for her ever urged him to alter the retelling of events?

"There's nothing for ye to worry about, lass. Ye and yer sister, as well as the three wee ones, are safe here." He grasped her chin and looked deep into her eyes. "As I knew she would, my grandmother didna hesitate to answer Grandma Edie's call. So long as ye are here with us, ye will have the protection of the MacKinnears."

Tears blurred Sarah's vision; her heart deeply touched. And yet there was still that part of her that always doubted and questioned and wondered why Keir's grandmother had agreed. Had it truly been out of sheer duty? Out of respect for Grandma Edie, perhaps? Or were the MacKinnears truly the kind of people who so easily opened their hearts to others?

Sarah wanted to believe so, and yet she had had far too many experiences, met far too many people who cared very little about anyone but themselves.

"Get some sleep, little wisp," Keir murmured, gently trailing his fingers down her temple before his hand slipped to the back of her neck, once more pulling her closer. "I shall see ye in the morning." He dipped his head and kissed her gently, then pressed his forehead to hers for another few heartbeats as they breathed in the same air. "Good night."

The moment Keir stepped away and then out the door, Sarah felt cold. Always had she regretted his absence, but lately it felt like a deep ache in her chest, growing more acute and painful with each day. "I love you, Keir," Sarah whispered, cursing herself for not having had the courage to tell him. Would he have returned her affections?

'Even if he does care for you,' her mother's voice suddenly snapped in her head, and Sarah flinched, 'his family will never accept you! They will want a Scottish bride for their son. Someone from their own clan.' Sarah could all but see her mother's face in her mind, her brows drawn down in a disapproving scowl. 'You're a fool!'

Tears filled Sarah's eyes. "Go away!" she told the voice, anger tightening her jaw. "Your advice never served me. After all, you never cared for me. Not truly." Feeling utterly lost, Sarah sank to the floor in front of the fireplace, her limbs suddenly weak, her body exhausted. "Why can you never encourage me? Make me believe and trust?" Hanging her head, Sarah closed her eyes, grateful for the soft touch of the fire's warmth reaching out to her. "Couldn't you have stood by my side just once?"

A soft touch upon her arm made Sarah open her eyes, and she found herself looking at Loki. The feline sat before her, his amber eyes widened and directed at her, something almost gentle upon his features. For a moment, he remained still, as though studying her. Then he moved toward her, brushing his face against her arm and purring softly.

With tears still clinging to her eyelashes, Sarah smiled, drawing Loki into her arms. "Thank you," she murmured into his fur, hugging him to her chest. "I don't know what I would ever do without you." She lifted her head and looked into his amber eyes. "Don't ever leave me. Promise?"

A faint meow drifted to her ears, and Sarah rested her forehead against Loki's little head as he continued to purr, the soft rumble in his throat soothing her rattled nerves. "I love you," Sarah whispered to the little feline. "If only I could have told Keir."

Chapter Eighteen

SIMPLY GONE

The moment Keir closed the door to Sarah's chamber behind him, he knew that something had been on her mind, something she had not said. He had all but seen her desire to speak, to confide in him whatever lingered upon her mind, and yet she had not. Again, concerns and doubts had crowded her thoughts; Keir had seen it plain as day.

For a moment, he had been tempted to press her. Still, perhaps all she needed was some more time, time to realize that good things happened after all and that they were not inevitably followed by something life-shattering.

Although fatigue weighed heavily upon him, Keir decided to see to the horses before finding his own chamber. Autumn, especially, always felt uneasy in unknown places, and he wanted to reassure the mare.

Venturing back downstairs, Keir stepped into the great hall. The place held many wonderful memories of Yuletide seasons and sweeping banquets as well as spring festivals and spooky All Hallows Eves. He could not help but imagine Katherine's three little ones among the children of the clan, and he smiled. Perhaps everything had happened the way it had been meant to. Perhaps Sarah and her sister had always belonged here, and everything they had done these past few months had played right into Fate's hands.

Keir rather liked that thought. He liked it very much.

Focusing his thoughts, Keir made to cross the hall when he suddenly heard footsteps fast approaching from the other side. He angled his head toward the front entrance and spotted a young woman sprinting toward him. Her dark hair was streaming down her shoulders, and the light from the fire in the hearth flickered across her soft features.

"Kenna!" Keir exclaimed in a laugh. "Ye look as though hellhounds are lapping at yer heels! Where are ye off to in such a hur—?"

Without stopping, Kenna flung herself into his arms, hugging him tightly. Her breath came fast beside his ear, and he could feel the flushed warmth of her skin.

"Is something the matter, lass?" Keir asked, chuckling. He tried to look into her face, his hands settling upon her arms and urging her back. "Why are ye out this late?"

Kenna huffed out a long breath, her cheeks flushed and her brown eyes dancing with eagerness. "Why would ye ask such a silly question, Keir MacKinnear?" she snapped, slapping his shoulder. "Ye left without a word and returned just the same."

Keir grinned at her. "'Tis been only a several months, and yet ye act as though ye havena seen me in decades."

The smile Keir expected did not come. Instead, Kenna lowered her chin, her eyes closing briefly as she drew in a slow breath. When she looked at him again, tears clung to her lashes.

Keir stilled, his gaze narrowing as he reached out a hand to place upon her shoulder. "What's the matter, lass? Did Eoghan send ye? Is it Bonnie?" Keir remembered well the last time Kenna had come to the castle in the middle of the night. Bonnie had run a terrifyingly high fever, and Eoghan had sent her to fetch help.

Kenna shook her head, and Keir breathed a sigh of relief.

"What then?"

At his repeated question, Kenna's lips seemed to thin, anger flaring in her eyes. "I missed ye!" she snapped, glaring at him. "Is that truly such a far-fetched notion to ye?" She gave his chest an angry shove—as she did when she was frustrated or furious with him. "Ye left so abruptly, I didna even have the chance to bid ye farewell."

Contrite, Keir offered her an apologetic smile. "I'm sorry." Carefully, not wishing to have his hand bitten off, Keir reached to pull her closer, slowly enveloping her in a tight embrace. "I'm sorry I didna bid ye farewell, lass. I never expected to leave that night, but the message was urgent, and I asked Eoghan to give ye my best." He looked down at her face. "Did he not do that?

Kenna's brows furrowed. "He did, but it wasna the same!" She shoved against his chest, breaking his embrace. "I woke up the next morning, and ye were simply gone." Shaking her head, she crossed her arms over her chest. "We were having a wonderful time at the spring festival, and then all of a sudden ye were called away to speak to yer grandmother." Her eyes narrowed, and her nose wrinkled into a disapproving frown. "Ye simply never came back, and the next morning ye were gone! Why didna ye say something? Why didna ye come talk to me?"

Keir heaved a deep sigh as wariness spread through his body. After explaining everything to his family in great detail, he truly did not feel up to doing it again. "I apologize for my rushed departure, lass, but 'tis a rather long story, and I'm too tired right now." He took a step toward her, trying to look into her down-turned eyes. "Come to the gathering tomorrow night and ye'll understand." When she would not look at him, Keir placed a hand upon her shoulder. "Kenna? Are ye truly angry with me?"

Tentatively, her gaze rose to meet his. "I thought we were friends," she retorted with a pout. "I thought..." She closed her eyes and briefly shook her head, then looked at him once more. "Eoghan said that... ye brought two English ladies back with ye." Her brows rose in question.

Keir chuckled. "How does Eoghan know they're English?"

Kenna gave him a bit of an exasperated look. "Ye know as well as I do that there are no secrets on this island, Keir MacKinnear. Dunna pretend otherwise!"

Keir nodded knowingly. "Aye, 'tis true; I can tell ye that. However, if ye wish to know more, then come to the gathering tomorrow night." He gave her shoulder an affectionate squeeze. "Good night, Kenna."

Then Keir turned away and hurried outside, reminding himself why he had come downstairs. Still, he knew he would not stay long, feeling fatigue tugging on every weary bone in his body. More than anything, he needed rest; after all, tomorrow would be a trying day.

Chapter Nineteen

IN A FAIRYTALE

When Sarah woke the next morning, the sun was already high in the sky, its light shining in through the windows almost blinding. Her entire chamber seemed to glow golden, and Sarah slipped out of bed feeling lighter than ever before. She quickly dressed, wondering about the routine in this place. How did people have breakfast? Did they all eat together?

Accepting that no answers could be found in her chamber, Sarah went to knock upon her sister's door. From inside, she could hear Augusta's and Dorothea's voices, suggesting they were involved in some sort of role-playing.

Not bothering to wait, Sarah entered, smiling as she found her two nieces upon the floor near the fireplace, playing with the toys Mrs. Murray had provided for them so kindly. "Good morning," Sarah greeted them, and received only distracted smiles in return as both girls were completely absorbed in their game.

Closing the door, Sarah approached the bed where Kate was just finishing nursing Frederica. The exhausted expression upon her sister's face spoke to a sleepless night. "How are you this morning?" Sarah inquired, seating herself on the edge of the bed.

Kate gave her a weak smile.

"Is there anything you need?"

"I could do with a spot of breakfast."

In that moment, a knock came on Kate's door, and both sisters turned their heads toward it. "Enter," Sarah called, rising from the bed.

Relief flooded Sarah when she saw Keir enter, a smile coming to his face as he saw the girls playing in front of the fireplace. "Good morning, ladies," he greeted them with a formal bow, and Augusta and Dorothea dropped into rather adorable-looking curtsies. Then he turned to smile at Sarah, and to her, it felt as though the sun was rising for a second time that day. "I found yer chamber empty and thought ye might be here." He stepped closer and reached for her hands, then quickly looked beyond her shoulder toward Kate. "Good morning, Katherine. I hope ye slept well. Would ye care for some breakfast?"

Sarah nodded gratefully. "Yes, in fact, we are quite famished."

Bouncing around the room, the girls ended up by the window, both their little noses pressed to the glass. "Can we go down to the beach?" Augusta asked excitedly before craning her neck to look back at their mother. "The weather looks so nice."

Kate heaved an exhaustive breath, dark circles still beneath her eyes. "I'm sorry, my dear, but I do not feel up to a walk right now. Perhaps some other time."

Instantly, the gleeful expressions upon the girls' faces fell.

"If ye dunna mind," Keir interfered, his hand squeezing Sarah's gently as he spoke, "I am more than happy to show the girls around." He looked at Augusta and Dorothea. "I have to admit, the beach sounds like a marvelous idea."

The girls squealed in delight, jumping up and down and clapping their hands together. In answer to their racket, Frederica waved her little fists about, her blue eyes wide open as she lay in Kate's arms, observing her two elder sisters with sudden interest.

Kate nodded in answer to Keir's question, gratitude in her eyes. "But you will look after them, won't you?"

Keir smiled at her, honesty in his eyes but a bit of teasing still twitching his lips. "Of course, ye have my word. I shall guard them with my life."

"But I'm hungry, too," Dorothea protested, placing a hand on her belly. "I already heard it rumbling in there."

Keir lowered himself to one knee to meet her eyes. "I'm certain we can find something along the way. Are ye up for a wee bit of an adventure?"

Instantly, Dorothea's eyes lit up like two beacons, and she nodded her head eagerly. Augusta quickly chimed in.

Stepping back to open the door, Keir once more reached out to grasp Sarah's hand. "I shall send up some breakfast and then take the girls down to the beach. Dunna worry and see that ye find some rest."

Sarah smiled at him gratefully, knowing that the second half of his words were meant for her sister. In truth, she would like to join them, to walk along the beach and feel the wind upon her face. Still, it had been a long time since Sarah had had time alone with her sister, and perhaps it would be good for them to stay back and speak to one another over a bite of breakfast. "Have fun and I'll see you soon."

As Keir shooed the girls out into the corridor, Loki followed them. Then the door closed, and yet the girls' eager voices still echoed back to their ears. With a heavy sigh, Kate fell back against the pillows. "It does not seem quite fair, does it?" she asked, looking up at Sarah. "They never seem to tire while I can barely bring myself to lift my head even after a good night's sleep."

Chuckling, Sarah seated herself beside her sister upon the bed, Frederica between them. The girl's shiny blue eyes moved back and forth between her mother and her aunt, her hands raised and grasping at thin air. Rising once more, Sarah retrieved a small wooden hound from the toys still scattered upon the floor and handed it to her niece. Frederica grasped it eagerly, turning it from side to side, her eyes wide with fascination, before plucking it into her mouth.

Soon, a young maid brought them a tray of breakfast with tea and pastries with cream, as well as two small jars that smelled of jam and honey. The sisters ate eagerly, their bellies empty, and for the first time in weeks, they truly savored the moment, this meal they shared with one another.

Eventually, Frederica fell asleep, and her soft breaths lulled the sisters into a deeply relaxed state. "This is like a fairytale land," Kate remarked with her eyes closed, a contented sigh drifting from her lips. A moment later, it was replaced by an amused chuckle. "With Mrs. Murray as the fairy godmother!"

Sarah laughed. "Oh, she does seem magical, does she not?" She sat up and looked at her sister. "Do you truly believe she was telling us the truth? That she's seen ghosts in this castle?"

Kate shrugged. "Perhaps not ghosts as we imagine them," she murmured, and a shadow passed over her face. "White sheets floating through the air, dragging chains behind them that rattle through the night." Her voice sounded distant, and a faraway look lingered in her eyes. "Perhaps these ghosts are more of an earthly nature."

Sarah reached out to grasp her sister's hand. "You're safe here. You know that, don't you?" She looked deep into her sister's eyes, needing Kate to believe her. "We are finally here, finally safe, but if we do not believe that we are, we will forever remain trapped in a place of our own making." She squeezed Kate's hand, relieved to see the touch of a smile come to her face. "This is our happily ever after, Kate. We did it! We're finally safe. The both of us."

Tears rolled down Kate's cheeks, and yet the smile upon her face stretched wide. "We truly are, aren't we?" Disbelief lingered in her eyes, despite the obvious truth of her words. "Perhaps we truly are in a fairytale... with Keir as the hero who came to free us from the tower." A giggle escaped Kate's lips.

It was infectious, and Sarah joined in with her. Yet the moment she did, she heard a voice whispering in her head—and this time it was not her mother.

Meeting Kate's eyes, Sarah sighed, her heart suddenly lighter than before. "You know, according to Keir." She smiled at her sister. "I'm the hero of my own story, and he is simply someone who... lent a hand."

The expression upon Kate's face spoke of many things: surprise, disbelief, emotion. In the end, though, the look in her eyes reminded Sarah of someone who had never known that the very thing they had searched the world to find had always been right there... and they had simply not known.

If only they had.

Chapter Twenty
OLD FRIENDS

Keir grinned as he watched Augusta's and Dorothea's eyes grow wider and wider with each delicious thing Mrs. Murray set down in front of them upon the table in the castle kitchen. The smell of warm pastry and fresh baked goods filled the air, their aroma only matched by the scent of honey, cinnamon and fresh cream. "Ye said ye wanted breakfast," Keir said with a chuckle, nodding toward the laden table. "Now, eat up."

Augusta licked her lips. "Is this all for us?"

Mrs. Murray nodded, pouring each of them a glass of milk. "Eat enough to fill yer bellies. After all, ye got a wee bit of growing to do."

As Dorothea reached for the cream, Loki launched himself off the stone floor and in one giant leap stepped in between the little girl and the mug of cream. While the look in his amber eyes gave him a rather innocent expression, the way Loki angled his head suggested otherwise. He clearly demanded his share and thought himself very much entitled to it.

"It would seem Loki is hungry as well," Keir remarked, nodding toward the feline and wondering how Mrs. Murray would react to him.

To his surprise, the old housekeeper seemed not in the least taken aback by this additional guest at her table. "Aye, right ye are," she mumbled, then poured Loki some cream and milk into a small bowl and set it down for him at the other end of the table.

Keir grinned. "I take it ye've met Loki before, Mrs. Murray."

The old housekeeper nodded, observing the feline for a moment before turning to look at Keir. "Aye, he joined us on our way to the guest chambers last night." She reached out a wrinkled hand and brushed it across Loki's head. "He seems very protective of yer lass." Her eyes rose to meet his, and Keir could see a question there. Perhaps not a question but a suspicion, one that did not require a confirmation from him to be considered a fact.

"Thank ye for this fine breakfast, Mrs. Murray," Dorothea said to the old housekeeper around a mouthful of food. "'Tis delicious."

Mrs. Murray smiled; a smile Keir remembered from his own childhood. Indeed, at first glance, the old woman looked rather stern and forbidding; however, those who got to know her, those who won her good opinion, soon discovered that the housekeeper of Clan MacKinnear possessed a heart of gold.

"What are ye up to today?" Mrs. Murray inquired, her gaze wandering to Keir. "'Tis a rather pleasant day, not one made for remaining indoors." She grasped a scone on her way around the table and thrust it into his hand. "Eat up," she told him with a wicked grin. "Ye still have some growing up to do."

The girls chuckled, crumbs flying from their mouths before they could cover them with their hands.

"I suppose I shall take them for a walk around the island," Keir informed Mrs. Murray, then he took a bite from his scone. "As ye said, 'tis a perfect day for it."

The old housekeeper nodded in agreement. Then, though, she lifted a finger in warning, her eyes meeting his. "But dunna take the wee dears near the cliffs, mind ye. 'Tis no place for children."

"Why not?" Augusta inquired, her eyes now wide with curiosity. Keir had often found that children possessed a sixth sense for things they were not meant to hear.

Mrs. Murray turned to look at them. "Why, dears, because 'tis haunted, of course." She shook her head at them, as though they ought to have known.

Dorothea swallowed hard, her green eyes large and round and staring. "H-haunted?"

"What do you mean?" Augusta demanded to know, half-leaning on her breakfast in her eagerness to hear Mrs. Murray's answer. "Are there ghosts there?"

Laughing, Mrs. Murray shook her head. "Ah, no, of course not. Ghosts rarely venture far from the livings' side. They dunna care for wind and water but prefer a warm, dry castle." With a weary sigh that betrayed her age for the first time since Keir's return, Mrs. Murray seated herself at the table. Her gaze swept over the girls' breakfast. "Will ye not eat up?"

Augusta glanced down at her plate and then back up at Mrs. Murray. "We want to hear the story." She looked at Dorothea, who immediately nodded in agreement. "Please!"

Mrs. Murray sighed yet again. Still, Keir saw amusement spark in her eyes before she turned to the girls. "People are not to go there," she began, leaning forward, her gaze fixed upon the girls, "because 'tis the place where the enormous sea serpent dwells in an underwater cave." She looked at him pointedly and then nodded.

While Dorothea merely continued to stare at Mrs. Murray, Augusta's jaw dropped. "Truly? We heard of the serpent. Auntie Sarah told us about it." The touch of a frown came to her little face. "But she said it was a good serpent, one that protects the people of this island."

Clearly impressed by the girl's knowledge, Mrs. Murray nodded. "Indeed, it does. At least, that is what the legends say. However, there are also stories of those who dared disturb the serpent's slumber... and were never heard from again." The old woman's brows rose pointedly. "It doesna take kindly to those who disturb its slumber."

For a moment, Keir wondered how Katherine would react to seeing her daughters entertained by such gruesome stories. Surprisingly, though, the girls did not seem frightened at all. Quite on the contrary. More than anything, Dorothea, in particular, seemed most intrigued.

"Do ye truly mean it?" Dorothea inquired with an almost hopeful gaze, her words once again imitating a Scottish accent with ease. *She seems to have a gift for languages.*

Mrs. Murray nodded, the expression on her face absolutely serious.

"Of course, I do. Sometimes on a bright, cloudless day, if ye stand in the right spot, ye can see scales glistening below the water's surface." She looked from Augusta to Dorothea. "I've seen them myself."

Sounds of awe emerged from the girls' mouths, and they stared with rapt attention at Mrs. Murray, as though she were some sort of magical creature herself.

Clearing his throat, Keir swallowed the last bite of his scone. "Well, I suppose we'd better be going." He helped them to their feet, handed each one of them a scone for the walk, and then bustled them out of the kitchen as quickly as he could. On his way out, he looked back at Mrs. Murray. "Do ye truly think it wise to speak to the wee lassies of such things?" Again, Keir wondered what Katherine would say. On the other hand, he had spoken to Dorothea of the faerie dog, had he not? Perhaps not his wisest choice.

Mrs. Murray chuckled. "Since when do ye speak to me of being wise?" She shook her head at him, grinning. "Do ye not remember, lad, how much ye always loved the stories when ye were little? Will ye truly deny them the same excitement?" With a wave of her hand, Mrs. Murray sent them out of the castle and into the bright daylight. "Have a good day, and dunna come back too soon. Their mother could do with a bit of rest."

Smiling, Keir hastened after the girls, who clearly did not believe they needed a guide. Their little legs carried them onward, their eyes fixed upon the sea ahead, meeting the horizon.

As Keir caught up to them, Dorothea lifted her chin, her green eyes looking into his. "Do ye believe in the sea serpent, Keir?"

Keir breathed in deeply, needing a moment to consider his words. "I dunna know. Still, in my experience, there are things that are not easily explained." He shrugged, not wishing to destroy the hope he saw shining in her eyes. "I suppose anything is possible."

A joyous smile came to Dorothea's face at his words, and she directed her gaze back to the sea, her little legs picking up the pace to catch up with her sister.

Together, Loki alongside them, they walked along a well-trodden path that led from the castle down through the meadows, past the village and toward the beach. The girls chatted animatedly, pointing to every fluttering creature they spotted, stilling at every sound they could not make sense of. Keir smiled at their delight, their eagerness to discover this new place. He pointed out the village and the harbor farther below toward the other side of the path, and the girls stuck their heads together, counting houses and people alike.

"But we're not going to the village right now, are we?" Augusta inquired with a pout. "We want to see the sea."

Again, Dorothea nodded along enthusiastically.

"Dunna worry." Keir lifted his head and pointed beyond the slope of a gentle hill ahead of them. "We're almost there."

As the girls quickened their pace, a shout suddenly rang out, and they all turned around to look.

From around a bend in the path, Eoghan and his daughter Bonnie emerged. Red-haired and green-eyed, the six-year-old girl looked like a dainty little fairy—especially compared to her father's tall stature. Keir grinned. *But a mischievous little fairy*, he reminded himself.

"Keir!" Bonnie called, rushing up to meet them. "Father said ye brought visitors." She pulled to a halt right in front of them, her wide green eyes going back and forth between Augusta and Dorothea. "Ye're English, aren't ye? Say something! Something English, please!"

Keir met Eoghan's eyes, and both men suppressed a chuckle.

Dorothea looked up at her older sister and then directed her gaze at Bonnie. "What do ye want me to say?" she said in her imitation of a Scottish accent, and Keir almost broke out laughing.

With a confused frown upon her face, Bonnie turned around to look at her father. "But ye said they were English," she addressed him chidingly before her arm whipped out and her forefinger pointed at Dorothea. "She doesna sound English. She sounds like us."

Keir stepped forward, going down onto one knee beside Bonnie. "They are English," Keir explained with a smile at the girls. "'Tis simply that Dorothea here has been practicing speaking like a Scot. Perhaps ye all can teach one another."

"He is right," Augusta remarked, standing just a little bit taller, her chin just a little bit raised. "We are English. In fact, we are English ladies. Our father is an earl."

At Augusta's innocent words, Keir pondered why she was not

speaking of her mother instead. After all, from Keir's understanding they had never had a close relationship to their father. And yet, children were taught early on that what mattered the most was their father's standing in life. It was as though Katherine did not matter in this regard. To her husband, she had certainly not mattered beyond his demand she provide him with an heir. *Aye, 'tis a sad world out there.*

Fortunately, though, the three girls did not care about the world at large. All they cared about was their own little world, and in that world, they were delighted to have come upon one another. Within moments, all three of them were racing across the hill and toward the sea, laughing and chatting and trying their best to speak as the other. "Come faster!" Bonnie called over the wind, doing her best to speak like Augusta. "I can show you where to find the best sea shells."

Instantly, Augusta and Dorothea doubled their efforts, picking up their skirts and racing each other across the pebbled beach, Loki close upon their heels.

Side by side, Keir and Eoghan followed.

"How does it feel to be home again?" Eoghan inquired with the sidelong glance. "Did ye find it much changed?"

Keir stopped, looking at his friend. "I saw yer sister last night," he remarked, knowing from the look upon Eoghan's face that his friend already knew.

Eoghan nodded. "Aye, ye did."

Chuckling, Keir rolled his eyes. "If ye have something to say, please do so."

Venturing onward, Eoghan shrugged. "Nothing in particular." Still, a faint grin appeared upon his face, which he tried rather unsuccessfully to hide by turning his face into the wind. "Ah, 'tis a beautiful day today."

Keir exhaled a rather impatient breath. "She seemed..." He wondered how to best put the impression he had received of Kenna, the night before, into words. If only he knew what she had said to Eoghan. Clearly, they had spoken to one another.

"Taken with ye?" Eoghan pulled up short, his green eyes serious. A moment later, though, a wide grin stretched across his face, and he slapped a hand upon Keir's shoulder. "Sometimes, ye truly can be a fool. Kenna has always sort of fancied ye. Dunna tell me ye didna notice!"

Casting his friend an apologetic look, Keir nodded. "Aye, only I had hoped she had outgrown it by now."

Eoghan chuckled. "Well, clearly she didna." He took a step closer, his gaze fixed upon Keir's. "I hope ye set her right." His brows rose in challenge.

Keir cringed inwardly. The last thing he wanted to do was hurt his best friend's little sister. Yet Kenna had never been more to him than a friend, and he had hoped that during his absence, she had come to see that and perhaps given her heart to another.

Eoghan scoffed. "Clearly, ye didna." He simply looked at Keir for another moment before humor returned to his eyes. "And just as clearly I can tell that yer thoughts are with another lass, am I not right?"

Even if he had tried, Keir could not have smothered the smile that broke free in that moment. Over the past weeks, he had more than once felt the urge to speak to his best friend about his affection for Sarah. Always had the two of them shared everything with one another. Often life had seemed more real, more true after Keir had discussed whatever had happened with his best friend.

Eoghan laughed once more and slapped him on the shoulder. "I'm happy for ye, my friend. Granted, I havena seen much of her, but she seems like a wonderful young woman." His gaze narrowed a bit. "And she likes ye as well? How on earth did ye manage that?" he chortled.

Not taking affront, Keir shrugged. "That, my friend, is a rather long story." Lately Keir felt as though he was saying these words a lot. Far too often. "As ye guessed, there will be a gathering at the castle tonight. I hope ye'll come."

Eoghan nodded. "As will Kenna," his friend pointed out helpfully. "I suggest ye make up yer mind—if ye havena done so already—and set things straight."

Keir nodded. "I assure ye, I have every intention of doing that. Sarah is..." He sighed, grateful for this chance to speak to his friend about Sarah. "I never thought much of marriage before meeting her, and now I canna seem to stop."

Eoghan smiled at him, and yet there was wistfulness as well as a touch of sorrow in his eyes. "I'm glad to hear it, Keir. I always hoped ye would find her someday. Ye know, the one meant for ye."

Keir nodded, uncertain what to say, knowing better than anyone how deeply his wife's passing had wounded Eoghan.

"Have ye asked for her hand yet?"

Keir shook his head. "A lot happened in her life lately; she was forced to leave everything she ever knew behind. I needa be respectful of that. I dunna wish to pressure her into deciding something she's not yet ready for." That smile returned with full force, and Keir was helpless against it. "Soon, though, I shall ask her."

"And I shall hope she will accept ye," Eoghan replied with a wide grin before he seated himself upon the top of the slope, his gaze directed downward at the beach, where the girls were chasing one another along the water's edge, now and then stopping to pick seashells. "That is an odd cat," he remarked as Keir settled himself beside him. "Look how he watches the girls. I've never seen nothing like it before."

Keir grinned. "That's Loki."

Eoghan slapped his knee, laughing. "Oh, that name doesna bode well." He looked at Keir. "I've never heard of people traveling with a cat. A dog, certainly. But a cat?"

Keir shrugged. "Well, to tell ye the truth, we're not entirely certain he is merely a cat. We have a wide range of theories, from a reincarnated king to a reincarnated bloodhound to a reincarnated guard."

Laughter lingered in Eoghan's eyes. "But ye're certain he is reincarnated?"

"Look at him," Keir remarked, nodding down toward the beach and the feline. "Look into his eyes. He seems far too... wise and knowing for this to be his first life. Get to know him, and ye'll see what I mean."

In that moment, Loki was approaching the water's edge but quickly retreated when the waves came rolling toward him. His soft paws dug into the ground, pushing aside pebbles until he found something. With a rather authoritative meow, he pointed it out to the girls. Immediately, Augusta, Dorothea, and Bonnie came rushing over, then snatched up whatever Loki had found and held it up to the sun. Most likely, it was another seashell; yet the joyous expression upon the girls' faces suggested it was rather pretty, or perhaps a rare one.

With thoughtful eyes, Eoghan nodded. "Well, I see what ye mean."

For a long moment, the two men simply sat side by side before Keir asked what had been on his mind for a while. "Would ye ever consider... marrying again?" He shifted to look at his friend.

A rather curious expression came to Eoghan's face. "What makes ye ask me that?"

Keir shrugged. "I know well what 'twas like between ye and Fiona, and when ye lost her..." He did not quite know how to put his memories into words, for he did not wish to cause his friend grief. Still...

Eoghan nodded, a wistful expression upon his face. "Well, I canna quite answer that right now. I mean, I'm not set against marriage, against marrying again." He sighed, and his gaze moved to look at Keir. "But it needs to feel right, ye know? It needs to feel just as right as it did that first time."

"Ye still love her, do ye not?"

Eoghan's nod came without hesitation. "Of course I do, and I always will."

"Do ye think it possible... that ye could love another the way ye loved Fiona?" Even though Keir had always known that there had been the deepest sort of love between Eoghan and Fiona, he had never quite understood what that meant. At least, not before meeting Sarah. Now, the thought of losing her felt crippling.

Worse even.

Seated beside his friend, Keir listened to the girls' squeals as they delighted in their treasure hunt, and he looked at Eoghan, wondering for the first time how his friend had been able to go on after losing Fiona. How had he stayed sane? How had he been able to rise in the morning?

Keir's gaze flickered to the little red-haired girl beside Augusta and Dorothea, and it seemed, perhaps, the answer was quite simple.

Bonnie.

Keir had never been the man to fear the future, to fear what might come or happen. He had experienced his fair share of unexpected events, good and bad. And yet, only now, with the thought of losing

Sarah upon his mind, did he realize how vulnerable he suddenly was. It was a new sensation that lingered these days, one he could not make sense of quite yet. Still, it felt good to speak to Eoghan about it. Better than anyone, Eoghan knew the risk of giving one's heart to another.

His friend smiled at the sight of his wee lassie. "I suppose everything is possible." He turned to meet Keir's gaze, the hint of a smile teasing his lips. "Is that not what yer grandmother always says?" His smile stretched into a grin.

Keir nodded, breathing in deeply of the familiar Scottish air. "Aye, that's precisely what she says."

Chapter Twenty-One
THE GATHERING

Sarah felt every inch of her skin crawling with nervousness. She was not necessarily concerned, but she also could not help the flutter of her nerves. Her hands trembled, and every few steps, she almost tripped over her own feet. "Oh, perhaps I simply should not attend," she exclaimed to Loki, who sat in the corner by the windows, eyeing her curiously. "This can only end in a disaster."

A quick knock came on the door, and before Sarah had even taken a single step toward it, Keir's voice asked through it, "What can only end in disaster?" A chuckle followed his question, and he added, "Ye're overthinking things again, aren't ye, lass?"

Blushing in spite of herself, Sarah hastened to open the door, then quickly pulled Keir across the threshold. She did not care for the thought of the entire castle hearing their conversation. "Would you lower your voice?" Sarah hissed as she closed the door behind him, not even daring to peek out into the corridor.

Keir chuckled, clearly amused by her fluttering nerves. *The scoundrel!* "Sarah, look at me," he murmured, his hands reaching out and gently cupping her face. He moved closer, his blue eyes fixed upon hers, gentle and kind and yet insistent somehow. "Ye're safe here... in every way. I assure ye." He held her gaze a moment longer, and Sarah felt her tense muscles relax.

Closing her eyes, Sarah counted to five, exhaling and inhaling slowly. When she looked up at Keir again, she felt a smile tease her lips. "I can't help it," she murmured, shrugging her shoulders.

Keir nodded. "I know, lass." Stepping forward, he pulled her into his arms and held her tightly, allowing her to breathe, to calm herself.

"A part of me would rather stay here," Sarah admitted, grateful that she did not have to see his eyes in that moment. She felt like a coward, and she did not wish to see whether he agreed. "The idea of walking into a room and having everyone look at me, knowing they..." She shivered.

Grasping her chin, Keir tipped her head backward. "If ye run now, ye'll be running for the rest of yer life. Ye know that."

To Sarah's relief, she saw no disappointment in his gaze. "I know."

The corners of Keir's mouth quirked in amusement. "Ye faced moments much more trying than this one before. Remember that, lass. As I said, ye're safe here. 'Tis time ye believe that."

Sarah nodded and then allowed Keir to pull her out of her chamber and into the corridor. Instinctively, her gaze went up and down the long hallway, on the lookout for people watching her every step, judging her every step. Alone with Keir in the woods or on the road, Sarah had not felt so self-conscious. Yet, back among people, it was second nature to her to doubt herself.

Keir, though, did not pause, did not give her another moment to reconsider. He grasped her hand and pulled her along, then knocked upon Kate's door.

"Thank you for seeing to the girls today," Sarah murmured, leaning into him. "They had a wonderful time, and I think it was good for Kate to—"

"Enter!"

Keir smiled at her, then quickly dipped his head and placed a kiss upon her forehead. "'Twas my pleasure," he whispered before opening the door and tugging her inside.

"I'm not quite certain what to wear," Kate exclaimed the moment they stepped across the threshold. Her gaze went back and forth between Keir and Sarah before she looked down at her simple blue linen dress. "I'm afraid I have little else."

Sarah had found herself in the same situation. All the dresses she had brought with her to Scotland were more of a practical nature, perfect for everyday use, but not quite so fitting for a societal event. At the same time, Sarah had no experience in what would be appropriate for a gathering at a Scottish castle. How did people dress?

Keir smiled at her sister. "Ye look lovely, Katherine. Dunna worry." His gaze darted to Sarah. "Ye're safe here. The both of ye are." His smile widened into a grin as he looked at the girls. "All five of ye are."

After having slept all afternoon, clearly exhausted after the excursion to the beach, Dorothea and Augusta were once again bouncing with energy, their little feet carrying them around the chamber, twirling them in circles, as their hands fluttered about, tugging at their dresses here and there and rearranging their curls. "Is this a ball?" Augusta inquired with shining eyes. "I've never been to a ball. Do people dance?"

Sarah felt quite at a loss, as did Kate, judging from the look on her face. Keir, though, simply smiled at the girls, leaning down to look into their eyes. "No, 'tis not a ball. Yet I believe there will be dancing." He straightened and looked from Sarah to Kate. "There'll be music and dancing and good food in the company of wonderful people." He stepped toward the door. "Shall we?"

Sarah saw her own nerves reflected back at her in her sister's eyes. Yet there was no choice. And so, she accepted Keir's arm, grateful when he offered his other to Kate, and together, they stepped out into the corridor. The girls quickly dashed ahead, every once in a while stopping to inquire where they were headed. Yet their feet would not keep still. Sarah knew it was a great relief to Kate to see them so happy and carefree. Clearly, the dark cloud of the weeks and months before had disappeared, and they once again felt sunshine upon their faces.

As they moved down the corridor and then ventured downstairs toward the great hall, voices and music echoed to their ears. The sounds were equally familiar and strange, the music beautiful and yet not quite what Sarah had expected. Voices spoke in English and Gaelic alike, laughing and chatting, and despite the differences, Sarah felt reminded of so many balls she had attended, never quite fitting in. Then Sarah breathed in the scents of the hall, one scent overpowering the others: roast pig and apples.

"It smells good," Dorothea exclaimed, craning her neck to look back at Keir. "What is that?"

"Mrs. Murray's pastries," Augusta replied, her face lighting up as she quickened her steps.

Dorothea, though, shook her head. "No, not that." She wrinkled her nose, sniffing loudly. "It's meat, isn't it?"

Keir grinned. "Roasting on a spit," he confirmed, chuckling, then led them toward the wide arch that led into the great hall.

Sarah's eyes widened as she beheld the crowd gathered before her. Her muscles involuntarily tensed, her hands clamping down upon Keir's arm. Her gaze moved from face to face, all unknown, and for a moment, a short moment, Sarah wished she had never left England. At least, back home, faces looked familiar. It was only a small mercy, and yet Sarah wanted it. She had so hoped to enjoy tonight, to look toward the future with hopeful eyes. Yet it would seem the past was not quite yet forgotten.

Rows upon rows of wooden tables lined the great hall while off to the side musicians had gathered and there was room for dancing. Couples twirled past, dressed in colorful plaids and tartan-patterned dresses. The women's hair, adorned with beads, swayed to and fro, their movements matching the music. Men beat drums and rattled wooden pipes, their chants entrancing listeners. The song they played was lively, its tune quickening with a sudden burst of energy. The walls of the great hall were covered in tapestries of bright and vibrant scenes of battle, hunting, and feasts.

Down the rows of tables, Sarah spotted Keir's family seated together. Duncan spoke in his booming voice, and then the others laughed in reply, their faces aglow and full of joy. Others—people Sarah had never seen before—looked the same, their joy contagious, beginning to buzz beneath Sarah's skin. She saw young couples gazing adoringly at one another, and children weaving through the crowd and vanishing under the table laden with food. For a moment, Sarah's gaze lingered on a tall, red-haired man, his eyes directed at her when he suddenly broke away from the crowd, a dark-haired woman and a red-haired little girl by his side, and he moved toward her.

"Bonnie!"

At Augusta's joyful exclamation, Sarah blinked. Her gaze focused upon the little red-haired girl, who was now darting toward them. Clearly, Augusta and Dorothea knew her, for their joy at seeing one another reminded Sarah of long-lost friends meeting again after years of absence.

Feeling herself smile, Sarah lifted her gaze to the red-haired man standing behind the little girl, a welcoming smile upon his face as he looked from Keir to the rest of them. The dark-haired woman by his side, though, looked far from pleased, her brown eyes slightly narrowed.

"Ladies, allow me to introduce," Keir began, the sound of his voice calm and soothing, "my oldest friend Eoghan MacKinnear as well as his sister Kenna and his daughter Bonnie."

The red-haired man—Eoghan—smiled broadly, and Sarah thought to see a glimmer of amusement in his gaze as he looked at Keir. "Welcome," he greeted them all before his gaze moved to her and then on to Kate, "to our little corner of the world. I assure ye, the people here are not as ill-mannered as they might seem sometimes." His brows rose teasingly, and the two friends shared a laugh, one that echoed with shared memories.

Sarah looked up at Keir and then over at his friend. "Thank you," she replied, uncertain what else to say. "We are very grateful to be here."

"Come!" Bonnie exclaimed, gesturing toward Augusta and Dorothea before any more words of greeting or gratitude could be exchanged. "Let's go see what pastries Mrs. Murray has put out today." She turned to dash away toward a large table laden with food, and Augusta and Dorothea made to follow.

The expression upon Kate's face instantly turned to one of alarm, and she stepped forward, one hand lifted and an objection upon her lips. "Oh, perhaps it would be better for you to remain near us," she said to her two oldest daughters, her green gaze flitting from the girls to Keir's old friend and then to Sarah, uncertainty there. "It is rather crowded here, and you are unfamiliar with..." Her voice trailed off, and Sarah could see that Kate felt torn.

Clearly, she did not want to be the kind of mother who stole such joy from her children, especially considering that she, herself, had been an equally adventurous child long ago. Yet at the same time, life had made her cautious, and these days, it was far from easy for her to part with her children.

Even if only for a moment.

Or across a crowded hall.

Eoghan stepped forward then, one look in his green eyes halting Bonnie's steps. The girl sighed rather dramatically as she crossed her arms, tapping her foot impatiently. Yet she stayed, waiting, as her father turned to look at Kate. "I understand yer concern," he said kindly, like a parent speaking to another. "Sometimes 'tis difficult to let them go, considering all that could happen." He looked down at Bonnie, a meaningful look in his eyes and an amused curl to his lips. "Considering all the mischief they do like to get themselves into."

Rolling her eyes at her father, Bonnie set her hands upon her hips. "I dunna get into mischief," she insisted, a rather annoyed tone in her voice. "Sometimes I simply forget—"

"—where ye are," Eoghan finished for her with a grin upon his face. "Or how late it already is."

Bonnie shrugged, as though none of his objections possessed any validity.

Brushing his hand over her red curls, Eoghan then squeezed her little shoulder and looked back at Kate. "What I'm saying is that the girls are safe here. Of course, ye are not familiar with everyone, but as someone who has grown up with this lot." His gaze swept affectionately around the people in the great hall. "I can assure ye that there is nothing to worry about. We keep an eye on our own." He nodded toward the crowd behind him.

Although Kate still looked hesitant, Eoghan's words as well as his kind demeanor eased Sarah's nerves. Like Keir, he possessed a very open and straightforward nature, making her think that even after only a few words, she already knew him.

"Oh, Mama, please!" Augusta and Dorothea begged, turning pleading eyes to their mother.

Finally, Kate nodded. "Very well," she agreed with a careful glance at Eoghan. "But behave yourselves."

The girls nodded eagerly and, within seconds, had vanished in the crowd, following Bonnie's lead.

In that moment, Frederica stirred, drawing Kate's attention away from her other two daughters. She softly rocked the child, making quiet cooing sounds, trying to calm her.

"How old is she?" Eoghan asked as he stepped closer, his demeanor that of kind interest. Sarah could see that he understood Kate's fears and sought to ease them.

Kate answered tentatively, apprehension in her wide eyes. Clearly, she felt overwhelmed by the situation after having been all but isolated these past few years. Perhaps it would do her good to be forced back among people. After all, once upon a time, Kate had thrived in the company of others. Perhaps this would help her remember who she was at heart.

Sarah certainly hoped so.

"How are ye today, Kenna?" Keir inquired as Kate and Eoghan exchanged a few tentative words.

Sarah eyed the young woman carefully, aware that she did not possess the same cheerful disposition as her brother. Not a word had passed her lips thus far, and Sarah could not help the thought that Kenna did not like having them here. Sarah sighed. *Perhaps some of my concerns are justified after all.*

Allowing her gaze to sweep over the many faces in the great hall, Sarah wondered who else might object to their presence here. Perhaps not openly but deep down.

The moment Kenna turned toward Keir, her demeanor changed. The frown vanished from her face, and a smile transformed her. *Then it is true*, Sarah thought. *She does object to me.* "I'm all right. 'Tis good to see ye back home. Yer mother was quite put out when ye didna write more often." The look in Kenna's eyes was teasingly chiding, and yet Sarah stiffened at the thought that Keir's mother might consider her, Sarah, the reason her son had not come home for such a long time.

"Ye're doing it again, lass."

At Keir's whispered words, Sarah's head snapped up. "Sorry?"

A gentle smile came to his face as he lowered his head to whisper in her ear. "I can feel every inch of ye tense, lass." He eased back to look into her eyes. "Dunna worry. If ye wish, I shall remain at yer side all evening."

Exhaling slowly, Sarah nodded. "Yes, I think I'd like that." There was never a moment when Sarah did not enjoy Keir's presence; however, tonight, in such an unfamiliar crowd, she needed him nearby more than ever.

Once more, Keir held her close as they stepped forward further into the great hall. Sarah willed a smile onto her face and then quickly glanced over her shoulder at her sister. Tentatively, Kate accepted Eoghan's offer to escort her inside, her green eyes wide as she took in their new surroundings. Kenna remained behind, arms now crossed over her chest, her narrowed eyes following them.

A shiver crawled down Sarah's back, and she wondered if the young woman's reaction was simply a precursor to what was to come. Were there more people in Keir's clan who objected to their presence here? Would Keir eventually be faced with the decision to choose between the family he loved and the promise he made her, Sarah?

In the next instant, all of Sarah's thoughts vanished when the great hall all of a sudden fell silent. The absence of voices echoed through her bones, and her head snapped up, her eyes wide. To her utter shock, she found herself the sudden center of attention, all eyes turned to her and Kate. Instantly, Sarah wanted to turn and run or hide in that ever elusive hole in the ground.

"Hush, little wisp," Keir murmured beside her, his other hand coming to rest upon hers, keeping her grounded by his side. "I'm here with ye." Then he straightened, smiled, and faced the crowd. "What is the matter with all of ye?" he demanded in a booming chuckle that reminded Sarah of his brother Duncan. "Have ye never seen English ladies before?"

Laughter broke out in the hall, good-natured and kind, and Sarah exhaled deeply when she failed to detect disapproval upon the surrounding faces. They certainly looked curious but not angry.

Keir guided her onward, nodding toward a long table beneath the tall windows on the western side. Sarah spotted his family seated there, his grandmother, as well as his parents and Duncan. She also saw faces she had not seen before, wondering who they were and how they would receive her.

To Sarah's relief, Keir's mother smiled at her, beckoning them forward. "Oh, my dear, ye look well-rested today. Does yer chamber suit ye? Is there anything else ye require?"

For a moment, Sarah could not speak a single word, and so her head began nodding up and down before shaking from side to side. She felt like a fool, and yet the expression upon Keir's mother's face did not change.

His father laughed, again a good-natured and kind laugh. "Dunna worry, lass. We dunna bite."

Rising from her seat beside her husband, Keir's mother moved around the table and came toward Sarah. "I'm certain 'twill take some time to get used to this new place. Ye've never been to Scotland before?"

Sarah shook her head, casting a quick glance at her sister. Kate looked equally at a loss, uncertain how to behave, all her training failing her; after all, it had never meant to carry her to such a distant place.

"Well, I suppose Scots are perhaps a bit louder than the English," Keir's father remarked, making them all laugh and nod in agreement.

Keir smiled at Sarah, squeezing her hand reassuringly. "Breathe, little wisp," he murmured near her ear.

"I'm not so certain that is true," Keir's grandmother remarked in that quiet yet attention-demanding voice of hers. "In my experience, the English are just as loud, only they would never admit to it."

Again, booming laughter echoed through the hall, and even Sarah felt the corners of her mouth twitch with amusement. In what ways the English differed from the Scots, she could not be certain. However, these people reminded her of the family she had always wished to be a part of—the Whickertons. Indeed, there was kindness here and affection, the urge to tease but not to offend. It was a precious balance, one that Sarah cherished because she had never known it in her own family. Indeed, perhaps it had been wise to come here. Perhaps this was, indeed, the place for them. If only they were wanted here. *Are we?*

Chapter Twenty-Two
LETTING GO

Kate felt her heart beat wildly in her chest as she stared wide-eyed at her surroundings. She saw people everywhere, unfamiliar faces looking back at her, smiling at her. Her ears rang with the noise, and yet part of her did not wish for it to stop, for it warmed her deep inside in a way she had not known in a long time. She could almost feel herself swaying along to the sound of the music, her feet tapping beneath the table, enraptured by the joy she saw on people's faces, their eagerness for life, for happiness. Once she had known it as well. Once she had been like Augusta and Dorothea, stealing away with their new friend, sneaking treats and finding a place to hide out and watch the proceedings in the hall.

Indeed, Kate remembered moments like these from her own childhood. She had loved them beyond everything. They had been those very few moments that had truly made her feel alive and wish for just such a future of her own.

Seated at the large table, Frederica in her arms, Kate watched the hall, the dancers, the musicians, everyone. Keir's family did their utmost to make them feel welcome, offering drinks and food and asking after their journey. She saw Sarah relax, Keir's hand upon hers, reassuring and calm. A part of Kate wished he would do the same for her.

"Yer two eldest are quite the little rascals themselves, are they not?" Eoghan remarked with a grin. He was seated beside her at the table, his green eyes full of mirth as he looked at her.

Still, Kate paused, her eyes upon his face. Only too well did she remember her mother-in-law's chiding comments, criticizing her daughters' behavior. "I apologize," she quickly said, making to rise from the table. "Perhaps I should—"

Eoghan's hand touched her arm, stilling her every move. "No, ye misunderstand," he interrupted, nodding to her to sit back down. "What I said was meant as a compliment, I assure ye." He looked over his shoulder to where Bonnie pulled Augusta and Dorothea onto the dance floor. Holding each other's hands, they twirled around in a circle, laughing and singing.

Settling back upon her chair, Kate shifted Frederica from one arm into the other. Her youngest seemed quite content with watching the scene around her as well, her blue eyes wide open.

Lifting her gaze from her child, Kate looked across at Keir's friend. Turned away from her and toward the dancers, Kate could only see his face in profile.

A smile curled up his lips, wistfulness in his eyes as he watched his little girl. "She's a wild one," Eoghan said with a chuckle, deep affection in his voice. "She goes where she wants and does what she pleases." He turned to look back at Kate. "And I wouldna dream of taking that from her." He shrugged almost helplessly, that wide smile still upon his face. "Yet sometimes I wish she were a little more careful."

Kate nodded, understanding his concern. While Augusta and Dorothea had never done anything adventurous, she knew what it meant to fear for them. Seeing them tonight, with their eyes and cheeks aglow, playing and laughing, children their age by their side, Kate knew she would do everything within her power to ensure they would always be this happy. Not long ago, thoughts of happiness had seemed like a fairytale. Now, though, they played out before her very eyes.

Kate blinked, afraid that what she saw was nothing more than a mirage.

Perhaps caught up by the music and the dancing around her, Frederica suddenly began waving her little fists about. She squealed and cooed delightedly. Then she grasped one of Kate's curls and tugged upon it rather strongly.

"Let me hold her," Eoghan offered, holding out his hands to receive Frederica. "Ye havena had a chance to eat anything."

At the expectant expression in his eyes, Kate froze, staring at him. The thought of handing over her child paralyzed her. She knew it to be foolish, but she could not help it. She could not make her muscles move or her heart stop hammering in her chest.

"Kate, are you all right?" came Sarah's concerned voice, her sister's hand settling gently upon her shoulder.

Kate swallowed. "I'm all right," she managed to say, struggling to contain Frederica's sudden exuberance.

Sarah nodded, quickly drawn back into the conversation with Keir and his parents. She seemed almost at ease; her smile genuine. Keir's hand held hers, their fingers intertwined.

Kate swallowed hard.

"When Bonnie was born," Eoghan began, and the sound of his soft voice jarred Kate out of her thoughts, making her turn her head to look at him, "I had a hard time getting my wife to let me hold her." He smiled at her. "Believe me, I know how protective new mothers are of their children, and rightly so." His gaze drifted lower and settled upon Frederica's face, a smile coming to his own that was unique to parents. It held that deep sense of utter devotion to this new life, the understanding that all of a sudden, nothing and no one else mattered more.

Kate heaved a deep sigh, willing the panic to subside, reminding herself that this was a new place, a different place. Not everyone was like her husband and her mother-in-law.

Eoghan's gaze met hers, understanding in his green eyes. "Ye needa eat, lass. Ye needa keep yer strength, especially if ye wanta keep up with that wee one and her two sisters." He held up his hand, as though swearing a solemn oath. "I promise that I willna move from this spot. Ye have my word."

For a long moment, Kate held his gaze, unable to decide, unable to take this sudden leap of faith. She knew Eoghan was right, and yet this was hard. She heaved a deep breath and then slowly loosened her hold on Frederica. Try as she might, she could not bring herself to hand her over, though.

And then Eoghan suddenly moved closer. He held out his hands toward Frederica, and as though the two were in league with one another, Frederica reached out toward him as well.

Eoghan chuckled. "Hello there, wee lassie. What do ye say ye come sit with me for a spell and let yer mother eat?" Gently, he took hold of Frederica, all but tugging her out of Kate's arms. He settled her comfortably in the crook of his own, rocking her gently with the practiced ease of a father. "See? Yer Mama is right there." He held Frederica so she could see Kate. Then he looked up and met Kate's eyes. "Eat up, lass. Before ye know it, yer hands will be full again, with none left over to move food into yer mouth." He chuckled warmly, tickling Frederica under her chin.

Kate blinked, overwhelmed by this sudden change. Yet she felt strangely light, almost weightless. Tentatively, she began to eat, realizing how famished she was and how wonderful everything tasted. She kept glancing up at Frederica and Eoghan, wondering about the tall, red-haired man. "Is your wife here tonight as well?"

The expression in Eoghan's eyes immediately darkened. "She's not," he said in a tone that made Kate feel chilled. "We lost her a few years back."

Sorrow swept through Kate at his words; yet before she could find a way to express it, loud voices echoed through the hall, along with clapping hands and stomping feet. A frown drew down Kate's brows as she looked from the people around her back to Eoghan, a question in her gaze.

"What's happening?" Kate heard Sarah inquire, and the two sisters exchanged a confused glance.

Keir chuckled. "They're demanding a story."

Kate saw Sarah still, as though some sense of dark foreboding had come over her, before she asked, "What story?"

Keir leaned closer, a teasing twinkle in his eyes. "Yers," he whispered just loud enough for Kate to hear.

Chapter Twenty-Three
WITHOUT WARNING

Still standing in the arched doorway to the great hall, her arms crossed over her chest, Kenna glared at the woman by Keir's side. Tension lingered in every muscle, and her teeth pressed together so hard her jaw hurt. Yet she could not avert her eyes, could not stop staring at the golden-haired English lady with the wide blue eyes, who blushed every time Keir smiled at her or leaned closer to whisper something in her ear, the woman who now stood in *her* place.

He's mine, a voice deep down whispered again and again, and each time the words echoed through Kenna's head, she felt her teeth press together a little harder. *He's mine. He's always been mine.*

And then her gaze locked upon the small braids woven in to the lady's hair, running along her temples and meeting at the back of her head. They were a mirror image of Keir's, and Kenna stared at them in utter shock. *Why would she—?*

"There ye are! I've been looking all over for ye."

At the sound of Brenda's voice, Kenna flinched. She had to blink her eyes twice to focus her thoughts when her friend suddenly stood before her, as though risen from the ground. Brenda's cheeks shone rosy with excitement, and she had weaved white beads into her mahogany tresses for tonight's gathering.

"Are ye all right?" Brenda inquired, a slight frown coming to her pretty face. "I thought ye'd be happy. Have ye not been waiting for Keir to return all these months?" Her hands reached out and grasped Kenna's upper arms, giving her a little shake. "Why the frown?"

Kenna exhaled a deep breath. Then, she nodded past Brenda's shoulder toward the table where Keir was just now whispering something into the English lady's ear. "That's why," Kenna spat, and her muscles tensed beneath Brenda's hands.

Looking a bit befuddled, Brenda craned her neck to look over her shoulder. "What do ye mean? I dunna see what—" Her voice broke off, and despite her own tension, Kenna could feel Brenda still, her hands now clamping down upon Kenna's arms. "Oh," she all but released a breath, and that one little sound felt like a knife to Kenna's heart.

"Aye," Kenna grumbled. "Oh."

Spinning back around, Brenda's brown eyes looked into hers, an expression of bewilderment upon her face. "What does this—? I mean, does this mean that he—" She shook her head, as though to clear it. "I mean, I'd heard that he had brought two English ladies back with him. However, I did not know that..."

Kenna's shoulders slumped, and in that moment, she felt utterly defeated. "Neither had I," she murmured, hating that almost pitying look in her friend's eyes. "I spoke to him last night, and I hoped that..." Tears misted her eyes.

"Oh, Kenna," Brenda exclaimed compassionately, and her arms flew forward, pulling Kenna into a tight embrace. "I'm so sorry. I know how much he means to ye. Are ye certain that—?"

All of a sudden, the hum of voices in the hall grew louder, accompanied by clapping and stomping. It slowly rose to a crescendo until Keir finally rose from his spot at the chieftain's table, a wide smile upon his face and a look of indulgence in his eyes.

Kenna sighed inwardly, her heart twisting at the sight of him. Never before had she felt like this. Always had she savored each and every glimpse of him, those piercing blue eyes that had a way of seeing right into her heart. The way Keir knew how to smile, with every inch of himself. Every little touch he had bestowed upon her, grasping her middle and spinning her out in a circle, or pulling her close and pressing a kiss to her temple. Always had she thought of him as hers. Never had there been any doubt in her heart…

… not until the day he had left.

Without a word.

Without any warning.

Still, Kenna had counted the days until his return, convincing herself that once he did, all her dreams would finally come to pass. *Was I a fool?* No, Kenna refused to believe that. After all, she knew him. She had known him all her life, and he had always looked at her with love in his heart. She was certain of it.

"Would ye rather leave?" Brenda whispered gently, tucking a curl away from Kenna's forehead and back behind her ear. "Perhaps we should go for a walk or—?"

Kenna shook her head vehemently. "No, I willna leave. This is my home, not hers. I needa hear. I needa find out what happened. I needa find out… who she is to him."

"Very well." Brenda nodded in understanding, then moved to stand beside Kenna, tugging her arm through hers and holding on tightly.

Standing tall, with his hands linked behind his back, Keir waited patiently until the voices in the hall had quieted down enough for him to speak. Then he lifted his chin and began his story.

Kenna had always loved listening to Keir. Yet she was certain that she would not care for the story he was about to tell.

"I know ye've heard the rumors," Keir began with a wide smile that made Kenna's heart ache. "I can see that ye're all dying to know what happened in England and why I stayed away for so long." He seemed to draw out his words until finally someone in the back of the hall yelled, "And dunna forget the ladies! We want to know about the English lassies!"

Joyous laughter echoed through the hall, and Kenna cringed, feeling it like a slap in the face.

Keir chuckled in amusement, and his gaze lowered to meet the eyes of the golden-haired lady seated beside him. Instantly, she blushed, embarrassment darkening her cheeks as she looked timidly around the hall. "If ye insist," Keir gave in with a laugh, then waited until the hall quieted once more. "I assume ye've heard it whispered that the English fancy marrying their young daughters to old men." His brows rose in question as his gaze swept over the assembled clan.

"Aye, men like Dougal!" Old Arthur exclaimed, grinning his toothless grin at his childhood friend.

Again, laughter swelled to the ceiling.

"I wouldna mind a young wife!" Dougal responded with a laugh, wriggling his bushy, gray eyebrows meaningfully.

"Aye, but the young wife would mind!" Keir's brother Duncan exclaimed in his booming voice.

More laughter filled through the hall, and Kenna wished Keir would simply get on with it. She did not care to hear the English lady's story, and yet perhaps it was wise to know what she was up against, what had made Keir look at her the way he did.

"The Dowager Countess of Whickerton," Keir began in his familiar storyteller voice, and immediately the hall fell silent. "The same woman who long ago prevented my grandmother's arranged marriage to an English Lord and allowed her to marry the man she loved, Cameron MacKinnear." Wistful sighs echoed through the hall as people turned to smile at Keir's grandmother. "Called me to England to prevent another match that was not meant to be."

Along with everyone else, Kenna felt her own breath catch, her ears now completely tuned in to Keir's story, her mind and heart demanding more. *Oh, why can I not be furious with him?*

And so, even against her will, Kenna listened as Keir spoke to them all of the match the young lady's parents had arranged for her. A match to an old, vile man! Kenna shuddered at the thought, applauding Keir inwardly for coming to the woman's aid. And yet could he not have done so without...?

Kenna closed her eyes, part of her wishing she could simply cover her ears and not hear more. Yet her hands would not move but clung to Brenda instead, needing her friend's support to make it through this evening, through this moment.

"After a fortnight of hiding out in the woods and evading her fiancé's henchmen," Keir continued, his blue eyes once more fixed upon the golden-haired lady. "We finally returned to London where the dowager countess ensured Sarah would never be forced into another such match by making her her companion and removing her from her parents' household."

Applause and approving comments echoed around the hall, and Kenna saw people nodding and cheering, congratulating Keir and voicing their support.

"And what of the other lady?" someone demanded, and quickly everyone joined in, asking for the story to continue.

For the first time that night, Kenna's gaze shifted from the golden-haired lady—Sarah!—to the other young woman. Her eyes were green instead of blue, and her hair shone in a slightly darker color. Still, Kenna could see a distinct resemblance between the two, making it obvious that they were related.

"Some years ago," Keir began, and his gaze drifted to the other young woman, all amusement now gone from his gaze. "Katherine, Sarah's sister, was married to the Earl of Birchwell. Though she gave him three beautiful, wee lassies." Keir smiled at the two little girls seated beside Bonnie, their hands filled with pastries and their eyes wide as they, too, listened to the story. "He desired a son, an heir, above all else… as English lords are wont to do."

Kenna saw the way Katherine briefly closed her eyes, a deep breath rushing from her lungs, before she turned to Eoghan, seated beside her, and her hands reached for her child. Eoghan complied instantly, gently settling the babe back into her mother's arms.

Keir's gaze moved to the girls beside Bonnie. He cast them a reassuring smile and then continued, "Unfortunately, in his quest for an heir, Lord Birchwell deemed it right to separate Katherine from her children, sending the girls to a remote estate."

Without a second of delay, outrage echoed through the hall as mothers and fathers and grandparents voiced their shock, their disapproval at such behavior. Kenna, too, felt something hot simmer in her veins, and her gaze involuntarily swept to the two little girls, their eyes wide as they listened and watched. Kenna could tell that Keir had phrased his words carefully, concerned for the girls, tempering his storytelling. Yet people understood. How could they not?

And they were appalled!

As was Kenna. As much as she wanted to dislike the two English ladies, a traitorous part of her heart felt for them, for their fate. But did they have to come here? Could that dowager countess not have sent them elsewhere?

Keir straightened and looked around the hall. Then, he placed his left hand upon Sarah's shoulder so she would meet his eyes. Her own were wide and misted with tears, her cheeks shining in a rosy glow. "I ask ye now," Keir asked in a strong voice that easily carried around the vaulted hall, "will ye stand with me to protect them against injustice as the MacKinnears have stood against it for generations, ever since Yvaine and Calen came to these shores centuries ago?"

As one, people rose to their feet, responding with a booming *Aye!*

Even Brenda cheered alongside them, her face flushed with the excitement of the moment. Kenna swallowed hard, realizing that in one short evening the two English lassies had conquered the hearts of her clan, their story one that would forever be told.

Gazing across the hall, Kenna felt tears collect in her eyes as she watched Keir pull Sarah to her feet. He embraced her, his powerful arms wrapping around her shoulders as he hugged her close. And she clung to him as well, tears running down her cheeks as she laughed and cried, her hands reaching to cup Keir's face a bare moment before Keir dipped his head and kissed her.

In front of everyone.

And everyone cheered.

Everyone but Kenna.

Chapter Twenty-Four

A DREAM COME TRUE

Standing in Keir's embrace, Sarah savored the echoing voices around her, the cheers of the people, the smiles upon their faces. *Is this a dream?* Indeed, it felt surreal. Never had Sarah experienced this kind of approval, this kind of support. She had been so terrified to be faced with rejection that she was utterly unprepared for this moment.

Tears streamed down her face, and she clung to Keir as though he were a lifeboat and she in danger of drowning.

"Are ye all right, little wisp?" Keir murmured, his lips brushing against her temple as he lowered his head. "Ye look quite fetching with that blush."

Sarah laughed, brushing the tears from her eyes. "I was so afraid, and now..." She shrugged, words failing her.

Keir nodded, the look in his eyes as always one of understanding. "I know, lass. But now ye see, that 'twas unnecessary. Ye're safe here. I swear it."

Again, Sarah sank into his arms, savoring the warmth of his embrace, the promise she felt in the way he cradled her in his arms.

And then voices rose once more, growing louder, demanding more stories. Keir chuckled, waving them away; yet people would not allow him. Sarah could already feel him pull away, loath to leave the warmth of his embrace, when his grandmother rose to her feet and the hall instantly quieted.

Her eyes shone warmly as she looked at her grandson, a smile upon her lips. Then she inhaled a deep breath, lifted her chin and met the crowd. "As you all know, decades ago I faced an arranged match," she began softly, her voice quiet, and a hush fell over the hall as everybody strained to listen. "Though a duke's son, he was a good man." She chuckled, and many joined in. "He was titled, rich and kind, and at least among the *ton*, that was considered by many to be a fortunate match." With expectant eyes, she looked around the crowd. "But is that the true definition of marriage? The absence of suffering?" Slowly, Keir's grandmother shook her head, her brown eyes warm and yet defiant. "Back then, I was a young girl, and without my friend's encouragement, I would have agreed to the match because I loved my parents, because I wished to honor them, because I did not believe I had a choice."

Sarah exhaled a slow breath as Keir's grandmother met her eyes, understanding shone in them. Indeed, Sarah remembered well how she had felt not too long ago when she had thought it her duty to sacrifice herself in order to protect her family and do what society demanded of her. Yet more than that compelling sense of duty, it had been the deepest hopelessness that had steered Sarah in those days. She had been convinced that there had been but a single path for her to walk. That there was no other choice.

Now, she knew differently.

"But there's always a choice," Keir's grandmother continued, her voice strong and hopeful. "My friend Edie fought to convince me of it. She stood at my side and pushed me to believe in a better tomorrow, to fight for what I wanted." A wistful smile came to her lips, and her eyes glowed with distant memories. "The moment I saw him, I knew I wanted Cameron MacKinnear."

The hall cheered loudly, clapping and stomping in approval and excitement.

Sarah laughed along with the others, delighted by this wonderful story. Her eyes swept around the hall, seeing many smiling faces. Even

Kate looked hopeful, for even though her own path had led her into an arranged marriage, she had found a way out. A new life stretched out in front of her, and now it was her choice which way to go.

"I knew I wanted him," his grandmother continued to tell her story, "and yet I knew I could not have him." Instantly, people's voices died down, their expressions stilling, something expectant in their eyes. "My match was arranged, after all, and we all met at a house party near the Scottish border so that I might get to know my betrothed." She sighed, shaking her head as though she still could not believe the situation she had found herself in all those years ago. "I found him to be a kind and decent man, and yet I knew within moments that we were not a good match. Yet what could I do?"

Silence lingered, and Sarah could see upon everyone's faces they were eager to hear more—even though, undoubtedly, they had all heard this story a hundred times.

Keir's grandmother chuckled, small creases framing her eyes. "Quite frankly, I did not know what to do, and without my friend, I would have done nothing. I would not have known what to do without breaking my parents' hearts, without disappointing my fiancé, without breaking all the rules and condemning myself."

"What did ye do then?" Old Arthur demanded in his raspy voice. "How come ye've never told us that part of the story?"

Many chuckled, as did Keir's grandmother. "Well, you've never asked me for more details, have you?"

Now, though, they did. Clapping loudly, people encouraged her to continue, to share the details of how her match had come to be all those decades ago.

"Did she ever tell you?" Sarah murmured to Keir, looking up into his blue eyes. After all, she remembered him speaking to her of this only weeks ago when they had stopped at an inn on their way to her sister's estate.

He grinned at her. "Aye, I always loved the story. I suppose it felt rather personal, and I never shared it beyond the close circle of my family. I always wondered why she never spoke of it at our gatherings."

Keir's grandmother lifted a hand, and immediately the voices in the hall died down again, all eyes expectant. "Well, in retrospect, it was all quite simple. In order to free me from my match without disappointing either my parents or my fiancé, my dear old friend… simply saw to it that he fell in love."

"With ye?" a raspy, old voice asked from somewhere.

"Of course not, ye old fool!" another responded lightning quick, followed by what sounded like a slap upside the head.

People roared with laughter, and Sarah wished that this evening would never end.

"As fate would have it," Keir's grandmother explained, a touch of disbelief upon her face as though even after all these years she could still not believe that everything had played out the way it had. "The woman of his dreams happened to be at that very same house party that year. And so, my dear old friend, who could always tell with a single glance what lived in another's heart, ensured that their paths would cross, that they would have moments alone together, that they fell in love." She shrugged, a wide grin upon her wrinkled face. "To her, it was quite simple, quite obvious. To me," her gaze moved to Keir and then Sarah, "it was nothing short of magic."

Again, the hall erupted in joyous exclamations. Only this time, many eyes were misted with tears, and Sarah smiled as she saw Keir's father rise to his feet and embrace his mother. Indeed, they were a wonderful family, and more than anything, Sarah wanted to be one of them.

One day.

Perhaps.

"Does anyone else wish to tell a story?" Keir's grandmother asked, her kind brown eyes drifting around the hall before they suddenly paused and came to linger upon someone near the large wooden table laden with food.

Sarah turned, and to her surprise, she saw little Dorothea hop down from the bench where she had sat beside her sister and step forward. Her green eyes were wide, and her fingers fidgeted with the hem of her sleeve; yet she did not pause but moved to the center of the hall.

Beside her, Sarah could hear Kate draw in a sharp breath, and for a moment, the sisters looked at one another.

"I wish to tell a story," Dorothea began in her soft, timid, slightly accented voice, her green eyes wide as she looked at Keir's grandmother. "'Tis a story about a fairy."

Keir's grandmother stepped forward, moved around the table, and then approached the girl. "About a fairy? Now, that sounds wonderful." Someone pulled out a chair for her to sit, and she beckoned Dorothea over, helping her climb onto her lap. "We're all ears. Please tell us."

Tears stood in Kate's eyes as she watched her little daughter lift her chin determinedly. "My sister and I used to live with our mother, but one day, our father sent us away. We didna know why." She shook her little head, then looked up at Keir's grandmother, as though asking for an answer. "Every day, we asked our governess when Mother would come to see us, but she always said that she didna know. A lot of time passed, and we were very sad." Her wide green eyes moved to look at Kate, and for a moment, her little chin trembled. But Keir's grandmother grasped her hand and clasped it within her own. "And then one day, a fairy came. I didna see her, but my sister spoke with her. The fairy asked my sister what her dearest wish was, and Augusta said that we wanted to see our mother again. The fairy then told her not to speak to anyone about her and promised she would return by nightfall and take us to see our mother."

Sarah listened, enraptured by Dorothea's simple retelling of the events of that night. Of course, she had known the essentials, and yet the story Dorothea was telling now meant so much more. She could see it upon everyone's faces.

"My sister didna tell me that the fairy had come," Dorothea continued, then looked up at Keir's grandmother. "I'm not very good at keeping secrets, and perhaps 'twas better that she didna tell me. I might have said something foolish." She shrugged, her fingers still tugging upon the hem of her sleeve. "That night, the fairy came, and my sister woke me. She told me to dress and be quiet. Together with the fairy, we left the house and then we had to ride in a carriage for a long, long time while the fairy went off to fetch Mama. We came to a big house where the fairy lived with her family. Everybody was very nice to us, and then the next day, we ran out of the house, and there was Mama." Tears shimmered in Dorothea's eyes, and yet the look upon her face spoke of pride.

"That was a wonderful story," Keir's grandmother exclaimed, giving the girl a soft hug. "Thank you so much for sharing it with us." Then she lifted her head and looked around the hall, and in the next instant, booming applause erupted. People cheered and whistled, tears still in their eyes but laughter falling from their lips.

A wide smile came to Dorothea's face, and a fetching blush bloomed upon her cheeks.

"She's blushing," Keir remarked near Sarah's ear. "Just like ye, little wisp." He chuckled teasingly, his hand still upon her arms, her back resting against his broad chest.

Ignoring him, Sarah reached out to grasp Kate's hand. Her sister had tears in her eyes as well. "I had no idea," Kate whispered, gazing at her beloved child. "She's often so quiet. I had no idea that she could be so brave." She laughed as tears rolled down her cheeks. "I love seeing her so vivacious, so full of life and joy."

Sarah squeezed her sister's hand, and Kate looked at her. "You, too, used to be vivacious. You used to be just like her and Augusta and Frederica." She glanced down at her newest little niece. "Perhaps you can find that part of yourself again. We both need to find out who we would have been without life's interference."

Smiling deeply, Kate nodded. Then, in the next moment, Dorothea raced across the hall and threw herself into her mother's arms. Besides Kate, Eoghan chuckled, snatching little Frederica from Kate's arm so she could embrace her daughter. He stood beside them then, rocking the child, just as touched by this moment as everyone else in the hall.

Indeed, the evening could not have gone better. Not in her wildest dreams would Sarah have expected to be welcomed like this, to have people look at her with such acceptance and compassion.

Before long, Kate and the girls retired to bed. Sarah, though, stayed, loath to leave Keir's side, completely overcome by the many people who stopped by to welcome him back and welcome her to their home. Sarah saw smiling faces and joyous expressions, and not for a moment did she feel as though ulterior motives or hidden agendas lingered upon anyone's mind. What she saw looked genuine, and Sarah allowed herself to believe that she had found perhaps the one place in this world where she was meant to be, where she was wanted.

"Welcome back, lad," Old Angus exclaimed, clasping Keir's shoulder. As the old man was of rather short stature, he had to push up onto his toes and stretch his arm to the fullest to do so. "And congratulations on finding such a bonny lass." He winked at Sarah good-naturedly. "Dunna be a fool and let her slip away." A deep sigh fell from his lips. "I'm ashamed to say that I once did." And then he launched into his own life's story of how he had once loved and lost because he had not dared speak his heart.

As the evening wore on, Keir drew Sarah onto the dance floor, and that night, Sarah did not mind people looking at her. She was far from accomplished in the dance preferred by Keir's clan, and yet she did not mind stumbling. After all, whenever she did, Keir was there to catch her, and she had never minded being in his arms.

Indeed, it was a wonderful night and Sarah knew she would never ever forget it.

Chapter Twenty-Five

BROTHERS

A strong breeze blew in from the sea, ruffling Keir's hair as he walked along the coastline to the south with his father and Duncan. Seagulls circled overhead, and waves rolled onto the beach, the sound of their movement soothing to Keir's ears. It had been a long time since he had heard it, and only now did he realize how much he had missed the sounds of his home, as well as the smells and sights. There was the touch of salt in the air and the coolness of the breeze upon his skin. He had missed the way the sun peeked over the horizon every morning, that soft orange glow growing as it rose, warm and comforting. And then when night fell, the streaks of violet upon the sky shimmered almost magically, and Keir was certain that many storytellers had been inspired by it.

"What do ye know of Sarah's fiancé?" his father inquired, scratching his chin as they walked. "What sort of man is he?"

Keir's jaw tightened briefly. "Her *former* fiancé," he pointed out, unable to stop himself.

Duncan grinned widely. "He might disagree," he teased, slapping Keir's shoulder good-naturedly.

Ignoring both his sons, their father went on. "And Katherine's husband? After what ye've told us, he will undoubtedly be most determined to retrieve his wife. I dunna wish to alarm the ladies, but I needa know what sort of men they are, what to expect."

Keir nodded, and although he knew he had done the right thing, he disliked the burden his choice had placed upon his father's shoulders. "Katherine's husband has a temper, and he has made it clear upon numerous occasions that he doesna care for his wife's well-being. Still, truth be told, I suspect that 'tis the dowager, Lord Birchwell's mother, who is the true threat. Her son seems like a puppet and she his master." Keir paused in his steps and lifted his head, gazing out across the sea toward the mainland. "But ye're right," he continued, turning to meet his father's steady gaze. "Without his wife, Lord Birchwell will never have an heir to his title. He canna afford to let her slip through his fingers." An icy shiver crawled down his back. "He will have no choice but to try to get her back."

While his father looked contemplative, clearly considering every word Keir had said, the expression upon Duncan's face darkened with emotion. Keir almost smiled at the anger he saw flash in his brother's eyes. Clearly, the MacKinnears now considered Katherine theirs to protect.

"And what about Sarah?" his father inquired as they once again fell into step side by side, continuing their way down the beach. "What about her *former* fiancé?" The ghost of a smirk played across his father's face as he glanced over to him.

Keir willed himself not to react but to consider his father's question most carefully. "Truth be told, I've never met the man," he admitted, wondering now if that had been a mistake. "I only ever saw him from a distance as he and Sarah's father came to the clearing in the woods to collect her after the ransom had been paid. Yet from what Sarah and Grandma Edie told me, Lord Blackmore is a most proud man. He no doubt considers what happened an affront committed against him, and I fear that he willna let it slide."

Duncan grasped his shoulder. "Are ye saying he will seek retribution?" His eyes narrowed as he looked at Keir. "Or do ye still believe he wishes to marry her?"

Keir almost cringed at the mere thought of it. "No, I dunna think that he intends to make Sarah his bride. He values his reputation too much, and the kidnapping has already dealt it a serious blow." In truth, Keir did not know what Blackmore might intend. Yet deep down, he doubted they had heard or seen the last of that man. It was a thought that made his skin crawl.

Their father heaved a deep sigh, looking from one son to the other. "Well, then 'tis clear that this is not the end of the story. These men—one or both of them—will seek to retrieve the sisters. We needa know what they might plan and how they intend to proceed."

Keir nodded. "The dowager will no doubt keep us informed. She seems to have her ears and eyes everywhere."

"But what if she doesna discover it?" his father asked with a raised brow. "From what ye told us, both men know that the Whickertons are involved. They are no fools. Undoubtedly, they will take care to mask their next steps."

Duncan nodded, meeting Keir's eyes. "Aye, Father's right. We needa stay alert." His gaze shifted from Keir back to their father. "I shall post sentries at the watchtowers and send a message to the mainland."

"I believe that would be wise," their father agreed, grasping Duncan's shoulder affectionately.

Keir smiled, for he had seen this sort of conversation before. His father had begun to groom Duncan for the chieftainship of the clan, always providing counsel, offering suggestions and voicing concerns. Ultimately, though, he allowed Duncan to make his own decision. Keir knew that step by step, his father would retreat, and slowly hand over the responsibility for their clan.

Suddenly, Duncan chuckled, and Keir frowned at his brother. "And what of Sarah?" his brother inquired, crossing his arms over his broad chest like a stern father questioning the intentions of his daughter's suitor. Still, amusement glimmered in his green eyes. "Ye clearly care for the lass, and she cares for ye. What do ye intend to do about that?"

A knowing smile came to their father's face, and his brows rose meaningfully as he looked at Keir. "I shall return to the keep and speak to yer mother." He chuckled, nodding to both his sons. "'Tis truly good to have ye both here again." Then he turned and walked back the way they had come.

Keir exhaled a deep breath, torn between joy about having

returned home and the tension that lingered because of an uncertain future.

"Well?" Duncan prompted, clearly unwilling to drop the subject. "Do ye intend to marry the lass?"

Keir grinned at his brother. "Ye've never been one to hold back, have you, Duncan?"

His brother shrugged. "If I wish to know something, I ask for it. In my opinion, it saves time."

Keir had always agreed with that assessment. He had always favored direct conversation over suspicions, concerns and contemplations that would eventually lead nowhere. Still, lately, he had come to realize that speaking one's mind was not as simple when one's own heart was on the line. He remembered well how he had advised Juliet, one of the Whickerton sisters, to speak to the man she had loved all her life and ask him how he felt about her. It had seemed prudent advice, and in the end, it had brought Juliet and Christopher together, forcing them both to realize what was between them.

Still, Keir could not deny a nervous tingle at the thought of revealing to Sarah that he loved her or that he wanted to marry her.

"I love her," Keir told his brother with a pointed look, surprised how good it felt to say so out loud, to reveal that part of himself to someone he loved.

Duncan grasped Keir's shoulders and gave him an enthusiastic shake, a wide grin stretching across his face. "Ah, I knew ye did the moment I saw the two of ye together. Did ye already ask for her hand?" He glanced up toward the castle. "Have ye spoken to Mother yet? Ye know she will be delighted to plan a wedding."

Keir chuckled, lifting his hands to halt his brother's steps before he could rush off and do something unwise. "As always, ye rush into things without thinking, Brother," he teased affectionately, then continued walking along the beach, nodding to Duncan to join him. "To answer yer question, I do intend to marry her, but I havena yet told her so."

A frown descended upon Duncan's face, and for a moment, he looked utterly confused. "What stands in yer way, Brother?" he asked, rather mockingly. "The fact that she cares for ye, that she's right here, that marrying her will forever protect her from Lord Blackmore's reach?" His brows rose demandingly. "Quite frankly, I've never known ye to be so indecisive."

Hanging his head, Keir smiled. "Neither have I," he admitted, running his fingers through his hair in an almost helpless gesture. "Believe me, ye will understand when yer time comes to have yer heart stolen. All of a sudden, simple things no longer seem simple."

If possible, Duncan's brows furrowed even more. "Ye're not making any sense."

Keir paused, looking out to sea for a long time before facing his brother again. "I met her only a few months ago," he shrugged his shoulders helplessly, "and now, here I stand, certain that I wish to marry her. How did that happen?" He chuckled. "Sarah asked me that very thing."

"The lass already told ye she loved ye?"

Keir shook his head. "She hasna, and yet I think we both know we do." Again, he raked a hand through his hair, his ring finger snagging on one of his braids. "I barely know her, and yet I feel as though I've known her forever."

An oddly earnest expression came to Duncan's face, and he reached out and grasped his shoulders. "Ye may not have known her long, Brother, but ye do know her. Ye know ye do. A blind man could see it. What is it that holds ye back? Truly?"

Keir sighed, once again realizing how precious it was to have someone to speak to so openly and without fear of giving offense. Duncan spoke his mind as Keir had throughout most of his life, and yet when it mattered the most, he could not... not as much as he wished. "I thought it better to wait and allow her time to settle in, to feel safe." He exhaled a deep breath. "Within a matter of weeks, her life was turned upside down, and I want to be certain that she chooses me because she wants me—truly!—and not because she simply feels safe with me." In the back of Keir's mind, Sarah's voice echoed words she had spoken to him not long ago. Was that not what she had told him? That she felt safe with him, that she wanted to keep him close because she wanted to hold on to that feeling?

A wide grin stretched across Duncan's face. "Ye truly have become a fool for love, little brother." He slapped Keir on the back and then wrapped an arm around his shoulders as he moved them both along farther down toward the water's edge. "Ye love her, and she loves ye. 'Tis as simple as that." He moved to step in front of Keir, his green eyes finding his. "By all means, allow her a few days to settle in, but then ask for her hand. Ye know what ye want. Dunna waste any more time. After all," Duncan's grin widened, "at yer age, ye've got no time to lose."

Keir laughed, and he felt his heart grow lighter. "Ye're one to talk, *older* brother. I dunna see a wife on yer arm."

"Well, of course not," Duncan exclaimed, a chiding look in his eyes. Yet, his lips still twitched with amusement. "I'm a warrior. I fight for our clan. You're a lover." Keir guffawed. "Ye ensure there'll be a next generation."

"And Magnus?" Keir asked, his sides aching from laughter.

Duncan scratched his chin, a gesture that reminded Keir of their father. "He's a thinker. He watches over us all, one eye always on the future." Duncan heaved a contented sigh, and together they turned their gaze away from the far sea and back toward their home. "Together, we're strong and we shall brave every storm." He met Keir's gaze, giving a quick nod, reminding Keir that he was not alone and never would be. As always, his family would be at his side, supporting him in whatever he chose.

And deep down, he knew he had made his choice long ago.

His choice was Sarah.

Chapter Twenty-Six

NEW BEGINNINGS

Although Sarah had enjoyed the gathering the night before, she felt a tad apprehensive about setting foot outside her chamber the next morning. Still, she was determined not to hide, and so she made her way toward her sister's chamber and invited them all for a walk outside. The sun shone overhead, and fluffy white clouds were pushed across the sky by a fierce breeze. Everyone tugged their cloaks tighter around them, and Kate wrapped Frederica tightly in her shawl, the little girl once more strapped to her chest. Kate had found it to be simpler to carry her daughter like this, allowing her arms to relax and her hands to be free if needed.

"I see friendly faces wherever I look," Kate murmured once they had left the castle and followed the girls along the narrow path toward the beach. "I keep expecting to find someone glowering at me, but I do not." A hopeful smile teased her lips, and Sarah could feel her sister's exuberance return. There was something in her eyes that reminded Sarah of the girl Kate had been long ago. She had lost her faith in the world and the goodness of people years ago, but now, perhaps, this was a chance to retrieve it.

To begin again.

Like the phoenix rising from the ashes to start a new life.

From the path that led upward from the village, Eoghan and Bonnie appeared. The girl darted toward them without a moment's hesitation. Eoghan, though, lifted his hand in greeting before he looked over his shoulder, addressing his sister. Kenna stood nearby, arm in arm with another young woman. Once again, the look upon Kenna's face was far from friendly. The moment their eyes met, if only for a second, Sarah could not shake the feeling that the young woman was displeased to see her. More than that, that she disliked having Sarah here.

Perhaps I'm imagining it, Sarah thought to herself, remembering all the friendly faces she had seen this morning, all the happy greetings she had received. After the gathering, everyone knew their story and thus far, everyone had been beyond welcoming. Sarah would have never expected this, and so the young woman's rejection bothered Sarah far more than she would have liked.

The three girls greeted one another with delighted squeals and then raced off down toward the beach. Laughing, Eoghan walked over, offering a warm greeting. "Bonnie has been speaking of her new friends all morning," he remarked with a chuckle, his green eyes shining with delight, "and she dragged me out of the house the moment she had finished her breakfast."

From the first, Sarah had liked Eoghan. He possessed such a cheerful disposition, such kindness in his eyes as he looked at Kate that Sarah could not help but adore him. Kate, however, seemed hesitant, and Sarah even thought to see suspicion in her eyes. Only too well did Sarah remember what it felt like to doubt the people around her. Even today, she still often wondered about people's motivations, wondering if they had any hidden agendas. Thinking like that had become second nature to her, and it seemed that it had to Kate also. Only that was no way to live, to be happy.

"Will you walk with us, Eoghan?" Sarah inquired with a smile, stepping to Kate's other side, hoping that prolonged conversation might ease Kate's concerns. "The girls wish to return to the beach."

Eoghan offered a polite bow. "'Twould be my pleasure."

For a moment, silence lingered as they walked, and Sarah wondered what she could say to prompt a conversation. Then, however, Eoghan turned to Kate. "How is Frederica? She seemed quite in her element at the gathering last night."

Kate smiled, gazing down at her sleeping daughter. "Yes, I've never quite seen her like that before. She truly seemed to enjoy herself."

Eoghan chuckled. "When Bonnie was born, I thought children needed silence in order to sleep." Laughing, he shook his head. "As it turns out, the more ruckus is around her, the better she sleeps."

Kate chuckled, and Sarah thought to see the strain upon her features slowly ease away. Indeed, perhaps all her sister needed was to meet genuinely good and decent people.

And so, Sarah slowed her steps, and with each spoken word, she fell a little farther behind. Eventually, it made her realize how soothing the sudden quiet was. She listened to the wind and the seagulls above, and her eyes swept over the far horizon as her chest filled with the salted sea air.

At the top of the path, where it sloped down toward the water, Sarah stopped and then seated herself on a large rock. She watched the children run around, squealing and laughing, before their heads turned abruptly when suddenly Loki showed up out of nowhere. As always, the feline came and went as he pleased, sometimes disappearing for days before returning rather unexpectedly. Sarah wondered where he went on his expeditions, envying the freedom he possessed coming and going as he wished. How did he see the world? What places did he explore?

She wished she knew.

All of a sudden, Kate craned her neck, her eyes looking about until they fell upon Sarah. Seeing Kate pause, Sarah lifted her arm and waved, hoping Kate would not feel abandoned. However, it seemed Eoghan was good company as he quickly drew Kate's attention away from whatever concerns might have found her in that moment. Before long, they continued their conversation, and Sarah felt herself relax. She pulled up her knees and wrapped her arms around her legs, sighing contentedly as she enjoyed the peaceful moment.

"'Tis a pleasant day, is it not?"

Startled, Sarah flinched, and for a brief moment, she thought it was Keir speaking to her; the voice sounded so familiar. Yet when she turned her head, she spotted Keir's father, Aidan, standing only a few paces away, a warm smile upon his face.

"Yes, it is wonderful," Sarah replied, suddenly feeling self-conscious again, wondering what to say.

On quiet feet, Aidan approached, then settled himself upon the rock beside her, about an arm's length away. His gaze followed hers, and for a moment, he watched the children play on the beach, a smile coming to his face. "Ye're safe here, lass. Ye have my word."

Taken aback, Sarah's head whipped around to look at him, surprised by his words, by the direction of his thoughts.

"'Tis easy to see that ye're not used to feeling safe," Aiden observed, his voice free of judgment as he shifted to look at her. "'Tis there in yer eyes, and the way ye look at us, the people around ye." Again, there was no judgment in his voice.

Sarah sighed. "You're not wrong," she finally admitted, surprised that her voice did not fail her now. "In my experience, there are few places and even fewer people that offer safety without demanding something in return." Her gaze met his for a brief second, and she prayed she had not offended him, that he would not consider her words a comment upon his clan's hospitality.

Fortunately, Sarah could see no anger on his face. He simply nodded. "Our clan rose from a need for safety," he told her, his voice now swinging with a note of a storyteller. "I dunna know if ye are aware, but our clan was born out of two warring clans."

"Keir told me."

During their time together hidden away in the woods, Keir had told her many stories of his clan. One story Sarah had liked in particular had been the story of Yvaine. She had been the one Keir's sister had been named after, the very woman who had centuries ago been the origin of their clan.

A twinkle came to Aiden's eyes as he regarded her. "My son cares for ye."

Caught off guard, Sarah almost flinched for the second time that day.

"Are ye truly surprised? After all, 'tis there in the way he looks at ye, the way he always knows where ye are, never hesitates to move to yer side the moment he senses yer need for him."

As always, Sarah felt heat rise to her cheeks, accompanied by the sudden urge to flee from this moment and hide somewhere. "I do see it," she whispered, her voice barely audible.

"But ye dunna trust it," Aiden concluded, a questioning frown coming to his face.

Closing her eyes, Sarah exhaled slowly. "Where I am from, I..." She shook her head, trying to clear her thoughts as they ran rampant through her head. "After everything that happened... there's not a single man in my world who would still want me." Never before had Sarah spoken these words out loud, and their finality almost knocked the air from her lungs. She knew Keir's clan to be different, had seen so with her own eyes, and yet this sense of wrongdoing that had been with her ever since she had agreed to the kidnapping was not something she could shake. It had ingrained itself into her bones and become the origin of every doubt and concern.

Aiden nodded, as though he understood precisely how she felt, his gaze once more directed toward the far horizon. "The world is far from a perfect place, and every bit of change takes time." He inhaled a deep breath, savoring the freshness of the sea air. "Perhaps ye were meant to find joy here. Our shores often feel like a place outside the normal course of time, a place far removed from the usual restraints one might find in the world outside." He looked at her then. "Ye were not wrong to demand yer own path, lass. I can see ye have doubts, and I understand where they come from. But ye must not allow them to keep ye from walking steadily onward." He swept his gaze over their surroundings, the nod of his head encompassing everything they saw. "Every single man and woman and child on this island is a MacKinnear," he told her, his gaze intent upon hers, "not because they were all born MacKinnears, but because they made the choice to be. In that way, we're different from other clans. We chose one name to represent who we decided to be. It began long ago with Yvaine and Calen, and it continues to this day. We're all one. We all belong here. Whether we were born here or came from another place does not matter. 'Tis our choice."

Overwhelmed by his words, Sarah all but stared at Keir's father, understanding in that moment how Keir came to be the respectful man he was. Indeed, what would the world be like if everyone were like the MacKinnears?

Chapter Twenty-Seven
KNOW THY ENEMY

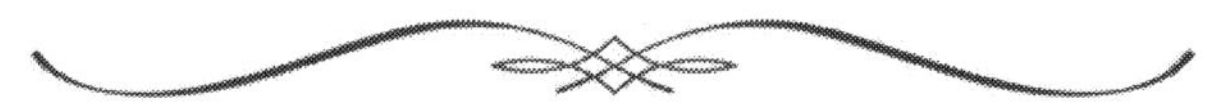

Kenna happened to be in the great hall when Keir's father entered, the English lady Sarah upon his arm. Words passed between them, and Kenna wondered what they were discussing. She did not care for the kind smile upon Aiden's face, nor for the joyful delight she saw upon Sarah's. It seemed that their visitors had won everyone's hearts within a single evening, their story deeply touching, persuading Kenna's clan to welcome them without a second thought.

Anger simmered in Kenna's veins at the mere sight of the English lass, for she doubted that the woman was as innocent and lovely as she portrayed herself to be. No doubt dark secrets lived in her past, ones she sought to hide. And so, as Aiden bid Sarah farewell and strode away, Kenna decided to keep an eye on the young woman.

For a moment, Sarah seemed a bit lost, her eyes sweeping around her surroundings, uncertainty in her gaze. Then she moved forward, peeking around corners and along corridors. Clearly, she had no notion of where she was going, and Kenna had no trouble trailing after her at a safe distance. She followed Sarah through several sitting rooms and watched her peek into the occasional alcove, a smile coming to her face, as though the discovery meant something to her. The woman's reaction only made sense to Kenna when she heard Sarah exclaim, "Oh, the girls would love to hide here. I must remember to tell them."

Kenna disliked that even her own family had fallen under the newcomers' spell. While Eoghan seemed fascinated by the woman named Katherine, Bonnie delighted in her new friends. That made Kenna an outsider, the only one who wondered what intentions the two English ladies had in coming here.

Next, Sarah stepped into the library, and Kenna hid in the doorway as she watched Sarah explore the rows upon rows of books. Joy flickered across the woman's face as she tentatively ran her fingers along the delicate spines. Eventually, her feet carried her to the window and the telescope set upon a small platform in front of it. She glanced out the window, a slight frown coming to her forehead.

Kenna quietly inched closer, hiding behind the tall shelves and peeking around their edges. She watched Sarah standing by the window, looking down into the courtyard, that puzzled expression still upon her face. As Kenna continued to observe her, Sarah slowly lifted her head, as though her gaze were following a movement. *Perhaps someone is riding down the path to the village*, Kenna mused. *Is it Keir?*

The thought of the English woman watching Keir had Kenna's hands curling into fists. Her teeth pressed together as she fought the urge to reveal herself and fling harsh words at Sarah's head, demanding she leave immediately.

Demanding she leave Keir alone.

Closing her eyes, Kenna inhaled a deep breath, struggling to calm herself as her mind raced with thoughts of how to break the spell this woman clearly had on Keir. *How on earth did this happen? He was mine. Mine!*

At the sound of footfalls, Kenna's eyes flew open.

Sarah had left the window and now stood upon the small pedestal, slightly bent forward to look through the telescope. Only it was not directed upward at the sky but down toward the village. *Who is she watching?*

Without another thought, Kenna stepped out into the open, leaving behind her hiding place, thinking that perhaps it would be wise to speak to Sarah. If she learned more about this English lady, perhaps she could think of a way to convince her to leave, to return to where she had come from and leave here in peace.

Straightening her shoulders, Kenna lifted her head, willing a polite smile on her face before she stepped forward, no longer concerned with moving silently.

As expected, at the sound of Kenna's approach, Sarah's head lifted and she turned around, her eyes widening. "Oh, I wasn't aware someone else was here." A hesitant smile came to her face, her blue eyes wide and yet not daring to linger upon Kenna's face for too long. Indeed, the English lady seemed nervous and uncertain of herself.

Inwardly, Kenna smiled. Perhaps it would be far easier to persuade the woman to leave than Kenna had first thought.

"What are ye looking at?" Kenna asked, watchful that her voice did not betray her discontent as she nodded toward the telescope. "I suppose 'tis far too early for stargazing."

A slightly embarrassed chuckle escaped Sarah. "I admit I was looking at Aiden and Duncan riding down to the village." A deep blush came to her cheeks, and she worried her lower lip, clearly ashamed. "I didn't mean to watch them, but I saw them mount their horses and then ride out of the courtyard. I could not help but wonder where they were going."

Kenna stepped forward and toward the telescope. "May I see?"

Sarah nodded her head a bit too enthusiastically, undoubtedly relieved that Kenna did not hold her spying against her. "Of course."

Pinching one eye shut, Kenna looked through the telescope, her gaze quickly finding Aiden and Duncan as they stood among others of the village, their coats cast aside as they assisted in the rebuilding of the house that had come down in the last storm. "Oh, aye, that's old Morag's house. The roof caved in a few days past." She stood up and looked at Sarah. "Sometimes the storms can be quite fierce near the coast."

A shiver seemed to shake Sarah, and she wrapped her arms around herself. "That sounds awful. Does it happen a lot?"

Kenna shook her head. "No, 'tis quite rare." She glanced toward the telescope. "They will no doubt have rebuilt it by nightfall."

A warm smile came to Sarah's face, and she turned her head toward the window, as though she could glimpse what was happening below in the village. "Does Keir's father often help with such work?" she asked then before returning her gaze to Kenna.

Kenna rather disliked the sound of Keir's name upon the Englishwoman's tongue. Still, she fought to hold her features in check. "They do. Why would they not?"

"No, it is simply that as leader of this clan, I would not have expected him to do so." She heaved a deep breath, and her gaze became distant. "Where I am from, the lords of the land would never consider doing such a thing." She blinked; her gaze focused upon Kenna. "There is such a distinction between people of the upper classes and those of the lower classes. It feels like a wall that no one could ever bridge."

Kenna frowned. "That is not something ye will find here," she remarked, a bit of an edge to her voice that she could not prevent.

Sarah's eyes widened immediately. "Oh, you misunderstand. I'm quite pleased to see how things are done here. I'm simply surprised." She sighed. "A part of me feels as though this place is too good to be true."

"What's it like," Kenna began, determined to learn more about the Englishwoman, "to be so far from home? Do ye not miss yer family?"

A thoughtful expression came to Sarah's face. "Well, fortunately my sister and her daughters are here with me, and... I was never close with my parents."

Kenna nodded, remembering the story from the gathering. "Aye, there's a strong bond between siblings, is there not?"

A deep smile came to Sarah's face as she nodded. "I suppose it is the same for you and Eoghan, is it not? He seems like a very dedicated father. Bonnie is fortunate to have him."

"And unfortunate to have lost her mother," Kenna retorted, beginning to get annoyed with the sweetness Sarah displayed. Was there no edge to this woman? There had to be! Only what would bring it forth?

At Kenna's words, Sarah's expression darkened. "Of course. That must've been awful for the both of them."

"Is it not the same for yer sister's daughters? After all, they are now growing up without their father."

An expression of guilt came to Sarah's face, and inwardly, Kenna rejoiced. "Is it not yer plan to see them returned, eventually? Perhaps distance will make him realize what he had in his family, and he will change his ways."

Sarah's lips pressed into a tight line as she shook her head, each movement becoming a bit more forceful. "I do not think that to be possible. Otherwise, we would not have taken such a drastic step. It was our last resort, and yes, I do feel awful for what happened. I wish it could have gone otherwise." She blinked her eyes, and then her chin rose a fraction, suggesting she wished to leave that topic behind her. "And you and your brother are close?" She chuckled a bit shyly. "I only have a sister, so I have no knowledge of what it is like growing up with a brother."

Kenna moved around past the telescope and toward the window, leaning her back against the wall. "Aye, we've always been close. He's a good man, and so is Keir." Curiosity sparked in Sarah's eyes. "They have been the best of friends since the moment they could walk." She chuckled, smiling warmly at the memory, wanting Sarah to see what connected them all. Something that did not include her as a foreigner. "I, too, often went along on their adventures, and it brought us closer."

Kenna rejoiced as she saw the smile upon Sarah's face dim. Clearly, the other woman had noted the underlying meaning of Kenna's words. Encouraged, Kenna continued, her gaze once more drawn to the young woman's small braids. "Keir and I have always shared a special bond, and I must say I missed him terribly when his grandmother urged him to go to England and help her friend. Of course, he didna wish to go, but he knew his duty. He is a most honorable man, ye know?" Kenna smiled warmly at Sarah, watching the other woman swallow hard, the expression in her eyes now overshadowed.

"Even though I missed him," Kenna added with a deep sigh, "I am quite glad that he went, for yer story touched me deeply." She pressed her hand to her chest for emphasis. "And I am so relieved that Keir could lend a hand in securing yer freedom. I see how he watches over ye and yer sister as well as yer nieces, and I simply love that about him, the way he tends to everyone in need."

Sarah swallowed hard, and once again her arms rose to wrap around herself. Yet Kenna detected a spark of something defiant in the woman's blue eyes as she lifted her chin and met her gaze. "I believe I know of what you speak," she murmured, her gaze watchful. "I grew up very close with my best friend's family, and she and her sisters became like sisters to me as well. It is such a bond that I see everywhere I look here. You are most fortunate."

Kenna felt a touch of anger spark in her veins at Sarah's suggestion that Keir might be like a brother to her. "Of course, I consider Keir family, but I must say that he never looked at me the same way he looked at his sister." She smiled at Sarah and then winked conspiratorially. "There was always something… different in his gaze."

Deeply pleased, Kenna watched Sarah's face pale. For a moment, her blue eyes remained unblinking, staring straight ahead through Kenna, her attention directed inward. Indeed, there was a spark of pain and disappointment in the young woman's gaze, and for a brief moment, Kenna felt remorse. Of course, she did not wish to hurt Sarah; however, it was better to make her see the truth now before her heart was misled into believing that Keir could ever truly love her.

Sarah mumbled a few rather unintelligible words and then hastened away, the expression upon her face quite telling. Aye, she had understood Kenna's meaning, and it had hurt her. Yet it had been necessary.

After all, Keir belonged here in Scotland.

At Kenna's side.

Chapter Twenty-Eight
CHOICES

Only a few days had passed since their arrival at Castle MacKinnear, and already the girls seemed to have settled in fine. Keir often saw them sneak treats from the kitchen with Bonnie or read stories in the library or run along the hills and down to the beach, Loki upon their heels. Every once in a while, children from the village joined in; however, the three girls—Augusta, Dorothea and Bonnie—had become as thick as thieves.

One afternoon, Keir was walking down a corridor and then came around a corner when he heard someone giggling. He paused, his gaze sweeping over the curtained off alcove when he saw Thea peak out, a finger to her lips, urging him to be quiet.

Smiling at the girl, Keir nodded at her reassuringly and then walked on as he heard the other two girls drawing closer. He was about to turn another corner when Loki suddenly crossed his path.

As was his habit, the feline once again appeared as though out of nowhere, seating himself by Keir's feet, his chin raised and his amber eyes looking up at him, a rather chiding look upon his face.

"Where have ye been?" Keir asked Loki, overcome as always that he felt compelled to speak to the cat.

Unfortunately, Loki did not respond. He simply continued looking at Keir in that way of his, and Keir had to admit he would not have been surprised if Loki had suddenly started shaking his head at him.

Keir chuckled. “What did I do? It must’ve been something awful, for ye clearly disapprove of it.” He cocked his head to the side, watching the feline most intently. “I must say that look upon yer face is rather unsettling.”

As though satisfied that his message had been received, Loki hopped to his paws and then darted away down the corridor, vanishing once more.

Chuckling, Keir headed downstairs and then entered the great hall, momentarily surprised to see Katherine—Frederica in her arms as always—and Kenna sitting by the fire and talking. A quick glance around told Keir that Sarah was nowhere nearby, and he wondered where she had gone. Lately, she seemed distant to him, and he worried that something might have upset her.

Fortunately, Katherine seemed to grow more and more accustomed to this new life, her demeanor now more relaxed than before. She no longer looked as fearful and apprehensive, able to relax her grip upon her daughters a bit more every day. Though, while she allowed Augusta and Dorothea to move about the castle freely—not that she had much choice!—she always kept Frederica by her side. Thus far, only Eoghan had managed to persuade her to hand over the child for brief moments at a time. There was still fear there, Keir knew. Yet he hoped that with time, Katherine would regain some faith in the world.

Pleased to see that Kenna was doing her best to help Katherine settle in, Keir smiled at her gratefully as he stepped closer. “Have ye seen Sarah?”

Katherine shook her head, and Kenna shrugged. “Perhaps she’s simply exploring the castle or the grounds beyond,” Kenna suggested, patting the seat beside her invitingly. “Come. Join us.”

Sighing, Keir took the seat, his thoughts once again drawn to Sarah, and the overshadowed expression he had seen upon her face lately. He thought perhaps deep down she missed her home, missed England and the Whickertons, the life she used to have. More than that, he worried that, perhaps, Sarah might not want to remain in Scotland for good.

Chapter Twenty-Nine
SECOND NATURE

In the past few days, Sarah had taken to walking the countryside, finding the solitude of being outdoors comforting. The castle and the grounds seemed too crowded all of a sudden, full of people Sarah did not know, people who smiled at her and greeted her... and now that had made her wonder about all the many things she was simply not a part of. They had had their lives, and she had had hers, and it felt as though they were miles apart.

Over her shoulder, Sarah watched the castle grow smaller with every step she took in the opposite direction. Somewhere inside were Keir and Kenna, not necessarily together in that moment, and yet to Sarah, that did not matter.

Try as she might, she could not shake the thought of the two of them, of the life they had shared, of the life that Kenna clearly still wanted. But what of Keir?

Of course, Sarah felt her heart unwavering. She knew what she wanted. She knew she loved Keir. She knew that she wanted a future with him. And until that day in the library when she had spoken with Kenna, Sarah had been almost certain that Keir wanted that, too, that he... loved her as well. And now doubts returned, and Sarah hated them. She wished she could simply chase them away and return to that state of tentative hopefulness. It had felt so wonderful to have faith, to expect good things to happen in the future.

Now, dark clouds lingered again, the same dark clouds that had been with her all her life. She knew she simply ought to ask Keir, speak to him and find out what was truly between him and Kenna. Had they been in love before he had left Scotland? Did he still love her? Or had things changed for him?

Yet she was uncertain if she was ready to find out.

Sarah had never truly dwelt upon the possibility that Keir had loved before, that there might have even been someone waiting for him to return home. *I am a fool!* Of course, a man like Keir was spoken for, had stolen hearts and known love. *How could it be any different?* Yet it had been so wonderful to think of the bond between them as unique, as one of a kind, something that came along once in a lifetime.

'You foolish child,' snapped her mother's voice in her head, and Sarah jerked to a halt, completely caught off guard. 'You acted despicably, and you expect to win hearts with such behavior? No, a decent man would never choose you.'

A furious growl rose from Sarah's lips as she pressed her hands to her ears as though that might shut out the voice. Would she hear it until the end of her days? Would her mother forever encourage her doubts? Would she never be free of them?

"He cares for me," Sarah whispered to the wind as she pushed onward, following the path to wherever it might lead her. "I know he does. He said so himself. I should not doubt him. I should not doubt what is between us."

Yet the thoughts continued to come, suggesting that what had happened between her and Keir was simply one of those things that happened when two people were thrown together in close proximity. Of course, Sarah would not know from experience. She knew nothing of love or men. Perhaps she truly had allowed herself to be fooled.

Torn in two different directions, Sarah quickened her pace, her fury racing down to her legs, almost making her run. Run from herself. Run from all the doubts that simply would not leave her alone.

And it brought her a measure of peace.

Indeed, it felt invigorating to move, to see new places as she explored first the area surrounding the little village, walking a little farther every day, before heading for the land farther inward. Keir's home was beautiful, and wherever Sarah went, she heard his stories echo through her head. Some days she would walk along the shore, enjoying the brisk breeze tugging upon her curls and the chill of the wind upon her cheeks. Other times, she would pick her way through the woods and across meadows. Winds often blew harshly, and Sarah had to keep walking to stay warm this early in the year. Still, winter was retreating, and spring was on the horizon. She could hear birdsong and spot the occasional blossom, daring the cold, unwilling to bend its head.

Sometimes Sarah all but stumbled onward blindly, lost in thought with no idea where she was going. And so, one day, she suddenly stood in front of a large rock outcropping, jutting upward and barring her path. It stood surrounded by thick foliage, thorny brambles growing at its base. Try as she might, Sarah could not see beyond or around it; and yet, the sound of the sea drifted to her ears. She knew it had to lie somewhere beyond. Only it was lost to sight.

Intrigued, Sarah moved closer, wanting a view of the sea, of the distant horizon. Yet there seemed to be no way through the thicket, the rock jutting upward in a way that would not allow her to climb. Disappointed, Sarah turned back the way she had come when a sudden sound echoed to her ears.

A sound almost as familiar as her own voice.

Spinning back around, Sarah swept her gaze over the thicket, her breath all but caught in her throat. The wind tugged upon her curls, blowing them in front of her eyes, and she brushed them away impatiently, annoyed to have her view obstructed. And then, out of the thicket, two amber eyes found hers.

Almost entranced, Sarah sank to her knees. "Loki?" A slow smile spread across her face as she watched the little feline slink out of the bramble bushes, seemingly unbothered by the thorns. "What are you doing here?" She held out her hand, and he came toward her, his gaze still upon hers, something almost beckoning there.

Loki's fur felt soft against her skin as he rubbed his head on her hand and purred. Yet it was not that sleepy purr he often emitted when he felt the most content, completely at ease. No, it was rather a greeting, something to draw her attention.

"What is it, Loki?" Sarah murmured, wondering if the feline had followed her there. Yet she had not seen him once, and he had to have found a way inside the thicket before she had even gotten here. "What brought you to this place? If only you could tell me."

Loki's gaze still held hers when he slowly inched backward, a soft meow drifting from his throat.

Crouching on the hard ground, Sarah followed him, her eyes moving back and forth between the little feline and the impenetrable thicket barring her way. "What is it you want? I cannot go in there. I—"

Sarah stilled when another sound suddenly drifted to her ears. For a brief moment, she thought it sounded like the fussing cry of a child, and her heart stopped.

Then, however, her eyes caught movement within the thicket, something black and white moving there. She heard a soft whine, and in the next instant, Sarah realized what Loki had been trying to tell her. "It's a puppy!"

With wide eyes, Sarah looked at Loki, all but expecting him to shake his head at her for stating something so very obvious. Yet instead, he once more tiptoed toward the thicket and the little creature trapped within, his meow urgent.

"Yes! I'm coming." Sarah inched closer, ducking her head as she carefully pushed branches out of the way, thorns scraping against her skin. She kept her gaze focused on the pup, its soft whine urging her onward. "Don't worry, little one. We'll have you out of there in a moment."

Seeing her approach, the puppy's whine grew louder, and he scrambled eagerly against the confining brambles, trying to push through, trying to get to her. Sarah was surprised that it was not cowering in fear. After all, how could it know she meant it no harm?

"Ouch!" Sarah jerked back her hand, blood welling up from a scratch on the back of it. She drew in a sharp breath, allowing a muttered curse to fall from her lips before fetching the handkerchief from her pocket and winding it around the wound. Then she turned back toward the little creature, moving carefully, bending away the branches and creating a hole big enough for the pup to slip through. "Almost," she murmured, beckoning it forward with her voice. "Come on, little one. You're almost out." Sarah gritted her teeth against another sharp poke of a thorn against the side of her neck; yet she held onto the branches until the pup managed to squirm free. Then she slowly ducked her head, released the branches, and backed out of the thicket.

The pup sat shivering upon the cold ground, and Sarah quickly swept it into her arms, wrapping her heavy cloak around it. "We need to get it back to the castle," Sarah told Loki as he fell into step beside her. "Without its mother, it will not survive." As she walked away, she turned to look over her shoulder at the thicket, wondering how the puppy had gotten there. Where was its mother? Was she still somewhere around? Had they been separated? Sarah did not know, and there was no time to linger and search.

With her eyes fixed upon the castle in the distance, Sarah walked quickly, holding the little creature clutched in her arms. At first, the pup seemed rather agitated. Eventually, though, he settled down, his heartbeat slowing as he grew warmer in her embrace.

Entering the castle grounds through one of the smaller gates to the west, Sarah spotted Keir's mother in the herb garden, an apron over her dress. Again, Sarah blinked in disbelief for a moment to see the lady of the keep do such ordinary work. But those were the MacKinnears, were they not? Just like the chief of the clan had gone to help rebuild a house, his sleeves rolled up, lending a hand where it was needed. Indeed, this was a different place.

A better place.

And Sarah wished she could stay.

"Sarah!"

Jarred from her thoughts, Sarah blinked.

Keir's mother had raised a hand in greeting, her gaze watchful. Then she nodded, beckoning Sarah over.

Sarah stepped through the small opening in the fence and into the herb garden, Loki at her side. "Good morning, my lady," she greeted Keir's mother. "It is a beautiful day, is it not?"

The other woman chuckled, smirking at Loki in greeting. "Please, call me Heather. Ye know that we dunna stand on ceremony here." The look in her eyes was insistent, and Sarah felt herself relax. "Now, tell me what's happened."

Sarah drew back the cloak, revealing the small pup. "I found him over by the cliffs. He had gotten caught in the thicket." She looked down at the black-and-white pup, its eyes now sleepy as it lay in her arms.

Heather smiled at the small creature. "Take it to Mrs. Murray. She'll see that it will be fed." She brushed a gentle hand over the pup's head. Then her gaze rose and met Sarah's. "Did my son put that look in yer eyes?"

Taken aback, Sarah stared at Keir's mother. "W-What?"

A rather indulgent expression came to the other woman's face. "Before, ye looked at him differently than ye do now." She took a step closer, and her hand settled upon Sarah's arm. "Tell me what he did, and I'll set them straight."

Sarah could not help the smile that stole onto her face, touched by Heather's offer. "It is nothing," she insisted, though, wishing she could confide in the other woman and see her doubts chased away for good. Yet not even Keir's mother could know his heart.

Not truly.

Heather sighed in disbelief. "All my sons have keen eyes, and yet sometimes they're as blind as a bat." She smiled at Sarah warmly. "Go and see to the little one, but if ye need someone to talk to, I'll be here."

Blinking back tears, Sarah nodded. She liked Keir's mother. In fact, she liked all of them. She liked all of them too much, and it broke her heart.

If only.

Chapter Thirty

A TERRIBLE MATCH

Entering the great hall, Keir spotted the girls tending to the stray pup Sarah had found the other day near the cliffs. To everyone's amusement, Thea had named the pup Faerie. In fact, she called him her faerie dog, which had caused old Morag to nearly drop dead as the little girl happily presented the creature.

Despite having discovered the pup, Loki seemed to dislike him. Curled up near the fire, the feline watched the girls and the little dog with apprehension. Keir wondered if perhaps Loki was a bit jealous, for Faerie now monopolized the girls' attention. They cooed over him, hugging him and stroking his fur, always offering treats.

The scent of roasted meat lingered in the hall as people gathered for the evening meal. Warm flames danced in the fireplace, and every candle throughout the vaulted room had been lit. Laughter and conversation echoed to Keir's ears as he strode through the rows of tables, his gaze falling upon his own family seated together...

... Sarah among them.

As though she could sense his approach, her gaze rose, and their eyes met.

Keir felt it like a spark, setting him aflame, and for a moment, the breath faltered in his lungs. Always had Sarah had such an effect on him, and yet lately life at the castle had drawn them apart, further apart than ever before. While Keir spent most of his days with his father and brother, discussing how to handle the potential threat of Lord Birchwell, Sarah often tended to her sister and her nieces. Yet over the past sennight, he had often found her strangely absent from the castle. More than once, he had wanted to seek her out, to have some time with her, but he had found her nowhere.

"What did ye do?" his mother had asked him the other day, and from the look in her eyes, Keir had known that she had spoken about Sarah. Something had happened, and yet Sarah clearly did not wish for him to know.

Barely a second after their eyes met, Sarah dropped her gaze, once again making Keir wonder if he had upset her. *Only what can it be? I needa speak to her.*

In that moment, though, the sound of the fiddle filled the hall, and people got to their feet, eager for a bit of dancing. Kenna appeared beside him, a wistful smile upon her face. "It has been forever since we last danced," she exclaimed, grasping his hands and pulling him toward the other dancers. "Dunna even try to deny me," she cut him off when he made to object. "Ye owe me this dance."

"I owe ye this dance?" Keir inquired with a chuckle as they stood up together.

Kenna nodded as they began to move to the music. "Aye, ye do, for all the dances ye missed. Do ye not remember the fun we had together?"

Keir laughed. "Aye, I do remember."

"I missed ye," Kenna exclaimed, slapping him playfully on the shoulder. "Ye daft man! I missed ye every day ye were gone."

Keir sighed, giving her hand a gentle squeeze as it slipped back into his own. "I missed ye as well," he told her earnestly. "Ye and Eoghan."

As the fiddler continued to play, Keir felt his feet move without fault. Indeed, it felt good to be home, to once again experience all that had always felt familiar.

Over Kenna's shoulder, Keir spotted the pup snuggling up beside Loki. Loki, though, looked annoyed by the pup's show of affection. He instantly got to his paws, retreating a few steps before settling himself again. However, rather undeterred, the pup followed, once again seeking the feline's side.

Keir could not help but smile at the sight, and yet it made him think of Sarah. Not unlike Loki, she seemed displeased with his presence lately, her demeanor changed, not as affectionate as before. And so, as the dance ended, he returned to his family's table, determined to seek her out.

Kenna, though, held him back, her hand upon his arm. "Can I speak to ye for a moment?" Concern rested in her eyes, and Keir could tell that something weighed heavily upon her.

"Verra well." He nodded, and they moved over to the side, out of the way of the dancers and into a corner where they could speak privately. "What is it, lass? Are ye all right?"

Kenna nodded. "I'm fine. But I'm worried about Katherine." She glanced sideways toward where Katherine sat next to Sarah and Eoghan. "She seems very sad and rather nervous."

Keir sighed. "Aye, she does. Well, I suppose that was to be expected, considering what she has been through." He smiled at Kenna, placing a hand upon her shoulder. "I am grateful she found a friend in ye. She could do with a bit of help settling in. All of this must be rather foreign to her."

Kenna smiled at him. "Of course. I am more than happy to help." She paused, and her gaze drifted sideways once more before returning to look up into his eyes. "Will they stay for good?"

Keir heaved a deep sigh, wishing he could respond with a confident nod. Instead, all he could say was, "I hope so."

"Let me hold the wee lassie." Eoghan held out his hands, the look in his green eyes telling Kate that she could trust him. "I promise I shall stay right here. Right beside ye."

With a glance at Frederica, Kate lessened her hold upon her daughter and then settled her gently into Eoghan's arms. "Thank you," she murmured, still feeling apprehensive.

Kate wished that feeling would go away, but it stubbornly remained.

"Go ahead, lass, eat," Eoghan urged her, glancing down at her untouched plate. "Ye need it." A warm smile came to his face as he met her eyes, and Kate felt something within her stir.

Still, Kate remembered that sort of smile from her husband. Long ago, he, too, had had an easy smile. It had charmed her, made her believe in him, and then...

Eoghan regarded her through slightly narrowed eyes. "Dunna worry," he whispered, rocking Frederica back and forth. "I dunna have an ulterior motive. I simply know what 'tis like to live with a small babe and feel as though where two hands used to be enough, they suddenly are no longer." He winked at her.

Surprising even herself, Kate laughed.

"Ye oughta do that more often, lass," Eoghan replied with a wide smile. "It'll do ye good." He held her gaze for a moment longer, then glanced down at Frederica. "Would ye give me permission to take the wee one for a walk around the hall?"

Kate felt the breath catch in her throat.

"I promise I willna venture far. Ye'll always be able to see us." His right brow rose challengingly.

Kate swallowed hard, glancing across the table at Sarah, an encouraging smile upon her sister's face. Then she drew in a slow breath and nodded to Eoghan.

As he rose from his seat, Frederica in his arms, Kate followed Eoghan's every movement. The food on her plate forgotten, she watched him like a hawk, every muscle in her body screaming at her to rush after him and retrieve her child.

"Breathe, Kate," Sarah whispered from across the table, and the moment Kate met her sister's eyes, she exhaled a deep breath. "All is well. Trust me."

Holding her sister's gaze, Kate nodded, the movement soothing, for it eased her breathing and allowed her muscles to unclench. Forcing herself to reach for the food upon her plate, Kate allowed her gaze to sweep around the hall, now and then, glimpsing Eoghan and Frederica but not daring to linger. "I need to let this go," Kate whispered to herself silently. *I need this fear to be gone. I need to be myself again.*

Kate's gaze jarred to a halt when she suddenly spotted Keir and Kenna across the hall. They stood off in a far corner, speaking to one another quietly, their heads bent close. The expression upon Kenna's face as she looked up at Keir was one Kate did not care for. Indeed, when the young woman reached out to touch Keir's arm, Kate tensed.

Glancing across the table, Kate saw Sarah's face bear a similar expression to her own, hurt in her eyes and her hands clenched.

"And we're back," Eoghan's voice exclaimed beside her the moment before he reclaimed the seat he had left only moments earlier.

Kate smiled at him, relieved to see Frederica slumbering peacefully in his arms.

Eoghan held her gaze. "'Twas not so bad, was it?"

Kate shook her head, grateful. "I… I never doubted you, but…"

Eoghan placed a hand upon hers, holding her gaze even as Kate startled. "Ye needna explain yerself. Ye do what feels right, and whenever ye need a wee bit of help, ye'll know where to find me."

Touched, Kate nodded. "Thank you." She truly liked the kindness in his eyes, the honest concern she saw there. And yet, it made her feel flustered, and she quickly averted her eyes.

As coincidence would have it, her gaze once more came to linger upon Keir and Kenna. "Did they ever have intentions toward one another?" Kate asked without thinking, feeling every muscle in her body still the moment the last word had left her lips.

Eoghan, though, merely looked at her with curiosity. "Who?"

Kate swallowed. "Your sister."

Eoghan followed her gaze, a touch of annoyance coming to his eyes. "Well, Kenna took a shine to him early on." He met her gaze. "I suppose 'tis probably just the natural reaction of a young girl toward her elder brother's best friend." He scoffed, then chuckled. "They'd make a terrible match."

Kate felt her pulse calm. "Why?"

"Keir is a very honest and direct man," he told her in hushed tones, "while Kenna likes to play games and keep secrets. They're simply not suited to one another."

"Has he ever… shown interest in her?" Kate could not stop herself from asking, her pulse once more picking up as she waited for Eoghan's reply.

Eoghan's gaze was watchful as it lingered upon her, then briefly darted to Sarah before returning to her. "He has not."

A heavy weight lifted off Kate's shoulders, and suddenly she felt like she could breathe again.

Chapter Thirty-One

UPON THE BEACH

The sun shone brightly overhead, and there was a touch of warmth in the air as they headed down toward the beach. Sarah and Kate walked arm in arm as Eoghan followed a few steps behind, Frederica asleep upon his shoulder. The girls had raced ahead and were now, near the water's edge, trying their best to entice Faerie into a game. The pup, however, seemed more interested in following Loki around, who tried his utmost to discourage the canine with an occasional hiss and a well-aimed swipe in the little pup's direction.

"He is wonderful with her, is he not?" Sarah inquired, casting a glance across her shoulder at Eoghan and Frederica. "She seems utterly content in his arms."

Kate exhaled a deep breath. "I know," she whispered, tugging Sarah closer so she could hear. "Truly, I do not doubt him. He is wonderful with her, and I believe... I'm beginning to relax. It is not as hard for me to hand her over as it was in the beginning." An almost shy, deeply self-conscious smile teased Kate's lips. "Somehow, Eoghan... he puts me at ease."

"I'm glad to hear it," Sarah replied with a smile, relieved to see Kate settling in, to see the sister she had once known peek through more often these days. Sarah also liked that wistful expression Eoghan seemed to have inspired. *Interesting!*

"And what of you?" Kate inquired; her green gaze slightly narrowed as she looked into Sarah's face with the practiced eyes of a sister. "You've seen the way Kenna always hovers around Keir, have you not?"

Her sister's words felt like a punch to the stomach, and Sarah cringed. "I have," was all she could manage in that moment.

"And it worries you," Kate observed simply. "You no longer look as hopeful and... mesmerized as you did in the beginning."

Wanting to weep, Sarah shrugged her shoulders. "This is a beautiful place full of wonderful people," she exclaimed as loudly as she dared without attracting Eoghan's attention. "I should be happy here. I *want* to be happy here. Yet, lately, I cannot help but wonder if this is truly the place I'm supposed to be. I cannot help but wonder if Keir even intends for us to stay, for me to stay."

Kate nodded, sorrow in her eyes. "Sometimes things are not what they seem," she whispered, and Sarah could see that her sister's thoughts drifted back to her old life, her husband. She closed her eyes briefly, and then shook her head, determinedly ridding herself of these thoughts. "You should speak to him. You cannot know what is in his heart unless you ask him."

Of course, Sarah knew Kate was right, and yet the thought of confronting Keir made her knees go weak. What if he told her that returning home had made him realize he belonged with Kenna? Safe or not, Sarah knew she could not stay here if Keir were to choose Kenna.

As though her thoughts had conjured them, Keir came walking toward them from the opposite side of the beach, Kenna beside him, her hand upon his arm, their heads bent toward one another. Words passed between them, and more than anything Sarah wanted to know what was being said. Were they whispering words of love? Reminiscing about the old days? Or was it something simple and far from noteworthy?

"Eoghan said that Kenna and Keir would not make a good match," Kate remarked, disapproval heavy in her voice. "He told me she fancies him, but that Keir has shown no interest in her."

As far as he knows, Sarah thought to herself, wondering if Eoghan could know all that went on between Keir and Kenna. Perhaps there had been secret moments, a kiss shared here and there. Who knew?

All of a sudden, Sarah could not shake the image of Keir kissing Kenna the way he had kissed her, Sarah, and she pictured them sharing the same precious moments. *Am I special to him? Or is it foolish of me to believe so?*

'Why would he want you if he can have another?' Her mother's voice snapped in her head, seizing this moment of weakness. 'Not even a barbarian like that man would want you after what you've done. It is precisely what you deserve.'

Sarah closed her eyes, wishing she could simply disappear into thin air.

Keir was relieved when Bonnie dragged Kenna away, demanding she help them gather seashells, for his thoughts were with Sarah. Again, her face looked overshadowed, and he knew he could not wait any longer to find out what burdened her.

As he moved to approach her, Eoghan stepped into his path, Frederica once more in his arms. "Ye need to speak to her, and ye need to do it right now." His green eyes shone with insistence, his jaw set, the usual humor gone from his face.

Keir paused. "'Tis precisely what I had in mind." Then he frowned. "What do ye know?"

Eoghan scoffed. "'Twould seem that ye're a fool." He shook his head at Keir. "Ye've spent a lot of time with Kenna lately."

Keir shrugged. "She said she... We were only talking and... It doesna mean that—" He stared at his friend as realization slowly dawned on him.

Eoghan's brows rose in challenge. "Is that so?"

"She's like a sister to me. Ye know that."

Eoghan glanced in Sarah's direction. "Does she know?"

Keir exhaled a slow breath, wondering how he could have been so daft. Was it truly possible that Sarah believed him to hold affection for Kenna beyond that of a friend or sister, perhaps? The idea seemed ludicrous, and yet perhaps it only did so from his point of view. "Pardon me," he said to his friend. "I needa speak to Sarah."

Eoghan grinned. "Truer words have never been spoken."

Ignoring his friend's amused chuckle, Keir strode down the beach toward Sarah and Kate. He could see the expression upon Sarah's face waver, something nervous sneaking into her eyes. She almost dropped her gaze, but then she forced her chin back up.

Inwardly, Keir smiled. Indeed, he had been a fool. He had been a fool to wait this long to make it clear to Sarah how he felt about her. Again, foolishly, he had thought she already knew. Of course, certain words had been spoken, and yet he had never told her he loved her, had he?

Smiling at the two sisters, Keir looked at Katherine. "Would ye mind giving us a moment?" he said softly, with a sideways glance at Sarah. "I needa speak to yer sister."

Katherine nodded, something almost wistful in her eyes before she smiled at Sarah and then hurried away toward Eoghan and Frederica.

"What do you wish to talk about?" Sarah inquired, her gaze barely meeting his as she continued down the beach, forcing him to fall into step beside her.

A devilish smile came to Keir's face. "Are ye jealous, lass?"

Instantly, Sarah spun around, her eyes wide and staring as a deep blush stole onto her cheeks.

Keir chuckled, unable to help himself. "Ye're blushing, little wisp," he murmured, savoring the moment, for once again time had stopped, and there was nothing and no one in the world but them. He stepped toward her and took her hands within his own, finding them chilled and trembling.

Bowing her head, Sarah closed her eyes, her teeth sinking into her lower lip.

"Tell me the truth," he urged her gently. "Are ye jealous?"

Forcing her gaze back up, Sarah met his eyes. "Why are you asking me this?"

"Because I want to know. Something has changed between us over the past few days. Ye canna deny it. I dunna care for the way we drifted apart."

Defiance lay in Sarah's gaze. "Well, you seemed rather busy lately," she snapped, a bit of an accusing tone in her voice.

Keir grinned, seeing his suspicion confirmed. "Then ye are jealous."

Glaring at him, Sarah spun around upon her heel and stalked back the way they had come.

Determined to see this settled between them, Keir went after her, quickly catching up. He grasped her arm and pulled her back around, forcing her to face him. "Have I not made it clear that I care for ye?" He held her tightly; his gaze fixed upon hers. "Why would ye think that to have changed?"

Sarah's lips trembled. "Everything feels different here," she whispered, looking deeply vulnerable. "This is your home, your family, your people." She glanced past his shoulder, and he wondered if she was looking at Kenna. "You have a past here. There are people here who—"

"Kenna is family," Keir interrupted, his voice hard and determined, his gaze fixed upon Sarah's, "and I care about her. But I never once looked at her the way I look at ye, little wisp. Do ye hear me? Never."

Chapter Thirty-Two

A BRAVE, LITTLE WISP

Stunned speechless, Sarah stared up at Keir. His words echoed through her head, and she felt that familiar warmth return. Whatever she had expected him to say, it had not been that.

'He's lying!' Her mother's voice growled in her head. 'He only wants what all men want.'

Sarah pinched her eyes shut, willing the voice away. She felt her head shake from side to side, desperate to clear her mind, to cling to this moment and Keir's words.

"Dunna listen to her," Keir's voice urged, and Sarah's eyes flew open. "I dunna know what she's saying, but whatever it is, is not true. Do ye hear me, Sarah?"

Sarah nodded, touched by Keir's insightfulness, and the tension slowly flowed out of her body. She had spoken to him of this before, had told him she sometimes heard her mother's voice whispering to her, urging her to doubt those around her, Keir in particular.

Gently, Keir grasped her chin, his blue eyes compelling as they looked into hers. "Tell me honestly, lass. Are ye jealous?"

As she could not turn her head away, Sarah closed her eyes. "Yes." That one quiet word felt almost deafening to her. "I miss that it is no longer the two of us," she rushed to add, unable to bear the silence, unable to look at him. "Your family is wonderful, and I'm so grateful. Still, I wish I knew if—"

"I missed ye as well, little wisp," Keir interrupted her.

Once again, Sarah's eyes flew open, her heart reaching out and holding on to the promise of his words. She felt his arms close around her and then his right hand reached out, the tips of his fingers brushing along the small braid in her hair.

"Ye still wear them," Keir remarked, his eyes drifting back to hers. "It gave me hope, for I thought ye did so because ye wanted people to know that ye belonged with me."

Sarah felt her heart stumble in her chest. "Do I?" she asked boldly, then quickly added, "I mean, I know your braids are not only for me, but..."

Keir sighed. "Aye, life is difficult sometimes, but for me, nothing has changed." The hand upon her back urged her closer as his other slipped to the back of her head, holding her tightly against him. "I still want more time with ye, lass. I still miss ye when ye leave the room." He lowered his forehead to hers, his warm breath teasing her lips. "I missed ye so much these past few days."

Again, Sarah's heart did that odd little flip that threatened to pull out her legs from under her and send her soaring into the sky at the same time. "I missed you, too."

And then Keir was suddenly kissing her, passion and longing fueling his embrace, and Sarah knew how deeply the distance between them had weighed upon him as well. He kissed her deeply, ardently, as he held her crushed against his chest, her feet almost lifting off the pebbled beach.

When Keir set her back down, they were both out of breath. "I know I asked ye this before, lass," Keir said, still holding her close, his fingers upon her chin. "What do ye want out of life? What do ye dream of?"

Indeed, Keir *had* asked her this question before, and Sarah could not answer it at that point. The truth had been that she had never thought any further than avoiding marriage to a horrible man. She had never had dreams of her own...

... until now.

"What is it that ye want, lass?"

Still, Sarah hesitated, her mother's voice urging her to bow her head. 'A lady ought never be so bold as to reveal her affections. A lady can only ever reciprocate.'

Keir grinned at her, and Sarah could tell that he once more guessed her thoughts. "This is not London," he told her markedly. "If ye want something, ye need to make that clear."

Sarah felt her mouth open and then close before her teeth sank into a lower lip, biting down hard. *Why is it so hard to speak openly?*

"Ye've always been brave, little wisp," Keir reminded her gently. "Dunna cower now. What is it that ye want?"

Emboldened by his words, Sarah lifted her chin another fraction, and her eyes looked directly into his. "I want you," she finally said after all this time, not even caring that a deep flush once more stole onto her cheeks.

The corner of Keir's mouth twitched. "Why?" the scoundrel dared to ask.

"Because I love you," Sarah replied without hesitating, without flinching, without averting her eyes. No, this time, she held his gaze and saw his expression change as her words sank in.

Keir's eyes seemed to glow as he looked down at her, and suddenly Sarah realized that, despite his own confidence, Keir, too, had felt uncertain about their future.

About her.

"I love ye as well, little wisp," he murmured, utter joy upon his face as he pulled her close once more and placed a kiss upon her lips.

In her mind, Sarah heard her mother scoff disparagingly. It made her realize that despite Keir's declaration, Sarah could not quite believe him. After all, what was her mother's voice than a manifestation of her own fears?

Tears streamed down Sarah's face. "You cannot mean it," she whispered, realizing that she would never rid herself of these doubts if she did not give them voice. "Men do not want women like me, not truly, not because—"

Rather forcefully, Keir grasped her chin. "Look at me, Sarah." His gaze drilled into hers, daring her to doubt him. "Forget everything yer mother ever told ye, for no one's opinion matters more than yer own." He sighed, the pad of his thumb gently brushing across her chin. "Are ye not proud of what ye've accomplished lately? Saving not only yerself but also yer sister and yer nieces, taking a stand against Blackmore and Birchwell?"

Deep down, Sarah realized she was proud of herself. Never had she allowed herself to realize it, though, because it went against everything she had been raised to be.

According to the *ton*, she had acted despicably.

According to her own judgment, though, she had been brave.

"Ye're kind and strong and compassionate. Ye're the most impressive woman I've ever met. Tell me, why on earth would I not want ye?"

Keir's face blurred as more tears ran down Sarah's cheeks. "Do you truly mean it? I thought perhaps that you were uncertain because of Kenna. Whenever I saw the two of you together, I..."

Keir shook his head. "I told ye I never cared for Kenna that way, and I meant it." He exhaled slowly. "Perhaps I was a fool for not telling ye sooner, lass. I didna realize ye had such doubts." He grasped her hands, holding them tightly within his own. "The truth is that I was overwhelmed by the way ye swept me off my feet. I never expected to find love so quickly or so completely. I admit, at first, I didna quite know what to do about it." He chuckled rather self-consciously, and in that moment, Sarah's heart fully opened to him, allowing him in, not holding anything back.

"I didna want ye to feel caged by putting another choice to ye so soon after ye gained yer freedom," Keir told her passionately, his warm hands holding hers. "I believed it better to wait, but perhaps I was a fool for thinking so. I need ye to know that ye will always be free to make yer own choices. I will never take that from ye." He inhaled deeply; his blue eyes fixed upon hers. "But the truth is that I love ye and I want ye to stay here with me. Forever."

Sarah flung herself into his arms, sobbing loudly as joy shot through her body, setting every cell aflame. "Yes, I want to stay." She felt Keir's chest tremble with liberating laughter as he clutched her in his arms.

Then Keir pulled back and looked down at her. "Will you marry me, little wisp?"

Sarah felt swept off her feet. "Aye," she breathed, pulling him down to her for a kiss. "Aye, I'll marry you."

Oh, this has to be a dream! But what if it isn't?

Sarah's heart sighed. Perhaps sometimes dreams came true after all.

Chapter Thirty-Three

A WEDDING IS ANNOUNCED

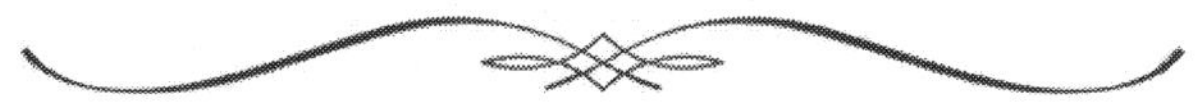

No explanation was needed for Kate to know what had happened between Keir and Sarah. She had almost cringed at the sight of them, her heart aching painfully; and yet she had not been able to avert her eyes. She had seen them speak, seen the way Keir had reached for her sister, the way his fingers had traced the delicate braids upon her temple, had grasped her chin and pulled her close. She had seen them kiss, and she had seen Sarah's face light up with utter joy and happiness.

They are in love. Kate knew that to be true. She had known so for a while. *And they shall be married soon, no doubt.*

Kate knew she ought to be happy for her sister, and yet strange as it was, what she felt was something entirely different. But why? Why did she cringe at the thought of Sarah marrying the man she loved? Indeed, Kate remembered an echo of this feeling from before. She remembered standing at her window at Birchwell, looking out into the gardens and seeing Keir and Sarah together. She also remembered coming upon them one night in the library. Yes, these moments had stayed with her, had touched Kate more than anything else ever had. They had been moments of love and devotion, of tenderness and trust, moments Kate had never known herself.

After all, her own husband had never cared for her, let alone loved her.

Even then, Kate had known herself to be envious of what her sister had found, and yet, here in this moment, standing upon the beach, Kate wondered if perhaps it might be a bit more than simple envy she felt.

One glance in Kenna's direction told Kate that the young Scottish woman felt it as well, the expression of crushing pain and stunned disbelief upon her face echoing Kate's own feelings.

Her heart ached in a new, yet profound way when Sarah and Keir ushered them back into the castle, calling upon the rest of Keir's family. As they all gathered together, Kate saw a questioning gaze here and there. Others, though, only needed a single glance at Keir and Sarah to understand.

"My son must've done something right," Keir's mother whispered to Sarah, a joyous smile upon her face. "Ye look flushed with happiness, lass. It suits ye." She squeezed Sarah's hand, then moved to stand beside her husband, her hand settling within his, their eyes meeting.

"So, what was so important for us all to gather here?" Magnus inquired, his gaze slightly narrowed, as though he, too, had his suspicions.

Duncan laughed his booming laugh. "Do ye truly not know?" He slapped his brother on the shoulder. "Truly Magnus, it doesna do yer mind well to be sitting all day with yer nose stuck in a book."

Keir and Sarah smiled at one another, their hands linked and their eyes aglow. Sarah's face was deeply flushed, and she clung to Keir's arm, as though she felt uncertain about the steadiness of her feet.

Kate felt that yearning deep inside her grow with each moment that passed, and one look at Kenna told her that the young woman felt the same. A scowl rested upon her face as she glared at Sarah, and Eoghan elbowed her gently in the side, a warning look coming to his eyes. *Oh, why can I not be happy for them? No one deserves this more than Sarah!*

Once they all stood gathered in Keir's grandmother's parlor, the happy couple looked at them all with glowing faces. "We called ye here," Keir began, squeezing Sarah's hand, "to share the good news with ye. It mightna come as a surprise to any of ye," his grandmother chuckled loudly, "but we wish to inform ye all that we are to be married." He turned and met Sarah's eyes. "Soon."

Augusta and Dorothea instantly began cheering, overjoyed at the thought of their aunt's wedding. Duncan, too, voiced his joy rather loudly as his father stepped toward Keir and Sarah. He held out one hand to each of them, a wide smile upon his face. "Welcome to the family, Sarah," he said, warmth in his voice. "I've never seen my son happier."

Keir's mother was next to embrace the happy couple, her eyes shining with pride and joy. "I'm glad my son found a strong woman to stand by his side." Briefly, she lifted her gaze to meet her husband's eyes, one of those enchanted smiles upon her face, before she once more turned to Sarah and whispered rather conspiratorially, "The MacKinnear men would be lost without us." Then she embraced Sarah warmly, hugging her close.

Standing beside her sister, Kate could not seem to move, to voice even a single word. She stood as though frozen, listening to the cheerful voices echo around her. Her eyes felt glued to her sister's face, utterly entranced by the joy she saw there, the tears that streamed down her face and the laughter that continued to bubble up, as though Sarah did not quite know how to handle these overwhelming emotions.

After hugs and congratulations, everyone settled near the fireplace. The atmosphere that lingered was one of familial bliss, one of hope and faith. The sun glowed golden outside the windows as it began its descent, orange and violet streaks gracing the darkening sky. An echo of these colors danced inside the hearth. Flames licked at dry wood, and a soft crackling filled the soothing silence.

"We heard Sarah's story the night of the gathering," Keir's grandmother remarked into the hushed stillness, her warm eyes moving around the room before coming to linger upon her grandson. "But we have yet to hear your story." Her gaze moved from Keir to Sarah and back; the smile upon her face one of wistful excitement.

"Aye," Duncan echoed, nodding to his grandmother before turning to Keir. "When did ye see her for the first time?" He wiggled his brows teasingly.

Before either Keir or Sarah could answer, though, a deep frown drew down Magnus's brows. "But they already told us that," he objected, looking from Duncan to his grandmother. "They first met the night he *kidnapped* her from her London home, did they not?"

Again, Duncan rolled his eyes, then slapped his brother's shoulder affectionately. "Dunna be daft, Magnus. I'm not speaking of the first time they saw one another; I'm speaking of the first time they *saw* one another."

Magnus's frown grew more pronounced. "That doesna make any sense." He looked to his parents as though for help, and his grandmother leaned forward, placing a comforting hand upon his shoulder.

Keir chuckled. "I think I know what he means, Magnus." Still holding Sarah's hand within his own, he turned to look into her eyes, and for a moment, Kate felt her own heart paused... waiting for... something. "I first saw her standing in the shadows as I was waiting, seated upon the box of the carriage, uncertain who that young lady was I was supposed to *kidnap*." He wiggled his brows, and Sarah blushed even more. "Yet the first time I truly saw her was when she fainted in the woods."

Roaring laughter filled the parlor, and as Sarah blushed to the very tips of her hair, Keir continued his story. "Apparently, Grandma Edie failed to inform Sarah that part of our journey would be completed upon horseback." He looked at his family. "Ye see, Sarah was... terrified of horses at the time, and when she realized we would be leaving the carriage behind and continuing on without it," he looked at Sarah, and Kate could see the memory of that moment pass between them, "she simply fainted."

"Was she hurt?" Magnus inquired, concern upon his face.

Eoghan laughed, and Kate's gaze shifted to him, her mind briefly distracted by the dazzling green of his eyes. "Nah, I bet he caught her." He grinned at Keir, then winked; and Kate shook her head to clear her thoughts. "Was it not so?"

"Aye," was all Keir said for a long moment, his gaze fixed upon Sarah.

Kate saw smiles on everyone's faces. This was the kind of joy that parents, that family felt when one of their own found profound happiness, and it showed in their eyes, in the way they seemed to glow.

Even the girls were mesmerized. Augusta and Bonnie sat side by side, their little arms slung around one another and their eyes looked almost hypnotized. No doubt, they, too, were caught up in the fairytale of love found in the most unlikely of places and moments. They might not yet know what it was all about, but they could sense the meaningfulness of what was spoken of. Dorothea snuggled into Kate's side, and she shifted Frederica more firmly into her other arm to pull her middle daughter close. Loki and the new puppy Faerie had settled themselves in front of the fire, curled up side by side, despite Loki's attempts to maintain a certain distance. It seemed Faerie's insistence had served him well.

Only Kenna sat a bit farther away, her arms crossed over her chest, and that same scowl still upon her face. Yet beneath the young woman's anger, Kate thought to see a broken heart. Kate was rather surprised that Kenna remained and did not excuse herself as Keir continued his story; after all, it had to be painful for her to listen.

"Sarah wore a cloak that night," Keir recounted in his storyteller voice, "with the hood pulled deep into her face. I only ever caught a faint glimpse of her features as she entered the carriage and later alighted from it once we had reached the woods. She kept her distance," he grinned at her teasingly, "clearly wary of the stranger Grandma Edie had sent to spirit her away."

"Ye didna know who it was she had sent?" Marcus inquired, his brows rising as he looked at Sarah and then back at Keir. "How could ye then know that ye could trust him?"

Sarah shrugged; her face still aflame as she found herself facing Keir's family. "I didn't know," she said a bit helplessly. "However, I did not have a choice. I did not wish to marry Lord Blackmore, and I knew if I did not leave that night, I would have to."

Eoghan nodded approvingly, respect in his gaze. "That was some choice."

"And then?" Duncan prompted with a wide grin.

Sarah once more dipped her head as Keir returned his brother's questioning grin. "As ye so rightly presumed," he said, glancing at Eoghan. "I caught her when she fainted and gently settled her down upon the ground." He looked at Sarah then, and her eyes lingered upon him as well. "Her hood fell back, finally revealing her face, now bathed in the moonlight. She looked almost serene, yet terribly frightened and alone. I felt this overwhelming need to protect her, to see her safe and earn her trust." He sighed deeply, then he reached out and his fingers touched the small braids upon Sarah's temple. "Her hair curled around her face," he murmured, tugging gently upon a loose strand.

"'Tis why ye call her *little wisp*," Magnus concluded, clearly enjoying when things made sense.

Entranced by the way Keir gazed at Sarah, Kate exhaled a deep breath. She had never known love, and now she could not help but think she might be falling in love with her sister's future husband. Why? It was the one question Kate wanted to see answered. After everything she had been through, why did this have to happen now and with him? Everything could be perfect if not...

"When did ye first kiss her?" Duncan inquired; clearly not shy to ask whatever it was he wished to know.

Looking utterly embarrassed, Sarah buried her face in her hands. Yet Kate thought to see laughter shake her delicate frame before she dared to peek up at their small gathering once more.

Keir, though, laughed openly, something wicked in his gaze. "Ah, that I willna tell ye," he said, much to everyone's displeasure. Sarah, though, looked relieved. "That moment shall forever remain ours."

Thus, the evening continued with questions asked and sometimes answered. Everything Keir spoke of sounded like a fairytale, though, the kind Kate and Sarah used to imagine when they had been children. Fairytales of gallant heroes and daring princesses. Fairytales of undying love and magical moments. Those days had been wonderful, and yet as Kate had grown up, she remembered thinking that these fairytales would never exist in real life. No one could find such happiness.

Not ever.

Now, Sarah had.

Chapter Thirty-Four

BETROTHED YET AGAIN

Arm in arm, Keir and Sarah walked down the corridor toward her chamber. He felt pleasantly exhausted after the long evening spent in his family's company. Yet he had enjoyed their teasing as much as the retelling of his time with Sarah. Indeed, he had wanted to share it all with his family, needing them to know how deeply he cared for her, how special she was to him, and how lucky he felt to have found her.

Perhaps the evening had also served in making Kenna realize that Keir's heart belonged to Sarah. He had seen the crestfallen look upon Kenna's face, and it had pained him. He had never meant to hurt her and hoped that she would soon find happiness elsewhere. Still, before they had left his grandmother's parlor, Eoghan had urged him to speak to Kenna and set things right. Keir knew his friend was right, and so he had assured Eoghan that he would do so on the morrow.

As they walked, Sarah's face still shone crimson in the faint light from the torches lining the corridor. It was why Keir had held back from sharing every little detail of their time together with his family, for he knew Sarah would feel deeply embarrassed. Perhaps she was right, though. Perhaps there were some moments that they simply ought to keep to themselves.

"Do ye regret the first time we kissed?" Keir asked lightly, elaborating when he saw her eyes grow around. "Not *that* we kissed. Simply the way it happened."

Understanding came to Sarah's gaze. "No, I do not. I don't regret the kiss or how it happened." She bit her lip shyly. "What I regret is that I lied to you and that you revealed my lie through a kiss. I'm still sorry I ate both tarts."

Keir chuckled. "I am not. As I told ye before, it gave me an excuse to kiss ye." He stopped and tugged her closer, one hand grasping her chin, ensuring that her eyes would not stray from his. "I knew ye had eaten the tarts the moment I stepped back into the parlor. I didna need the kiss to tell me that."

Sarah blinked. "Then why did you—?"

"Because I wanted to kiss ye." Keir held her gaze as he had done all those weeks ago and then slowly lowered his head, brushing his mouth against hers. "I knew I shouldna, but I couldna stop myself."

Sarah's breathing quickened. "Why shouldn't you have?" she asked as her arms snaked around his neck, and she pulled herself closer.

Keir slid his hands over her back down to her waist. "Because I was to protect ye, lass, and I needed to keep a clear head to see ye safe. Yet the more I thought about ye, the more my thoughts became consumed by ye." He nipped her lower lip. "Ye were all I could think about. Kissing ye was all I could think about, and then, there we were in that little parlor with ye barely an arm's length away..." He exhaled a slow breath, once again feeling this overwhelming need to feel Sarah in his arms. "We shouldna—"

Footsteps echoed to their ears, and Sarah surged out of his embrace, old instincts taking over. Her expression was one of alarm, but then quickly changed, the heat of embarrassment coloring her cheeks. "I'm sorry. It's simply..."

Keir nodded and grasped her hand, pulling her onward. Within moments, they made it down the corridor toward Sarah's chamber and quickly slipped inside, closing the door firmly behind them. Then he spun her around, walking her back against the sturdy wood of the door, and kissed her the way he had not done in far too long.

And Sarah kissed him back, her hands in his hair and her lips as eager as his own. In his arms, she had never been shy. Not after that first kiss in the cabin in the woods.

Keir held her close, his hands trailing up and down her arms. He traced his fingers up the slender column of her neck, gently cupping her face. She felt almost tiny in his arms, delicate and breakable, her head tilted back as he kissed her. "Are ye all right, lass?" Keir murmured against her lips, unwilling to step back. Still, he needed to see her eyes.

"I am," Sarah responded, her breath coming fast as her hands rose to touch his face, as though wanting to pull him back down to her and resume what they had started. "I'm perfectly fine." She smiled at him then, and Keir could feel it in every cell of his body.

"Good," he murmured and kissed her again, rejoicing in the way Sarah's hands slipped into his hair. His hands settled upon her waist and then lifted her off the ground, holding her between the door and his body, her feet dangling in the air.

Now, they were eye to eye.

Sarah smiled against his lips. "How can you hold me up like this?" she murmured, her mouth brushing against his.

Keir met her eyes, delighting in the slight twitch of her lips. "Ye weigh next to nothing, lass."

"Dorothea weighed next to nothing when I carried her up the stairs at the inn," Sarah retorted with a questioning gaze that made Keir smile. "And my arms still felt as though they might fall off after only a few steps."

Keir chuckled, then slowly set her back onto her feet. "If ye dunna like it when I pick ye up, all ye have to do is say so." With one hand upon her shoulder, he held her gaze. "Ye know that, lass, do ye not?"

A somewhat puzzled expression came to Sarah's face. "Are you worried that I… I will not say it if there is something I… do not want?" Her gaze fell from his for a second.

Keir remained where he was, his own gaze not wavering. "Aye, sometimes I worry that ye might feel compelled to do as ye were taught, lass." He grasped her chin, needing the feel of her skin against his. "I dunna want ye to bow yer head ever again. Not to anyone, ye hear me, little wisp? Ye have a voice, and I want ye to use it whenever ye see fit."

Tears stood in Sarah's eyes, and Keir knew that as confident as Sarah had grown over the course of the past months, there was a part of her that still doubted her own worth, as though no one could truly care for her if she did not fulfill the role that had been intended for her. "I promise," she vowed, her breath shuddering past her lips.

Keir smiled, giving her chin an affectionate pinch. "How do ye feel about finding yerself betrothed yet again?" he asked lightly, not wishing to conjure dark memories. Yet he had to know if she felt any apprehension. "Is there anything that worries ye?"

To Keir's relief, the look upon Sarah's face was not one of relived pain. "I don't simply *find* myself betrothed," she told him, her voice determined and a fierce look in her eyes. "You're *my* choice," she told him boldly, her eyes lighting up in a deeply compelling way. "I want you, and I am not afraid. I know you would never hurt me. This," she stepped closer, her right hand reaching up to cup his cheek, "is what it's supposed to feel like."

Keir wrapped his arms around her once more, savoring the feel of her hand upon his cheek. "I'm relieved to hear it, lass, but I needed to be certain."

"I know," Sarah murmured before a slow smile curled up the corners of her mouth. "I never thought I'd ever be married." Her voice was only a whisper, a faraway look suddenly in her eyes. "After all, escaping marriage was the only thought on my mind for so long." She smiled at him then, before her expression changed once more.

"What is it, little wisp?" *Aye, something weighs on her.*

Sarah heaved a deep sigh. "When Frederica was born, I suddenly realized that I would never be a mother." She shook her head. "Before, I only ever thought about protecting myself from my parents' scheming, and never once about missing out on motherhood." Sadness and regret rested in her eyes. "It was only then that I realized what I had lost in gaining my freedom." She blinked back tears, and yet before Keir could say a word, her eyes found his and she said, "Before I met you, I was so certain I could live without love." Keir could see that there was more she wished to say; her lips, though, remained sealed.

"Do ye wish for children?" Keir asked, taking both her hands within his own.

Sarah nodded, and a lone tear rolled down her cheek. "I do," she whispered, a question in her gaze.

Keir smiled at her, gently wiping away her tear. "Ye'll be a wonderful mother, lass. I have no doubt."

The joy that came to Sarah's face nearly brought Keir to his knees. "And what of you? Do you wish for children?"

Keir sighed. "Truthfully, like ye, I never thought much about being a father. Though, lately, I found joy in spending time with the girls, watching them discover the world, holding their hands and sharing their joy." He nodded to Sarah. "Aye, I do."

Utter disbelief now glowed in Sarah's eyes as she gazed up at him. "We'll have it all, won't we?" she whispered, awe in her voice. "I never expected any of this. I never expected to... find you." Her hand reached out to touch his cheek before it settled upon his chest, right above his thundering heart. "I never..." Tears clung to her lashes. "All of my childhood dreams are coming true." She laughed disbelievingly. "Is this real? Would you pinch me?"

"I have a better idea," Keir murmured before he leaned in and, without warning, kissed her soundly. "Does this feel real?" he asked against her lips, their breaths mingling.

"Aye," Sarah replied, pushing herself up onto her toes, her hands eager as they reached for him. "But kiss me again... just to be certain."

Keir chuckled, happy to comply.

Chapter Thirty-Five

TRUTH BE TOLD

Upon waking the next morning, Sarah felt almost deliriously happy. Not only because of the events of the previous night. More than even in her engagement, Sarah found bliss in opening her eyes and finding Keir lying beside her, a teasing smile upon his lips.

The night before, she had been most reluctant to bid him good-night, and so Sarah had asked him to stay. Yes, her cheeks had been aflame, and her mother's voice had offered countless objections, adding insults when Sarah had remained steadfast in her request.

Yet Sarah had persisted.

As they had sat with Keir's family the night before and Sarah had listened to Keir telling their story, she had become overwhelmed by the memory of the night they had slept in each other's arms. "Would you stay?" she had asked him when he had turned to go. "Would you hold me again as you did that night in the woods?"

And Keir had.

Still wrapped in each other's arms, Sarah gazed into Keir's eyes as the sun streamed in through the windows, giving the chamber a golden glow. "You're still here," she murmured, unable to hide a smile.

Keir chuckled. "Aye, I am." Then his brows furrowed, and yet Sarah could see the wicked gleam that lay in his blue eyes. "Have ye already grown tired of me, lass?"

"Never," Sarah told him earnestly, inching closer for another kiss when the sound of little feet suddenly sounded from the corridor, quickly followed by a most insistent knocking upon her door.

"'Twould seem our moment of bliss is over," Keir remarked, sliding out of bed and pulling his boots back on. Then he shrugged back into his coat and moved to open the door.

"Wait!" Sarah called out quietly, suddenly feeling mortified. "Should we—? What will they—?"

Keir grinned at her wickedly. "Do ye want me to hide under the bed?" He wiggled his brows teasingly.

Sarah buried her face in her hands. "No, of course not. I'm sorry."

"We did nothing wrong," Keir told her reassuringly as he walked over, his warm hands settling upon her trembling shoulders. "Look at me, lass."

Sarah lifted her gaze. "I know you're right."

"Do ye?" He raised one eyebrow.

Sarah nodded. *Yes, he's right! I will not cower.* Then she reached up to grasp his face, planted a kiss upon his mouth, and moved toward the door with confident steps. "Good morning," she greeted her nieces, a smile upon her face despite the slight trembling in her hands. "Is there anything I can do for you?"

The moment the girls spied Keir their jaws dropped. "A lady is not supposed to meet a gentleman without a chaperone," Thea mumbled, her words an echo of her governess's instructions. Still, the conviction Sarah had heard in her voice before when Thea had shared what she had been taught had lessened, as though the girl suddenly doubted the truth of what she had learned.

"Sarah, would you—?"

Sarah cringed when she saw her sister's face fall the moment Kate beheld Keir. With Frederica clutched in her arms, she stood in the corridor, staring at Keir, her face paling.

Sarah felt deeply unsettled by her sister's reaction. Yet she knew it had become second nature to Kate to judge according to society's standards. After all, Sarah, too, still felt the need to do as she had been taught. Was that not why she had reacted with sudden panic the moment the knock had come upon her door?

"Good morning," Keir exclaimed, striding forward and coming to stand beside Sarah at the door. He smiled at her nieces and her sister, his right hand coming to settle in the small of her back. It was warm and reassuring, and Sarah smiled up at him.

Kate cleared her throat, looking a bit flustered. Sarah hoped that with time, her sister would find herself set free of these old restrictions and once again become the woman she had once been. "I... I simply wish to ask," Kate began, her gaze flickering back and forth between Sarah and Keir, never quite daring to linger. "What I mean to say is that the girls wish to see Bonnie." Her gaze drifted to Keir and then quickly returned to Sarah. "Would you know where to find her?" The moment the last word left her lips, Kate all but bowed her head, not daring to look up again.

Sarah frowned, confused to see her sister so upset. Perhaps, though, there was no reason to be. Perhaps all Kate needed was a bit more time.

"I'll take them," Keir interjected, grasping Sarah's hand and giving it an affectionate squeeze. Then he stepped past her, and Kate instantly retreated toward the other side of the corridor. "Dunna worry. I shall see them safely to Eoghan's house." He smiled at Kate and then turned to the girls. "Have ye had breakfast? Or should we stop by the kitchen?"

Augusta's and Dorothea's faces lit up, and they nodded eagerly.

Keir grinned at them. "Well, then lead the way." As the girl dashed away, Keir placed a gentle kiss upon Sarah's cheek. "I'll see ye later." Then he nodded to Kate and hurried after the girls down the corridor.

Looking after Keir, Sarah felt deliriously happy. This was precisely what she had always dreamed of. This ease. This natural closeness. To look into Keir's eyes and know precisely what he saw when he looked at her. To know his heart. To have faith in him and in them together. Indeed, all her dreams seemed to come true.

"Will you go for a walk with me?" Sarah asked Kate, feeling the sudden need to move, to explore the castle and its grounds. "It seems to be a beautiful day."

The distracted look upon Kate's face vanished as she seemed to force a smile. Then she nodded, settling Frederica more comfortably in her arm. "Yes, I… I suppose that would be nice."

As Kate turned to go, Sarah reached out and grasped her arm. "Are you all right?" She stepped closer, seeking her sister's eyes. "You seem… unsettled somehow. Did something happen?"

Again, that forced smile appeared on Kate's face. "No, I'm perfectly fine. Don't worry." Then she strode away quickly, as though wishing to outrun Sarah.

Concerned, Sarah hurried after her sister, wondering what had happened. She knew Kate had been worried from the start that Keir's people would not accept her. Strangely enough, Sarah had felt quite the same way. Now, though, she knew better, and with time, perhaps that feeling deep down that still had doubts—irrational as they were!—would change and turn into something wonderful. Perhaps it was no more than that that also plagued Kate.

The sun shone brightly overhead as they stepped out into the courtyard. People were bustling everywhere. Everyone seemed to be busy tending to one task or another. Still, many looked up from whatever they were doing and turned in their direction. Sarah felt herself tense, an old instinct taking over. Then, however, she realized people were smiling at her, nodding their heads in greeting. Some even called out to her, joy upon their faces, their words clearly suggesting that the news of her betrothal to Keir had already spread through the clan.

"Never thought he'd ever find a lass special enough."

"Ye stole his heart. Finally!"

"'Tis right there in his eyes."

Sarah felt warmed by their words, the smile upon her own face no longer strained. Yet when she looked at her sister, Sarah paused. "Kate, please, you're clearly not all right. What is the matter?"

Kate merely shrugged. "It is nothing. I'm simply… cold. We should've brought our coats." A slight shiver shook her before she turned away and headed back inside.

Sarah could not deny her sister's reasoning. It was cold this early in the year, and not even the sun managed to warm her sufficiently. Still,

Sarah knew that there was something else on Kate's mind, something that upset her deeply. If only she knew what that was.

Suddenly very aware of the cold, Sarah followed her sister's footsteps, returning inside the castle. She stepped into the great hall and was just about to approach the stairs when someone called out to her. She turned and found Keir's mother moving toward her, a wide smile upon her face and her gentle eyes warm and welcoming.

Sarah instantly felt better.

"Do ye have a moment, my dear?" Heather inquired, looping her arm through Sarah's and pulling her along. "As ye are to be my son's wife, I believe we should spend a little more time together. Would ye mind?"

Sarah shook her head. Still, a chill chased down her back at the thought of being weighed and measured. What if Keir's mother found her wanting?

Up the stairs they went and then down a long corridor. For a moment, Sarah was confused where they were headed. Then, however, she remembered this part of the castle from the night before. Shrouded in darkness with only torches to light their way, it had looked different somehow.

A moment later, they stepped into Keir's grandmother's salon, where a warming fire burned in the grate. Its flickering flames danced softly, their orange glow mingling with the golden rays of the sun streaming in through the windows. Not unlike Grandma Edie, Keir's grandmother was settled in an upholstered armchair, a blanket upon her lap. In that moment, Sarah wished she could see the two women side by side.

"Ah, good morning, Dearest," Keir's grandmother exclaimed, gesturing toward one of the chairs opposite her. "Do sit down. Heather, do you mind tending to the tea?"

Keir's mother smiled at Sarah, then released her arm and moved over to the tea cart. "Dunna be nervous," she told Sarah with a look over her shoulder. "We have no intention of devouring ye. We simply wish to talk and get to know ye a little better."

Sarah exhaled a deep breath as she settled herself across from Keir's grandmother, still uncertain where to look and what to say.

"Tell me, Dearest," Keir's grandmother inquired, leaning forward in her chair as she gazed at Sarah curiously, "did you ever learn Edie's true reason for calling Keir to England?"

Sarah frowned. "True reason?"

Handing Sarah a cup of tea, Heather settled down beside her, amusement twinkling in her eyes as she looked at her mother-in-law and then back at Sarah. "Aye, we canna help but wonder after all the stories Addie told us."

Still confused, Sarah looked from one woman to the other. "I'm afraid I do not know what you speak of."

Adele chuckled. "Are you not aware of my dear old friend's reputation for being the most... what shall we call it?... persistent matchmaker in known history?"

Adele and Heather laughed, exchanging another one of those glances. "Truth be told," Adele went on, the shrewd look in her eyes reminding Sarah of Grandma Edie, "I suspected something the moment I received her letter."

Sarah stilled when a sudden memory returned to her. Not long before leaving for her sister's estate, she had sat in her chamber with Christina, her oldest friend and one of Grandma Edie's granddaughters. At the time, Sarah had been distracted by the thought of having to bid Keir farewell for good. Yet remembering that moment now, she recalled Christina mentioning something. "My friend," Sarah began tentatively, "told me that, at first, they believed Grandma Edie had called Keir to England because she sought to match him with Juliet, one of her granddaughters."

Adele and Heather both nodded along to Sarah's words, then paused and looked at one another, the smiles upon their faces spreading wider. "Clearly, though, that was not the case, was it?" Adele inquired with a chuckle.

Sarah shook her head.

"Did she say anything else?" Heather asked, setting down her teacup. "Any other suspicions?"

As much as Sarah willed it not to happen, she could feel heat creep into her face. She instantly dropped her gaze, unable to meet the other two women's eyes. "Well, Christina said that after that initial suspicion did not prove true, she got the impression that perhaps Grandma Edie had called Keir to England to..." Mortification now burned in Sarah's cheeks, and once more, she felt like sinking into a hole in the ground.

A warm chuckle drifted to her ears a moment before Heather's hand settled upon hers, squeezing it gently. "There's no need to be embarrassed, dear. 'Tis a wonderful story; one we will no doubt tell for generations."

Sarah looked up and met her future mother-in-law's gaze. What she saw there eased the tension in her shoulders and cooled the heat in her cheeks.

Adele nodded. "Quite true. Quite true. What else is life than a good story? And Edie always knew how to make them happen." She grinned at Sarah. "Why do you think I instantly sent Keir to her? I knew she would find him the best match possible." With a satisfied smile, she leaned back in her chair. "And she did."

Sarah felt deeply warmed by Adele's words, and yet she had to speak her mind. "How do you know?" Sarah wanted to be accepted and welcomed by these people; still, she wanted their respect to be real, based on something genuine. "We've only just met. You don't... even know me." A little apprehensively, her gaze drifted back and forth between Adele and Heather, and she felt relieved not to see their smiles waver.

"What you say is true," Adele said, in agreement. "I may not know you." Again, she leaned forward and met Sarah's eyes. "Yet I know my grandson. He's always been a good man, but when I look at him now, I see that you've made him an even better one." Her brown eyes shone with warmth and affection. "That is all I need to know to be absolutely certain that you are the woman meant to be by his side." She patted Sarah's hand affectionately. "Everything else will come later. There'll be plenty of time for us to get to know one another, dearest."

Air rushed from Sarah's lungs, accompanied by an odd chuckle that spoke of nervousness and disbelief alike. Indeed, Keir's grandmother did remind her of Grandma Edie. Both were deeply affectionate people, honest and direct in their demeanor. And despite the distance between them, Sarah was no longer surprised that their friendship had survived to this day.

A wistful expression came to Adele's eyes as she settled more comfortably in her chair, pulling up her blanket. "Oh, knowing what I know today, I would not hesitate to trust Edie with my life… but even more so with my heart." She smiled deeply, a faraway look coming to her eyes, and Sarah suspected she was reliving those moments long ago when she had found her own perfect match. "I wish I could see her again," Adele murmured, a glimmer of tears coming to her eyes. "It's been an awfully long time."

Sarah felt a heavy lump settle in her throat at the depth of friendship between Grandma Edie and her old friend, and she wondered if perhaps one day she would find herself in the same position, wishing to see Christina one last time. Would that happen? Now that she was to marry Keir and remain in Scotland, it seemed likely.

Before more could be said, a knock sounded upon the door, and Sarah saw Keir's grandmother blink away the tears that had come to her eyes. "Not a moment of peace one can find in this castle," she grumbled under her breath. Still, amusement made her smile before she called for the visitor to enter.

Sarah turned her head and saw three young men step into Lady Adele's parlor. Two of them she knew to be of Keir's family, while the other looked unfamiliar to her.

"Good day, Grandmother, Mother," Keir's brother Magnus exclaimed as he strode forward, running a hand through his brown curls. "I apologize for interrupting upon yer morning." He glanced back at his cousin Hamish, then waved the other young man forward.

Sarah watched as Lady Adele's gaze narrowed in surprise, a warm smile gracing her features. "Finnigan MacDrummond," she exclaimed, a shrewd expression coming to her eyes. "Back so soon? Why is it, dear boy, that you cannot seem to stay with your own clan?" She cocked her head, eyeing him curiously. "This is about a lass, is it not?"

The young man's jaw tensed instantly, his green eyes overshadowed with pain and an almost desperate longing. It echoed within Sarah's heart, and looking at him now, she was almost certain that he was in love and unhappily so.

"Do not fret, Mr. MacDrummond," Lady Adele chided him kindly.

"Of course, you are always welcome here." She smiled at her grandson. "Magnus, please try to cheer him up."

Magnus grinned at his rather uncomfortable-looking friend, then nodded to his grandmother. "I shall do my best, Grandmother." A moment later, the three men left, and the door closed behind them.

"Love is not always simple," Heather remarked knowingly, another one of those looks passing between mother-in-law and daughter-in-law that gave Sarah felt a moment of envy, hoping that one day she would be just as close with them.

Lady Adele nodded. "Aye, Edie is right to aid it as she does, and no one will ever convince me otherwise." Her gaze moved to Sarah. "You're here, lass, because you were meant to be here. I have no doubt. You're one of us now." A sudden grin overtook her face, something wicked lurking in her eyes. "May Heaven help you."

The two women laughed, and even Sarah felt laughter bubbling up in her throat. Indeed, she wanted them to be right. She wanted to belong here. What if she had not agreed to Grandma Edie's ludicrous kidnapping scheme?

It was a thought that frightened Sarah, and so she refused to dwell upon it.

Chapter Thirty-Six

HEART TO HEART

Having a word with Kenna proved to be far from simple. After taking the girls to Eoghan and Bonnie, Keir searched most of the castle, and yet caught not even a glimpse of her. Oddly enough, he felt reminded of their childhood when she had hidden from him whenever he had upset her. Still, whether or not Kenna liked it, he needed to clear the air between them.

Crossing the courtyard, Keir came upon Magnus and Hamish, once again accompanied by Finn MacDrummond. Keir grinned. "I heard ye only just left?" he teased, wondering about the tight expression upon the young man's face. "If I didna know yer name, I'd pick ye for a MacKinnear."

Magnus and Hamish laughed good-naturedly, and Hamish clasped a friendly hand upon Finn's shoulder. "Dunna mind him," he said, winking at Keir. "He only just now became betrothed and has been in a devilishly good mood ever since."

Keir laughed; still, he did not miss the look of intrigue that came to Finn's eyes, as though he wished to ask a question but did not dare.

"Let me ask ye, Finn," he addressed the young man, seeking to distract him, "did ye see or hear anything odd on yer way to the coast?"

He looked to his brother and cousin. "Did ye tell him?" The two of them nodded.

Relief reflected in Finn's eyes, and he eagerly turned to Keir's question. "Aye, they said that there are currently two English ladies at the castle." He paused for a moment, thinking, then shook his head. "I canna say that I saw anything suspicious; however, I went across country and didna stay at an inn."

Keir nodded, wishing that there was no need for suspicion at all. More than anything, he simply wanted to be happy here with Sarah.

"If ye wish," Finn offered, "I'll send word to my friend Cormag and ask him to keep an eye out."

Keir nodded, grateful. Cormag MacDrummond was the current clan chief's son, a rather serious young man, but with good instincts and a watchful eye. "I thank ye."

As the three young men headed toward the stable, Keir, too, saddled Scout and made his way down to the village and the harbor. The gelding was eager to move, tossing his head and stretching his legs, clearly wishing for a longer ride across country. "Soon," Keir told him, patting his neck as he dismounted and then tied the prancing horse to a pole near the docks.

Duncan stood on deck of one of their larger ships, overseeing repairs. "I didna expect to see ye today," he remarked with an insinuating grin. "Where is yer betrothed?"

Keir shook his head at his brother, deciding that it was best to ignore him completely. "I wish to send letters to our neighboring clans, asking our allies for help."

At Keir's words, the smile upon Duncan's face vanished. "I thought about it myself." He nodded. "Perhaps 'tis wise to ask for their help. After all, these are times of peace, are they not?"

Keir exhaled a deep breath, casting a frowning look at the horizon where dark clouds gathered. "It seems a storm is coming."

A noncommittal grunt escaped Duncan's throat. "If ye have Father write the letters, I shall deliver them."

"Thank ye." Keir grasped his brother's shoulder. "Let me know the moment ye hear anything."

Duncan nodded, and Keir hurried back to the castle, quickly

discussing their plan with his father before hurrying back to the harbor. The sky had grown even darker, the bright sunshine from this morning gone, as Keir handed Duncan the letters. "Is it safe to sail now?"

Duncan grinned. "If ye know what ye're doing."

Shaking his head at his brother, Keir held his gaze. "Take care of yerself, Brother. I expect to see ye back here tonight."

Duncan nodded, and Keir walked down the gangplank, lifting his hand in farewell as Duncan ordered the ship to be readied. Mounting Scout, Keir returned to the castle. There, he brushed down the snorting gelding, hoping that all their precautions would prove unnecessary.

As he crossed the courtyard, Keir's gaze traveled upward, coming to rest upon the windows to the library, and suddenly, he remembered Kenna's favorite hiding place.

Far in the back of the vaulted room, there was an alcove, half-hidden behind tall shelves. As a wee lass, she had often crawled in there, her lips pouting and her face streaked with tears whenever Eoghan, Duncan, and Keir had refused to let her join their games.

Although she might not fit in there anymore, Keir decided to try his luck. He did not wish to put off their conversation any longer, wanting peace of mind for his future with Sarah. And, of course, he did not wish to see Kenna upset, praying that he would find the right words to see them made friends once more.

A hushed silence hung over the library as Keir stepped inside. A fire burned in the grate, and yet its dancing orange flames did not break through the gloom of the day and illuminate much of the interior. Most of the room lay in shadows, and Keir moved slowly through the rows of shelves, peeking around each one, straining his eyes to see if anyone might be nearby.

At first, he found nothing, no sign that anyone had been here recently. Then, however, his ears picked up the soft sound of someone breathing nearby. His steps quickened, and he rounded another shelf, now remembering where precisely the alcove was. Indeed, he had not been here in a long time.

"Kenna?"

At his call, there was a pause before the sounds of breathing continued. He heard the rustling of fabric and then the soft fall of footsteps approaching.

"What do ye want?" Kenna demanded; her arms crossed over her chest as she stepped toward him. "I wish to be alone."

Keir heaved a deep sigh, raking a hand through his hair. "Do ye not think we need to talk, lass?"

Kenna stared at him, tears shimmering in her eyes even in the half dark. "What is there to talk about? Ye are betrothed! Betrothed!" She shook her head, then suddenly shot toward him, accusation burning in her eyes. "How could ye? How could ye do this to me?"

Caught off guard by the vehemence of her emotions, Keir was at a loss. "I thought we were friends," he began tentatively, not wishing to upset her more. "Was I mistaken?"

Kenna inhaled a slow breath, her chest rising and falling slowly, her eyes fixed upon his face. "I thought we were more than friends," she retorted, her voice sharp. "Ye almost kissed me that night."

Keir sighed, remembering the night she spoke of. Only in his memory, there had been nothing romantic about it.

Clearly, Kenna disagreed. *Eoghan was right. I oughta have spoken to her sooner.*

It had been the night of the spring festival when the air had grown warmer again, bringing forth blossoms and shades of green otherwise lost to winter. There had been music and dancing, banquet tables set in the great hall laden with food, a feast worthy for kings. As custom had it, many young men and women alike adorned themselves with an early bloomer, such as a bluebell. While women tied them into their hair, men often fixed them with a brooch onto their plaids. It signaled not only the beginning of a new season but also represented a willing sign for another age-old tradition similar to that of the mistletoe.

"Ye know that 'twas only because of the old tradition, lass, do ye not?" Keir reminded her, remembering how Kenna had suddenly stood before him, pointing to the small flower attached to his brooch. Only Keir had had no notion how it had gotten there.

"I dunna believe ye," Kenna snapped, and then she suddenly stood right in front of him just as she had that night. "I could see it in yer eyes. Ye wanted to kiss me. But then ye were called away and..." She swallowed hard, her lips pressing together tightly. "If yer grandmother hadna sent for ye, ye would have kissed me."

Keir nodded. "Aye, I would have," he admitted, concerned by the look of triumph that came to her face. "But," he rushed to say before she could draw the wrong conclusion, "that woulda been it. Only a kiss, nothing more."

Stunned, Kenna stumbled a step backward, staring at him.

"We're friends, Kenna," Keir told her, needing her to understand. "I love ye as I love yer brother. Nothing more would've ever happened between us."

Pain stood in Kenna's eyes, and Keir made to reach for her, wanting to offer comfort. Yet before he could, she snapped, "I dunna believe ye. Ye're only saying that now because she bewitched ye." Seeking his gaze, Kenna stepped toward him, her hands settling upon his upper arms. "Had ye kissed me that night, ye would've known."

Slowly, Keir shook his head. "I would've known us to be friends, Kenna. Nothing more."

As anger sparked in her eyes, her fingers dug into his arms. "No, 'tis not true! Kiss me now, and ye'll see." Suddenly reaching for him, Kenna pushed herself up onto her toes, her lips seeking his.

"No." Keir turned his head, his hands finding her arms, urging her back. He met her eyes then, shaking his head. "No, Kenna." He sighed, seeing tears collect in her eyes. "It pains me to see ye like this, and I wish I could—"

"Are ye afraid to be proven wrong?" Kenna demanded, once more inching closer, her chin raised and her gaze straying to his mouth as she spoke. "Are ye afraid of what a kiss would prove to ye?"

Keir stepped back, holding her at bay. "I need no proof." He paused, his hands still holding her wrists, his eyes imploring as they looked into hers. "Hear me, Kenna." He waited as she drew in a slow breath. "My heart belongs to Sarah. I love her, and that will never change."

Her lower lip trembled, and yet she continued to glare at him.

"Yer time will come," Keir counseled gently. "Believe me. One day, ye'll find love, and it'll knock ye off yer feet. There willna be a single doubt in yer mind that ye're meant to be with that person."

Fresh tears gathered in the corners of Kenna's eyes. "But I want ye." Her eyes closed, and the tears that had lingered spilled over and ran down her cheeks. "I've always wanted ye." She raised her eyes to his once more. "How could ye not have known?"

Keir hung his head. He felt awful for doing this to her. Truly, how could he not have seen how deep her affections for him were? Yet he had not. "Why?"

Kenna frowned. "Why what?"

"Why do ye want *me*?"

For a moment, Kenna simply stood before him, the picture of misery, her mouth opening and closing, as though, for the first time that night, she did not know what to say. "Because... Because I love ye."

Smiling at her, Keir slowly shook his head. "I dunna think ye do," he murmured, thinking of Sarah and how she had spoken to him of how he made her feel. She had been so expressive, words flowing from her lips with no need for thought. "Perhaps ye love the idea of us. Nothing more." He looked into her eyes. "Ye know that there's never been more than friendship between us, and so I beg of ye, do not cling to this or ye'll not notice when love finally does show its face."

As much as Keir had hoped that Kenna would heed his words, the look upon her face became defiant. "Dunna treat me like a child! I know what I feel, and I know what I want. Perhaps ye are the one who is confused." She glared up at him, her hands balling into fists. "Ye left, and then months later ye return with a woman ye barely know." She shook her head at him, holding up her hands as he tried to console her. "No, I dunna want to hear anymore." Tears still clung to her lashes. "Leave me alone." Then she dashed past him, the sound of her footsteps swallowed up by the heavy rugs upon the stone floor.

Keir heaved a deep sigh, raking his hand through his hair once more. If only Grandma Edie were here, he mused. No doubt, she would have Kenna fixed up with her true love in a matter of days.

At the thought, Keir chuckled.

If only.

Chapter Thirty-Seven

A KINDRED SPIRIT

Standing by the window, Kate gazed out at the starry night. The wind howled around the castle towers, and she could make out the soft pelting of rain upon the windowpane. Yet the shimmer of the moon above the harbor cast everything in a beautiful light. It seemed surreal and sort of magical, as though this was a night where anything was possible, where the border between wishing and existing became blurred.

With a smile upon her face, Kate moved closer to the bed where her eldest daughters slept peacefully, their eyes closed and their faces relaxed in slumber. Nearby stood Frederica's crib, her little fists raised as though she were prepared to fight some sort of nightmarish creature. In the next moment, though, an almost angelic smile flitted across her little face, and Kate exhaled the breath that had briefly lodged in her throat.

Indeed, she could not remember the last time she had seen her children like this. The world they had been born into had been harsh and treated them ill, forcing them away from their mother at such a tender age. Kate still felt guilt well up in her heart whenever she thought about it, knowing she ought to have interfered, knowing she ought never to have allowed that to happen. And yet she had. To her great shame, she had. *Yet what could I have done? I did the best I could, or didn't I?*

Another deep breath raised her chest, then she let it fall softly. It felt good simply to breathe in the night, her thoughts now free of a mother's duty, able to stray back to moments of the day and truly savor them.

Never would she forget the eager look upon her daughters' faces, seated in Lady Adele's parlor with Bonnie and other children from the village. To Kate's surprise, Keir's grandmother had taken it upon herself to teach the children of her clan Latin and Greek. As a duke's daughter, she had received a formal education and now sought to pass that knowledge on to the next generation.

Only Lady Adele did not go about teaching dry subjects, such as Latin to the children, in the usual manner that Kate and Sarah knew from their own childhood. Never had their tutors made them laugh or even attempted to do so. Everything had always been strict and serious, for, clearly, the *ton* believed that learning had to be grueling and painful in order to be effective.

Lady Adele, though, proved them wrong.

Instead of boring old texts, she made up almost nonsensical sentences devised as riddles and encouraged the children to decode the message.

Even now, a smile came to Kate's face as she remembered standing in the doorway earlier today. She had watched the boys and girls as they flitted through the room, sticking their heads together and discussing how they would best go about solving this riddle. They fetched books to aid them, took notes, and in the end all came together to exchange their ideas.

The chamber had been filled with their voices, their laughter, their excitement, and in the end, they had done it.

They had succeeded.

"This is a wonderful place," Kate whispered to the night, to her sleeping children. "Had I been allowed to grow up in such a place..." She left the thought unfinished, knowing that it would do her no good. Still, it lingered.

And Kate felt a shadow pass over her. After all, they had been through, why did this have to happen?

Turning back to the window, Kate hung her head, a desperate ache growing in her heart. This place was the perfect place for her children, and they deserved it more than anyone. They deserved to be happy and carefree and see each day as an adventure, never knowing the cold censure and disparaging comments life could hold. Indeed, this was it. This was where they were meant to be.

And yet...

Try as she might, Kate could not seem to banish the sight of Keir and Sarah together, of their embrace on the beach, of their joyous proclamation of marriage, of the way Keir had stood in Sarah's bedchamber earlier this morning. She knew her thoughts to be wrong, traitorous even. Yet she could not rid herself of them. She could only bury them, keep them to herself. But if she did, what sort of life did that mean for her?

'You're married,' her mother's voice snapped in her head, and Kate flinched. 'How despicable of you! You are a disgrace!'

Kate hung her head, knowing her mother's words to be true. After all, within a matter of weeks, Kate had committed numerous affronts, betrayed her husband and stolen away his children, robbing him of any chance for an heir. And now? Now, she had lost her heart to...

Burying her face in her hands, Kate sank down onto the edge of the bed. Tears stung her eyes, and her heart felt so heavy, all she wanted was to curl up into a tight ball and weep.

As though Frederica could sense her mother's turmoil, a slight whimper fell from her lips, her little fists once more waving through the air.

Grateful for this distraction, Kate rose to her feet and picked up her youngest daughter, settling her comfortably into her arms, softly cooing under her breath. Still, tears persisted. She could feel them lingering, waiting for her guard to come down. And so, Kate flung a cloak over her shoulders and stepped from the chamber.

Rocking Frederica gently in her arms, she walked up and down the corridor before turning down another and then another. She had done so with all her daughters, walking the halls of Birchwell at night to sooth them, and in doing so, Kate had found that it also soothed her own nerves.

And so she walked.

Along darkened corridors.

Across barely lit halls.

And past firmly closed doors until...

Lost in thought, Kate only noted the young woman standing a little ways down the corridor when she was near enough to hear her voice. Her feet instantly drew to a halt, her eyes wide as she stared at Kenna.

Also wrapped in a cloak, Eoghan's sister stood pacing outside a door, her feet carrying her away and then back toward it, occasionally rooting her to the spot and making her seem almost like an ancient column, immobile and lifeless. Yet there was fury upon her face, and Kate could see raw emotions bubbling close beneath the surface. "He isna even here," Kenna spat, casting another hateful glare at the door. "He's with her, is he not?" Her hands balled into fists, and she shook them at the door, then suddenly rushed toward it, her right fist raised as though to knock. Only a hair's breadth away from the wood, Kenna managed to still her movements, her eyes closing and her forehead coming to rest against the door.

In that moment, Kate realized—perhaps belatedly—that this must be the door to Keir's chamber. Only he wasn't inside, was he?

He's with her, is he not? That was what Kenna had said, and Kate felt drawn back to that morning when she had come to her sister's chamber and found Keir there. Neither one of them had offered any sort of explanation, and yet Kate had known that he had not merely stopped by for a visit. No, he had spent the night, had he not?

A part of Kate felt appalled, knowing her mother would have been outraged at such scandalous behavior, as would have the *ton*. Fiancé or not, Sarah ought never to have allowed a man into her bedchamber. Another part of Kate, though, understood. She knew the love Sarah felt for Keir, and in her sister's place, Kate knew she would not have been able to send him away, either.

"They're not even married yet," Kenna growled at the closed door, her feet once more carrying her away, "and he already canna stay away from her." She shook her head then spun around, a look of utter disgust on her face… until her gaze fell on Kate.

Finding Kenna's eyes upon her, Kate flinched, and Frederica mewed disapprovingly in her sleep.

"What are ye doing here?" Kenna demanded as she stormed toward her, fury lighting up her eyes. Then, however, her gaze dipped lower and found Frederica, and almost instinctively, the young woman lowered her voice. "Did ye follow me?"

"No," Kate rushed to assure her. "Of course not." Almost mesmerized, her gaze lingered upon the closed door to Keir's chamber, and her heart almost paused in her chest when she realized that if Keir truly was with Sarah, he had not been far away. Before Kate had left her chamber, the only thing separating them had been a thick stone wall.

At least physically.

"Ye care for him as well."

Kate flinched despite the softly spoken words of Kenna's observation.

For a long moment, the two women stared at one another. Although Kate saw displeasure upon Kenna's face at this newest revelation, she also thought to see understanding and a sort of kinship. Indeed, it felt good to have this awful secret out in the open, to have it known to someone who understood, someone who knew how painfully a heart could ache.

Swallowing hard, Kate bowed her head in shame. "Ever since," she murmured, her voice almost inaudible, "he came to save us, I have been feeling… certain things." She raised her eyes once more, afraid to look at Kenna.

For a long moment, Eoghan's sister did not utter a word, her face half-shrouded in darkness. Then she exhaled slowly, and Kate could sense her fury being replaced by resignation. "Would ye care for a cup of tea?"

Surprised but pleased, Kate nodded, and together, the two women headed downstairs into the kitchen. The remnants of a fire remained in the hearth, and Kenna stirred it back to life. Soon, the scent of tea filled the air, and the two women sat down at the worktable, each a cup in front of them.

"I wonder how he does it," Kenna voiced with a scoff and a roll of her eyes. "It must be witchcraft. Perhaps we oughta ask Mrs. Murray for a cure." Something utterly helpless rested in her gaze, and yet Kate knew this woman to be brave. "I've loved him all my life, and then he left and I..." She closed her eyes, shaking her head. "I truly thought he'd declare himself upon his return." Another scoff left her lips. "I must be a daft fool!"

"No," Kate objected without a moment's hesitation, her free hand reaching out and grasping one of Kenna's. "No, you're not. Of course, you're not. You're... You're in love, and I suppose that makes one blind to many things. At least, that's what I've heard."

Kenna eyed her curiously. "What ye've heard?"

Almost embarrassed, Kate bowed her head, not daring to cast more than a furtive glance at the other woman. "I've never known love myself."

"But ye're married," Kenna objected, the frown upon her face deepening.

This time it was Kate who scoffed. "Where I'm from, people do not marry for love." She heaved a deep breath, reluctant to go on and yet eager to do so at the same time. "My husband never cared for me. Perhaps he could have once, but now it is too late." As Kate continued to tell her story, she found an eager listener in Kenna, and it felt good to speak to someone other than Sarah, to someone who also felt a little bit broken.

Like herself.

Chapter Thirty-Eight

A MOTHER AT LAST

Tentatively, Sarah stepped across the threshold into Heather's chamber. It was a comfortable room, delicately furnished with warm colors and a dedicated hand. It possessed soul, and Sarah could see Heather's generous and kind spirit in every corner of the room.

"You asked me here?" Sarah spoke up as Heather rose from an armchair near the hearth, setting aside her sewing. "Keir said—"

Holding out her hands, Heather swept toward her, a wide smile upon her face. "Aye, I did. There's something I must show ye, and I hope that ye will cherish it as much as I did." Excitement twinkled in Heather's eyes, and Sarah wondered what this could be about.

Allowing Keir's mother to pull her toward the enormous bed on the opposite side of the chamber, Sarah's eyes grew wide. A most exquisite gown had been laid out upon it. The fabric seemed to flow like the water of a stream, small waves rippling along its path. At the same time, it shone almost golden in the late afternoon sun. Intricate patterns had been embroidered along the sleeves and down the front, like the swirls of an ancient language, its meaning long forgotten while its beauty persisted through the ages.

Awed, Sarah reached out her hand and tentatively touched her fingertips to the soft, cool fabric. "I've never seen anything so beautiful," she gasped, overcome by the thought that this dress had been worn by many generations of MacKinnear women. Of course, she knew nothing about it, and yet there was not a single doubt in Sarah's mind.

A wistful expression came to Heather's face, and she sighed, clasping her hands together. "Aye, 'twas my wedding gown and my mother-in-law's before me," she confirmed Sarah's thoughts. "I felt wonderful the day I wore it, and I hope that ye will as well."

Sarah's heart paused in her chest as she stared at her future mother-in-law. "You want me to wear it?" she asked disbelievingly.

Heather nodded. "Of course, only if ye wish, dear." She reached out and grasped Sarah's hands. "Since yer mother canna be here and offer ye her own wedding gown, I am most happy to offer ye mine." She squeezed Sarah's hands affectionately. "I've always wanted a tenacious woman at my son's side." She chuckled. "Believe me, he can do with a bit of a challenge in his life. It makes him a better man."

Moved to tears, Sarah shook her head, unable to accept these kind words. "I am not tenacious," she objected, afraid her mother-in-law had the wrong impression of her and would find herself disappointed down the line. "I am..."

Heather's gaze narrowed; her blue eyes fixed upon Sarah's. "Why would ye doubt yerself, lass? Ye stood against opposition and fought for yerself as well as others." She dipped her head in an affirmative nod, emphasizing her words. "I'll be proud to call ye my daughter. Verra proud." Amusement teased her lips. "Believe me, the MacKinnear men need women like us."

Sarah almost slumped to the floor at Heather's words. Her knees grew weak and threatened to give out, her body wholly unprepared for such praise. Never once had her own mother voiced anything remotely like pride in her daughter, and now, here, Sarah stood in front of a woman who had become very dear to her over the past few days and who offered her her heart with such ease that Sarah feared she had strayed into a dream. Always had she wanted a mother like Lady Whickerton, who loved her children with all her heart, dried their tears, held their hands, and stood at their side no matter what, always proud, always supportive, always full of faith.

The compassionate expression that came to Heather's face told Sarah loud and clear that her future mother-in-law understood her inner turmoil. "Ye're one of us now, Sarah, and whatever happened in yer life before no longer need matter." She gently grasped Sarah's chin; her blue eyes insistent as they held Sarah's. "Ye determine yer own fate. Ye choose who ye are, who yer family is, who ye love and at whose side ye stand." A warm smile came to her face, one that whispered of encouragement and trust. "That, my dear, is freedom. That is what family means. That is what the MacKinnears have always believed ever since Yvaine and Calen first came to these shores." She gave Sarah's chin a playful pinch and then once more took both her hands within her own. "'Tis a clan tradition, one as dear to us as life itself, and we're ready to fight to uphold it." She gazed down at the golden gown. "Do ye wish to wear it? And dunna worry, I willna be offended if ye say no. 'Tis yer choice."

Sarah's vision blurred as tears streamed down her face. Never would she have expected to find a family on top of the man she loved. "I'd feel honored to wear it," she murmured, her voice choked with tears. Sniffling helplessly, she wiped her cheeks with the backs of her hands, trying to regain her composure.

Heather smiled, her eyes shining with joy. "Ye'll look beautiful in it." She heaved a deep sigh, and a touch of sadness came to her gaze. "I had hoped my daughter would one day wear it." She shrugged her shoulders in an almost helpless gesture, unable to explain how her life had been turned upside down by Yvaine's disappearance. "My son said he spoke to ye of her."

Sarah nodded. "He did."

During their time in the woods, Keir had not only spoken to Sarah of the legend of Yvaine, a woman who had lived centuries ago and been the origin of the MacKinnear clan, but he had also told her of his adopted younger sister, who had been named after their clan's founding lady. His family had stumbled upon Yvaine out in the woods one day, unable to discover where the girl belonged. After that, she had become their daughter, their sister, their family... until the day she had vanished, not a trace of her left, as though the earth had swallowed her.

A sudden smile came to Heather's face, one that whispered of perseverance rather than joy. "Mrs. Murray believes that Yvaine was never truly from this world, and that the fairies fetched her back home."

Sarah reached for her future mother-in-law's hands. "Yes, she told me so. Everyone loved her dearly, did they not?"

Heather nodded, tears misting her eyes. "Aye, they did. She was one of a kind. I wish ye could've met her."

Sarah nodded, wishing the same thing, saddened by the thought that as dear as Yvaine had been to everyone, she would forever remain intangible to Sarah. Only a story. Not even a memory. Nothing she had beyond the words of others, the joy in their eyes and the smiles upon their faces.

If only Yvaine would return.

For all their sakes.

Chapter Thirty-Nine
NEWS FROM THE MAINLAND

"Will a fortnight do?" Keir's father inquired with a chuckle, the look in his gaze meaningful beyond his words.

Keir smiled. "I'd marry her rather today than tomorrow," he replied, warming his hands upon the fire in the hearth. "Yet I would never dream of depriving Mother of preparing a celebration fit for a queen." The great hall stood almost empty this time of day, everyone busy tending to one task or another. Only Loki and Faerie had settled themselves in an armchair, curled up together. The sight of them made Keir smile, for he knew how hard Loki had tried to rid himself of the newcomer. Yet the little pup had proved most persistent, slowly wearing Loki down. These days, feline and pup seemed inseparable.

His father laughed, clasping his hand upon Keir's shoulder. "I remember that eagerness," he said wistfully, memories shining in his eyes. "'Twas the same when I married yer mother. She insisted upon a lavish feast that needed a fortnight in preparations." He rolled his eyes, a rather impatient sigh leaving his lips. "Quite frankly, I'm convinced she only did so to torture me." He grinned. "She knows me too well. Always has."

Keir laughed, for it warmed his heart to see his parents so happy.

Their love had always seemed effortless, and growing up, Keir had never once doubted that one day he would have the same. Only when he had become a man had he realized how precious their love was, and for the first time, he had experienced doubts, wondering if he, too, would be as fortunate.

"Ye look happy, my son," his father remarked, a wide smile upon his face. "She's a rare woman, is she not?"

Keir nodded. "Aye, she—"

"Keir!"

At the call of his name, Keir turned toward the entry hall from where quick footsteps approached, thundering upon the stone floors as they drew closer. He exchanged a tense glance with his father as they stepped forward, meeting Magnus, Hamish and Finn MacDrummond halfway, the expression upon their faces far from relaxed.

"What happened?" Keir demanded, his gaze moving from his brother to Finn. "Did ye hear from Cormag?"

Finn nodded; a piece of parchment clasped in his hand. "He writes that a traveling clansman returned the other day from Glasgow," he rushed to explain, his breath coming fast. "He heard a rumor of Englishmen traveling the country, asking after two English ladies."

Keir felt every muscle in his body tense, his apprehension increasing when he saw the look upon his father's face. "What else? Does he write anything else? What direction were they headed?"

Finn shook his head, regret in his eyes. "I'm afraid since the clansman had no notion of the importance of that information at the time, he didna pay attention to it."

Keir nodded, exchanging another glance with his father. "Thank ye," he murmured, his thoughts already turning to what to do next. "At least we know they're here. In Scotland."

Magnus's usually so calm demeanor had been replaced by one of nervous apprehension. "Do ye truly think they will come for them? Here?" He looked to their father. "They will never make it onto the island, will they?"

Their father heaved a deep sigh, then parted his lips to speak. Yet before he could, a terrified gasp made them all spin around.

There, in the doorway, staring at them wide-eyed and pale-faced, was Katherine, Frederica clutched in her arms.

Keir cursed under his breath, nodding to his father, before striding toward her. The moment she saw him coming, though, she shrank back as though finding herself face to face with an enemy. Her feet retreated, and a moment later, she dashed away, fleeing blindly toward the stairs.

As Keir hurried after her, he heard his father call out to him. "I'll post watchmen at every tower and send out scouts! No one will get onto our island!"

Taking the stairs two at a time, Keir caught up with Katherine as she rushed down the corridor toward her chamber. He fell into step beside her, glancing down at Frederica, the little girl's face alert, her eyes wide and staring up at her mother. "Let me hold her," Keir insisted, reaching for the babe and taking her from her mother's limp arms. He settled her within the crook of his own, rocking her gently as he hurried after Katherine.

Her feet moved as though someone were lapping at her heels, her eyes unseeing and panic clouding her expression. She pushed open the door to her chamber and then rushed toward the armoire in the corner, yanking clothes out and throwing them onto the bed. "I need to leave," she murmured, her voice barely audible and yet frantic. "I need to leave. We need to leave. He will come, and he will find us. I never should've left. Never. Now, he will make me pay."

As gently as he could, Keir settled Frederica into her crib. Then he turned to Katherine, crossing the chamber in a few large strides. He stepped into her path and grasped her hands, halting her movements and forcing her to face him.

Her green eyes were wide and filled with tears as she looked up at him, her lower lip trembling. Her face was so pale that for a moment Keir feared she might faint, and yet her chest rose and fell with rapid breaths.

Holding her gaze, Keir rubbed her chilled hands, forcing warmth back into them. "Katherine, listen to me," he implored, realizing in that moment that he had never seen her so fearful. "Ye're safe here. I promise ye. Nothing will happen to ye. Do ye hear me?"

Still staring at him, Katherine blinked her eyes, and yet Keir could not rightly say that she had understood him.

"Ye're safe here," he repeated, reaching to grasp her chin, pulling her closer, his gaze drilling into hers, willing her to see him, to hear him. "My clan will protect ye. I will protect ye."

A shuddering gasp passed her lips, and when she blinked her eyes once more, they finally focused upon his. "Keir?" It was an almost desperate plea, and as tears welled up in her eyes, her whole body started to shake.

Keir pulled her into his arms then, wrapping her in a tight embrace, willing the shivers to cease. He held her close and ran his hands over her back, murmuring words of comfort. Perhaps if he were to repeat his assurance of protection over and over again, she would believe him.

His mind strayed to Sarah, wondering how she would react when she found out. *Will she be as terrified? Or will she trust in me... and my clan?*

Keir closed his eyes and inhaled deeply, willing his own mind to calm and think. Thus far, they knew very little. Cormag's letter had spoken of Englishmen. Since Keir could not imagine Birchwell himself traipsing the Scottish countryside, he wondered if the term *Englishmen* simply referred to those Birchwell had hired to bring him news of his wife or if perhaps it was not only Birchwell seeking answers.

Did Blackmore still seek to see Sarah returned to him? Keir cringed at the thought, wondering what the man's motive could be. After all, now ruined, the man's reputation would surely suffer if he were to wed Sarah. *What does he want with her?*

Whatever it was, Keir was now even more determined to marry Sarah quickly, ensuring that Blackmore could not get his hands on her. Perhaps it would be wise to have that information circled around the *ton* in order to discourage any plans Blackmore might pursue. No doubt Grandma Edie would see to it immediately. He had to get a letter to her.

As soon as possible.

Chapter Forty

DESPERATE NEED

Sarah thought she was floating on air as she left Heather's chamber, humming under her breath. She felt light and carefree and happy in a way she had never experienced before. Tears still clung to her lashes, and yet even though Sarah knew tears, these ones were different. They were tears of joy and affection, and she did not mind them at all. Finally, she had found the one place where she was meant to be, the family she was meant to have.

"I'm going to have it all," she whispered to herself, still in disbelief over how everything had turned out. "I am to marry the man I love." As many times as Sarah whispered these words to herself, a part of her still felt as though it was a lie, a dream hoped for but never achieved.

Turning around a corner in the corridor, Sarah paused when she saw the door to Kate's chamber standing ajar. A frown drew down her brows as she moved closer, wondering if her sister had simply forgotten to close it or if—

Heartbreaking sobs echoed to Sarah's ears, and they instantly quickened her steps. She dashed forward...

... and then came to an abrupt halt upon the threshold as her gaze fell upon her sister...

... wrapped in her fiancé's arms.

An odd feeling settled in the pit of Sarah's stomach, only she could not quite say what had caused it. Perhaps it was the way Kate clung to Keir, her face half buried against his shoulder and her fingers digging into his arms. Perhaps it was that look of almost desperate need upon her sister's face, as though she never wanted to move from this spot ever again. Perhaps it was the way the expression upon Kate's face suddenly reminded Sarah of Kenna, of the way she had spoken of Keir that day in the library.

As her heart tensed painfully, a shuddering breath left Sarah's lips, and in the next instant, Keir's head turned, and his eyes found hers. His gaze held concern, and yet his expression instantly changed the moment he saw her face, something puzzling coming to his eyes.

More than anything, Sarah was relieved not to see guilt upon his face. What on earth was happening here?

"Katherine," Keir murmured, and he looked down at Kate's head, still resting against his shoulder. "Sarah's here."

At his words, Kate blinked and finally released her claw-like grip upon his arms. She turned toward Sarah, and tears filled her eyes, her face looking pale, fear etched into her features.

Sarah's jaw dropped. "What happened?" She shot forward, instinct urging her to her sister's side. She grasped Kate's hands and pulled her into her arms, then looked up at Keir. "Is she all right?"

Before Keir could answer, Kate's voice, subdued and fearful, echoed to Sarah's ears. "He found us. He found us. We have to leave. We have to go somewhere safe. We..."

Ice settled in Sarah's heart, its cold slowly spreading throughout her whole body, and her eyes flew up to meet Keir's.

Tension lingered upon his face as he stepped toward her, gently placing his hand upon her shoulder. "We've received word, lass, of a rumor that Englishmen are searching for two English ladies. That is all."

Sarah shivered, for despite the reassuring tone in Keir's voice, she could tell that he was deeply concerned. "How do you know?"

"A few days ago, Finn sent a letter to his clan. Their answer arrived today." He held her gaze. "We knew this could happen," he reminded her gently. "We expected this to happen, and we are prepared." He glanced at Kate. "There is no need for panic. Ye are safe here."

Staring into Keir's eyes, Sarah nodded, allowing his warm voice to chase away the icy chill.

"Watchmen are being posted as we speak," Keir continued in that smooth voice of his. "No one is allowed onto the island without my father's permission. Still, it might be wise for ye to remain within the castle and not go out on yer own until we know more. 'Tis simply a precaution."

Sarah nodded, feeling comforted by his reassurances. Never had she known Keir to take things lightly or to speak without reason, and she found she trusted him beyond doubt. As much as her instincts told her to run, told her to panic, told her to expect the worst, Keir's promise now stood against all that.

And it felt good.

Over the next few days, Keir's family worked without pause to fortify the island. Watchtowers were manned, and scouts were sent out on a regular basis. Every ship to land in the harbor was checked, every person upon it questioned. More letters arrived, replies from other clans, answers to the MacKinnears' request for information.

Apparently, the rumor of Englishmen searching for two English ladies had spread far and wide, and yet it was nothing more than that: a rumor. No one knew any details. No one had ever seen the men before. No one quite knew where they were headed.

Westward.

That was all.

Throughout it all, Sarah remained calm, doing her utmost to ease her sister's terror and to keep her nieces occupied and clueless. Yet once again, Kate was watching the girls with hawk's eyes, terrified whenever she would lose sight of them. Eoghan was constantly at her side, taking Frederica from her without asking so she would eat. He often took the girls down to the beach, assuring Kate that he would not leave their side and return them safe and sound. And to Sarah's surprise, Kate never once doubted him. Yet she seemed not even to realize to what degree she had come to trust Keir's oldest friend.

Loki, too, appeared more watchful these days, always alert, always nearby. As often as he had disappeared into nowhere the weeks before, suddenly there was no place he would rather be than at their side.

One afternoon, they managed to coax Kate outside, the children running ahead as they followed the usual path toward the beach. Laughter echoed through the air, and Sarah exhaled a deep breath as she walked on Keir's arm, wishing for a moment of peace. Still, her thoughts continued to circle, her gaze constantly drawn to Kate, her shoulders tense as she clung to Eoghan's arm. "I cannot help but wonder," Sarah murmured out loud, lifting her chin to look up at Keir, "why Grandma Edie has not sent word. Usually, she is so well-informed."

Keir smiled at her, his hand holding hers a little tighter. "Perhaps the answer is rather simple. Perhaps there simply is nothing to report because there is nothing to worry about."

Resting her head against Keir's shoulder, Sarah breathed in the sea air, praying that he was right. Still, that icy chill lingered, constantly putting her on edge. Only Keir's presence seemed to ease it, warming her, body and soul. Every night, Sarah slept in his embrace, the comfort of his presence priceless. Still, she longed for the day of their wedding. Only she had hoped for a truly joyous occasion, free of worry and doubt. Now, it was anything but.

As they approached the beach, Eoghan pulled Kate to a halt. Then he took Frederica from her arms. Indeed, Kate looked exhausted, dark circles under her eyes, suggesting that her sister slept very little these days. Keir and Sarah stopped beside them, and Sarah helped Eoghan settle the little girl upon his shoulder, wrapping the small blanket tightly around her little niece to keep her warm.

"They're running too far ahead," Kate exclaimed in a fearful voice as she followed Augusta, Dorothea and Bonnie with her gaze. "I told them to stay close." Her hand settled upon Keir's arm, and she all but tugged him forward, her gaze fixed upon her daughters.

Casting a look at Sarah over his shoulder, Keir escorted Kate down to the beach, his lips moving as he spoke to her, no doubt seeking to alleviate her fears.

Still, once again, Sarah felt that odd sensation settle in her stomach at seeing Kate upon Keir's arm. Something had changed; she was certain of it. If only she knew what it was. Yet it needled her, sending cold sensations up and down her back.

"Are ye coming?" Eoghan inquired with a kind smile upon his face as he waited for her by the small slope that led downward.

Sarah nodded and then hurried to fall into step beside him. Her gaze, though, remained upon Keir and Kate as they walked arm in arm toward the girls playing upon the beach.

"How are ye doing?"

Sarah started, then looked up at Eoghan. "I can hardly say," she remarked with a shrug. "I am worried for Kate. She seems..." She exhaled a deep breath, welcoming the gentle sensation of the wind tugging upon her tresses. "I've never seen her so frightened. I had hoped freeing her of her husband would bring back the girl she had once been. Yet even before..." She swept an arm outward, her gesture encompassing everything that had happened these past few days.

Again, her attention wandered down the beach, aware of the way her sister clung to Keir's arm, her face occasionally lifting to look up at him. Sarah told herself that it meant nothing, and yet she could not quite believe it. It made something well up in her heart she had hardly ever known before, she hardly ever had reason to feel.

Jealousy.

"'Tis not real," Eoghan remarked, interrupting her thoughts.

Sarah lifted her face and looked at him. *What does he mean? He cannot possibly—*

Eoghan nodded toward Kate. "The way she feels for him isna real," he elaborated, and Sarah stilled, shocked that he had guessed her thoughts. "She doesna truly want him. She wants the safety she feels only he can guarantee."

Overwhelmed, Sarah wrapped her arms around herself, suddenly feeling icy cold. Now that Eoghan had echoed her thoughts, she could no longer convince herself that she had merely imagined the way Kate looked at Keir these days.

"Ye needa be worried," Eoghan counseled, not a flicker of doubt in his green eyes as he looked at her. "'Twill fade. She will come to see that Keir isna the man for her."

Sarah stared at him, shaking her head. "How can you possibly know that?"

Eoghan grinned at her. "Because Keir's the man for ye, is he not?" His grin widened, and he shook his head, glancing down the beach toward his friend. "As observant as Keir often is, he seems wholly unaware." He shrugged. "Or perhaps I am mistaken."

Deeply unsettled, Sarah met Eoghan's eyes, afraid to ask and yet equally afraid not to know. "He always seems so concerned for her," she whispered, glancing toward her sister and her fiancé. "He's always asking about her." She felt her arms tighten around herself. "Perhaps he does not even realize that he would rather be with..."

Eoghan stepped closer, careful not to stir Frederica awake as he settled his free hand upon Sarah's shoulder. "He does so for ye," he said gently, and once again, his eyes shone with conviction. "Aye, Keir is a good man, but the devotion he shows Kate is because of ye, Sarah, because Kate is *yer* sister." He smiled at her. "He does it for ye."

"How do you know?" Sarah demanded, afraid to trust him. A part of her knew she was being unreasonable, that Keir had not given her a single reason to doubt him. Yet doubting people was second nature to Sarah, and to her great shame, it came so easily to her. She hated it, the fact that she could not escape this part of herself. She had been so happy these past few days, and yet when something like this happened, she instantly fell back into that old habit.

Eoghan laughed good-naturedly. "Because I've known Keir all my life, and I've never seen him in love... until now." He looked down into her eyes. "Until ye came."

Tears collected in Sarah's eyes, and she pressed her lips together to keep them at bay. "Thank you," she whispered, reminding herself that impressions did not always represent the truth. Sometimes, one had to look deeper to find it.

Sarah was glad Eoghan had reminded her of that.

Chapter Forty-One

A LEAP OF FAITH

Every day, Kate expected to see her husband striding into the castle, demanding she be handed over to him, their daughters along with her. And every night, she conjured terrible scenarios of what he would do to her, of what he would do to them. And so, Kate looked at every sunset with horror in her heart, dreading the moment she would have to lie down her head and close her eyes.

Only Keir's presence seemed to hold the demons at bay.

Grateful for the massive walls surrounding the castle, Kate strode through the inner garden. She savored the hesitant warmth upon the air as spring drew closer; yet a sense of dread lingered. Countless times, Kate found herself peering over her shoulder, afraid that someone might linger behind one of the tall columns.

No one was there, though, and so she walked on.

However, the next moment, Kate detected movement at the other end of the garden. Her feet instantly drew to a halt, her heart tensing in her chest as panic flooded her being. She could barely breathe. Bright spots danced in front of her eyes before she finally realized that it was only Keir and Sarah.

Together, their hands linked, they stood near the southern wall, whispered words passing between them.

The sight of their closeness weighed heavily upon Kate's heart. It was a feeling of loss, harsh and painful, that quickly mingled with the by now familiar sense of guilt and shame. Keir and Sarah were beginning a new life together, and here Kate stood looking at them, wishing she were the one in Keir's arms.

"There ye are," came Eoghan's voice from behind her. "I've been looking for ye."

Slightly startled, Kate turned around to face him, her gaze quickly noting Frederica's absence. "My daughter? Where—?"

Eoghan held up a staying hand. "They're fine," he assured her. "I left them with Lady Adele. They are perfectly safe, I assure ye."

Exhaling slowly, Kate briefly closed her eyes. "Good."

Eoghan's gaze remained upon her and continued to linger, his green eyes watchful, as though he were searching for something. Then he nodded past her shoulder and remarked in a rather conversational tone, "Ye dunna want him."

Right away, Kate felt herself tense as she stared at him, a part of her wishing she had not immediately understood the meaning of his words. "I... I do not know what you mean," she stammered, mortification sweeping through her.

Eoghan took a step toward her, his head lowering slightly as he spoke in a hushed tone. "They're in love."

Kate's hands balled into fists, anger and disappointment giving her the strength to lift her chin and meet his eyes. "I know," she snapped, instantly regretting her outburst.

"Yet ye're not happy for them."

"Of course I am!"

Instead of taking affront at the hostile tone in her voice, Eoghan smiled at her, humor in his green eyes. "Keir is not the only decent man in this world, ye know."

Kate swallowed hard as sudden memories assailed her of choices that had not been her own, of decisions made without regard for what she wanted. "I've never met one," she murmured, a heavy weight settling upon her shoulders, making her struggle to hold up her head.

"Then open yer eyes, lass," Eoghan urged, his right hand reaching out and grasping hers, making Kate gasp. "Not to toot my own horn."

He grinned at her rather wickedly. "But I, too, am a good man." He held her gaze, his hand warm against her own chilled ones.

"I know," Kate whispered, wondering at what point she had come to that conclusion. Still, it felt true.

Eoghan nodded, the look upon his face encouraging. "There are many good men among the MacKinnears but also elsewhere. More than once, I've heard Keir and Sarah speak of the Whickertons. Although I've never met them, I've heard enough. Ye know them yerself, do ye not?"

Kate nodded, oddly entranced by this moment.

"There are many decent men in this world. Ye dunna have to cling to Keir." His gaze softened, and his hand squeezed hers. "I know ye feel as though ye do, but 'tis not true. That's nothing but fear speaking." He held out his other hand to her. "Trust me, lass."

Trust me. Eoghan's words echoed through Kate's head, their effect reaching even further, making her yearn for something she feared all the same. Still, as much as Kate felt compelled to cling to Keir, she knew deep down that Eoghan was right. And so, with one last glance over her shoulder at her sister's fiancé, Kate took Eoghan's hand and with it a leap of faith.

Chapter Forty-Two

A FIERCE ONE

Wanting a moment alone with Sarah, Keir pulled her outside for a walk. In less than a fortnight, they would be married. Everything was being prepared, and excitement lingered in the air. Smiling faces met them as they walked out across the courtyard and then into the garden.

Yet Sarah seemed distant.

Thoughtful.

"What's on yer mind, lass?" Keir asked as he drew to a halt and took her hands within his. "Something plagues ye. I can see it."

Sarah's lips pressed into a tight line, and he could see that she was reluctant. Yet the look in her blue eyes was troubled. "I'm not certain I should tell you."

Keir frowned. "Why?"

Sarah's eyes closed, and she bowed her head. "Because I do not wish to betray my sister." Her hands tensed upon his, yet she did not look at him. "All of a sudden, I feel so helpless. Everything I feel is making me wonder and imagine and fear and—"

"Yer sister doesna truly care for me."

Sarah's head flew up, and she stared into Keir's eyes. "How would you know this?"

Keir shrugged, then he reached out and touched her cheek. "I dunna know. Yet there was something in her eyes..." He shrugged again. Then his gaze settled more firmly upon hers. "It means nothing, though. 'Tis the same with Kenna."

Sarah felt his hand briefly tense upon hers and then relax.

"Ye know about Kenna, do ye not?" Keir murmured, his gaze sweeping over her face. "Did she speak to ye?"

Sarah swallowed hard, sorrow clouding her eyes. "She said that—"

"I can imagine what she said," Keir interrupted, reaching for her and tugging her closer, not wanting there to be any sort of misunderstanding between them. "'Tis not true, though. There was never anything between us." He searched her eyes.

Heaving a deep sigh, Sarah nodded. "From the way she spoke, it sounded more like something she'd always wished for than something that truly happened." She shrugged. "Still..."

Keir slipped a hand into her hair, pulling her closer, wanting to feel her. "Sometimes people are in love with a dream or an idea, and they cling to it in such a way that, to them, reality bends," he murmured, feeling Sarah's warm breath against his lips. "They no longer see the truth but what they wish for or fear."

Sarah's eyes closed. "I know what that's like. For me, it was fear, always seeing the worst in people, always being on my guard." Her eyes rose to meet his again. "I don't want that anymore. I want the truth. I want to know what is real." A smile teased her lips. "I want you."

Keir delighted in her bold declaration. Not long ago, she would not have been able to give it voice.

Rather daring, Sarah lifted her chin yet another fraction, her wide blue eyes holding his, unashamed. "I love you," she told him, and her voice resonated with strength. "I never truly expected to find love for myself. Perhaps when I was younger but not after seeing how the *ton* handles marriage and all those awful unions my parents planned for me, their disregard for my happiness obvious in each one." Her chest rose and fell in a slow breath, and she stepped forward, her hands reaching up to cup his face. "When I found you, I... I did not dare believe. I tried to convince myself that it could not be." Shrugging almost helplessly, she shook her head. "I was so afraid to allow myself to love you, so afraid of having my heart broken."

Deeply moved by her words, Keir wrapped his arms around her, feeling slight shivers trail up and down her back. "Ye took a risk, and 'twas worth it, was it not?" She smiled at him, one of those smiles that always threatened to bring him to his knees. "Of course, not everything ends happily, but if ye never dare risk anything, nothing ever will."

Sarah nodded. "I know that now, and I hope I will never forget. I don't want to be fearful anymore. I want to savor what I have and be happy." She grasped the lapels of his coat, giving him a little tug. "With you."

Sliding his hands further onto her back, Keir dipped his head. "That sounds like an awfully good plan, lass," he murmured against her lips before his mouth claimed hers in a passionate kiss. He held her close, felt her heart beat fast against his own, the pulse in her neck hammering below his fingertips. Her skin felt chilled, and yet she was warm, heat simmering wherever he touched. She was everything. To him, she was love and life and happiness, the only future he could imagine.

Lifting his head, Keir looked deep into her eyes, wishing this moment would never end, wishing they were already married. Utterly drawn to her, Keir once more lowered his head, determined to steal another kiss, when movement flickered at the edge of his vision. He glanced sideways, past Sarah's shoulder…

… to see Kenna standing there, her eyes narrowed to slits as she glared at them.

Keir heaved a deep breath.

"What is it?" Sarah asked, before she craned her neck to look beyond her shoulder.

Keir knew the moment she spotted Kenna because he felt the muscles in her arms and back tense. Yet when she turned back to look up at him, there was confidence in her eyes.

"Will you give us a moment?"

Rather surprised, Keir smiled at her and nodded his head. "I always knew ye to be a fierce one." He released her hands and watched her step away, then turn around and walk toward Kenna.

Aye, she's the one.

Chapter Forty-Three

HE'S MINE

Sarah's hands trembled as she made her way across the garden and toward Kenna. The young woman's face showed a hint of surprise; however, it vanished quickly, replaced by the same scowl Sarah had seen upon her face from the first.

Kenna crossed her arms over her chest as Sarah came to stand in front of her. "Why are ye here?" she demanded in a hiss, her brown eyes cold and yet filled with pain.

Compassion welled up in Sarah's heart; after all, she knew the pain of losing Keir. How often had she imagined the next moment to be their last together?

"I think we should talk," Sarah said gently, hoping that Kenna would see reason and they would not have to part as enemies.

Kenna scoffed. "Aye, perhaps we should." Her arms fell to her sides, and she took a step toward Sarah, her eyes sparking with animosity. "Ye dunna belong here, and ye should return to where ye come from."

Holding Kenna's gaze, Sarah slowly shook her head. "I will not. I cannot. You know that."

Kenna's jaw tensed. "How arrogant of ye," Kenna snapped. "The English have already taken far too much from us. And now..." She settled her hands on her hips, leaning forward. "Now ye claim one of our men for yerself and see nothing wrong with that."

Kenna's accusation made Sarah feel defensive; yet she could see that the young woman's anger was merely a mask to hide something much more painful. And so, Sarah refused to rise to the bait. "Do not pretend this has anything to do with fairness," she said calmly. "This is not about being English or Scot. This has nothing to do with borders and treaties. There is no need for us to be enemies. You know that, Kenna." Sarah raised an eyebrow, daring the other woman to acknowledge the rightness of her words.

Yet Kenna's anger still blazed. "Before ye came here, Keir was mine."

Sarah shook her head. "That is not true."

"How would ye know?"

"Keir told me, and I believe him." Indeed, there was not a single doubt in her mind or heart that nothing had ever been between Keir and Kenna.

With her lips pressed into a tight line, Kenna glared at her. Her hands balled into fists, trembling as her whole body seemed to shake with emotions she barely managed to hold in check. "Before he left for England, he kissed me."

Again, Sarah shook her head. "No, he did not." Somewhere in the back of her mind, Sarah felt amazed at the certainty of her words. Indeed, Keir had not told her everything, and she was uncertain if she wished to know. Yet he had told her enough, and she knew that whatever else might have been had been of no importance.

Kenna looked more and more aggravated as her words failed to anger Sarah. "I've wanted him all my life," she spat, and now her voice rang with sorrow rather than fury. "For years, I pictured the life we would've had together. And now?" She shook her head, an almost forlorn look upon her face.

"Do you truly want him?" Sarah inquired gently, remembering what Keir had said about Kate's feelings toward him. "Or did he perhaps simply suit the dream you held dear?"

"I dunna care what ye say," Kenna shot back, a furious glare back in her eyes. "I want him."

Sarah inhaled a slow breath, then she straightened, squaring her shoulders and lifting her chin as she met Kenna's gaze. "I want him as well," Sarah replied calmly. "I will not give him up. Never. I spent my entire life doubting myself, doubting whether I even have the right to demand happiness." She shook her head, determination sparking in every cell of her body. "No more. Now that I found Keir, I will never give him up." She took a challenging step toward Kenna. "There is no need for us to be enemies, but if you intend to fight me, then beware. He is mine, and you cannot have him." Sarah felt strength flow through her as never before as she held Kenna's gaze, her own unwavering, staking a claim upon the man she loved.

For a long moment, neither one of them moved, their eyes locked, each testing the other, trying to glimpse what would happen next. And then Kenna began to tremble as the dam broke, tears welling up in her eyes. Her lips were still pressed into a tight line, and Sarah could see that the young woman was furious with herself for showing such emotion.

Such weakness, perhaps.

"I'm sorry," Sarah whispered, wishing there was something she could say to ease Kenna's pain. "I truly am. I never meant to hurt you."

Kenna's eyes closed, and she bowed her head. A shuddering breath made it past her lips before she lifted her chin once more and met Sarah's gaze. "Ye're not the woman I thought ye to be," Kenna murmured, her voice now almost gentle, devoid of anger but filled with resignation and sadness.

Sarah sighed. "For a long time, I did not know who I was. Only now, I'm beginning to discover who I truly am."

A sob escaped Kenna's lips, and she clasped her hand over her mouth, embarrassment widening her eyes. "I've only ever..." She cleared her throat, hesitant and yet almost desperately determined. "I've only ever seen this one future." She shrugged helplessly. "What am I to do now that I've lost him?"

"Anything you wish," Sarah replied with an encouraging smile. "That is the beauty of freedom, is it not? You live here in this beautiful place where your choices are your own. Yvaine made certain of that long ago."

Wiping the tears from her face, Kenna managed a tentative smile. "I always loved her story," she murmured, her shoulders slumped and the look upon her face one of uncertainty. "And I often wondered where Yvaine found the strength to begin again."

Sarah nodded, remembering how deeply in awe she had been from the first after hearing Yvaine's story. "I suppose sometimes there simply is no other way. Sometimes we might only find our true strength once we need it." She smiled at Kenna. "You will find your place as I found mine, and I suppose more often than not, the path that leads us there is not a straight one."

Clearly thoughtful, Kenna nodded, and as Sarah turned away, crossing the garden once more on her way to the great hall, she was fairly certain that they did not part as enemies.

Chapter Forty-Four

A RAY OF SUNSHINE

As his wedding day approached, Keir was happy to see the skies clear and the sun peek out once more. The breeze blowing in from the sea no longer felt as chilled upon his skin, and the countryside slowly grew more vibrant in color. Greens intensified, and tentative blossoms could be spotted here and there. Soon, the spring festival would be upon them, and Keir mused that only a year ago he had not even known Sarah. Indeed, a lot had happened in so short a time. After all, he could no longer imagine his life without her.

"It appears the Fey smile upon ye, little brother," Duncan remarked with a chuckle as he looked up at the bright blue skies. "I suppose they always have."

Keir elbowed his brother good-naturedly as they walked along the ramparts, their eyes sweeping out to sea as well as over the harbor and the village. "Any news?"

Sobering, Duncan shook his head. "No one's been spotted, and the sea has been clear and the weather fine these past few days." He nodded toward the harbor where a two-masted ship lay at anchor. "Only a trade vessel returned from the continent, but with no unwanted passengers on board." Duncan turned to meet Keir's eyes. "I searched it myself."

Keir exhaled a breath of relief, nodding gratefully to his brother. He had always stood at his family's side, ready to support his father and brother in leading their clan whenever they needed him. Yet lately, with his wedding coming up and the threat of Birchwell and Blackmore, Keir had often found himself distracted.

Laughing, Duncan slapped a hand on Keir's shoulder. "Now, stop looking so concerned. In only two days, ye'll be married. If that is no reason for celebration, I dunna know what is." Duncan grinned at him broadly. "Especially with a fetching bride like dear Sarah."

Keir playfully lunged at his brother, but Duncan easily sidestepped him. Indeed, it felt good to laugh again, and he heard an echo of his grandmother's voice circling through his head, *There is always a ray of sunshine even on the darkest of days.*

As Duncan once more shifted his attention to the fortification of their island, Keir headed back inside. The great hall was filled with people, breaking their fast together, and Sarah and Katherine were seated with the girls at his family's table.

"Where have you been?" Sarah asked him as he seated himself beside her and pressed a quick kiss to her temple. She smiled at him, and her hand reached out to touch his face. "I've missed you," she whispered, dropping her voice low enough so only he would hear.

Keir traced the braid at her temple with the tips of his fingers, delighting in the little wisps that always seemed to escape, curling around her face. "I've missed ye as well, little wisp," he whispered in her ear, feeling her warm breath against the side of his neck.

Someone cleared their throat rather loudly. Keir glanced up to see Eoghan standing beside the table, a broad grin upon his face. "Ye're aware that this hall is full of people, children included, are ye not?" his old friend teased before his gaze moved sideways to indicate not only his own daughter but Sarah's nieces too. Augusta and Dorothea were staring at them with unabashed fascination.

Keir chuckled while Sarah blushed rather profusely before she buried her flaming face in her hands.

"Da, can we go down to the beach?" Bonnie inquired in that moment, breaking the slightly awkward silence that had fallen over the table.

Eoghan kneeled down in front of his little girl. "Again?"

Bonnie nodded eagerly, and Augusta and Dorothea quickly appeared at her side, joining in. "We want to go find seashells."

Eoghan heaved a deep breath. "More seashells?" He glanced up at the adults seated around the table. "Frankly, every cup and bowl in our house is filled with seashells. By now, the sea must be empty."

Everyone laughed, smiling at the girls.

"Verra well," Eoghan gave in, hugging Bonnie as she surged into his arms for a quick hug. "We'll go the day after tomorrow." Bonnie's face fell. "How about today the three of ye play in the gardens?" He glanced at Augusta and Dorothea, their expressions as crestfallen as Bonnie's. "Are ye not excited for Sarah's and Keir's wedding?"

Though the girls nodded, sadness rested in their eyes as they trotted off, their shoulders slumped.

Keir noticed Katherine's lips part as though she wished to object, and he quickly rose to his feet, calling for Loki. The feline lay stretched out by the fire but immediately rose to his paws and hurried over at Keir's call, his amber eyes attentive. "Go with them," Keir instructed, feeling foolish to be speaking to a cat like this. Yet he did not doubt for a moment that Loki knew precisely what he wanted. "Keep an eye on them."

Eoghan chuckled, clearly amused, as did many others. However, they all fell silent rather quickly when Loki did precisely as Keir had ordered. The moment the girls hurried away; the feline followed.

As did Faerie.

A frown rested upon Eoghan's face as he stared after the cat. "Did ye train him?" he asked with a glance at Keir.

Meeting Sarah's eyes, they both laughed. "What can I say?" Keir remarked with a shrug. "Loki is Loki." He sought Sarah's gaze, remembering the many times when Loki had stood at their side, always watchful, always protective. "He is family, loyal and faithful." He lifted his eyes to Eoghan, allowing a smirk to play across his features. "And perhaps he was in a former life."

Again, everyone laughed, easing the hint of tension that lingered at the unspoken threat that might or might not present itself.

Still, the expression upon Katherine's face remained tense, and when Keir caught her eye as she looked across the table, she immediately dropped her gaze. Indeed, she looked rather self-conscious and seemed to avoid looking at him. Kenna, too, appeared different this morning as she hurried by, casting only a furtive glance in their direction. That loathing expression in her eyes was gone, replaced by something akin to sadness. Still, Keir saw a determined spark in her eyes not to be pushed down by the heavy weight upon her heart, and he wondered what had passed between Sarah and Kenna that day in the garden.

Wanting a moment alone with Sarah, Keir pulled her away from the table the moment she finished her breakfast. They climbed the stairs to the upper floors, higher and higher, until they stepped out onto the ramparts. The wind blew briskly, and yet there was a touch of warmth in the air, the icy chill of winter gone. "How are ye this morning, lass?" Keir asked as he watched her lift her face to the sky, her eyes closed and a soft smile teasing her lips.

Sarah sighed in contentment. Then she turned to him, and the look in her blue eyes made him forget everything around them.

Within two heartbeats, Keir held her in his arms, his mouth dropping to hers.

Sarah's lips parted on a gasp, and Keir dove into their kiss with fierce passion, thrusting his hands into her hair and cupping the back of her head, holding her to him. He felt her tremble, and yet there was nothing shy in the way she returned his kiss, her hands just as eager as his own.

The world around them disappeared, and for long moments, they were the only two people in existence. "Ye seem quite eager this morning, lass?" Keir murmured against her lips, kissing her again.

"As do you," Sarah retorted with a smile, the tips of her fingers tracing the line of his jaw, sending teasing shivers down his back. Then she stilled, and something in her gaze changed. "I told Kenna that she could not have you, that you were mine."

Keir felt the breath lodge in his throat, and for a long moment, he simply stared at her, mesmerized by the sudden fire in her eyes. "Fierce and brave," he murmured, awestruck, "and utterly bewitching." *Aye, I chose well. There's no other like her.*

Sarah chuckled, a touch of crimson blossoming upon her cheeks. Yet she did not bow her head. Her eyes, though, took on a thoughtful expression. "And I think Eoghan spoke to Kate. She seems... different these past few days. I thought of speaking to her myself, but perhaps it would be better to give her some time."

Keir nodded. "Aye, that seems wise." He grasped her hands, delicate and small within his own. "Ye'll always be her sister, but ye're no longer the only one who cares for her, who watches over her." He thought to see a touch of regret flash up in Sarah's eyes. "Dunna be saddened by it, lass. 'Tis a good thing. Yer sister will find her place here, and she will come to see that she isna alone. 'Twill give her strength to explore the person she wants to be."

Sarah heaved a deep sigh. "You're right," she murmured, and a tentative smile appeared upon her face. "Long ago, it was only the two of us, and I suppose a part of me clung to that bond. But it will not lessen simply because she now has other people in her life as well, will it?"

Keir pulled her close. "Never," he told her, then grasped her hand and pulled her along. "Come, lass. There's something I wish to show ye."

Chapter Forty-Five
A SHARED LIFE

Sarah stood outside a door, belatedly realizing that it was the door to Keir's chamber. In all this time, she had never been near it, never been inside it, never ventured close. Keir had always been the one to come and find her.

"Will ye come inside?" he asked, holding the door open for her. "After all, in a mere two days, this will be yer chamber as well."

Feeling strangely nervous, Sarah nodded, then tentatively stepped across the threshold, Keir following her inside.

Through the large windows of his chamber, Sarah could see the vast expanse of the sea to the south. She could hear it crashing against the rocks below as well as the cries of seabirds circling overhead, hunting for fish. Inside were only a few pieces of furniture, but the most prominent was the large bed placed by the eastern wall. An ancient tapestry of a red-haired woman, whom Sarah assumed to be Yvaine, the legendary figure, hung above a wooden chest beside the fireplace, and a large broadsword had been mounted on the wall across from the bed.

"Of course, we can make changes," Keir remarked with a smile, his blue eyes seeking hers, as though he suspected her slight unease. "Ye need to feel at home here." He reached out a hand and grasped hers, his gaze still watchful. "Tell me what's on yer mind, lass."

Sarah shrugged, her mouth opening and closing. "I don't quite know," she replied honestly, uncertain what the tingle meant that trailed down her back. "As much as I…" She sighed, her gaze sweeping around the room. "I never quite pictured…" Indeed, in her mind, her future had only ever been an abstract concept. Now, here she stood in Keir's chamber, and suddenly images unfolded of the new life they would have together.

It was overwhelming.

"Life will be different, no doubt," Keir remarked as he moved toward her. One hand settled upon her shoulder while the other grasped her chin, his blue eyes slightly narrowed as they looked down into hers. "Is there something that causes ye concern?"

Again, Sarah felt at a loss, uncertain how to answer him, not because she did not wish to share her thoughts, but simply because she did not know what they were. "What will our life be like?" she asked instead of replying.

A smile tugged on Keir's lips. "Well, I certainly hope 'twill be easier to have time alone with ye. To speak without being interrupted. To sneak down to the kitchen in the middle of the night or dance in the moonlight." He chuckled. "Ye'll not be rid of me ever again."

Sarah sighed, feeling her heart warm and the images in her mind take shape. They came into focus, their edges no longer blurred. "That sounds wonderful."

Keir leaned down and placed a kiss upon her lips. "I'll be seeing ye first thing in the morning and falling asleep to the feel of ye in my arms." He sought her eyes, then glanced sideways at the bed.

Sarah followed his gaze and swallowed, understanding his implication.

"Are ye apprehensive about sharing a bed?" Keir asked, his voice gentle; yet the clasp of his fingers upon her chin remained insistent.

Sarah looked up at him nervously. "We've shared a bed before," she replied as her face went up in flames, heat searing her skin as though a fire engulfed her whole.

"Aye," Keir murmured, and she felt his gaze linger upon her heated cheeks. "Yet never in that way." His eyes looked into hers, and Sarah was surprised when she suddenly saw a touch of unease flare up. "Do ye know...?" he broke off, drew in a slow breath, and began again. "Has yer mother ever spoken to ye of—?"

Understanding his concern, Sarah broke free of his grasp, her feet carrying her to the other side of the chamber. "I don't want to speak of it," she declared, lifting her chin and meeting his eyes.

A frown drew down Keir's brows. "Why not?"

Sarah swallowed, determinedly pushing the memory his question had conjured from her mind. "Because... Because it will not be like that, will it?" *No, it will not!*

Keir stilled; his gaze trained upon her. "Yer mother did speak to ye," he murmured, then nodded as he moved toward her. "Aye, of course she did. The night I *kidnapped* ye was the night before yer wedding."

Sarah nodded, remembering the distant look in her mother's eyes. There had been no concern for her daughter in her heart. She had merely performed a duty, informing Sarah in a few brisk and rather emotionless words of what to expect from her future husband. "She said it would be... painful and degrading and," she swallowed hard, struggling to hold Keir's gaze, "awful." Her hands clenched. "Yet I would have to endure it as any wife must."

Anger sparked in Keir's gaze as he approached, his steps quickening as he hurried to her side. "Lass, yer mother—"

"No." Sarah held up a hand before he could reach for her, bewilderment coming to his gaze. "There will be no enduring. I've never felt like that with you." She licked her lips, remembering the many times she had been in Keir's arms. "Whenever you touch me, I feel... wonderful, and I refuse to believe that—" She paused, suddenly awestruck by her fortune in life to crave the touch of the man she was to marry.

It seemed her mother had never known that feeling, and for the first time in her life, Sarah wondered how her mother had felt as a young woman, finding herself married to a man who had not been her choice.

"Lass?" Keir came to stand in front of her, reaching out a tentative hand to touch her cheek.

Blinking, Sarah lifted her chin, and a smile claimed her face. All of a sudden, everything felt simple.

Determined to reclaim the bond that had always been between them, she met Keir halfway, her hands trailing up his arms, over his shoulders and into his hair as she pressed closer, wanting to feel him. "I'm not worried," Sarah whispered, loving the way his eyes looked into hers, "and I'm not apprehensive. I'm... perhaps a little nervous." She chuckled, delighting in the warm glow that came to his face. "Is that all right?"

Keir smiled at her, relief in his gaze as his arms cradled her. "Aye, 'tis all right. Quite frankly, I'm a bit nervous myself." He leaned in and kissed her. "'Twill be a new life for the both of us."

Sarah nodded in complete agreement. "That, too, sounds wonderful. A life without fear and regrets and..." She paused, and a heavy sigh drifted from her lips.

The expression upon Keir's face froze before his brows furrowed. "What is it, lass?"

Able to guess the direction of his thoughts, Sarah smiled up at him. "I do not have any regrets... only perhaps that this place is so very far from England, from London, from..." She bit her lip.

Keir nodded knowingly. "The Whickertons."

"I received a letter today," Sarah told him, her mind drifting back to earlier that morning. "From Christina."

Immediately, Keir tensed, his eyes narrowing in concern.

Offering a smile, Sarah shook her head to dissuade his line of thought. "No, she wrote to tell me that Anne's baby was born. A little girl." She exhaled. "I don't know if I'll ever meet her. Or Christina's children. Or..." She shrugged, suddenly feeling homesick.

Indeed, in a perfect world, Sarah saw herself walking through life with Christina and the others by her side, and it filled her with sadness, knowing it to be impossible. Yet Sarah was determined not to dwell upon it, and so she lifted her chin and blinked away her tears. After all, the distance between them was one easily bridged for a visit, at least. "It was the same for Grandma Edie and Lady Adele."

"Aye, 'twas; and yet they never lost one another, did they?"

Sarah knew his words to be true. Years might have passed since they last saw one another; still, they remained close to this day, never hesitating to answer the other's call.

"Perhaps we could invite them to visit us here in summer," Keir suggested, his blue gaze searching her face, "when traveling is easier."

Sarah nodded eagerly. "That is a wonderful idea."

"And what of yer family? Yer parents?" His gaze lingered upon her mouth as Sarah began to toy with her bottom lip. "Do ye wish to send word to them?"

Sarah heaved a deep breath, knowing that as her parents, they ought to be at her wedding. And yet they had never acted as such. Searching her heart, Sarah realized she did not need them to come. "I feel no longer burdened by the desire to gain their approval or their affection." She reached out her hand and touched his face, teasingly tracing the line of his jaw. "I found affection elsewhere."

A wide grin came to Keir's face, teasing and endearing at the same time. "Aye, ye did." Then he stilled, and Sarah could see thoughts circling in his mind.

"What is it?"

Blinking, Keir shook his head, his gaze once more focusing upon hers. "I just thought that if yer parents had granted ye a choice in who ye'd marry, we would never have met." The blue in his eyes seemed to grow darker, become more intense, suddenly overshadowed by a deep sadness. "As much as I regret all that ye've suffered," he murmured, leaning closer, his forehead almost touching hers, "a part of me is grateful that it happened because it brought ye here." He kissed the tip of her nose. "To me."

Tears pricked the backs of Sarah's eyes, and yet her heart overflowed with a deep sense of belonging. Never had she known anything like it, and part of her still struggled to believe that she was awake, that this was not a dream. Not too long ago, she had thought her life in ruins, like something burned to ashes, never to rise again. And yet, here she was, happy at last, after no longer believing it possible. Perhaps that was how life worked sometimes. Perhaps sometimes what was needed was to go up in flames, and then out of smoke and ashes something new arose.

Something wonderful.

Something perfect.

Chapter Forty-Six

A GRAY CLOUD

To Kate's utter surprise, she spent a most wonderful afternoon seated in the great hall with Eoghan. While their daughters had retreated to the gardens, no doubt planning their next adventure, Kate listened to his gentle voice, telling her one story after another, some amusing, others deeply touching; yet throughout it all, Kate felt a sudden lightness steal over her. It was the absence of worry and fear that felt so unfamiliar, and, at first, she did not even recognize it.

"Yer arm must be falling off soon," Eoghan remarked before he moved closer and scooped Frederica out of her arms. "Come, we'll take a turn about the hall, stretch our legs."

Kate followed him gladly, stretching and bending her arm, feeling her muscles ache with the strain of holding her growing daughter.

Frederica cooed happily as Eoghan made faces at her, and Kate watched, utterly entranced by the man at her side. Truly, he was a good man, like Keir, who offered his help out of compassion and not because he wanted something in return.

Looking at him now, Kate realized he had become her friend. She could not quite say when it had happened, but she realized that she no longer tensed whenever he scooped Frederica out of her arms and settled her into his own. As a father, Eoghan knew how to look after a babe, and Kate realized with stunned disbelief that he made her feel safe.

"Is something wrong?" Eoghan inquired, a quizzical expression upon his face. "Ye sort of look a bit… taken aback."

Blinking her eyes, Kate tried to clear her mind, overwhelmed by the sudden revelations. "Yes. No, I mean…" She looked up and met his gaze. "Nothing is wrong. I'm simply…" She shrugged.

Eoghan nodded knowingly, as though he truly understood the chaos in her head. "Aye, sometimes life makes us stumble and almost trip, and yet we love the way it makes our hearts beat faster." He inhaled a slow breath, and Kate saw something painful flash in his eyes. "When my wife passed," he murmured, his gaze distant and not meeting hers, "I thought I could never get back onto my feet. I didna even wish to." He closed his eyes and breathed in deeply, then he opened them once more, and a smile flitted across his face as he looked down at Frederica. "But there was Bonnie, and she made me realize that I couldna simply lie down and die, that I had to rise again no matter how painful 'twas." He lifted his gaze, and his green eyes met hers. "More than that, she made me *want* to rise once more."

Tears stood in Kate's eyes as she nodded. "Sometimes I think I do not have the strength."

"I know," Eoghan murmured, "but ye do. Never doubt that." He smiled at her. "If ye ever need a hand, ye know where to find me."

Eoghan winked at her, and Kate laughed. She laughed! A true, genuinely felt laugh, and it felt wonderful.

"Ye should do that more often, lass. It suits ye." He grinned down at Frederica, tickling her chin. "Does it not, wee Freddie?" Yet as his gaze strayed toward the windows, a frown slowly fell over his face.

"What is it?"

Eoghan exhaled a slow breath and then settled Frederica back into her arms. "It'll be suppertime soon," he told her, not quite meeting her eyes. "I'll go see to the girls." A smile meant to be reassuring flickered across his face but fell far short of its purpose.

Kate felt her heart tense painfully, resettling into the familiar clench that stole her breath and made it hard for her to stand tall.

Eoghan's hand grasped hers, his green eyes imploring. "I am certain 'tis nothing. They probably only lost track of time." He chuckled, and his expression no longer seemed as tense. "After all, what could happen to them with a loyal guard like Loki by their side? No doubt, he'll chase them back inside soon."

Still, Eoghan did not remain. Instead, he turned to leave but stopped when he spotted his sister and her friend Brenda?—as far as Kate recalled—enter the hall in that moment. "Kenna!" he called, waving her over. "Have ye seen Bonnie and Katherine's daughters?"

Kate's heart sank when Kenna shook her head, exchanging a glance with Brenda. "Yes, they were in the gardens," she replied, offering a quick smile to Kate before her eyebrows drew down in a concerned frown. "But that was a while back. Is something wrong?"

"No, nothing," Eoghan assured his sister. "They probably lost track of time playing." He turned away. "I'll go fetch them."

Kenna reached out a hand to stop him. "They're not there," she told them, her gaze moving from her brother to Kate and back. "They left before we did." She glanced at Brenda.

Brenda nodded. "Aye, they went out the side door."

Eoghan cursed under his breath, the muscles in his neck tightening.

"What?" Kate demanded breathlessly, feeling the blood rush in her ears.

Eoghan heaved a deep sigh and turned to her. "They sneaked away and went down to the beach." Again, his jaw clenched. "I'm sorry. I bet 'twas Bonnie's idea. She's...a bit wild, at times."

"But..." Kate felt her head begin to spin; yet she forced herself to remain calm. "What now? Will they...? Do you think they're lost?" Kate interjected; her gaze fixed upon Eoghan. "What if they...?" She bit her lower lip to fight back tears as well as a fresh wave of panic.

Eoghan's hand settled upon her shoulder, warm and reassuring. "They're not lost," he assured her, his voice suddenly ringing with conviction. "Bonnie is an island lass. She willna lose her way."

Kenna nodded in agreement. "They probably just forgot about the time," she remarked, then grinned at her brother. "I canna even count how often that happened to us when we were little. We sneaked away all the time. Do ye remember?"

Eoghan nodded, yet the expression upon his face was far from carefree. "I'll go look for them." Then he spun around, and quick steps carried him out of the great hall. He weaved his way through the many people streaming in, laughing and chatting, hungry for food after a long day's work.

"Dunna worry," Kenna urged, grasping Kate's hand and gesturing for her to sit back down. "He'll find them. I'm certain they're already on their way back."

"I'll fetch ye some tea," Brenda offered, and quickly hurried away.

Kate nodded to her, her mind elsewhere, for it needed to believe in that moment that there was a chance her daughters would come rushing back into the hall any second now. After all, what was the alternative?

As hard as Kate tried not to think of it, her mind would not heed her. Instead, it kept whispering in her ear, urging her to contemplate the possibility that her husband had found a way onto the island after all.

"I cannot lose them again," Kate murmured as fear buried her under a boulder of ice. "Not again."

Chapter Forty-Seven

A DISTRACTION?

The moment Keir walked into the great hall, Sarah upon his arm, he knew that something was wrong.

The drone of voices usually carried a cheerful note as people sat down to supper. Now, though, tension lingered in the air, and one look into Sarah's eyes told him she had noticed as well.

"Magnus, send someone to the village," Duncan called above the noise, one arm gesturing toward his younger brother. "I'll organize a search party of the castle grounds."

Keir saw Magnus spin upon his heel and rush out of the hall. "What is going on here?" he murmured, then quickened his steps, pulling Sarah long, as he hastened toward his brother. "Duncan!"

In that moment, Katherine charged toward them, her green eyes wide and her face pale, Frederica clutched in her arms. "The girls are missing!" she exclaimed, her voice barely audible, weighed down by fear. "Do you think… Do you think…?" She broke off, her teeth sinking into her lower lip.

Keir saw Sarah's still, her face paling, and he felt his own heart clench against the possibility that despite all their precautions, Lord Birchwell had found a way to his family.

"Now dunna be hasty," Mrs. Murray cautioned as she moved to

Katherine's side, one arm wrapping around her shoulders while the other settled upon her fluttering hand. "Ye dunna know what happened. There is no use in conjuring demons." She nodded to Frederica, her eyes open, the expression upon her little face one of agitation. "Yer wee lassie needs ye to remain calm."

Shaking her head, Sarah recovered her senses and stepped toward her sister. Her gaze, though, moved to Keir. "Do you think it possible?"

Keir willed himself not to shrug. In his experience, very few things were truly impossible. "Stay with yer sister," he told her calmly. "We shall find the girls. I'll go speak to Duncan."

Swiftly, Keir weaved his way through the throng of people gathered in the great hall until he reached his brother's side. "Duncan, what happened?"

The look upon his brother's face was a dark one. "I doubt the lassies are anywhere in the castle," he remarked, his gaze calm as it held Keir's. "We think they went to the beach, but we've already looked there. It lies empty." He took a step toward Keir, concern in his dark green eyes. "Ye know yerself that when we were young, we would often go places we were not supposed to go." He shrugged. "They could be anywhere."

Keir nodded, calmly absorbing the information provided to him. Mindless panic served no one. "Do ye think it possible that someone took them?"

Duncan paused and shook his head. "I dunna think so, for I see no way someone could have sneaked in here." Still, a glimmer of doubt shimmered in his eyes. "If I'm wrong, though, the longer we delay, the smaller our chances of retrieving them are." For a long moment, he held Keir's gaze. Then he nodded. "I'll have the ship readied, just in case."

For a moment, Keir considered whether he ought to share this information with Sarah and Katherine; yet they had a right to know, and he could not keep this from them. As expected, Katherine almost fainted, fear etched into her eyes. "Take her upstairs," Keir told Sarah, grasping her arm and pulling her close for a moment. "I shall join the search. Try yer best to keep her calm."

Sarah nodded, her blue eyes wide; still, she did not crumble, her jaw set in determination. "Do not worry about us," she told him, her hand settling upon his cheek, her eyes imploring. "Take care of yourself." She surged forward and pressed a kiss to his lips before once more turning to her sister and joining Mrs. Murray in ushering Katherine out of the great hall and up the stairs.

On horseback, Keir and Duncan raced down to the village and the harbor. There, they met up with Eoghan, the expression upon his face the mirror image of Katherine's—only more controlled. "Anything?" Eoghan demanded, raking his hands through his hair in agitation.

After bellowing orders to the ship's crew, Duncan turned back toward them, his gaze going back and forth between the two of them. "Let's think about this," he said calmly, his gaze slightly narrowed in thought. "Let us assume for a moment that Lord Birchwell did find a way onto the island. Why would he take the children? I thought he needed his wife."

Eoghan gritted his teeth, fighting to remain calm. "Well... they're his children."

Keir shook his head. "He never cared for them." Of course, a father like Eoghan could not fathom that there were men out there who did not care for their own children. "I'm truly sorry Bonnie got caught up in this," Keir murmured quietly, casting his friend an apologetic look. *If only—Nah, I canna think like that!*

Eoghan gave only a quick nod of acknowledgment before turning back to Duncan. "So, he needs his wife," he stated, "but instead, he took his children. Why? What is his plan?"

Duncan shrugged. "Perhaps 'tis only a distraction. He took the children to keep us focused on them, and meanwhile he sneaks into the castle to get to Katherine."

Eoghan frowned. "But with everything going on, he could never spirit her away without anyone noticing." He shook his head. "If this is his plan, 'tis a bad one. What if he realizes that?"

Keir groaned, remembering the shrewd expression he had often seen in the Dowager Lady Birchwell's eyes. Indeed, more than once, he had thought their true adversary to be Katherine's mother-in-law, not her husband. Like a puppet, Lord Birchwell followed his mother's commands, his own cunning falling far short of hers. "What if his plan is not to take Katherine but to have her come to him?" Keir's brows rose as he looked from his friend to his brother. "And what better incentive is there than taking her children?"

Eoghan's face paled at the implication of Keir's words. "If what ye say is true, then he, at least, will have to get word to her somehow. We needa get back before she disappears, goes to meet him, and we dunna know where."

Duncan nodded. "Ye go while I ready the ship." He exhaled a sharp breath. "Who knows? We might need it after all."

Pulling himself into Scout's saddle, Keir raced Eoghan back to the castle, his thoughts spinning. How could this have happened? They had been so careful. How had Birchwell gotten onto the island? And where was he now?

If only they knew.

Chapter Forty-Eight

A LIGHT IN THE DARK

"This is my fault," Kate repeated, the anguished look upon her face twisting Sarah's heart. "I should never have left. I should never have gone against him." Her hands trembled as she paced her chamber, casting a frantic gaze at Frederica and her little crib every few seconds, as though to assure herself that her youngest daughter, at least, was still here.

Sarah exchanged a worried look with Mrs. Murray, then stepped toward her sister. "Kate, you cannot think like that. None of this was your fault. You had every right to leave after what he did."

"Aye," Mrs. Murray agreed, her shrewd gaze slightly narrowed, and the expression upon her face not brooking an argument. "Ye're a mother, lass, and that means that, first and foremost, 'tis yer duty to see to yer children." Determined, the old housekeeper moved toward Kate, grasped her hands and gave her a little tug so that Kate had to lean down, her eyes now at level with Mrs. Murray's. "Ye and yer daughters belong here, and we will find them."

Sarah saw her sister tremble, her tear-filled eyes shining with gratitude as she looked at Mrs. Murray. Then Kate sank into the housekeeper's arms, and for a moment, Sarah wondered if this was what it felt like to have a mother.

One who cared.

Truly.

Feeling her own limbs tremble, Sarah clenched her fists, then crossed her arms over her chest and stepped over to the window. Her gaze swept out toward the darkened sky where stars twinkled, beautiful and soothing. Yet as her gaze drifted lower, Sarah saw more lights, little dots that moved in the dark. For a second, she was confused. Then, however, she realized that those little lights were not stars. Of course not. They were the torches of all the people out there, searching for her nieces and Bonnie.

The sight touched Sarah, for she knew in that moment that the MacKinnears would search endlessly, their loyalty and support unwavering. Indeed, it appeared the entire village, the entire island, was out there looking for the girls.

Tears misted Sarah's eyes, and she dabbed the hem of her sleeve to their corners when she heard the door open. Turning around, she spotted Lady Adele striding into the room, holding a cup of tea, little puffs of steam drifting into the air.

Sarah offered Keir's grandmother a tentative smile, one which Lady Adele returned. Her hand briefly grasped Sarah's and squeezed it reassuringly. "Do not worry. All will be well." Then she strode over to Kate, handing her the cup. "Drink this, dear. It will settle your nerves."

Still looking distraught, Kate settled upon the edge of her bed and gratefully reached for the cup. She blew upon its hot content, then sipped slowly, her chest still rising and falling with each agitated breath. "Is there any news yet?"

Lady Adele shook her head. "Not yet, dear."

Kate's eyes closed briefly. She inhaled a deep breath, breathing in the aromatic scent of the tea. Indeed, Sarah thought it was a rather unfamiliar blend, its flavor failing to stir a memory within her.

For long moments, silence lingered about the chamber, and Sarah turned back toward the window, feeling restless. She remembered times at the cabin when there had been danger and Keir had told her to remain safely locked away. Then she had not listened. Ought she to listen now? After all, there was no danger to her, was there? No, it was her little nieces that had been taken... or were simply lost out there somewhere. Sarah wished she knew what had happened. She wished she could be out there helping with the search instead of in here, waiting and doing nothing.

Kate yawned loudly, and Sarah turned to see her sister's eyelids droop. Lady Adele quickly took the cup of tea from Kate's hands and settled it upon the bedside table. Then she and Mrs. Murray helped Kate lie down upon the bed, removing her shoes and draping a blanket over her.

Sarah frowned, thinking it quite odd that her sister could sleep at a time like this. Then she noted a shared look between Lady Adele and Mrs. Murray, and her gaze instantly drifted to the teacup. "What did you do?" She stepped forward, looking at the other two women. "What was in it?"

Lady Adele smiled at her. "Something to help her rest. No mother ought to have to endure this sort of fear for her children." She placed a hand upon Sarah's arm. "Now, we must do all we can to bring her daughters back before she wakes, so that this was nothing more but a bad dream."

Sarah nodded, glancing toward Mrs. Murray, who settled herself in a chair beside Kate's bed. "I want to help," she told Lady Adele, wondering how the woman would react.

Lady Adele nodded. "Then go and help. We shall see to yer sister and the little one. And do not worry; my son posted guards at every entrance to this castle. If Katherine's husband is truly on this island, he will not get in here."

Sarah inhaled a slow breath, overwhelmed by the sudden opportunity to aid in the search. "Thank you," she whispered, drawing strength from the confident look in Lady Adele's eyes. "Thank you for everything."

Lady Adele nodded. "No gratitude is necessary, my dear. It is what family does, is it not?"

With tears in her eyes, Sarah hurried from the chamber, returning to her own. There, she quickly pulled on boots and draped a thick cloak over her shoulders before hurrying back out into the corridor.

Quick steps carried her down the stairs and across the great hall. There, she spotted Heather standing by the fireplace. Her gaze was focused as she spoke to one group of volunteers after another, directing them to different places upon the island. "Where can I go?" Sarah inquired as she hurried toward Keir's mother. "I want to help." *I* need *to help. This is my family out there.*

Heather smiled at her, grasping her hands and squeezing them tightly. "Follow them." She nodded toward a small group of two men and three women who were preparing to depart. "They're heading land inward. Many are already searching the coastlines." She turned around and then handed Sarah a torch. "Light it in the hearth," she told her with a nod toward the enormous fireplace at her back. "And be careful. Dunna go too far."

Sarah nodded, doing as Heather had bid her, the torch sizzling and crackling as it caught fire. Sarah hurried after the small group of people heading outside. She turned back to look at Heather as she stepped through the arched doorway, nodding to Keir's mother, hoping that the next time they saw one another, all of this would be behind them, and the girls would be back safe and sound.

With the sun absent, the air felt chilly as Sarah stepped outside. She blinked and squinted her eyes, trying her best to see through the dark. The torches' light only cast a small circle, and everything beyond it lay in shadow. "Stay together," one of the men reminded them as he waved them onward. "And watch yer step."

Everyone nodded, and they hurried out of the castle, turning westward. The path sloped upward for a bit before it once more fell, curving to the south. To the north, a forest loomed like a dark wall in the distance, impenetrable and threatening, while the south seemed guarded by a tall outcropping of rock, the sound of waves drifting to their ears.

Sarah moved slowly, tripping every so often over her own feet. Unlike the others, she was not familiar with this terrain, her eyes darting from side to side and often down to the ground, afraid something might be in her path. "Don't rush," Sarah reminded herself, knowing that it would serve no one if she tripped and hurt herself, forcing the others to abandon their search and assist her. "There's nothing to worry about so long as you can still see the others' torches," Sarah murmured to herself, as she lifted her own torch, squinting through the darkness.

The path sloped farther down toward a meadow. It was open ground, and she could see the others fanning out a little, the light of their torches like little dots moving onward. Sarah quickened her steps, carefully lighting the ground in front of her, when she suddenly heard a sound that gave her pause.

She stopped and listened, and for a long moment, all she could hear was the sound of the waves nearby. Yet all Sarah could see as she turned toward it was an enormous rock formation blocking her path. "This is where I found Faerie," Sarah murmured to herself, relieved to have discovered her whereabouts. Indeed, in the dark, everything looked different, and she had felt completely confused by her surroundings.

Remembering how Faerie had gotten trapped in the thorny brambles, Sarah crouched lower, wondering if perhaps the girls had found a way inside, their sense for adventure making them careless. Had they become trapped? "Augusta! Dorothea! Bonnie!" Sarah called out, wanting nothing more than to hear their voices, to have this day come to a happy end.

Yet no sounds echoed to her ears beyond the lapping of the waves, and Sarah's heart sank. She called the girls' names a few more times, each time listening intently, hoping against hope that they had perhaps not heard her before. Still, each time, only silence met her.

With a heavy heart, Sarah made to turn around and head after the others when suddenly something caught her eye. Squinting into the darkness, Sarah crouched down and raised her torch, trying to see.

At first, she feared it had only been a trick of light, something there one second and then gone the next. After all, it had been only a spark, as though someone had struck flint, trying to light a fire. Had she imagined it? In the next moment, though, there was another flash of light somewhere in the thicket, and Sarah stilled.

Squinting even harder, she fixed her gaze upon it, afraid to lose it once more. It moved and grew larger as it headed her way. And then,

Sarah saw it was not one light but two. Two glowing disks in the dark, heading her way.

Sarah's heart tripped over itself as she stared, terror filling her heart as Mrs. Murray's ghost stories echoed through her mind. "What is this?"

Chapter Forty-Nine

NOT A TRACE

Keir and Eoghan pulled the horses to a halt in the courtyard, then jumped down and rushed inside. They took the stairs two at a time, then raced along the corridor toward Katherine's chamber. Keir slowed his steps, reaching out his hand to hold Eoghan back from bursting through the door. He quickly knocked, then stepped inside without waiting for an answer. Inside, he found his grandmother and Mrs. Murray seated by Katherine's bed, the young woman upon it, her eyes closed in slumber. Frederica lay sleeping in the crib beside her, and Sarah—

Keir felt his heart constrict. "Where is Sarah?" he demanded as he moved into the chamber, his eyes finding his grandmother's.

His grandmother rose to her feet and stepped toward him, her gaze moving from him to Eoghan and back. "She decided to aid in the search."

Keir cursed under his breath. He ought to have known. She had never remained behind and out of danger before. Of course, wanting to help was something Keir understood, and yet the thought of her in danger killed him.

"Is she all right?" Eoghan murmured as he stepped toward the bed.

His gaze narrowed as he looked at Katherine then back at Keir's grandmother. "She seems..."

Mrs. Murray patted his arm. "Dunna ye worry. The lass is fine, but she could do with some sleep. It serves no one if she walks a hole into the floor."

Keir could not resist the chuckle that rose in his throat. "Ye drugged her," he exclaimed, shaking his head in disbelief. "Why would ye do that?"

Mrs. Murray met his gaze, her own steady. "Because she needed it." She exchanged a glance with his grandmother before she stepped toward him. "Ye dunna know what 'tis like to fear for yer child, dear lad, and I pray that ye never will."

"What are you doing here?" Keir's grandmother inquired, a shrewd expression coming to her face. "Clearly, you have not found the girls. What is happening?"

Keir looked at Eoghan and then met his grandmother's eyes. "We canna be certain, but we think that perhaps taking the girls is to serve as a distraction. After all, Birchwell is after his wife, not his daughters."

His grandmother nodded. "You think he will send word to her, urging her to come to him, or she will never see the girls again?"

Keir exhaled a deep sigh, well-aware of the tension that lingered in Eoghan's shoulders. While they were fairly certain that Lord Birchwell would not harm his own children, Bonnie was a different matter. She was nothing to him, a complication at most. Would he stoop so low as to harm a child?

Keir did not know, and that thought sent icy cold shivers down his back. "Have ye seen nothing? Nothing suspicious?"

His grandmother looked at him a bit indulgently. "No one can get in here, lad. Your father posted guards."

Keir huffed out a deep breath. "Well, he got onto the island, and we also didna think that possible, did we?" He raked a hand through his hair. "Be careful," he told his grandmother and Mrs. Murray. "And dunna let her out of yer sight."

The two women nodded, the expression upon their faces determined, and a part of Keir felt bad for anyone who would try to get past them.

With Eoghan by his side, Keir rushed back downstairs, his mind racing. "What now?" he thought out loud, meeting his friend's gaze.

Eoghan looked utterly shaken. "I dunna know." Pale and frantic, he paced, his hands clenching and unclenching as he went.

Keir grasped his friend's shoulder. "Stay here and guard Katherine. Keep yer eye out and send word to Duncan the moment ye see anything suspicious."

Eoghan nodded. "And ye?"

"I have to go find Sarah," Keir replied, an apologetic expression upon his face. "I canna allow her to be out there by herself. After all, we dunna know if Blackmore is involved." He made to turn around when he spotted Magnus, Hamish and Finn rushing back into the hall. "Magnus!" Keir called out, then hastened toward his brother. "Any news?"

His younger brother shook his head. "We searched toward the north but found nothing. No tracks or ships ashore. Father said that riders were sent to the villages farther south." He paused, nodding toward their father striding into the hall in that moment. "They havena returned yet."

Keir exhaled a breath of relief at the news. It truly appeared no one had come ashore, but if that was the case, where were the girls? What had happened? "Will ye stay here and help Eoghan keep an eye on everything?" He looked from his brother to his friends. "Taking the girls might've been a distraction. We canna be certain at the moment."

Magnus nodded solemnly, as did Hamish and Finn. "Go. We'll stay here."

"Thank ye." He made to hurry out of the great hall when he spotted his mother. "Have ye seen Sarah?" he called as he hastened over. "Grandmother said she joined the search."

His mother nodded. "She was here. I sent her out with a group going toward the cliffs."

Without another word, Keir took the torch out of his mother's hand and then darted off. He almost flew down the steps toward the courtyard, then flung himself into Scout's saddle. The gelding seemed to sense his agitation, prancing eagerly and then charging off the moment Keir gave him free rein.

The farther they moved from the castle, the darker the night became, wrapping around them and hiding everything else from sight. Keir cursed under his breath, wondering why these situations always arose after the sun had set. Of course, he knew the answer to that question, and yet it did not annoy him any less.

Guiding Scout toward the cliff face, Keir tensed when he spotted the light of a single torch shining up ahead. He leaned forward, and Scout instantly quickened his pace. With his gaze fixed upon the small light, Keir frowned, wondering why it did not move. *Is it Sarah?*

Keir jumped to the ground when they approached the tall rock outcropping that barred his view of the sea. A thicket of brambles grew at its base, and Keir remembered that this was where Sarah had found the little pup. Yet right now, the place looked empty, the only sign that someone had been here, the lone torch, thrust into the ground, its flame flickering in the wind.

Frowning, Keir strode closer, his gaze sweeping over the thicket and the rock, always circling back to the torch. Had Sarah come here? But why had she left the torch behind? And where could she have gone?

"Sarah!" Keir called into the night as he moved along the base of the rock, peering into the thicket. Yet everything was pitch black, the light from his torch illuminating very little. Keir could not banish the thought that someone had come upon Sarah here. Why else would she have left behind the torch? Had it fallen to the ground in a struggle?

As a lad, Keir had played up here with his brothers and Eoghan. He knew this place well, and although they had tried countless times, they had never found a way down to the water from up here. The thicket was impenetrable, and the rock outcropping solid. Yet had Sarah gone? If she had ventured back down the way she had come, would they have run into one another?

Keir ran an agitated hand through his hair, contemplating what to do. He could not shake the feeling that by leaving, he would be leaving Sarah behind. Something deep down told him she had been here. That this was her torch. *If only I knew where she went.*

Cursing under his breath, Keir spun around and remounted Scout.

There was no point in lingering. Perhaps he ought to head back down to the harbor and board the ship. Duncan could take them around the island, and they could search from the water. At the very least, it was better than standing here waiting.

Chapter Fifty

THE LEGEND OF THE SERPENT

Sarah felt battered and bruised as she crawled along on her hands and knees. Try as she might, she saw nothing, the rock walls around her shielding her from any light. The air inside the tunnel was cold, as was the rock beneath her hands. Her whole body felt chilled, and she continuously worried that she might bang her head on something she could not see. Yet there was no going back.

Only forward.

"Loki?" Sarah called into the darkness. She could no longer see his glowing eyes as he moved silently ahead of her, like a ghost not of this world.

Indeed, the moment she had first seen his eyes glowing in the dark, her heart had almost stopped. It had taken her a few minutes to recover from the shock before she had thought clearly again, utterly surprised to find Loki here upon the cliff. Yet all questions had remained unanswered. *Of course!* Still, the look upon Loki's face had been insistent, and so Sarah had followed him into the thicket, leaving her torch behind, afraid to set the dry branches on fire.

It had been a tight fit, nearly impossible, and Sarah felt scratches all over her face. Yet she had continued on, and eventually the ground sloped down and then changed from dirt to rock. It had grown even darker then, all light from above cut off by a solid rock wall. Was this where the girls had gone? Sarah continued to wonder, her thoughts torn back and forth between Birchwell kidnapping them and them simply getting lost. Indeed, she could not imagine Birchwell to have been here. How would he have known about the tunnel?

The sound of water lapping nearby drifted to Sarah's ears, its echo slowly growing more pronounced. "Loki?"

A soft meow answered her, and Sarah lifted her head, spotting two glowing disks in the dark. "Where did you go?" she inquired, wishing he could answer her, wishing she could understand. "This is truly where the girls went?"

Sarah had to trust that it was. After all, Loki had left with them, and she was certain that he would not have abandoned them. How had they ended up here, though? Had Birchwell been involved, after all? Perhaps he had come upon them, and they had fled into the thicket. Of course, Loki could not have protected them from Birchwell. Last time, he had gotten hurt getting into the man's path, determined to protect Sarah.

When she closed her eyes, Sarah could still see Loki's little body lying across the chamber, motionless. She had been terrified at the thought of losing him; yet that time he had come back. He had recovered and remained by her side as before.

"Perhaps I ought to have gone for help," Sarah murmured as she followed Loki, slowly moving on her hands and knees. "Perhaps I ought to have told someone." Now, it was too late, for Sarah had serious doubts she could turn around in this narrow tunnel. The only way was the way forward.

"Why is there a tunnel here?" Sarah murmured to herself, preferring the sound of her own voice to the silence that lingered. "It must be man-made. But why?" For a moment, she feared it might end in the water, somewhere below the surface of the sea. "I should've gone for help."

Sarah stilled as these last words left her lips, for they did not echo back to her ears as the others had before. Was she reaching the end of the tunnel? Indeed, as she peered into the darkness, Sarah thought to see a faint touch of light. The blackness seemed brighter somehow, not quite black anymore but perhaps midnight blue. Yet the sound of waves remained, growing stronger, the soft swishing of the tide rolling to her ears.

Encouraged, Sarah quickened her movements and soon she saw starlight filtering into the tunnel, glistening on the softly swaying sea. As far as the eye could see—which was not far at all—there was nothing there, only the endless sea. "Why did you lead me here?" Sarah asked, craning her neck to spot Loki. "Where did you go?"

She crouched forward, her hands lifting to the walls. She felt the ceiling slope upward and cool air brush against her cheeks. The tunnel was wider here, and Sarah slowly rose to her feet, taking one careful step forward and then another. Her eyes grew wide as the clouds above shifted and the moon shone down upon the sea. Indeed, the water was only a few steps away, its waves lapping onto a small ledge that was the end of the tunnel.

Craning her neck, Sarah found herself on the edge of a small bay on the south side of the main island. The land curved inward, tall cliffs reaching into the sky, almost barring any view of the sea. Only ahead of her, a small distance from where Sarah stood upon the ledge, she glimpsed a small island sitting nestled in the bay, like a child embraced by its mother.

"Loki?" Sarah called once more as she stood at the black abyss, upon the last bit of solid rock. One more step, and she would sink into the waves. "Loki!"

His call made her head turn, and the moment her gaze fell upon the little feline, Sarah almost fell over backwards in shock.

Ahead and a little off to the side, Loki seemed to stand upon the water, his glowing eyes directed back at her.

Staring, Sarah shook her head and blinked her eyes, trying to clear her vision. Yet the image remained. "Loki, what are you...? How can you...?"

The little feline regarded her curiously, then shook his little paws, clearly disgusted with the wetness. Still, he lifted his head, his call urgent, demanding she follow.

Sarah shook her head. "I can't," she whispered, staring down into the black waves only a step in front of her. "Loki, how...?" Still, she stared at him. Indeed, he had always seemed to be far more than a mere cat, and yet she would have never expected to see him walking on water.

Again, Sarah's mind drifted back to Mrs. Murray's stories, to all the stories Keir had told her, all the legends and myths. Was it possible? Were perhaps some of them true? Was Loki a... water sprite? The thought seemed ludicrous, and Sarah shook her head, trying to focus her thoughts.

"I cannot go back," Sarah murmured, doubting she would find her way, knowing that it would take too long to fetch help. Whatever Loki was trying to tell her, it seemed urgent, and Sarah trusted him.

Bracing her hands on the rock walls to her sides, Sarah inhaled a deep breath, then slowly moved one foot forward, lowering it down to the water's surface. She felt her booted foot dip into the waves, sinking lower and lower...

... until suddenly...

... it settled on something solid and sturdy.

Carefully, Sarah put weight upon her right foot, testing whatever it was she stood upon, her heart hammering wildly in her chest. When whatever it was, did not give way, she lifted her other foot, moving it forward and setting it down as well. It, too, sank into the water over her ankle, soaking her skirts. There, however, it remained, not sinking deeper. "How is this possible?" Sarah gasped as the clouds above shifted, revealing a crescent moon, its silvery light reflecting upon the water's surface.

And there, just below the waves, right in front of her, Sarah saw something glistening beneath the water. It shimmered, reminding her of the scales of a fish or... *Oh, this is not—This cannot possibly—*

Sarah froze, remembering the legend of the sea serpent that was rumored to protect the island, always out of sight, just below the surface. "This is not happening," Sarah murmured, fear crawling up her back as she gazed down into the water, expecting the solid ground beneath her feet to move at any moment, to rear up and throw her off. "It can't be true. I am not standing on the back of a snake."

Feeling every limb tremble, Sarah eased her foot across the solid surface she stood upon. Her eyes squinted, trying to see through the churning water. She only ever caught faint glimpses of something underneath, glistening in the moonlight... like scales. Slowly, Sarah leaned forward, trying her best to keep her skirts from soaking through all the way, and reached out a tentative hand.

Ice-cold water sloshed into her boots and swirled around her ankles. Goosebumps chased up and down her arms and legs. Still, Sarah extended her hand farther and farther into the freezing water until the tips of her fingers brushed against something solid.

Something smooth.

Like... Like stone.

Cobblestone.

Straightening once more, Sarah followed the smooth path of the *snake* with her eyes. "Is this a road of some kind?" she murmured, taking another step forward and then another.

Loki called to her, his small body shivering as he stood up to his belly in the cold water. Sarah could tell that the tide was coming in. The water was slowly rising, and for a moment, she felt uncertain which way to go. Then, however, Loki turned and headed out toward the small island.

Huffing out a deep breath against the shivering cold that seized her, Sarah followed him. It truly was an odd sensation, to be *walking on water*, with nothing but water around her. She was a good distance from shore now, and it felt eerie to be out here by herself. She felt as though she was trapped in an old legend, wondering what lay to the right and left of this underwater bridge. How had it come to be here? Was this what had inspired the legend of the sea serpent? If so, it had to be ancient.

"Loki!" Sarah called again when she lost sight of the little feline. A few more steps carried her forward, and squinting her eyes, Sarah could finally spot him upon the bank of the small island ahead of her. He shook his little legs, trying to rid himself of the icy water, and then moved onward, disappearing into a shadowy thicket.

Sarah felt a deep sense of relief when she reached the small island, and she hurried farther up the small beach. Water sloshed inside her boots, and she quickly dumped it out. Her whole body shivered from the cold, and she knew she could not stay long. She was about to follow Loki when she paused, quickly collected a few pebbles and piled them about two feet from the water's edge.

"Loki!" Sarah called into the dark, her eyes glimpsing nothing but shadows, some large and looming and others small and shifting. There was some sort of rock formation near the center of the infinitesimal speck of land, surrounded by trees and brambles of some sort. It seemed impenetrable. "Loki!"

For a long moment, everything remained quiet, and Sarah feared she had lost the little feline. Yet why would he disappear if he had gone to such lengths to lead her here?

Then, a soft sound suddenly drifted to Sarah's ears, and she stilled, listening.

For a moment, everything within her tensed. She recalled Mrs. Murray's ghost stories, all the legends the old housekeeper had only been too happy to share. Indeed, in the dark, alone by herself, nothing seemed impossible.

"Aunt Sarah?"

Sarah flinched at the soft voice, and for a moment, she thought she might have imagined it. Then, however, it came again, more urgent and almost pleading.

"Augusta?" Sarah exclaimed, hurrying onward, her eyes running over the shadowy thicket, unable to catch sight of anything.

And then, out of nowhere, out of the blackness of the night, three little girls appeared, Faerie by their side and Loki trailing behind them. Their faces were pale and their eyes wide, and Sarah knew they were frightened.

The three girls almost threw themselves at her, hugging her tightly, words rushing from their lips as they voiced their relief and delight in seeing her. "We're so happy you're here, Auntie Sarah," Augusta exclaimed, clinging to her arm. "We couldn't find our way back. Suddenly it was dark, and we couldn't find the path anymore."

"How did you come to be here?" Sarah inquired, hugging them tightly as Dorothea buried her face against her shoulder, silent sobs escaping her lips. "This morning, you said you wanted to head down to the beach. Besides, you were supposed to stay in the gardens."

Bonnie straightened, a bit of a guilty expression upon her face. "I thought 'twould be fun to explore. Mrs. Murray always tells us these amazing stories about the cliffs, and when we got here, Faerie found a way through the thicket and disappeared. Of course, we couldna leave him behind," she stated matter-of-factly. "So, we followed him and—"

"We walked on water," Dorothea piped up, lifting her face to look up at Sarah. "Truly!"

Sarah nodded, hugging the girl close. "I believe you, Thea." She looked back at Bonnie and then at Augusta. "Why did you not come back, though?"

Augusta heaved a deep sigh and exchanged a look with Bonnie. "We forgot where the path was," she murmured, clearly disappointed with herself. "It got dark, and then we couldn't see much. We couldn't find it anymore." She shivered. "We were frightened."

Sarah nodded, then threw a look over her shoulder toward the small pile of pebbles she had stacked near the water's edge. It was almost completely submerged. "We need to go," Sarah exclaimed, grasping the girls' hands and pulling them along toward the water's edge. She stepped closer, the water once more sloshing into her boots, her eyes peering through the churning waters. Carefully, she moved in deeper, one foot ahead to test the ground. For a moment, Sarah feared that she, too, had lost the path. Then, though, her boot brushed across something smooth and solid. "Here. It is here." Moving onward, Sarah found that she now stood in the water up to her knees. She glanced back at the beach where the girl stood, her eyes moving to Faerie and Loki.

Even Dorothea looked too short to find her own way across. She might be swept into the deep by the waves. Still, they could not stay. The cold was already seeping into every fiber of Sarah's being, and the girls, too, had gotten wet. They stood with their little arms wrapped around themselves, shivering silently. No, they would never make it through the night. They had to get back.

Now.

"The way is not long," Sarah said as she waved the girls onward, "but we have to go now before the tide rises even more." She looked at Augusta and Bonnie, both girls a head taller than Dorothea. "Can you carry Faerie and Loki?"

The two girls nodded, and while Bonnie picked up Faerie, Augusta settled Loki into her arms. Sarah grasped Dorothea's hand, pulling her forward before picking her up and settling her on her hip. "Follow right behind me," she told the girls with a glance over her shoulder. "Stay on the path. We don't quite know how wide it is. Do you hear?"

Both girls nodded solemnly.

Then they waded out into the water. Sarah could almost hear the girls' teeth chattering as they moved onward. "It's all right," she murmured, willing her own shivers away. "It is not far. Do you see over there? That's where the tunnel is." Everyone squinted through the dark, and she saw the girls' heads bob up and down. "As you came here," Sarah asked, choosing her words carefully, "did you see anyone? Did someone speak to you? Or did you perhaps see a ship?"

Settled upon her hip, Dorothea frowned at her. "No, there was no one. People rarely come up to the cliff. They don't like ghosts." The hint of a smile dashed across the girl's face in the dim light of the moon. "I like ghosts. At least, I think I do."

Sarah smiled at the girl, then glanced over her shoulder. "So, you encountered no one?"

Augusta and Bonnie shook their heads. "Should we have?"

"No, of course not." Sarah exhaled a deep breath, realizing in that moment, perhaps a bit belatedly, that Lord Birchwell had nothing to do with the girls' disappearance. They had truly just lost their way. No one had come onto the island. No one was after them or Kate. They were all still safe.

All they needed to do now was get back to the castle.

"There!" Bonnie exclaimed all of a sudden, her right arm whipping out and pointing toward a small gap between the curve of the main island and the smaller one settled in its bay. Indeed, a light shone from there, moving closer, and as the clouds shifted once more, Sarah's breath lodged in her throat as she saw the white sails of a ship approaching. *Oh, please, don't let me have been wrong.*

Chapter Fifty-One

A GHOST UPON THE WAVES

Keir and Eoghan stood upon the deck beside Duncan as the MacKinnear ship made the tight curve around the coast, aiming for that small space between where the main island dipped inward and the tiny island lay to the south. The winds blew strong that night, pushing them onward, and the crew struggled to maintain control and maneuver the ship through the small gap. Never had there been a reason to seek out the small bay, the rocky coast of the island impenetrable.

"There is no way Sarah could've come down here," Duncan argued as he had before, convinced the journey here would be for nothing. "We've tried to find a way down to the water often enough when we were lads. We never succeeded."

Eoghan nodded in agreement. Yet Keir could see a glimmer of doubt in his friend's eyes.

"I have to be certain," Keir replied, squinting his eyes, wishing for the thick cloud cover overhead to disappear and allow the moon to shine through more permanently. "Sarah has surprised me before, and she has to be somewhere. I refuse to believe that...," he gritted his teeth, "... that she's lost to me, that she was snatched away, and I didna even notice."

"There!" came a shout from the crow's nest, and all three men glanced upward, seeing the crewman up there point toward the island. "'Tis a ghost!" he stammered, his voice tight and quivering. "'Tis gliding across the water!"

Within moments, everyone stood at the railing, gazing out across the water. Keir felt his heart thunder in his chest, his mind instantly arguing that there were no ghosts. Yet as his gaze focused, he did see something.

"Mrs. Murray was right," another crewman stammered fearfully. "We ought to turn back."

Keir squinted his eyes further, as did Eoghan and Duncan beside him. "What is that?" he murmured, allowing his gaze to sweep over the shadowy figure that seemed to hover in the air above the water.

"It canna be a ghost," Eoghan remarked, doubt in his voice.

Duncan scoffed. "Of course not."

"We have to know what it is," Keir stated clearly, knowing he could not leave without finding out what had happened. "We needa get closer." He looked at his brother, and Duncan nodded.

Slowly, carefully, they sailed onward, passing safely through the small gap and into the bay. Clouds still lingered above, hiding the bit of moon that shone that night, and despite the spyglass in his hands, Keir could barely make out anything. "It does look as though someone is walking there."

"How is that possible?" Eoghan remarked, taking the spyglass from him to see for himself.

Duncan laughed one of his booming laughs, then shook his head at the crew as they gazed on in fear. "Walking on water? Ye must be mad."

Still, all of a sudden, it was eerily quiet. No one dared say a word. The only sound was the howling of the wind and the soft lapping of the waves, carrying them onward, closer and closer.

"I shall sail straight through that ghost and prove to ye all," Duncan exclaimed, gesturing for them to pick up speed, "that ye're all mad." He laughed, slapping his knee.

Keir met his brother's gaze. "I'm not saying this is a ghost," he remarked, casting another glance out toward the water, "but 'tis something. And if it is not hovering in the air, it must be standing on something." His brows rose meaningfully. "Something solid just beneath the water's surface."

For a moment, Duncan frowned before understanding dawned upon his face. He immediately gestured to his crew and had them lower the sails, slowing the vessel. "What do ye think it is?"

Keir shrugged as they slowly drifted closer.

Sarah froze as the cloud shifted, and her gaze fell upon a ship with large sails, heading straight toward them. "We need to hurry!" she exclaimed, picking up the pace and ushering the girls onward. "We need to reach the other side!" Could this be Birchwell after all? But how could he possibly know to find them here?

"But 'tis a MacKinnear ship," Bonnie objected, her eyes expectant as they looked at Sarah. "Perhaps they can help us."

Sarah frowned. "How do you know?"

"Ye canna tell ships apart?" Bonnie asked rather incredulously. "'Tis Duncan's ship."

Nervous laughter fell from Sarah's lips. "Well, I've barely seen a ship in my life." Still, the certain expression upon Bonnie's face was reassuring, and the slowly rising water, now well above her knees, worried Sarah. After all, the ledge from whence she had embarked was still a good bit away.

"Wave to them," Sarah instructed, praying that she was not making a monumental mistake. "And call out."

Without a moment of hesitation, the girls did as she had asked.

Keir's heart slammed almost painfully against his rib cage when, from one second to the next, the image before his eyes suddenly cleared... and he recognized Sarah. "'Tis her!" he called, peering through the spyglass. "'Tis them!"

"What?" Eoghan jerked the spyglass from Keir's hands. "Bonnie?"

Duncan frowned at his brother. "Are ye certain? How can they possibly…?" He gestured out there, toward the *ghost* hovering above the water.

Keir shrugged. "I dunna know, but we have to go get them." He hurried toward one of the dinghies, calling for the crew to lower it down to the water. "Eoghan, come on."

Within moments, Eoghan was by his side as they waited rather impatiently for the dinghy to touch down upon the water. Then they climbed in and rowed.

Sarah held her breath as she watched a small boat being lowered to the water. She could see people moving on deck, but she could not make out any of their faces. The ship was still too far away, and the occasional ray of silver moonlight that shone through the cloud cover did not grant her a good view. She could only hope that Bonnie was right, that this was Duncan and not Birchwell.

And then the smaller boat came toward them, two men sitting inside, working the oars. Again, Sarah wondered if they ought to make a run for the shore. Yet she knew they would never make it. By now, the girls stood to their hips in the water, their lips turning blue and their arms growing heavy from carrying Faerie and Loki. No, there was no other way.

And then, the clouds finally did abandon this part of the sky, and in the white golden light from the crescent moon, Sarah finally recognized the faces of the two men coming toward them.

Keir and Eoghan.

Sarah almost slumped down into the water in relief, her body now shaking uncontrollably. Tears stung her eyes, and she bit her lip to keep them at bay.

Keir and Eoghan waved to them, calling out words Sarah could not quite make sense of; too overcome was she by the mere sight of them.

"It's Father!" Bonnie exclaimed, a wide smile coming to her face. "Father!"

The expression upon Eoghan's face spoke volumes, and Sarah could see that he had to force himself to remain in the boat and not jump into the water and swim toward his daughter.

Slower now, the small boat moved closer until it came to rest alongside them. Sarah instantly deposited Dorothea into the boat while Bonnie and Augusta did the same with Loki and Faerie. "What are ye standing on?" Keir asked, already swinging a leg over the edge of the boat.

In the next moment, Keir stood beside her. He embraced her quickly, then turned and picked up Augusta, setting her down next to Dorothea on the wooden bench. Eoghan already held Bonnie in his arms, hugging her tightly, tears streaming down his face.

And then, Sarah felt the ground underneath her feet disappear as Keir lifted her into his arms. "Ye're cold," he murmured, his warm breath a wonderful sensation against chilled skin. "We need to get back." He set her down in the boat, then with one last glance at the *snake* beneath his feet, he climbed back in himself. "It feels like a cobblestone road."

Sarah nodded, wrapping her arms around Dorothea and Augusta, hugging them close as they shivered. Keir quickly grabbed the oars, rowing them back toward the ship. "Send up the flare!" he called as ropes were tossed down and attached to the small boat. A moment later, it was lifted out of the water, swaying gently against the side of the ship. "Call off the search!"

"This is for you, Auntie Sarah," Dorothea murmured, snuggling closer into Sarah's embrace. "Thank you for coming for us."

Puzzled, Sarah looked down at the small string in Dorothea's hand. At a closer look, she could see that it was three strings braided together, each one a different color. Yet in the dark, she could not quite tell which ones they were. "Where did you get this?"

Dorothea shrugged. "I found it on the island."

"Then you keep it," Sarah murmured, pressing a kiss to the girl's forehead. "To remind you of this adventure.

Dorothea chuckled. "I won't need it for that. I'll never ever, ever forget this." She smiled at Sarah and settled the small braided string into her hand. "Thank you, Auntie Sarah." Smiling, she settled deeper into Sarah's arms and then closed her eyes.

Though touched, Sarah knew that more than anything it was the cold closing Dorothea's eyes. "We need to warm them," she called out to Keir through chattering teeth as he jumped out of the boat and onto the deck of the ship. "They're much too cold!" *Please!*

Instantly, blankets were brought forth and wrapped around the girls. Still, the shivering persisted as they sailed back around the southern edge of the island and returned to the harbor. Sarah felt her own limbs grow heavy as well, her eyelids closing again and again. Her mind became foggy, and after a while, she realized her eyes had closed.

Still, the shivers continued.

Sarah had no notion of how much time passed or how they got back to the castle. She heard Keir's voice speaking nearby now and then. His embrace tightened upon her whenever the darkness around her grew heavier, only interspersed by flashes of light like the warm glow of a torch or the silver ray of moonlight.

Eventually, Sarah found herself back up at the castle. She heard Lady Adele's voice, ushering commands, calling for a bath to be drawn for the girls and her as well. "The girls first," Sarah murmured, snuggling closer into Keir's embrace. "I am... all... right."

Then there was a sudden exclamation of joy as Kate burst into the chamber. Sarah's eyes opened briefly at the sound of her sister's voice, and the sight of Kate embracing her daughters warmed her heart.

"See to them, will ye?" Keir murmured, and through half-open eyes, Sarah saw his mother nod. "I'll take care of Sarah." Then he turned and climbed the stairs two at a time.

Chapter Fifty-Two

BREAKING EVERY RULE

The blue tinge of Sarah's skin worried Keir. She was soaked through, her skirts heavy with water, and by the time he reached his chamber and pushed open the door, his own clothes were wet as well. "Sarah!" Keir called, pushing the door closed with his right boot, grateful to see a fire burning in the grate. "Sarah, wake up!"

When she failed to react, Keir pinched her arm, relieved when she stirred, a murmured complaint falling from her lips before her eyes slowly blinked open. "Keir? W-Where are we?" she murmured; her voice barely audible.

"In my chamber." He waited until her gaze met his. "I'll set ye down now, lass. We needa get ye out of these wet clothes, ye hear?"

Sarah nodded, and yet her unseeing eyes suggested he could have spoken of flying pigs, and she would not have found that odd in that moment.

Gently, Keir placed Sarah back on her feet, his hands never leaving her arms as she swayed, her eyes blinking rapidly as she tried to focus. "Open yer eyes," Keir urged her when they fluttered closed once more. "Lass, open yer eyes."

Sarah did, and after a moment, her balance returned, and she no longer swayed upon her feet. The shivers, though, suddenly grew in intensity, and she wrapped her arms around herself. "W-What of that b-bath?" she stammered as Keir pulled the blanket from her shoulders. "Th-That s-sounds l-lovely."

Keir grinned at her, his fingers reaching for the laces of her gown. "I have a better idea," he murmured in her ear and then quickly divested her of her soaked gown.

Staring at him, Sarah gasped when the cool air hit her chilled skin. "Y-You do? What—?" Understanding dawned, and a slow blush claimed her cheeks, chasing away the disconcerting paleness.

Keir stilled, savoring the sight of the color returning to her cheeks. "Aye," he murmured, then leaned in and kissed her, his hands settling upon her upper arms, his palms almost hot against her skin. He held her close, willing his warmth into her body, willing the shivers to subside. "Next time, tell me where ye are going, lass," he murmured against her lips. "Ye almost killed me today."

"Sometimes there isn't time," Sarah replied, her voice no longer trembling, as she pressed closer, her arms coming around his neck. "My feet are freezing."

Keir chuckled against her lips, then pulled back and pushed her onto the edge of the bed. He pulled off her boots as Sarah watched him; her gaze now as heated as her flaming cheeks. Her skin felt cool to the touch, but no longer as icy as before as Keir ran his hands down her calves to pull off her stockings. He rubbed her cold feet, and she laughed. Yet her arms remained wrapped around herself as though to shield herself from his gaze; after all, the thin fabric of her chemise hid very little after the soak in the icy water.

"Would ye rather have the bath?" Keir asked, rising to his feet and taking a step back. "All I care is that we see ye warmed."

Sarah chuckled self-consciously. "All you care?" she teased, one eyebrow arching.

Keir grinned, loving that daring side of her. However, before he could reply, a knock came on the door. He nodded to Sarah and then strode toward it. On its other side, he found Duncan.

"Do ye have a moment?" his brother asked with a weary sigh, then he rushed on, clearly exhausted and eager for a good night's sleep. "The search has been called off. Everyone has returned safe and sound, and no one reported seeing anything unusual. It seems highly unlikely that Birchwell made it to the island. Of course," he held up a hand, "that doesna mean he willna try. I'll keep sentries posted. Should he try, we'll find out."

Keir nodded, the sound of soft footsteps padding about the chamber drifting to his ears from behind him. "I'm glad to hear it. Good night then." He made to close the door, but Duncan's boot stopped him.

His brother's gaze narrowed. "What's going on? Ye're acting—" He broke off, and a slow grin came to Duncan's face as his gaze swept sideways, as though he could see straight through the wooden door. "Ye're not alone, are ye?"

Keir chuckled, casting his brother a meaningful look.

Duncan laughed. "Good night to ye then," he remarked, "and give the lass a hug from me." He grinned devilishly at Keir and then walked off down the corridor.

Closing the door, Keir turned, surprised to find Sarah in bed, the blanket pulled up to her chin. "Still cold?" he asked, strolling closer. Then his eyes fell on the wet chemise Sarah had still worn only moments earlier; now, though, it lay crumpled upon the floor. Keir's gaze rose and met Sarah's. "No bath then?" he asked with a teasing grin.

Sarah chuckled self-consciously; yet she did not avert her eyes. "No bath."

Removing his own damp shirt, Keir stepped closer. He was well-aware of Sarah's inquisitive gaze. "May I join ye?" She nodded, and without giving her a moment to reconsider, Keir slipped beneath the blanket.

Sarah shivered as he reached out to touch her, her teeth sinking into her lower lip and her blue eyes wide.

"I can simply hold ye, lass," Keir offered, wondering if perhaps he was pushing her a bit far after everything she had been through today. "Warm ye." Perhaps she simply needed a good night's sleep.

Perhaps they all did.

For a long moment, Sarah held his gaze, a glimmer of uncertainty in her eyes. Then, though, she suddenly reached for him, and her mouth claimed his before Keir realized what was happening.

Her skin was still chilled, and Keir flinched as her bare skin came to rest against his. Yet the feel of her in his arms was indescribable, and he embraced her tightly, holding her to him without a second thought.

"Too cold?" Sarah asked, an apologetic expression upon her face, as she lifted her head to look at him.

"Aye, lass, much too cold," Keir murmured, then instantly reclaimed her lips, determined to see her warmed. His hands drifted over her body, teasing, exploring, and he felt her tremble, the breath hitching in her throat.

Pulling back, Sarah looked up at him, tears misting her eyes as she smiled. "This is how it began," she murmured, touching his face, the tips of her fingers tracing his brows, down his temple and along the line of his jaw, the touch tantalizing and utterly intoxicating. "Do you remember? That night in the cabin when you found me shivering?"

Every moment of it.

"How could I forget?" Keir chuckled against her lips, then kissed her again, rolling her onto her back and bracing himself above her. Her eyes were two dark pools as he looked down at her, and he suddenly felt an icy chill trail down his spine. "I was afraid for ye today."

Sarah bit her lip. "I'm sorry. I never meant..." Again, she reached out and touched his face, her gaze trailing the movement before returning to meet his eyes. "I'm sorry," she whispered, and her teeth sank into her lower lip once more, a smile tugging upon her lips. "Will you kiss me again?"

Keir smiled at her, sinking down onto his lower arms, feeling the soft touch of her body beneath his. "Is that what ye want?"

Sarah nodded; her voice breathless as she spoke. "It is." Yet the moment his mouth reclaimed hers, she melted into his embrace, her hands eager as they explored his shoulders and the planes of his chest.

Keir trailed kisses down her throat, nipping her skin gently, overwhelmed by the feel of her in his arms. There had been moments like this before; only now he wanted more. Every kiss, every touch, sent heat sizzling across his skin, and he struggled to contain his desire. After all—

"Why did you stop?" Sarah asked, her brows drawn into a quizzical expression as she looked up at him, her hands still locked at the back of his neck.

Keir chuckled. "We are to be wed tomorrow. There's no need to rush, lass." Yet deep down, every fiber of his being disagreed.

Again, Sarah's teeth sank into her lower lip as she regarded him. Then, the right corner of her mouth twitched. "We are to be wed tomorrow," she echoed his words. "There's no need to stop."

Thinking his hearing impaired, Keir stared down at her.

Sarah chuckled, the blush upon her cheeks deepening, her skin now warm to the touch. "I've already broken every rule at least twice. What is one more?"

Keir grinned, loving that she could still catch him off guard. "Are ye certain?"

Sarah nodded, and her hands pulled him back down to her. "Aye, I am," she whispered, claiming a kiss that stole the breath from Keir's lungs.

Today was definitely ending far better than he had expected.

Chapter Fifty-Three

THE ECHO OF LOSS

Waking the next morning, Sarah stretched out leisurely, a wide smile upon her face she could not seem to subdue. Every inch of her tingled, warm and languid from the previous night. Never had she felt so at ease, so much like herself, free and almost dauntless. Far from the way her mother had prophesied! Indeed, every whispered word, every touch had been perfect, making her wish the night would never have to end. Yet waking in Keir's chamber—in their chamber come today!—felt like a most wonderful promise of many more such nights to come, spent in each other's arms.

In some way, Sarah had always felt alone in the world. Yes, there had been people who had cared for her—the Whickertons—and yet they had not been her family, endowed with the right to protect her, to care for her. More often than not, they, too, had been forced to stand by and allow her parents to jeopardize her future, her happiness. Now, here at MacKinnear Castle, Sarah felt truly safe, no longer alone and only able to depend upon herself, for the first time in her life.

It was an exhilarating feeling.

Still, when Sarah finally cracked open her eyes, blinking them against the bright sunlight announcing a new day, she found herself alone in Keir's chamber. For a moment, she wondered if she had simply imagined the previous night. Yet every fiber of her being instantly argued against it, reminding her of everything that had happened the day before. *And it did, did it not?*

As though to answer her question, the door flew open in that moment, and Keir strode in, a wide grin coming to his face as he saw her awake.

Instantly, Sarah felt heat shoot into her cheeks, unable to prevent it. After all, as wonderful as she felt after what had happened between them, it was still utterly new, and she would need some time to truly feel at ease with it.

"Ye're blushing," Keir remarked with a chuckle as she had known he would. "It suits ye." He held her gaze as Sarah sat up, pulling the blanket all the way to her chin. "Dunna ever stop."

Sarah frowned. "Stop blushing?" She laughed. "I don't think I could. It has never been my choice after all, remember?"

Keir seated himself on the bed beside her and handed her a pile of clothing. "I am glad to hear it."

Sarah returned his smile, then reminded of the boldness she had felt the night before, leaned in and kissed him. "We are to be married today," she murmured against his lips before sitting back and dropping her gaze to the clothes in her lap.

Keir nodded. "Aye, we are." He stilled, his blue eyes searching hers. "Any regrets?"

Grinning from ear to ear, Sarah shook her head as she felt the blush upon her cheeks darken. "None," she told him boldly. "I am more certain than ever."

Clearly delighted with her answer, Keir seized her and dragged her into his arms, his lips finding hers in a passionate kiss. "There are people in yer chamber, awaiting yer return," he murmured, brushing his mouth against hers. "After all, we are to be married today."

Sarah frowned. "People?"

"Aye, my mother and grandmother, ready to prepare ye for our wedding." His brows rose, as though he were warning her of an impending doom. "Any regrets now?"

Sarah laughed. "Do not even try to dissuade me, for it will not work." She grasped his chin and held his gaze. "You're mine, Keir MacKinnear, now and forever." She arched up an eyebrow. "Any regrets?" *Don't you dare voice any!*

A rather booming laugh escaped Keir's throat, and it reminded Sarah of Duncan. "Never," he stated without a moment's hesitation, his voice strong and determined, not allowing for doubts. "Ye're truly one of a kind, lass, one of a kind."

Sarah basked in his words, allowing them to sweep through her and warm every inch of her. Indeed, she could get used to this loving care, this unerring devotion. It felt so good, so unbelievably good. For a long time, Sarah had hoped that her wedding day would never come, knowing that if it did, it would fill her with dread and apprehension.

Never in her life had she been more wrong, and she was glad for it.

"Ye should dress, lass," Keir murmured, tucking a stray wisp behind her ear. "I fear if ye dunna return to yer chamber soon, my mother and grandmother will come to find ye." He chuckled. "They are quite the intrusive lot. Ye might remember me warning ye about that."

"They are," Sarah agreed, feeling that same warmth sweep through her as before. "But I would not want to have it any other way."

Keir rose to his feet. "Then dress quickly and see that ye dunna anger them." He winked at her, then turned his back and began gathering up her wet clothes from the day before.

Sarah was grateful that he averted his gaze, allowing her to dress without feeling too self-conscious. "I wonder how the girls are?" she thought out loud as she slipped into her dress. "I hope they're well."

Keir nodded, glancing back at her over his shoulder. "They are," he assured her, shaking out her dress before laying it over his arm. "I ran into Mrs. Murray on the way, and she assured me that Augusta and Dorothea as well as Bonnie are well."

Sarah chuckled, not at all surprised that the housekeeper was well-informed. "I'm so glad." She closed her eyes, remembering the events of the previous day. "Dorothea felt so cold in my arms that for a moment I feared..." She swallowed hard, seeking to push the memory away.

Keir nodded, turning back to look at her. "I felt the same way when I carried ye up here, lass. Ye were icy cold and—" He broke off, his gaze falling to the floor as the small braided string Dorothea had gifted Sarah the day before fell from the tangle of her damp dress. In the daylight, Sarah now saw that each string had a different color: green, white, and blue.

"Oh, I had completely forgotten about that," Sarah murmured, rising to her feet. She brushed her hands down her skirts, smoothing out the wrinkles, and then step toward the braided string. "Dorothea gave this to me when—" All words lodged in Sarah's throat when she lifted her gaze and finally noted the expression upon Keir's face as he continued to stare at the braid by his feet.

He looked thunderstruck, his face suddenly pale and his eyes wide, their blue shining with an intensity Sarah had rarely seen. He remained perfectly still; only his chest moved with each slow breath. Yet there was something in his gaze that spoke of a broken heart, of an open wound, of pain and anguish.

But also of love.

"Keir?" Sarah spoke his name tentatively as she drew closer, reaching out a hand to touch his shoulder.

The moment the tips of her fingers made contact Keir flinched. He blinked his eyes and then lifted his chin, finally looking at her. "How did ye say ye got this?" His voice was only a whisper, and he still looked as pale as a sheet that for a moment Sarah worried he might faint.

Taking the clothes from his arm, Sarah set them aside. "Dorothea gave it to me last night."

Keir swallowed hard, then kneeled down and reached for the small braid, his arm extending slowly as though part of him did not dare touch it. Sarah watched as he brushed his fingertips over it, a shiver going through him, before he finally gathered the braid in his hand. His fingers closed over it, and he gripped it, closing his eyes as he rested his forehead against his fisted hand.

"Keir, what is it?" Sarah asked tentatively, touching her hands to his shoulders, wanting to offer comfort for whatever had shaken him so.

For a moment, Keir remained completely still. Then he slowly rose to his feet, his gaze going back and forth between Sarah and the braid in his hand. "Thea gave this to ye?" He stared at her. "How?"

Sarah stepped closer, the palms of her hands settling upon his chest as she looked up into his eyes. "She said she found it on the island. Why? What does this mean to you?"

Keir swallowed hard. "'Twas my sister's," he murmured, his gaze once more straying to the small braid. "Yvaine wore it the day she disappeared." His gaze met hers. "She wore it every day wherever she went." He exhaled a slow breath, and his brows knitted together. "Thea found it on the island?" He shook his head, disbelief widening his eyes. "We searched everywhere, turned over every rock and blade of grass. We found nothing."

Sarah felt her heart thundering in her chest, unable to utter a single word as she hung on each and every one of Keir's, her mind racing with the implications of this discovery.

"I have to go there!" Keir suddenly exclaimed, then instantly spun upon his heel and rushed toward the door. "I have to—"

In a flash, Sarah grasped his arm and pulled him back, her eyes finding his.

Keir swallowed. "I have to go there." There was something pleading in his voice, asking her to understand. "I have to..." He glanced down at the small braid again. "She was my sister." He seemed to flinch at his own words. "She *is* my sister. I have to go."

Sarah held onto him, her gaze holding his. "*We* have to go," she corrected, remembering the way Keir had always been at her side, had accompanied her to her sister's estate, done all he could to protect Kate and her children. Now it was Sarah's turn to stand at his side.

A smile touched his face, and the next moment, Sarah found herself in his arms, his lips pressed to hers in a crushing kiss. "Aye, we do," Keir murmured, his eyes shining in a blue so bright that they seemed almost devoid of color. "First, though, we'll get married."

"Aye," Sarah echoed and followed Keir out the door; yet deep down, she wondered what they might find out about Yvaine—if anything at all. How had the braid ended up on the island? Had Yvaine truly been there the day of her disappearance?

As much as Sarah hoped Keir would finally receive answers, she could not banish that chilling sensation suggesting that whatever answers they might find would break his heart. And what if they found nothing at all? From experience, Sarah knew that hope was a dangerous thing, for it held the power to crush one's heart and soul. Indeed, Keir had guarded his heart before. He had made his peace with his sister's disappearance as much as that was possible. Yet seeing her small braid now out of nowhere in front of him was different. Sarah knew Keir had been utterly unprepared for that. It had torn down his defenses, and hope had surged back into his heart.

What if we find nothing? Sarah continued to wonder as she followed Keir down the corridor toward her chamber. After all, Yvaine had been gone for three years. What could they possibly find on that island, small as it was?

Still, whatever the future might hold, Sarah knew she would forever remain at Keir's side. He had stood by her before, and now she would be there for him.

Always.

No matter what.

Chapter Fifty-Four

A PLAN HATCHED

London, England
A few days prior

Climbing the steps to Lord Birchwell's London townhouse, Albert Harris, Baron Blackmore, struggled to contain his disappointment. Indeed, disappointment was not quite the right word to describe this inner raging he felt whenever his thoughts strayed to his former fiancé, Miss Sarah Mortensen.

Unfortunately, his thoughts strayed to her quite a lot these days. After all, the woman had played him for a fool; Albert was certain of it.

Though the *ton* thought her a victim of a most fiendish kidnapping, Albert had his doubts. Too many things had raised his suspicion, and although he had no proof, he was certain that Miss Mortensen had never truly been kidnapped. Indeed, strangely enough, the moment he had paid the ransom to her kidnappers. who had never shown their faces, her father's gambling debts had mysteriously disappeared.

No, Albert was no fool; yet he had been played for one, a fact he could not allow to stand.

Handing his hat and gloves to a footman, Albert followed Birchwell's butler across the main hall and then down a long corridor to a lavishly furnished drawing room. There, near the imposing fireplace, sat the dowager countess, her eyes as shrewd as always as they glided over him upon his entry. Her lips twitched ever so slightly, and she raised her chin another fraction as though she wished to look down upon him.

Albert almost chuckled. Though he disliked anyone who thought themselves superior to him, he had to admit—even if only grudgingly—that he rather admired her shrewd wit as well as her haughty high-handedness.

"Good day, Lord Blackmore."

Albert inclined his head to the dowager, then seated himself across from her. "Good day, my lady."

For a long moment, neither one of them said a word, each quietly assessing the other.

"So?" the dowager eventually began, lifting one eyebrow. "What did you find out?"

Albert felt bile rise in his throat. "Your daughter-in-law as well as my former fiancé seem to have sought refuge with a Scottish clan by the name of MacKinnear."

The lady exhaled a slow breath, her lips flattening, as though she wished to bite off his head. "Kin to that man, no doubt," she grumbled under her breath, outrage lighting up her eyes.

Albert could not deny that he was rather surprised by her show of emotion. Thus far, the dowager countess had always maintained her composure. "He visited you?" Albert inquired, already knowing the answer to his question. "Alongside Miss Mortensen?"

The dowager gave a curt nod.

Albert felt his blood boil, certain that his former fiancé and the Scot were somehow involved. After all, what man would go to such lengths in aiding her to escape the country if he did not expect something in return?

"Do you have a plan?" the dowager inquired, curiosity sparking in her eyes, and Albert cursed himself, knowing that she was well-aware of his short temper these days.

Leaning back in his chair, Albert steepled his fingers. "Unfortunately, the MacKinnears are an island clan. They reside just off the coast, their land heavily fortified." He heaved out a deep breath. "My men have observed it at length and concluded that it is impossible to invade." He chuckled darkly. "I suppose it could be done if one had a large army at hand." Momentarily amused, he raised an eyebrow at the dowager. "I don't suppose you have one at your disposal."

Looking down her nose at him, the dowager ignored his remark. "So, you do *not* have a plan? Is that not so?" She looked at him pointedly.

Albert seethed quietly. "I have... certain ideas," he grunted out through clenched teeth, "and I have no doubt that with time I shall—"

The dowager chuckled mockingly, rolling her eyes at him. "Well, if it is, indeed, impossible to sneak onto the island and steal them away," she thought out loud, her gaze drifting toward the bustling street out front, "then perhaps we should pursue an alternative."

Albert frowned. "An alternative?" His hands clenched into fists, for he rather disliked following another's lead.

The dowager's gaze returned to him, and a sweet smile touched her lips. "But of course," she replied, as though he ought to know the answer to his own question. "Well, I should think the solution quite simple. If we cannot go there, then we will simply have to lure them back here." Her eyebrows rose challengingly. "All that is needed is the right incentive. Would you not agree, my lord?"

Albert could not help thinking that her words mocked him. Still, it would be unwise to anger the dowager. At least for now, they needed one another, their plan having a greater chance of success if they worked together.

"What sort of incentive did you have in mind?"

The dowager rested the tip of her forefinger against the corner of her mouth. Her gaze once more drifting to the window. For a moment, she did not say another word, paid him not the least bit of attention. Then, however, a slow smile spread across her features, one not speaking of joy but rather of deceitfulness and conquest.

Albert felt an involuntary shiver, serving as a reminder not to antagonize the dowager. After all, she would be a most formidable enemy.

Fortunately for him, though, she was not.

Miss Mortensen and her sister were.

And they would suffer for it.

Albert would make certain of it.

TO BE CONTINUED

Of course, Sarah's and Keir's story does not end here. How could it? There is more to come. So, stay tuned for the next part of their story as Keir and Sarah search for clues regarding Yvaine's disappearance while Sarah's former fiancé plans his revenge. And what about Kate... and Eoghan?

On the Wings of Cinders, coming soon!

In the meantime, have you read my *Whickertons in Love* series?

It is set in Regency-era England, portraying the at times turbulent ways the six Whickerton siblings' search for love - including their matchmaking Grandma Edie, and, of course, family friend Sarah, who is already trying to escape her parent's marriage schemes. We'll also get a glimpse of Keir in the last three books of the series.

Start with the Christmas prequel *Once Upon an Aggravatingly Heroic Kiss*, which tells Grandma Edie's story, matchmaking for her best friend, Keir's grandmother.

Once upon a time, our beloved Grandma Edie began her career as the best matchmaker in known history by using her extraordinary talent to bring about her own happily-ever-after...

Determined to perform a Christmas miracle by seeing her friend wed to the man she loves, Edith finds herself distracted from her task by a teasing gentleman with wicked eyes and a devilish smile.

Acknowledgement

A great big thank-you to all those who aided me in finishing this book and made it the wonderful story it has become. First and foremost, of course, there is my family, who inspires me on a daily basis, giving me the enthusiasm and encouragement, I need to type away at my computer day after day. Thank you so much!

Then there are my proofreaders, beta readers and readers who write to me out of the blue with wonderful ideas and thoughts. Thank you for your honest words! Jodi and Dara comb through my manuscripts in an utterly diligent way that allows me to smooth off the rough edges and make it shine. Thank you so much for your dedication to my stories! Brie, Carol, Zan-Mari, Kim, Martha and Mary are my hawks, their eyes sweeping over the words to spot those pesky errors I seem to be absolutely blind to. Thank you so much for aiding me with your keen eyesight!

About Bree

USA Today bestselling and award-winning author, Bree Wolf has always been a language enthusiast (though not a grammarian!) and is rarely found without a book in her hand or her fingers glued to a keyboard. Trying to find her way, she has taught English as a second language, traveled abroad and worked at a translation agency as well as a law firm in Ireland. She also spent loooong years obtaining a BA in English and Education and an MA in Specialized Translation while wishing she could simply be a writer. Although there is nothing simple about being a writer, her dreams have finally come true.

"A big thanks to my fairy godmother!"

Currently, Bree has found her new home in the historical romance genre, writing Regency novels and novellas. Enjoying the mix of fact and fiction, she occasionally feels like a puppet master (or mistress? Although that sounds weird!), forcing her characters into ever-new situations that will put their strength, their beliefs, their love to the test, hoping that in the end they will triumph and get the happily-ever-after we are all looking for.

If you're an avid reader, sign up for Bree's newsletter on www.breewolf.com as she has the tendency to simply give books away. Find out about freebies, giveaways as well as occasional advance reader copies and read before the book is even on the shelves!

Connect with Bree and stay up-to-date on new releases:

facebook.com/breewolf.novels
twitter.com/breewolf_author
instagram.com/breewolf_author
amazon.com/Bree-Wolf/e/B00FJX27Z4
bookbub.com/authors/bree-wolf